ALSO BY STEPHANIE DeCAROLIS

The Perfect Sister
The Guilty Husband
Deadly Little Lies

THE
WIVES OF
HAWTHORNE
LANE

THE WIVES OF HAWTHORNE LANE

STEPHANIE DeCAROLIS

BANTAM
New York

Bantam Books
An imprint of Random House
A division of Penguin Random House LLC
1745 Broadway, New York, NY 10019
randomhousebooks.com
randomhousebookclub.com
penguinrandomhouse.com

A Bantam Books Trade Paperback Original

Copyright © 2025 by Stephanie DeCarolis
Book club guide copyright © 2025 by Penguin Random House LLC

Penguin Random House values and supports copyright. Copyright fuels creativity, encourages diverse voices, promotes free speech, and creates a vibrant culture. Thank you for buying an authorized edition of this book and for complying with copyright laws by not reproducing, scanning, or distributing any part of it in any form without permission. You are supporting writers and allowing Penguin Random House to continue to publish books for every reader. Please note that no part of this book may be used or reproduced in any manner for the purpose of training artificial intelligence technologies or systems.

BANTAM & B colophon is a registered trademark of
Penguin Random House LLC.
RANDOM HOUSE BOOK CLUB and colophon are trademarks of
Penguin Random House LLC.

ISBN 978-0-593-72603-7
Ebook ISBN 978-0-593-72604-4

Printed in the United States of America on acid-free paper

1st Printing

BOOK TEAM: Production editor: Annette Szlachta-McGinn •
Managing editor: Saige Francis • Production manager: Chanler Harris •
Copy editor: Tracy Roe • Proofreaders: Amy J. Schneider,
Jane Scarpantoni, Brianna Rapoza

Book design by Alexis Flynn

The authorized representative in the EU for product safety and compliance is Penguin Random House Ireland, Morrison Chambers, 32 Nassau Street, Dublin D02 YH68, Ireland. https://eu-contact.penguin.ie

For Lauren—my partner in crime

THE WIVES OF HAWTHORNE LANE

HALLOWEEN NIGHT

Someone is always watching. It's what Detective Frank Olsen is thinking as he steps out of his sleek black town car onto the quiet cul-de-sac of Hawthorne Lane. His bad knee aches with the chilled wind that winds itself around him, lifts the ends of his salt-and-pepper hair. He takes in the scene before him—the stray paper cup rolling down the empty street like a tumbleweed, mulled wine staining the pavement a bloody red, a hand-painted banner for the annual fall festival twisting on a lonely breeze, and the candy apples that have been dropped from sticky hands, left to litter the sidewalks.

He can picture the lane as it was before, alive with the sound of laughing children, music playing, neighbors smiling, white teeth bared in a facsimile of fondness. Surely they believed they were safe here, in such a nice neighborhood. The houses in this part of town are magnificent—proud brick colonials with rows of mullioned windows and sweeping porches decorated with fat pumpkins that sit like sleeping cats curled upon their steps. The sprawling lawns are dappled with leaves fallen from the towering oaks that surround the little cul-de-sac, nestling it in a false sense of security.

The detective imagines the scream that ended the festivities, shattering the illusion that nothing terrible could ever touch a place like this. He can see it all, unspooling like a film reel in his mind: parents grabbing their children by the hand, noticing, for the first time, how the branches of the gnarled oaks reached for them like spindly arms, how the houses seem to watch you here, their glowing windows stretching into jack-o'-lanterns' taunting grins.

Detective Olsen looks out over the street, notes the white ovals of faces that watch him from every window now. The residents are curious, of course they are, but the feeling of watchful eyes on his back never ceases to unnerve him.

It's ghoulish, he thinks, the world's newfound fascination with death. True crime podcasts, Netflix specials, sensationalized headlines. Or perhaps it's not new at all. Perhaps it's always been there, this inevitable lure toward the macabre, only now it's more accessible. Death on demand. Murder at the click of a mouse. Either way, Detective Olsen doesn't approve. He finds it unnatural, morbid. These people, the ones who stare down at him from their ivory towers, they don't know what it's *really* like to see death up close, to know what it feels like when it doesn't go away at the end of a sixty-minute segment, when it stays with you, clinging to the fibers of your clothing. While they're binging on the stories, finding quick thrills from their tangential brushes against death, he's raking through the muck of it. And it's his job to tidy it all away, to catch the bad guys and make the world a little less gruesome. To make people feel safe enough that homicide can be consumed in bite-size squares of entertainment.

Detective Olsen analyzes the evidence in front of him—the position of the body on the wooded jogging path, lying just beyond the reach of the streetlights; the spill of black-red blood shining like onyx on the pavement around it. *Someone must know something.* He thinks again of the watchful eyes. In a town like this, someone is always watching. It's just a matter of finding out who.

THREE MONTHS BEFORE HALLOWEEN

Sterling Valley Community Board

Forum: Hawthorne Lane
7/31/2024

Poster: Georgina Pembrook

Hello, Everyone!

I hope you're all having a lovely summer! I know it seems silly to be discussing this already (it feels like the Fourth of July was just yesterday!), but the annual fall festival will be here before we know it! As always, this event will be held on the evening of October 31, Halloween.

As you all know, the fall festival is a huge event for our little cul-de-sac, and after last year's incredible turnout, I'm expecting this year to be bigger than ever! I've already applied for the necessary permits to close off the street and for vendors to sell some special treats for the little ones. We may even be able to arrange a fireworks show! (Fingers crossed!)

Please reply as soon as possible if you plan to participate in this year's festival. Looking forward to seeing all of your houses in their autumn best!

Georgina Pembrook

1
HANNAH
Hawthorne Lane

Hannah Wilson stands in the driveway of 5 Hawthorne Lane looking up at her new house. The drive up to Sterling Valley from New York City hadn't been a long one, yet Hannah feels like she's arrived in a distant, faraway land. As she and Mark traveled north, the scenery changed from gray to green, cold concrete giving way to lush foliage. Billboards were soon replaced with canopies formed by mature elm trees, and silvery rivers slicing through shorn stone gorges began to flow alongside the highway. As traffic dwindled to a few slow-moving cars trickling down a sinuous stretch of road, they finally reached the town of Sterling Valley. It looked to Hannah like something out of a fairy tale: quaint little shops— a bakery, a florist, a book store—with glittering display windows and carved wooden signs painted with gold; flower boxes brimming with summer blooms and trailing vines beneath open shutters; old-fashioned streetlamps with their long curved necks and ornate lanterns.

Hannah adjusts the moving box in her arms, shifting its weight to her hip. She's never lived in a place like this before. It all feels so... *big*. She knows this doesn't make sense, that she's coming from Manhattan—a city brimming with millions of people and soaring skyscrapers—but something about this place, about the expanse of blue sky overhead and the thick woods surrounding the cul-de-sac, gives her the impression that they could go on forever. And then there are the houses. Towering over her, stately and dignified with their neat rows of bricks and their white pillars gleaming bright in the summer sunlight.

She tilts back her head, squinting against the sun, to take in the details of the house in front of her. (*Her* house, she reminds herself.) The stiff peaks of its roof, the riotous colors blooming in the garden, the wide porch that stretches across the front of the house like a smile. It seems far too large for only two people. Hannah has never even been inside a house this big, never mind lived in one. She imagines what it will be like living here. She imagines herself and Mark wandering the halls, their footsteps echoing in the cold, empty rooms, and then she imagines filling them. It's why they chose this house, after all. She can vaguely picture the cribs and baby bottles, the soft blankets and impossibly tiny socks, but it all feels so far away. A daydream only half formed.

The box begins to feel heavy in her arms, and Hannah sets it down at her feet. Mark will want to start trying for a family as soon as they're settled in the new house, and Hannah is ready. At least she *thinks* she's ready. How is she supposed to be sure? How can anyone ever be sure? It's times like these that she misses her mother the most. If her mother were still alive, Hannah would have asked her. She doesn't know what her mother might have said. Hannah was too young when she died for them to have had the kind of relationship where they could talk like friends about adult things, about the things that Hannah would someday have to figure out on her own. But she likes to imagine that her mother would have poured them each a cup of tea and told Hannah that she once felt just like Hannah does now. That no one is ever sure about these things, but Hannah should follow her heart. It's not exactly the most helpful imaginary advice, but it's all she has to work with.

Hannah's phone buzzes in her pocket and she checks the screen. There's a new post in the Hawthorne Lane community forum. She only just joined on the drive up, and already she's received a notification. It's from someone named Georgina Pembrook about a festival being held on Halloween. She gathers from the effusive text that the fall festival must be an important event on Hawthorne Lane. Hannah scrolls past this post to find the one below it. This one was also shared by the same Georgina person.

```
Please welcome our new neighbors at 5 Hawthorne
Lane!
```

That post was Liked by Libby Corbin, Audrey Warrington, and a gaggle of others whose names she doesn't recognize but that she imagines she'll soon come to know as her new neighbors. She can already tell that living here is going to be a change. She'd grown accustomed to being another anonymous face in the ever-changing sea of New York City. But she likes the idea that here, she and Mark can belong to something bigger than themselves.

"I think that's the last of it," Mark says as he dusts off his hands, rubbing them on his jeans. He hooks an arm around Hannah's waist and plants a kiss on the side of her head.

She loves the scent of him, clean and crisp, even in the heavy summer heat. In his arms, she feels at home. For a moment she can see it, snapshots of their future here: children learning to ride their bicycles on the lasso-shaped street, tires crunching over piles of burnt-orange leaves; bare feet running across the Technicolor lawn in the summer, melting Popsicles clutched in tiny palms; shucked-off rain boots scattered haphazardly on the porch. A sense of peace washes over her and she closes her eyes, listens to the chirp of the birds, the buzz of a distant lawn mower, breathes in the loamy scent of the surrounding woods. They'd made the right decision coming here. This is the beginning of their Happily Ever After.

"The honeymoon phase," Kelly, her coworker at the coffee shop, had called it. "The shine wears off all of 'em sooner or later. You'll see." But Hannah doesn't believe that. It's true that she and Mark are newlyweds, having been married in a small, private ceremony (much to his mother's dismay) only six weeks ago, but Hannah knows that what they have is real. The kind of love that's built to last.

She looks up at him now, her husband. She loves that she gets to call him that. She loves *everything* about him. She loves the way his hair sticks up at odd angles on the days that he doesn't wrangle it with wax, and she loves the dated, wire-rimmed glasses he can't seem to part with. She loves the grays that have started to pepper his temples and the way his eyes crinkle in the corners when he smiles. Which is often. But most of all, she loves how easy it is to love him. From the moment they met—just over a year ago now—falling for Mark felt like the easiest thing in the world for Hannah to do.

Hannah knows that not everyone understands it. After all, she, at twenty-six, is nearly twelve years younger than Mark, the quiet, thirty-eight-year-old accountant she'd chosen to spend her life with, and she'd often heard his friends back in the city teasing him that she was out of his league. Mark would always laugh, play along with the joke: "I don't know what she sees in me." But it hurt Hannah's heart to hear him speak that way. She knows exactly what she sees in Mark: He's a good man. It's as simple as that. The easy, uncomplicated love they share is all she's ever wanted.

"I'll take this one too," Mark says now, lifting the last box from the pavement at Hannah's feet.

She watches him as he trots up the front steps of their new house, the contents of the box jangling in his arms. The memory almost overcomes her then. In her mind, she sees another house. A dusty porch, a single, empty rocking chair creaking in the wind. But she pushes it back into the dark recesses of her memory before it can break the surface.

They're going to be so happy here on Hawthorne Lane. No matter what it takes.

2
LIBBY
Hawthorne Lane

Libby Corbin's phone vibrates on her kitchen counter and she eagerly snatches it up, expecting a message from her ex-husband explaining why he's not yet at her front door to pick up their son, Lucas, as promised. He should have been here by now, and Libby is going to be late for work if he doesn't make an appearance soon. But it isn't a message from Bill that interrupts her anxious pacing. It's a new post in the Hawthorne Lane community forum from Georgina reminding everyone about the fall festival. Libby reads it, and it conjures an image of her neighbor in her mind—her homemade pies and flawless smile, her immaculate house and *Better Homes and Gardens*-worthy yard. Now *there's* a woman who can do it all, unlike Libby, who doesn't know whether she's coming or going most days. She likes Georgina—she might have once even considered her a friend—but most of the time she finds it difficult not to compare herself to the other woman, especially when Libby always seems to come up short. Libby closes the post with a twinge of guilt. She just has so much on her plate right now that the thought of taking on another obligation, even one three months away, is enough to make her eye twitch. She'll volunteer to help with the fall festival as it gets closer, she promises herself. She *wants* to. And she'll make it a point to go introduce herself to the new neighbors one of these days too. Yes, Libby is going to get around to all of it, just as soon as she finds a spare moment...

She clocks the time on her phone screen and frowns. *Where the hell is Bill?* Would it have killed him to let her know he was running late?

"Mom!" Lucas shouts from somewhere in the depths of his bedroom.

"Yes?" She drops her phone and picks up a sponge. She might as well get a start on the dishes piled up in her sink, do something productive with her time if she's going to be forced to wait on Bill. Again.

Jasper, her beagle, lets out a tired groan at her feet.

"I know, Jasp," she says as he looks up at her with his wide eyes surrounded by graying fur. "I feel exactly the same way." He's getting up there in years. Libby is beginning to see it in the way he moves, his legs a little stiffer, his pace notably slower. They've had him since he was just a puppy, and his frailty is not something anyone in the Corbin family is ready to deal with.

"Mom!" Lucas shouts again, irritation rising in his adolescent voice.

Libby drops a plate onto the drying rack and tries to force her mind back to the days when he was a child. Back to when Lucas was a sweet, loving little boy who worshipped his mother. So much has changed since those early, simpler days. *What's that expression? Bigger kids, bigger problems.* It certainly feels that way to Libby lately. Sometimes she doesn't know how she's going to survive his teen years.

"Yes?" Libby calls back, louder now, trying to sound as unbothered as possible. She often thinks that talking to teenagers is like approaching an animal in the wild: no sudden movements, speak in gentle tones, and never let it sense your fear. Although Libby knows that they're almost on the other side of things. At seventeen, Lucas is nearly a man now, and he's starting to look it too. It seems to Libby like he grew up all at once this past year. A light smattering of stubble now darkens his jawline, and there's definition in his long legs that were once gangly and thin, poking out from the bottom of his basketball shorts like two sticks.

"Where's my jersey?" Lucas shouts. Libby can picture him upstairs, his room a disaster of discarded clothes and dog-eared sports magazines. "Did you take it?"

Why on earth would she have taken his jersey? "No," she replies calmly as she blows a rogue lock of hair out of her eyes. The steam from the sink has turned her blond curls into a mess of frizz. "I'm sure it's up there somewhere. Have you looked in the hamper?"

Libby dries her hands and checks the time again. She's definitely going to be late. She opens her phone and sends a text to Erica, her assistant manager, asking if she's available to open Lily Lane, the flower shop Libby owns.

Erica, always efficient, responds almost immediately:

> Not a problem. I've got it covered.

Lucas bounds down the stairs just as Libby drops her phone into her purse. He's wearing a soccer jersey with a distinct green grass stain slashed across the back.

"I don't have a clean jersey," he remarks as he walks into the kitchen and immediately begins rooting through the refrigerator. "Dad's taking me down to the field to practice."

"Guess your laundry should make it from your bedroom floor to the washing machine every once in a while, then."

Lucas sighs dramatically, rolling his eyes at his mother.

Libby has always loved that he inherited her eyes, a smoky hazel green that is striking against his long lashes and his mop of dark hair, but every time she looks at him lately, she sees undeniable traces of his father. In the broadness of his shoulders, the crooked tilt to his smile. It's a painful reminder of the status of her marriage.

I think we need some time apart. Bill's voice floats through her head. As if a marriage is the type of thing you can simply press pause on, like a film that's no longer holding your attention.

"What do you two have planned for the weekend?" Libby asks, but Lucas doesn't seem to register the question. He's already absorbed in his phone, his thumbs tapping away at the screen.

Libby doesn't know when this happened, when her son stopped talking to her. They used to be so close, or at least she'd thought they were. There was a time when he'd tell her about school, his teachers, his friends. Now it feels as though, somewhere along the way, the door to his inner world has been slammed in her face, a dead bolt slid into place.

The doorbell chimes, saving Libby from having to have yet another talk with her son about prying himself away from his phone from time to time.

Jasper gets up from his favorite sunny spot by the back door with considerable effort, and Libby hears him doing his best to trot behind her while she goes to answer the door, his nails clacking in a lopsided pattern as he moves.

Libby yanks open the front door, and a wave of July heat pours into the house.

"Hi, Lib," Bill says, leaning casually on the door frame, a pair of aviator sunglasses perched on the end of his nose. He gives her one of his tilted smiles, the one that made Libby fall in love with him all those years ago. She feels her knees weaken, but she steels herself quickly, standing up straight, her chin held high.

"Lucas!" she calls into the house. "Dad's here to pick you up!"

"Uh, gimme a minute," he yells back. "I'm not done packing." She hears his feet clomping up the stairs toward his bedroom.

"You gonna let me in, then?" Bill asks, all rakish charm and breezy familiarity. He looks different somehow, Libby thinks. Younger. He's wearing a black cotton T-shirt that tapers at his waist in a way that suggests it probably didn't come in one of the plastic-bundled packs of five she always bought for him; his sandy-brown hair is a little longer than she's accustomed to, curling at the nape of his neck, and there's some new definition in his crossed arms that she definitely doesn't recall being there before.

"Sure," she replies. "But I only have a minute. I was supposed to leave for the shop ages ago."

Bill looks down at his watch; his brows draw together in puzzlement, as if he's only just realized the time.

"You didn't have to wait on me," he says as Libby turns and leads the way toward the kitchen. "I'm sure Lucas could have managed on his own."

Libby listens to the heavy thud of Bill's footfalls as he trails her down the hallway. A sound once so familiar now feels out of place in her house. There's a sadness in that, she thinks, in how foreign Bill's presence here is starting to feel.

"I know Lucas would have been fine," Libby replies as they reach the kitchen. "But there's something I wanted to talk to you about this morning. Didn't you see my texts?"

Bill leans down and gives a scratch to an excited Jasper, whose tail thuds against the tiled floor in delight. "No. Sorry, Lib, must've missed it."

Libby suppresses a sigh. Bill's phone is practically glued to his hand. He would never forget to open a text from one of his clients at his real estate brokerage, but hers? Those he manages to overlook.

"Anyway," she says, pressing on, "it's about Lucas and the car."

"He still driving you crazy over that?"

"Yes. He is. He's been practically begging me to buy one for him, but I've been standing firm, telling him that he has to earn the money to pay for it. I think it's an important life lesson, you know? That things aren't just handed to you even if your parents might be able to afford them. I want him to understand the value of money and hard work."

Bill nods, scratching at the stubble on his chin. When they were together, Bill shaved every morning, but Libby finds that the roguish look suits him.

"It's important," Libby continues, shaking away the thought, "that we present a united front on this. I'm sure he's going to apply the pressure to you this weekend."

"Yes, boss," Bill replies with a mock salute, a smile breaking across his face that threatens to crack open Libby's chest.

She hates how much power he still has over her, how much she still loves him, even after everything he's put her through over the past eight months of their separation.

"I just need some space." Bill had said it so casually, as if it weren't a grenade tossed haphazardly onto everything they'd built together. "It'll be good for us, Lib," he'd assured her as she gaped at him, struggling to find her voice.

"But what about Lucas?" Libby could barely conceal the humiliating desperation that weaved its way through her words. She'd never thought she'd be the type of woman who would beg her husband to stay when he so clearly wanted to go. But yet, there she was, clinging to his hand while his eyes were already cast out the open door.

"We'll figure something out," he promised her, his voice calm and smooth, no trace of the panic that swept over her like a tidal wave. They'd been together since they were nineteen. Bill was the only man Libby had ever loved. How could she possibly imagine a future without him?

She looks at him now, popping a pod into her coffee maker, the dog they'd adopted together as a puppy lying at his feet, and reminds herself that this is only temporary. They're just separated, not divorced. It's probably just some sort of midlife crisis. Bill just needs to feel like he has some freedom before he sees how good he had it here. He'll come around eventually, Libby is sure of it, and when he does, they can start to heal. Because as hurt as Libby is, when she said "Forever" in their wedding vows, she'd meant it. They're just going to have to put in the work. Maybe he'll even agree to see that marriage counselor Libby had suggested.

"Well, now that that's settled, I'm going to head to work," Libby says, sliding the strap of her purse onto her shoulder.

"Have a good day." Bill leans over and kisses her tenderly on the cheek, before turning back to his coffee and adding a splash of his favorite hazelnut creamer that Libby hasn't had the heart to remove from her weekly shopping list.

"Thanks," she squeaks, her voice unsure and girlish to her ears. What was *that*?

She walks outside as if in a daze, the tingling imprint of Bill's lips lingering on her skin. It's a gorgeous sunny day and she breathes in the laden smells of summer—citrus and fresh-cut grass, mossy wood and rich earth—savoring the feeling of sunshine warming her face as she tilts it skyward.

Libby slides into her car and makes the conscious choice to ignore the check-oil light as she turns the key in the ignition and starts driving. She tries not to overthink the kiss. It's something Bill has done thousands of times over the course of their eighteen years together. It could have just been force of habit, but Libby can't help but feel like it was something more. A rekindling of an old flame.

Maybe it's still there, the spark they'd ignited so long ago. Maybe it wasn't extinguished after all; maybe it has just been buried under years of marriage and mortgage payments.

Libby is so lost in her thoughts that she nearly doesn't see the pretty blond woman stepping around the side of the moving van. She jams on the brakes; her tires squeal against the asphalt as she skids to a stop. *That's* one *way to meet my new neighbor...*

3

AUDREY
Hawthorne Lane

Audrey Warrington hears her phone buzz on her nightstand, and she gropes for it with a groan. On the screen is a new post in the Hawthorne Lane community forum about the fall festival. *Halloween is three months away! Why the hell are we talking about it now?* She tosses her phone aside without giving it a second thought. Her prim and proper neighbor Georgina, with her buttoned-up cardigans and her strands of pearls, is the last thing Audrey wants to be thinking about right now as she sinks back down into bed, savors the feeling of her bare skin against her new sheets. They're mulberry silk and cost more than she'd be entirely honest with Seth about should he ever ask, but she knows that he never will because he never even noticed that she'd swapped out the old ones. In this moment, Audrey is certain they were worth every damn penny.

She hears the shower turn on in the en suite bathroom and pictures the hard lines of his body, the way the water will be running over his taut stomach, his muscular arms. The thought sends another wave of pleasure cascading through her body, curling at her toes. To say the sex was good would be an understatement. The sex was *transcendent*. Which, Audrey is fully aware, sounds dramatic but in this case also happens to be true. She felt like she was having an out-of-body experience, looking down on herself moving, speaking, moaning in a way she hasn't in years. Who *was* that person? God, she'd almost forgotten that her body was capable of feeling this way. How could she have forgotten?

The sudden sound of squealing tires grabs Audrey's attention. Curious, she gets out of bed, covering her bare breasts with her thick, white duvet, and pads to her open window, where her gauzy curtains billow in the gentle summer breeze. She parts them slightly and looks down into the cul-de-sac below just in time to see Libby jump out of her car and race toward the frightened woman standing, hand to her chest, inches from the hood. She can't hear what the two women are saying, but she watches as Libby gesticulates wildly, appearing to apologize profusely, while the other woman extends her hand, introducing herself. Audrey wonders whether the pretty young blonde is the new neighbor she'd read about on the community board. She's glad that a property developer had the good sense to buy the old house that stood at 5 Hawthorne Lane and flip it. It had been an eyesore when it was owned by Ms. McGreely, the bitter octogenarian who didn't believe in landscaping. But now it's a lovely modernized colonial that blends neatly with the rest of the block. *Well, no matter.* Audrey turns away from the window. It seems that everyone is just fine, and if all her neighbors are finished interrupting her postcoital glow, Audrey would prefer to return to bed and enjoy it for a little bit longer.

It's been hard, with Seth traveling so much, to keep the spark in their marriage alive. Audrey remembers now that it was like this in the early days. It's coming back to her like muscle memory. The passion, the hot, driving need that pulled them together. But once Seth's writing career took off, she felt like he was always gone—book tours, writers' conferences, speaking engagements. Audrey lost her husband to the fictional world of the Detective Marlow series. After a while, even when he was home, he felt far away. There was a time when Audrey had been bitter about it. Angry, resentful, that Seth neglected their marriage so heavily in favor of his career, but eventually she became ... indifferent. Which was probably worse, she's beginning to realize. She'd almost forgotten what it was like to feel wanted, alive, her nerve endings fizzing with desire. And now, as though a switch has been flipped, she remembers. Holy hell does she remember.

Audrey hears the shower turn off, and in moments he's leaning in the doorway, a towel wrapped low on his hips, hot steam billowing out behind him. She has the sudden urge to go to him and lick the water droplets that cling to his broad, soap-scented shoulders, but she refrains. It's been so long since she's had to *refrain*. Instead, she props herself on her elbows, the duvet barely covering her breasts, and turns to him with a salacious smile, letting a shock of hair fall tantalizingly over one eye. She's aware of her body, of how it looks to him as she lies here. Audrey knows she's beautiful with her thick, dark hair, her olive skin, the fullness of her breasts, and the toned muscles in her long legs. Men have looked at her all her life; it's something she's become accustomed to, the heat of the male gaze on her skin. And at some point along the way, she learned how to use that power to her advantage.

"You coming back to bed?" she asks, her voice a seductive purr.

"I wish I could, but I have a meeting I can't miss."

She nods, masking her disappointment.

He begins to pull on his clothes—a crisply pressed blazer, an Armani tie. "Perhaps we could go out for a late dinner tonight, though."

Audrey perks up at the idea of a repeat performance and then deflates just as quickly. "I have a drinks thing," she laments with a dramatic groan. "For work." Spending an evening sipping cosmos with her coworkers from *Top Cast,* the magazine where she works as an executive editor, suddenly feels like the last thing in the world she wants to do tonight.

"Well," he says as he draws closer and playfully bites her shoulder. "I guess we'll have to reschedule." His lips edge near her breast now, and she feels her heart pounding in her chest. *How bad would it be for me to skip one work event?*

"That is, if you really can't miss it . . ." His warm mouth closes around her nipple, and her body quivers with want. *Maybe I could feign a migraine?* She feels herself coming undone, giving herself over to his mouth, his tongue, his roaming fingers . . .

And then her phone buzzes on the nightstand yet again and shatters the moment. His hands leave her body as abruptly as if a spell had been broken, and he resumes knotting his tie. Audrey sighs in frustration as she reaches for the offending phone, ready to toss it out the nearest window if it's another asinine post from Georgina. But it isn't.

"Who's calling?" he asks her casually, adjusting his lapels in the full-length mirror.

"My husband."

4
GEORGINA
Hawthorne Lane

> Where are you?

Georgina Pembrook stares at her phone screen, willing her son, Sebastian, to respond, though she knows he won't. This is the third text she's sent him tonight, all of which have gone unanswered. Sebastian, who is turning eighteen in a few short weeks, might think he's too old to have to answer to his mother, but as long as he lives in Georgina's house, there are rules that he's expected to follow.

While she waits for the reply she knows isn't coming, she opens the Hawthorne Lane forum on the community board. Her post about the fall festival has gotten exactly zero replies. Her neighbors don't seem to grasp that three months is very little time to pull together an event of this magnitude, but no matter, she'll handle it. She always does.

With a sigh, Georgina sets down her phone and turns back to the stove, where a large pot of sauce simmers on the front burner. She's making Colin's favorite tonight—eggplant rollatini. Georgina usually loves to cook, but tonight her heart isn't in it. She's finding the process—the cutting, dipping, rolling, frying—tedious. She's made this meal so many times that she could probably make it in her sleep. But she reminds herself that she's doing this because her family loves it, and there's nothing that Georgina wouldn't do for her family.

After giving the sauce a stir, Georgina lifts her cleaning caddy from beneath the sink and begins to attend to the kitchen. She washes the cooking utensils sitting in her sink by hand, carefully puts each back in its designated place, then polishes the granite countertops until they sparkle and scrubs the stainless-steel appliances to a shine.

Satisfied with the state of her kitchen, she turns to get a start on setting the dining table when the ring of the doorbell calls her attention. She glances at the clock. It's too early for Colin to be home. She isn't expecting her husband for another half an hour. Perhaps it's Sebastian and he's forgotten his key again. She slides the tray of eggplant into the oven and wipes her hands on a tea towel before she makes her way to the front door, ready to greet her son with a reminder about the house rules and keeping better track of his things.

"Mom?" Christina calls as she appears on the stairs, a book tucked under her arm, her glasses pushed up atop her head. "Is someone here?"

"It's probably just your brother," Georgina replies as she pulls open the door. At least she has *one* child she doesn't have to worry about. "Oh!" She's surprised by the figure standing on her porch, and she struggles to place her. A petite blond woman with wide, cornflower-blue eyes and a nervous smile. She's too young to be one of the school parents and too old to be one of the kids' friends, and yet Georgina is struck by the feeling that she should know her somehow, that she already does.

"Hi," the young woman says, her voice soft and delicate. "My name is Hannah Wilson. I'm your new neighbor." She points to the house across the rounded bend of the cul-de-sac. "Just over there. My husband and I are in the process of moving in. Anyway." She thrusts a stack of papers toward Georgina. "It seems that some of your mail has been coming to our address. We only just found it. I hope it isn't anything too important."

Georgina takes the cluster of envelopes from Hannah's hand. Now she remembers. She saw this woman before, when she and her husband were taking a tour of the old McGreely house with their real estate agent, Libby's husband, Bill Corbin. "Thank you for bringing it over. I'm Georgina, and this is my daughter, Christina." She steps aside, allowing Hannah to see into the open entryway.

She notices the way Hannah's eyes widen as she takes in the soaring ceilings, the black-and-white family portraits hanging in their silver frames, the polished curved banister of the center staircase.

"Hey," Christina says with a small wave before darting back upstairs to her bedroom.

Hannah smiles. "You have a beautiful home, Georgina. You'll have to give me some decorating tips sometime. I don't have the first clue where to begin with our house!"

"Thank you. That's very kind. Would you maybe like to come in?"

She hadn't intended to invite the new neighbor inside, but it feels like the polite thing to do in the moment. And Georgina Pembrook is nothing if not polite.

"I wouldn't want to impose on your evening." Hannah shakes her head, her golden-blond hair rustling softly at her shoulders, but Georgina gets the impression that the younger woman wants to accept. There's something about her. Something that Georgina feels drawn to. She wonders if Hannah feels it too.

"Nonsense, I just popped dinner into the oven, and I'd be happy to pour us a glass of wine."

"Oh, uh." Hannah looks back over her shoulder toward her house, where the porch light shines as if awaiting her return. "Sure. Thank you."

Georgina leads her new neighbor through her house and into the kitchen. She motions for Hannah to sit, pulls out a pair of crystal wineglasses, and sets each one on a coaster on the table.

Georgina lifts two bottles of wine—a red from the rack and a chilled white from the refrigerator below it. "Red or white?"

"Whichever you prefer," Hannah demurs.

Georgina inspects the two labels. Colin likes the red, so she selects the white and uncorks the chardonnay with a pop.

"So where did you move from?" Georgina asks as she pours a finger of the pale gold liquid into each of their glasses.

"Manhattan," Hannah replies, lifting the glass to her lips.

"Ah, so not too far, then."

"No, Mark is going to be commuting into the city for work most days. He's an accountant and that's where his firm is."

"My husband's law firm as well. But I find it's so much more enjoyable living out here, away from all the noise of the city."

"Yes, that's part of the reason we chose this place. We were ready to live somewhere quieter with a little more space." She blushes. "Maybe think about starting a family."

"Well, this is the perfect place for it." Georgina smiles warmly. She remembers those days, when the promise of the future seemed to sparkle tantalizingly on the horizon. "It doesn't get much quieter than Hawthorne Lane. And the school district is incredible."

"So I'm told."

The front door opens with a whine. "Georgina?"

At the sound of her husband's voice, Georgina checks the clock above the stove. *He's early.*

"In here, darling," she calls. She hears his dress shoes tapping on the hardwood floor, growing louder as he approaches.

Colin appears in the entry to the kitchen in a tailored navy-blue suit and a crisp white shirt, his jacket casually draped over his shoulder. Georgina sees a look of confusion pass over his face as he registers their unexpected guest, but it's gone as quickly as it arrived.

"And I see we have company." Colin smiles, two dazzling rows of perfect white teeth.

"I'm . . . uh," Hannah stutters as though she's momentarily forgotten her own name. "Hannah."

Colin tends to have that effect on people, women in particular, Georgina has noticed. He's strikingly handsome, almost startlingly so. Like a movie star that's just stepped off the silver screen. They've been together for almost twenty years, and sometimes he still catches Georgina off guard.

"It's a pleasure to meet you, Hannah." Colin takes her hand.

"Hannah is our new neighbor," Georgina explains. "And she was kind enough to bring over some of our mail."

Colin laughs. "I doubt it will be the last time. Wait until you meet our mailman, Doug. He wears glasses as thick as Coke bottles. I doubt he can read a damn thing." Colin sniffs the air. "Hey, is that eggplant rollatini I smell?"

"Oh!" Georgina rushes to the stove and shuts off the burner

under the extra sauce. "I'd nearly forgotten I was cooking. It'll be ready in just a few minutes."

Hannah smiles graciously. "Well, I'll let you two get back to your evening. Thank you again for the wine." She pushes her glass forward, though Georgina notices she's hardly touched it.

"Anytime," Georgina replies as she walks Hannah to the door.

"And I really was serious about those decorating tips! Everything here is just *perfect*!"

The word rings in Georgina's head like struck glass: *perfect, perfect, perfect.*

5

HANNAH

Hawthorne Lane

It's late by the time Hannah starts her walk home from Georgina's house. The sky has turned dark, and the stars sparkle overhead in an array of constellations that Hannah could never see in New York City.

She hadn't planned on staying at Georgina's, but there was something about her, something that seemed to pull Hannah into her orbit. Everything about Georgina said *right* in all the places Hannah has always been wrong: Her hair, the color of a polished penny, fell in smooth waves past her shoulders, her clothes were elegant and refined, and the diamond tennis bracelet encircling her slim wrist gave the air of casual wealth. Not to mention her house—the largest on the block, sitting dead center at the end of the cul-de-sac—which was incredible. It's clear that Georgina has taste. Hannah saw it in the small details: the vase of fresh white roses in the open foyer, the original artworks adorning the walls, the curated throw pillows strategically placed to make the house feel homey yet elegant. That's the kind of taste that money can't buy. Not that Hannah would know what that's like, never having owned a piece of furniture that she didn't have to assemble with an Allen wrench. Mark had given her a credit card, told her to buy anything she wanted for the new house, but Hannah didn't even know where to begin. Preferences, as far as she's concerned, are for people who can afford them, and she's never been able to.

She has been worried about whether she'd fit in here, on Hawthorne Lane. This place is so different from what she's accustomed to. She knows that Mark was raised in a neighborhood very much like this one, where there were dinner parties and impromptu games of kickball in the street. Coming here is, for Mark, like coming home. But it's different for her. Hannah isn't even sure what home feels like. She'd known once, when her mother was alive, but that was a very long time ago. Hannah did most of her growing up in foster care. Which meant that she often wasn't in the same place long enough to find her footing, to make any real connections. And after a while, she'd given up trying. She accepted that she was a girl who belonged to no one and nowhere. Until she wasn't.

Hannah shakes her head. She's not that girl anymore. And Hawthorne Lane is going to be different. She's already met two of her neighbors, and despite the fact that Libby nearly hit her with her car, they'd both been warmly welcoming. Libby had apologized to Hannah profusely and explained that she'd been distracted and hadn't seen her coming around the side of the moving van. Hannah had offered an apology of her own, admitting that she hadn't been looking before she stepped into the street. In the end, they'd both laughed at the awkwardness of the introduction, and Libby had jokingly promised to try not to mow Hannah down again the next time they saw each other.

The house is quiet now as Hannah slips inside and locks the front door behind her. Mark must have fallen asleep after their long day of unpacking. Hannah feels it too, the exhaustion that is ready to consume her. She sets her purse on top of one of the many unopened boxes that dominate the space that will soon be her new living room. She dropped the mail there earlier as well. That was when she'd spotted Georgina's name, familiar from the community forum, on several of the envelopes and realized the mailman's mistake. The rest of the mail is still there, the pile of scattered flyers, bills forwarded from their previous address in Manhattan, and takeout menus. After being inside Georgina's warm and spotless home, Hannah finds that she suddenly can't stand the clutter of her own. She's eager to start unpacking, tidying away the mess, but it feels like a daunting task. One that she knows she'll mostly be doing alone once

Mark goes back to work in a few days. With a sigh, she quickly flips through the mail one last time as she makes her way toward the garbage bin.

That's when she sees it—an envelope marked only with the address of the apartment in Manhattan where she and Mark had been living before closing on their new house on Hawthorne Lane. There's no return address, which strikes Hannah as odd. She turns it over in her hand, inspects the back flap, and finds that it's held closed with a small piece of tape.

She slides her finger beneath the flap, opens it, and pulls out the single sheet of paper folded inside.

In bold block letters, the word LIAR has been printed in red ink, like a slashed wound across the white page.

Hannah's fingers start to tremble and her vision swims; the letters jumble and blur in her hands.

"Hannah?"

The sound of Mark's voice just over her shoulder nearly causes her to jump out of her skin. She whirls around to face him, holding the offending paper in one hand, the other rising to her chest to still her thrashing heart. "You scared the life out of me."

"Sorry. I thought I'd heard you come in." He takes off his glasses, wipes them with the hem of his shirt. "What are you doing down here?"

His eyes lower to the piece of paper clutched in her hand, and she quickly crumples it in her palm before stuffing it into a garbage bag with the rest of the junk mail, burying it beneath wads of peeled packing tape and bubble wrap.

"Nothing," she says, forcing a smile onto her face. Her lips tremble at the corners, but she's hoping that it's too dark for Mark to read the lie behind her teeth. "Just thought I'd tidy up a little before calling it a night."

"I have a better idea," he says as he takes her into his arms and lifts her onto the counter. "It's our first night here"—he nuzzles her neck—"all alone in our new house." He moves between her thighs as he continues, his teeth softly grazing her earlobe, "Why don't we christen the place?"

Mark trails his fingers down her arms, and Hannah feels herself softening beneath his touch. That letter could have come from anywhere. Maybe it wasn't even meant for her. She tells herself this as Mark lifts her top over her head, reaches for the clasp of her bra. She tells herself that she has nothing to worry about. But then again, Hannah is a liar.

HALLOWEEN NIGHT

Transcript of interview with Shelby Holt
October 31, 2024

Detective Olsen: So, Ms. Holt, I understand you're the one who found the body earlier tonight. Is that correct?

Ms. Holt: Y-yes.

Detective Olsen: That must have been very upsetting for you.

Ms. Holt: It totally was.

Detective Olsen: And how old are you, Shelby?

Ms. Holt: Sixteen.

Detective Olsen: Do you live on Hawthorne Lane?

Ms. Holt: No, I was just there for the festival.

Detective Olsen: And how did you come to be in the woods?

Ms. Holt: Oh, I . . .

Detective Olsen: Don't worry, you aren't in any kind of trouble, Shelby. I'm just trying to piece together what happened out there.

Ms. Holt: Well, see, a lot of kids go up to those woods at night. To, like, hang out or whatever. My friends and I made a plan to ditch our parents during the fireworks and meet up on the main path. When I got there, I saw someone lying on the ground. At first I thought it was one of my friends or something, maybe one of the boys just being stupid and trying to play a prank. Like, they were going to jump up and scare me or whatever. But when I got closer . . .

Detective Olsen: Would you like a tissue?

Ms. Holt: No, no, I'll be fine. It's just, I'd never seen a dead body before. And the blood, so much blood . . .

Detective Olsen: What happened next?

Ms. Holt: Well, I screamed, obviously. And then I ran out of the woods to find my mom. I was yelling that someone was dead, that we needed to call the police. People started just going crazy after that. Like, everyone started running, trying to get away from there as fast as they could.

TWO MONTHS BEFORE HALLOWEEN

6
LIBBY
Hawthorne Lane

Libby is in a rush. Again. She has less than an hour before she has to open her shop, and she still needs to make a stop at the grocery store. It's her assistant's birthday, and Libby wants to bring her one of the fancy cakes they have at the bakery counter of Grocers' Way. Erica deserves it. She works nearly as hard as Libby to make Lily Lane a success, not to mention that Libby owes her one for being willing to open at a moment's notice last month when she got caught up waiting on Bill. But as with most things, Libby left it until the last minute and now she's rushing.

She darts out of the house, the strap of her purse sliding down her shoulder as she pulls the front door closed, and trots down the brick steps of her porch. It's another scorchingly hot day. This summer has been a brutal one, the type of oppressive heat that brings the entire town to a boil. Patience has been in short supply—customers being snippy with Libby's staff, horns honking on Main Street. She wonders if the weather could be partially to blame for Lucas's recent attitude too (though she knows that's a stretch).

They'd argued again that morning. If you could even call it arguing. Lately, it seems to Libby like she can't say a single solitary thing to her son without setting him off. This morning it was as innocuous as her asking about his plans for the day.

"Where are you going?" Libby inquired when Lucas finally emerged from his bedroom and made an appearance in the kitchen.

"Out," he replied. He swiped a bagel from the kitchen counter and headed toward the front door without so much as a look in his mother's direction.

"And where would 'out' be located, exactly?"

Lucas stopped in the hallway, throwing his head back in exasperation. She could see the dramatic rise and fall of his shoulders as he sighed heavily. "What's with the interrogation?" he asked, finally turning to face her.

Libby swallowed her annoyance at his tone. "It's not exactly an interrogation to inquire about where my seventeen-year-old son is going. Pretty sure that's just basic parenting."

"Field at the high school."

"See? That wasn't so bad."

Lucas shrugged and slid in a pair of earbuds, once again tuning her out.

"It's been great talking to you," Libby huffed sarcastically as her son walked away. She threw up her hands in a sign of defeat, even though Jasper was the only one who was there to see it.

The entire exchange had thrown Libby off this morning as she turned it over and over in her head, trying to determine where she'd gone wrong. And now she's running late.

She slides into her car, jams her key into the ignition, and starts the engine. Something is going on with Lucas. She's certain of it. She just wishes he'd *talk* to her. Like he used to. Maybe it's her fault. Maybe she's been spending too much time at the shop, and it's affecting her relationship with Lucas. Ever since Bill left, Libby has practically buried herself in work. She knows it's a crutch and that there are probably healthier ways of dealing with the whirlwind of emotions she's constantly holding back, but working is the only thing that seems to distract her these days. In her store, she's in control—she can trim, cut, arrange, and set things in order. She can make something beautiful enough to hide the ugliness in her life. But as much as Libby loves her shop, Lucas has always been her priority. He knows that. Doesn't he?

Once again, Libby feels a stab of resentment toward Bill. She doesn't understand it, how he could put their family through this. How it's possible to just walk away from someone after eighteen years of building a life together. Sure, things hadn't been great those last few years, but life can't always be sunshine and rainbows. Libby thought Bill understood that. She thought they'd weather the storm. And yet here she is, braving the elements alone.

Libby shifts her car into reverse, carefully checks her rearview mirror. She can't risk another incident like the one she had with their new neighbor, Hannah Wilson. She'd practically run the poor girl over! Hannah was, thankfully, quite gracious about the whole thing, but Libby was mortified, stammering about how she'd been distracted that morning and issuing assurances that she's usually a much more cautious driver. What a first impression she must have left on her lovely new neighbor.

But this time, there is no sign of Hannah. Instead, Libby spots a woman pushing a stroller along the sidewalk at an efficient clip, occasionally checking the fitness watch strapped to her wrist. Libby remembers those days, when motherhood was all-consuming, when it felt like you were losing yourself in the sea of diaper changes and nap schedules. When it seemed impossible that you'd ever have another moment to yourself, and those extra few pounds clinging to your hips were just another reminder of all the sacrifices motherhood demanded of you. But she remembers the golden haze of all of it too, the languid mornings spent with a laughing toddler—witnessing wobbly first steps and clumsy attempts at forming words. She'd wanted more children after Lucas, but it just wasn't in the cards for her. No matter how hard she and Bill tried for another child, Lucas seemed destined to be their only. And so Libby put everything she had into raising her son—she gave all of herself over to being his mother. And now he's nearly grown up and wants practically nothing to do with her. Libby wishes she could tell the woman with the stroller to slow down, not to rush these days away, but she knows she won't understand, not until her kids are grown and she's looking back on this time in her own rearview mirror.

THE PARKING LOT OF GROCERS' WAY is surprisingly crowded for a Thursday morning. Libby checks her watch. She has only twenty minutes before she needs to open Lily Lane, but it should be enough time if she hurries.

She runs into the store, where a gust of cool air-conditioning and the smell of fresh produce greet her. The baked-goods section is at the back of the shop, and Libby makes a beeline for it, but she is quickly diverted from her mission.

"Libby Corbin?"

I don't have time for this, Libby thinks. But of course, she doesn't say that. Instead, she plasters a smile on her face, one that she prays looks more cordial than manic, and stops to chat with Beth Something or Other, the head of the PTA at the high school. Beth is standing with another mother whom Libby doesn't recognize, a pigtailed toddler happily licking a lollipop in the front seat of the woman's cart.

"Hi, Beth!" Libby trills.

"I thought that was you!" Beth gushes dramatically. "It's been so long since I've seen you up at the school! I hardly recognized you!"

Subtle, Beth. Very subtle. "Oh, you know how it is, busy-busy!" She resists the urge to check her watch again. She can almost feel the seconds ticking away as she stands here.

"I heard you have new neighbors up on Hawthorne Lane."

Libby sighs inwardly. She sometimes forgets what a small town Sterling Valley is. *Too* small, if you ask her. Of course word of the moving trucks coming and going from her block already hit the rumor mill. Something about the big houses, the secluded location, makes Hawthorne Lane and its residents a favorite topic of discussion.

"I do, but I'm afraid I don't know much about them yet," Libby says with a tight smile, and Beth's look sours. As the town's reigning gossip, she was probably hoping for some exclusive insight into the newcomers.

"I saw that Bill's brokerage was the listing agent for the property. I considered buying it myself, but the timing didn't work out."

Libby nods, distracted with thoughts about how to politely extricate herself from this conversation.

"Anyway," Beth plows on, "that must have been quite a sale for Bill. Good for him. How *is* that husband of yours anyway?"

Libby flounders over how to answer the question for a moment. She hadn't realized that Beth even knew Bill outside of a few times they'd met at school functions. But she shouldn't be surprised. Libby supposes that many people in Sterling Valley have a faux familiarity with her husband. After all, it's his face grinning out from SOLD signs all over town, his rakish smile on a park bench on Main Street, one rogue curl flopping disarmingly over his forehead. And isn't that the whole point? He's a familiar face, a friend, a neighbor, someone you can trust. Everyone except for Libby, that is. But even as she thinks it, she knows it's not true. That's the problem with Bill. It's hard to hate him. He's not a bad person. Not really. He's the guy who runs over with jumper cables if he sees that you're having car trouble; he's the neighbor who is happy to hold the ladder while you clean out your gutters and even happier to crack open some cold beers, glass bottles clinking, when the work is through. The thing is, Libby's husband is a genuinely *nice guy*. A fact that infuriates Libby to no end as of late. The only fault he has, as far as she can tell, is that he's stopped wanting her.

"Good," Libby manages, "he's good. Busy as ever." Beth is the last person Libby wants to discuss the details of her tumultuous marriage with. And anyway, soon this absurd separation will end, and no one will have to be the wiser.

"I'm sure," Beth replies, her tone betraying her boredom with Libby's surface-level response.

"Anyway, I really should be going, I—"

"Since I have you," Beth interrupts, "I know the new school year hasn't started yet, but I was hoping to get a few volunteers lined up for the goodwill auction—"

"Actually, would you mind shooting me an email with the details? I hate to cut this short, but I have to open the shop in a few minutes."

Beth's friend smiles wryly.

"Of course, of course," Beth replies with a shooing flick of her wrist. "You get going. I know how busy you must be, running your own business and whatnot! I simply *don't* know how you do it all!"

Libby flashes her a quick smile. She's almost out of time. "Thanks, Beth! Talk soon!"

Libby race-walks to the bakery counter and places her cake order, drumming her fingers on the countertop while she waits. *I should be able to make it to the shop on time if I don't run into any more delays.* She watches as the young woman attempts to write Erica's name in pink frosting with an unsteady hand; she has to scrape it off and restart the process twice.

"Sorry. I'm still training," the girl says sheepishly.

Libby realizes that she's probably making the poor kid nervous. "It's no problem, take your time," she replies through a forced smile, stilling her anxious fingers. She decides to leave the girl to it and distract herself by perusing the rows of rolls and French breads. Maybe she should pick up something to bring to the barbecue Georgina is hosting over the weekend to welcome Hannah and Mark Wilson to the neighborhood. Libby considers some of the packaged pastries, imagines them sitting in their plastic clamshells on Georgina's artfully arranged dessert table beside her own homemade confections and decides against it.

"It's really a shame," Libby hears, the words floating over the display and pulling her from her thoughts. She recognizes Beth's voice but can't see her. She must be in the next aisle. "I heard her husband just *left* her. Walked out on her and her kid."

"I can't imagine why." Her friend giggles. "She seems so pleasant."

"Oh, stop," Beth chides, laughter bubbling beneath her words. "You're so bad. Anyway, he's with some other woman now. At least that's what I've heard. Melissa Welton—do you know her? She said she saw Bill Corbin out with some woman, and it looked pretty hot and heavy from how she described it. I wonder if Libby knows about *that*. If she did, she'd probably be a little less smug, always bringing up her shop, how *busy* she is, and rubbing it in people's faces like we're supposed to be impressed."

The conversation continues—"By the way, have you seen the new principal at the high school yet? He's not hard to look at, I'll tell you that much!"—but the words are nearly drowned out by the ringing in Libby's ears. She slides to the floor, her purse landing with a thud next to her. She hardly even notices when the contents spill out onto the ground, her lipstick rolling away. She barely registers the salesgirl who's run around the counter to check on her.

"Are you okay, ma'am? Are you okay?"

All she can hear is Beth's voice, her nasty little words echoing in her consciousness: *He's with some other woman now.*

7

AUDREY
Hawthorne Lane

Audrey looks out her kitchen window across her vast green backyard. It's nearly dusk, but the gardener has only just arrived. He whizzes by on his ride-on mower and waves. She lifts her hand, gives him a slight nod and a tight smile in return. Everyone loves Tony Russo. They *rave* about him. He's the gardener of choice for all of Hawthorne Lane. Personally, Audrey doesn't understand what he's done to earn such a standing. She suspects there are plenty of other middle-aged men who are capable of wielding a hedge trimmer, but it is what it is. She was hardly going to be the only stuck-up bitch on the block who refused to let the guy ride his obnoxiously loud mower back and forth over her lawn. And so she and Seth dutifully leave a check for him in their mailbox once a week, just as their neighbors do, and she pretends not to notice the unnerving way he stares through their windows.

Audrey opens the wine refrigerator, pulls out a bottle of pinot grigio, and tips a generous helping into her glass. She needs a little something to take the edge off. It's been two weeks since Seth returned from the latest leg of his book tour, and things have been tense ever since. From what Audrey gathers, his new Detective Marlow novel isn't being received as well as he'd hoped, and as a result, there have been an endless slew of closed-door phone calls with his agent, his editor, his publicist. Audrey has largely just tried to stay out of the way.

There's a loud bang outside and she watches as Tony disentangles his mower from her wrought-iron garden bench. Audrey huffs. You'd think he might feel compelled to be a little more careful, what with all the money he makes on this block alone. *Perhaps I should take his job,* she thinks. *Get myself a ride-on mower, collect all the checks lined up in the mailboxes.* She can't help but laugh as she imagines Seth's reaction if she were to tell him she was going to quit her job at *Top Cast* to be the neighborhood gardener. It's not so much that they need the money she makes as an executive editor—Seth's books are certainly successful enough that they don't need Audrey's income—it's the principle of the thing. The optics. Seth Warrington's wife in khaki pants with a leaf blower strapped to her shoulders.

Audrey shakes her head at the very idea and turns to make her way into the dining room. As she does, she catches sight of the invitation stuck to the side of her refrigerator with a magnet. A barbecue being hosted by Georgina Pembrook to welcome the new neighbors. Audrey rolls her eyes at the formality of it all. A simple text would have sufficed, but of course Georgina ordered printed invitations on thick, creamy card stock and hand-delivered them to each mailbox. She never does anything halfway. Audrey once watched that woman serve a five-course meal in Louboutins without breaking a sweat. But it feels performative to Audrey, this pretense Georgina insists on keeping up that they're all the best of friends simply because they happen to live on the same block. It's not that Audrey particularly dislikes her neighbors, but she sees them as exactly that: neighbors. Friendly enough, but certainly not *friends.* If they were all real friends, maybe one of them might have noticed how unhappy she's been in her marriage these past few years. Maybe she'd have wanted to confide in them about how lost she's felt, how lonely. But none of that happened. Because the relationship among the wives of Hawthorne Lane is a surface-level one—no deeper than waves from the ends of their driveways, forced smiles over a shared fence. Audrey doesn't understand why they should pretend it's anything more than that.

At least, for once, she and Seth will be on the same page about something. He's not going to be thrilled at the prospect of attending this barbecue either. She recalls him once referring to Georgina as a Stepford Wife and her husband, Colin, as insufferably arrogant. It was the kind of thing they used to laugh about together.

Audrey carries her drink into the dining room, takes her seat at the far end of the table. Seth doesn't look up from his phone long enough to notice her arrival. She watches him, rolling the stem of her wineglass between her fingers. She's trying to look at her husband with fresh eyes, to spot the things that once drew her to him, see if they're still there. She and Seth and have been together a long time—coming up on fifteen years now—and, as far as Audrey is concerned, that's an awfully long stretch to assume that they're still the same people they were when they first met. At thirty-four, she's certainly not the woman she was at twenty. She wonders as she watches him now—absently sipping at his glass of whiskey, thumb scrolling over the screen in his palm—whether she'd still choose him if they'd met today. Given the fact that she's been sleeping with another man, she tends to doubt that.

"What are you reading?" she asks. She could venture a guess, but she's eager to shatter the stifling silence that's settled between them.

"Another review. Not good."

Audrey tries to suppress a sigh. She knows Seth hasn't been pleased with the early reviews (Seth has come to expect that his work will be met with nothing less than glowing accolades), but the damn book will still probably hit the bestseller lists. Every time he bashes out another half-hearted thriller, it climbs to the top of the charts simply because his name is printed on the cover. Audrey hasn't read this one, but she's certain it will be no different.

She hears her phone buzz against the sleek, polished wood of their dining table. Seth, of course, is paying her no mind, but even still, she slips it under the table before checking the incoming message, as if she knows, before looking at the screen, that it's from *him*.

> Meet me tonight

Audrey bristles slightly at the demanding tone but quickly brushes it off. She usually likes that sort of take-charge attitude in a man, but she already told him that Seth was home this week and she wouldn't be available.

> Can't. Shouldn't even be texting. Husband is here.

She silences her phone and puts it facedown on the table. "What's your agent saying?" she asks, turning her attention back to Seth, who is still staring into the blue-white glow of his own phone screen.

He grumbles an unintelligible reply.

Audrey sips her wine. *Is it any wonder I'm having an affair?* She is, of course, aware that it's not the *right* thing to do, but it was so easy to fall into it, to let herself be led by the heady temptation of feeling wanted and appreciated when she barely exists to her own husband anymore.

There was a time when Seth wanted her. God, there was a time when he'd *worshipped* her. Now she can't even manage to get him to speak a full sentence to her.

She sees the edges of her phone screen illuminate again and ignores it. Instead, she watches Seth as he scowls down at his phone, noticing all the ways he's changed since they met so many years ago. There are the physical changes, of course—the crow's feet marring the corners of his eyes, the deep lines etched around his downturned mouth, the thinning of his hair, the paunch in his midsection—but it goes much deeper than that.

She thinks back to the early days, to the tiny apartment they shared, the two of them talking late into the night about the successful careers they were going to build, the big house they'd live in, the exotic places they'd travel to together. Audrey can still see the way Seth's face would light up as she walked through the door, bone-tired, feet aching after a long day at *Top Cast,* where she'd started as a lowly intern, how he'd take her in his arms and kiss her deeply until all of her stress melted away. She remembers how eagerly she'd snatch up whatever pages he'd written that day, devour them before she even had a chance to change her clothes, poring over the prose, marveling over the way he could spin entire worlds out of thin air.

But she blinks and the memories melt away. They aren't those people anymore. It feels as if, somewhere along this journey that they started together, their paths diverged. Now Audrey watches from the sidelines as Seth tours the country alone, promoting his books, smiling no longer at her but at his adoring fans.

Seth slugs back his whiskey now, draining his glass. "Getting a refill." He barely looks at his wife as he stands, turning away from the table.

Audrey raises an eyebrow. She's noticed that Seth has been drinking more than his usual weekend glass of brandy since he's been home these past weeks. She opens her mouth to say something, but she decides against it, chalking it up to his stress over the new book. She doubts that discussion would be well received at the moment anyway. How did they get to this point where it feels like even having a conversation is a minefield not worth crossing?

She picks up her phone, taking advantage of Seth's absence to check the message that came in earlier.

> Make it work, and I'll make it worth your while.

Audrey huffs. Though such an offer from him would normally stir a warm tingle of want deep in her belly, today it's left her feeling annoyed. She doesn't appreciate that he's not respecting the boundaries she very clearly set for their relationship. Things may not be great with Seth these days, but he's still her husband. They have a history together, a nice life that they've worked hard to build. She's not interested in a messy divorce, especially one in which she'll be cast as the evil adulterer.

Audrey doesn't respond, deciding instead to switch her phone off entirely. She hopes that sends a clear enough message.

"What's this?" Seth asks, startling Audrey, who drops her phone with a clatter just as he walks back into the dining room.

Seth's brows are knit together in a puzzled expression as he stares down at something in his palm.

He holds it out to Audrey, unfurling his fingers. And there, in

Seth's hand, is a silver tie clip that Audrey is acutely aware does not belong to her husband. She sees a snapshot of *him* standing in their living room, eyes hungry for her as he pulled off his tie, the tinkling sound of something metallic hitting the hardwood floor . . .

Audrey swallows the nausea that creeps up her throat and shrugs. "Is it one of yours?"

Seth inspects the little silver clip. "No, it's not. I found it on the floor under the bar cart." There's a telltale slurring around his words, as though his tongue is a fat slug in his mouth. He's looking at her now. Really looking at her. Watching her appraisingly, the way an art dealer might inspect a potentially fraudulent painting. Wasn't this exactly what she'd wanted? Her husband's undivided attention? And now that she has it, Audrey feels herself withering under the intensity of it.

"Oh! It must have been from when you had your team here for drinks!" The lie springs lightly from her lips. "Someone must have lost it."

"But that was weeks ago."

"I know," Audrey says, nodding as the narrative gains momentum. "But I can't imagine where else it might have come from. I'll have to talk to Naomi about cleaning under the furniture. She's meant to be doing that, but I think she cuts corners sometimes."

Seth hesitates a moment before dropping the tie clip into his pocket. "Yeah," he says, sounding less than convinced. "Right, that must have been it."

Audrey nearly sags with relief as the offending object disappears from view. If Seth ever found out she was having an affair, Audrey doesn't know *what* he'd do, but she knows it wouldn't end well. He's a prideful man, her husband, hyper-concerned about appearances. And the wife of the famous Seth Warrington sleeping with another man certainly doesn't align with the public image he's going for.

Audrey takes a long sip of her wine, hoping the slight tremor in her hand isn't noticeable. Seth sits across from her, his eyes intent on his wife for the first time in as long as she can remember. He smiles, but there's a falseness to it, a chill that makes Audrey's blood run cold.

8
GEORGINA
Hawthorne Lane

The kitchen timer dings and Georgina slides on her oven mitts before slowly edging open the door to the oven. The sweet, nutty aroma of her famous amaretto cheesecake wafts out, filling the kitchen with evidence of her efforts. This recipe isn't an easy one. Georgina knows that a perfect cheesecake should cook slowly and evenly, and the top should never brown. The eggs in the batter need a humid environment to rise properly while not becoming dried out, so the key is the bain-marie, the water bath. Cooking the cake in a lined springform pan and adding just enough water around the base to keep the temperature regulated and the filling moist without oversaturating it ensures that the cake will lift slowly while maintaining its rich, creamy texture.

She gingerly slides the confection from the oven and places it on a trivet atop the counter. The center of the cake jiggles as she puts it down, as it should; it will set as the cake gradually cools. She usually leaves her cheesecakes inside an open oven, but it's already far too warm in her kitchen and she knows her neighbors will be arriving any minute.

This welcome-to-the-neighborhood barbecue for Mark and Hannah is long overdue, as Georgina had some difficulty juggling everyone's schedule, but it was important to her that they do it, even if only a few families will be attending. She had hoped that the family at the end of the block, the ones closest to Hannah's age, might come with their two children, but they hadn't been available. Georgina isn't entirely surprised by this, as they tend to keep to themselves. In fact, Georgina hardly ever sees the parents, both young professionals from what she's gleaned, just their nanny pushing their little girl in a stroller, holding their little boy by the hand.

It's a shame, Georgina thinks, that the residents of Hawthorne Lane aren't more connected. They're all cordial enough—bringing in each other's recycling bins should someone forget, loaning a cup of sugar here and there—but none of the neighbors are particularly close. It seems that the only occasion the entire block gets together for is the fall festival on Halloween. It's the neighborhood's biggest event—all the residents of Hawthorne Lane decorate their porches and set up tables in the street to hand out candy, and this year Georgina's even arranging for a fireworks display. The whole town of Sterling Valley comes to Hawthorne Lane for Halloween. It's what they're known for. And Georgina has, over the years, become the unofficial organizer of the event. Not that she minds. This is where she excels.

Georgina takes a bowl of lemons out of the refrigerator and begins slicing them for the fresh-squeezed lemonade she'll serve today with sprigs of lavender clipped from her garden. Even though it will be a small gathering, Georgina wants to do this for Hannah. It's been eighteen years, but she hasn't forgotten what it felt like to be the newcomer on the block. She was pregnant with Sebastian at that time, and she remembers how nervous she'd been, how alone she'd felt with Colin working long hours and no friends or family nearby. And then she'd met Libby. She rang Georgina's doorbell one morning, completely out of the blue.

"I know pregnant ladies are supposed to sit around eating bonbons or whatever," she'd said, her hand coming to rest on top of her belly, which was almost as full and round as Georgina's. "But I've been going a little stir-crazy lately. Thought you might be feeling the same. Up for a walk?"

Georgina had been so touched by the gesture, by Libby's easy familiarity. It might not have meant much to Libby, but it did to Georgina. Suddenly she had someone to walk through the neighborhood with as they pushed matching strollers, someone to chat to about the best brands of diapers and the exhaustion of sleep regressions. Even though their connection has faded over the years, Libby felt like a lifeline to Georgina back then, whether she knew it or not. Georgina wants that for Hannah too. No one should have to feel alone.

Georgina slides the first batch of lemons into a glass pitcher, the knife scraping along the cutting board. She recalls that Audrey Warrington once mentioned enjoying this lemonade at a previous neighborhood gathering, so Georgina wants to have it on hand for her. The two women might not be close, but Georgina prides herself on being an excellent hostess.

She feels a gentle breeze at her back, and for a moment it's refreshing. A reprieve from the oppressive summer heat. She allows herself to close her eyes and breathes in the fresh air, swirling with the clean, bright scent of the lemons. And then she realizes, too late, where the draft must be coming from—she'd cracked the kitchen window open earlier this morning.

Georgina whirls around to close it, but to her horror, she sees a crack—no, a canyon—opening down the center of her cheesecake. The rapid temperature change has ruined it. She remembers reading somewhere that running a hot spoon over the top of the cake can hide unsightly cracks, but she can't bring herself to do it. Even if no one else noticed the flaw, the spoon-smeared surface, she would. She slides the entire thing into the garbage can, where it lands with a judgmental thud.

Georgina made plenty of other desserts to serve, but that cake was supposed to be the centerpiece. She turns her back on it and resumes cutting the lemons with a renewed fervor.

She's so angry at herself for the oversight that she could scream. How could she have made such a stupid mistake? This is her *thing*. Her *one* thing. She knows it seems trivial in the grand scheme of things—her spotless house, her flawless cheesecakes—and maybe it is, but it matters to her. She doesn't have a high-powered corporate career like Audrey's or a business she can call her own like Libby's. All she has is this small corner of the world, and she should be able to make it perfect.

Colin strolls into the kitchen in the new white polo shirt Georgina picked up for him earlier in the week. "Smells great in here," he says.

"Thanks." She doesn't mention the failed-cake incident. "You're looking awfully refreshed today."

"I took one of the new sleeping pills the doc prescribed me. Woke up feeling like a million bucks." Colin grabs a cube of cheese off the crystal platter Georgina arranged them on and pops it into his mouth. "When is everyone expected to arrive?"

"Any minute now. Oh—" She notices the sales tag that dangles from the collar of Colin's shirt and pulls the kitchen scissors from the knife block. "Let me get that for you." She snips off the tag and hands it to him.

"Good catch," he says as he turns to throw it away.

He hesitates for a moment, his hand hovering over the garbage can. Perhaps he notices the ruined cheesecake at the bottom of the bin, but if he does, he doesn't mention it. He drops the tag in and closes the lid just as the doorbell rings, announcing the arrival of their guests.

GEORGINA UNLATCHES THE FRENCH DOORS leading out to the yard, a tray of maple bacon–wrapped water chestnuts balanced on one hand. As the door swings open, she's greeted with a wave of gentle music, the sound of light laughter. All in all, the party is off to a great start.

Colin is holding court by the drinks cart, mixing up mojitos with muddled mint leaves for Seth, Mark, and Hannah, while Libby and Audrey are seated under the shade of the patio table with drinks in their hands.

The kids, who would probably rather be anywhere other than here with their parents, have positioned themselves as far from the adults as possible: on the other side of the yard, by the pool. Christina is lying on a towel near the water's edge. She's on her stomach, kicking her legs up behind her, her nose in a book. Sebastian, meanwhile, sits surly and bored on a lounge chair, a plate of food on his lap and headphones plugged into his ears. Lucas, Libby's son, is his mirror image in a chair on the opposite side of the pool. Georgina and Libby had tried to foster a friendship between their sons when they were small, but sadly they never quite took to each other.

An image floats into Georgina's head of her children when they were small, Sebastian and Christina splashing in this very pool that sits empty now, inflatable water wings fixed around their upper arms. *Mommy! Watch what I can do!* But that was a long time ago, a faded-sepia memory.

She watches her daughter as she stands and stretches now, leaving her paperback splayed, facedown, on her towel beside her discarded glasses. She lifts her cover-up over her head, revealing a swimsuit that as far as Georgina can tell is nothing more than a few triangles held together with bits of string. She knows these tiny little suits are all the rage at the moment, but she's not certain it's appropriate for a neighborhood function. Especially for a girl Christina's age. Georgina doesn't have the first clue where her fifteen-year-old daughter procured such a thing, but she's positive that Colin would have an absolute stroke if he saw her in it. Georgina, still balancing the tray of hors d'oeuvres, hurries over to Christina.

"Oh, yum," Christina says, lifting a water chestnut from the platter.

Georgina studies her daughter, who suddenly looks five years older with her taut stomach, the golden tan on her long legs, the highlights in her blond hair brought out by the summer sun. Christina has always been the easier of Georgina's two children. The quiet, studious one, the agreeable one, the one she never had to worry about. She wonders now if that's about to change.

She picks up her daughter's sundress from the pool deck where she'd dropped it and hands it to her.

"Seriously, Mom?" Christina says in reply, spots of pink blooming on her cheeks. "It's just a bathing suit."

"Seriously."

Christina groans. "I'm not a baby, you know. I'm almost sixteen." But despite her protests, she pulls the dress back over her head.

"Thank you." Satisfied, Georgina turns and carries her tray over to the bar cart.

"Hello, darling," Colin says as he plants a kiss at her temple. "Mojito?"

"Please."

He begins to mix the drinks while Georgina passes around the hors d'oeuvres.

"Thank you again for hosting today," Hannah says. "Mark and I really appreciate it."

Georgina notices the blue beaded earrings dangling from Hannah's ears. They're simple, inexpensive things, but Georgina finds that she quite likes the boldness of them. She thinks of her own pearl studs that she wears for most occasions and wonders if it's time for a change. "It's our pleasure," she says. "Truly. It's far past time we all got together."

Mark nods his agreement as he takes a bite of a bacon-wrapped water chestnut. "I don't know how you do it. All the food today has been unbelievable. I feel like I'm at a Michelin-starred restaurant!"

"How strong has my husband been making those drinks?" Georgina jests.

"Don't be so modest," Libby says as she sidles up to the group. "Georgina actually went to culinary school!"

"Did you really?" Curiosity sparkles in Hannah's pretty young eyes. "That's so interesting!"

"Oh"—Georgina swats the topic away with a flick of her wrist—"no, it was just a few classes. I never even graduated." It feels like a lifetime ago when she made the decision to leave culinary school to follow Colin to New York. He'd just finished his law degree at Duke and was offered a job at a white-shoe firm in Manhattan. They both knew he couldn't turn down the opportunity, but they were also newly engaged. A long-distance relationship simply wasn't an option. She told herself that she had time, that she could always go back to school, finish her degree in New York. But before she knew it, she was pregnant with Sebastian, and her life had a new focus. She never quite got around to resuming her studies. And now that she's forty, the idea of being a student again feels so silly. She doesn't have the courage to sit in a class, knowing she's the oldest person in the room but with no culinary experience to show for it except hosting neighborhood dinner parties.

"Well," Seth says, licking his fingers, ice rattling in his near-empty glass, "those classes certainly paid off."

"Thank you."

"Colin," Mark says, turning to him and clapping a hand on his back. "You better hang on to this one. You're a lucky man!"

Georgina lifts the mojito from Colin's hand, searching his face for a reaction. It's as subtle as watching the tide change, the darkening around his irises. And as quickly as it came, it's washed away.

"Lucky indeed," he says, wrapping an arm around Georgina's waist and pulling her to his side.

She's certain he didn't much like Mark's compliment. Georgina is usually the one being told how lucky she is to have him. For his looks, his money, his status as a partner at one of the top law firms in New York. The luck, he's come to believe, is all hers.

"Mark here was just telling me what an avid golfer he is," Colin says, deftly changing the topic.

"Ugh," Hannah groans playfully. "Don't get him started again. It's bad enough I lose him for hours every weekend while he plays."

"You guys should really join me sometime," Mark says, nodding toward Seth and Colin. "And you too, of course, Georgina. If you play."

"Sure," Seth replies absently, though Georgina gets the sense that he's not paying much attention to the conversation anymore. He's busy watching his wife, Audrey, across the yard as she pulls off her sundress, uncovering a rather revealing white bikini. Georgina has always admired Audrey, her self-possession, her grab-life-by-the-horns attitude, though perhaps not her choice in swimming attire. She certainly has the figure for it, but the extent of her exposed skin is shocking enough that even Sebastian stops scowling for a moment, tilting down his sunglasses to watch as she wades into the deserted pool. Georgina catches Christina's eye across the yard; her daughter's arms are folded over her chest, her eyebrows raised, as if to say, *Unfair*.

"Count me in as well," Colin responds. "I'm sure Georgina wouldn't mind getting me out of the house for a few extra hours." She feels his grip tighten, ever so slightly, on her hip, and it snaps her attention back to the discussion. "After all, that's when she spends all of my money!"

He laughs good-naturedly, and Georgina forces herself to join in even though she doesn't feel much like laughing, even though his comment landed like a targeted blow.

But Colin isn't finished. "On things like this." He picks up the cheese plate Georgina had so carefully arranged earlier. "What do you even call this thing?"

"A platter," she responds, her voice as small as she feels.

"Right. A decorative crystal platter. We couldn't *possibly* serve cheese on anything less." He chuckles, tossing a thumb over his shoulder toward the house. "I'm sure we've got seven more just like it inside too."

There's a titter of laughter from their guests, but this time the most Georgina can muster is a polite smile.

"I'm just glad Mark will have someone to play with," Hannah says graciously. "I'm a terrible golfer."

Georgina reads something in Hannah's gaze, something so close to pity that it causes tears to prick behind her eyes. "Excuse me while I go get the desserts ready to serve," she says, turning away from the humiliating exchange—from Hannah's knowing look, her husband's subtle, triumphant smirk.

She walks quickly toward the house, her eyes cast down at the ground as she moves.

"I hope you made your amaretto cheesecake!" Colin calls after her. "That'll *really* impress them!"

9
HANNAH
Hawthorne Lane

"So, what did you think?" Hannah asks as she slides into bed next to Mark. He sets down his book, a hardcover spy novel with a splashy neon-green title, and looks at her over his reading glasses, which are still balanced on the end of his nose.

It's not often that she feels their age difference, but in this moment she sees it. In the tiredness around his eyes, the lines that wrinkle the corners. It's never bothered her, but when they first started dating, Mark had expressed some concerns about the twelve-year gap between them.

"I'm nearly forty," he told her over drinks in an overcrowded Manhattan bar. Mark had chosen the location—some trendy pop-up with floral walls and scripted neon signs—but as he looked around at the crowd, Hannah was certain it wasn't lost on him that he was the oldest person there. "Are you sure you're okay with that? I'm afraid I won't be able to keep up."

"Age is just a number. If you find a genuine connection with someone, why let something so trivial as that come between you?"

"Still, I wouldn't want to hold you back from living your life." He sipped slowly from his eighteen-dollar martini, a heaviness in his eyes as they drifted away from hers.

"Can I be honest with you?" Hannah asked, leaning toward him to be heard over the blaring music. She saw Mark wince, as if he were bracing himself for disappointment. "I hate this just as much as you do."

He laughed then, a full hearty sound that came from deep in his belly. "I think I might just fall in love with you, Hannah."

"About the party?" he asks now, pulling her from the memory.

"Well, yes. And the people." It was the first time Mark had met their new neighbors, not that it showed. He blended in seamlessly, as if he'd lived here all his life. He talked about golf swings and country clubs without missing a beat. Hannah was a little bit envious of it, if she's being honest.

"They all seemed nice," Mark replies. "Very welcoming."

"They were," Hannah concurs. "For the most part. Didn't you think that whole thing with Colin and Georgina was a bit off, though?"

"What do you mean?"

"You know, how he brought up the fact that he makes all the money in their relationship. I'd imagine it was kind of embarrassing for her."

"Did he really say that? I must have missed it."

"Not in so many words, but he implied it. When he made that comment about Georgina spending money while he's out of the house. It felt like he was putting her down."

"Oh, that." Mark scratches his chin. "I didn't take it that way. And I'm not certain Georgina did either. She laughed about it, if I'm remembering correctly. Seemed like he meant it as a joke."

"I guess . . ." Hannah takes off her wedding ring, sets it in the ceramic dish on her nightstand. "I didn't think it was very funny, though."

"I can see how you might not," Mark replies.

Hannah doesn't know if her husband can see the interaction from her perspective or if he's saying that because his credit cards are currently in her wallet too. Hannah just started a new job in the children's room at the Sterling Valley Library, but her income is nothing compared to Mark's. She is acutely aware that their house and everything in it was bought with her new husband's money.

"But," Mark continues, "Georgina seemed fine with it, and I suppose there's no need for us to worry about it if she's not." He takes off his glasses and folds them into their case. "I'm going to turn in for the night. Early day at the office tomorrow. Good night, my love." Mark leans over and kisses Hannah chastely on the lips before rolling over, his back to her, and tucking the blanket around himself.

Mark might be right. Hannah could be reading too much into the situation. After all, no one else batted an eye at Colin's comments, not even Georgina. She doesn't know the first thing about Georgina's marriage. Maybe Colin isn't the type of man who would knock his wife down simply because she was getting too much attention.

And yet... she can't shake the feeling that there's more going on with their new neighbors. She felt it in the things that weren't said, all the details that were lost in the gaps between their words. No one commented on Libby's fake brightness, the sadness behind her smile when she cracked jokes about being the only single one at the party. No one seemed to notice that Audrey and Seth barely interacted the entire time but that Audrey kept watching him across the yard as he chatted with the other men, or the number of times Seth topped off his drink. They'd all talked to one another for hours, but Hannah left feeling like they hadn't said very much at all, at least not about anything that truly mattered.

And then her thoughts move to her own marriage. To the things *she* hasn't said. It's been nagging at her ever since that note arrived in their mailbox last month. Hannah can still see the red letters, boldface and defiant, as if the word has been painted into her memory: LIAR. She hates that she's been keeping this from Mark. She doesn't want to have the kind of marriage where secrets grow between them like weeds, where they can spread and take root, killing every good thing. And yet she can't tell her husband the truth—not all of it, anyway.

This time, Hannah knows exactly what her mother would say. She remembers the first time she'd said it, her hand gently rocking Hannah's shoulder, rousing her from sleep: "It's time to go." Hannah can still feel the stiff motel blanket, scratchy on her skin, the darkness of the room, how confused she'd been, wondering where she was and how she'd gotten there. "Come on, baby, it's time to go. He found us."

Hannah looks over at Mark, who is snoring contentedly beneath the thick down duvet, and edges out of bed. She reminds herself that she's not that little girl anymore, that she doesn't have to run, that she's safe here, and she tiptoes out of their bedroom as quietly as she can.

Downstairs, she opens her laptop, balancing it on her knees. The screen fills the dark room with an eerie silver glow as it wakes. Hannah navigates to her email server and, for the first time in months, logs in to the account that Mark doesn't know exists.

She holds her breath while it loads, waiting to see if there's any new correspondence. There isn't. An empty inbox shines back at her. Relief, solid and sure, washes over her. She knows she's taking a risk, but she had to be certain.

The bed upstairs creaks; the sound of Mark turning over in his sleep. Hannah quickly logs out of her account, erases her browsing history, and sneaks back into bed beside her husband.

10

LIBBY
Hawthorne Lane

Lucas shuffles into the living room, his soccer cleats flung over his shoulder. "I'm going to the field," he declares succinctly.

Libby smiles at him, pleased that he decided to communicate in a full sentence for a change. "Have a great time!"

"Okay," Lucas replies, though it's more of a grumble than a word.

"Love you!" she yells at her son's retreating back just before the door closes behind him.

Libby turns to her laptop, where the inventory spreadsheet she's been working on stares back at her, the cursor blinking impatiently. The truth is that she should have finished with this ages ago, but her mind has been elsewhere. It's been elsewhere ever since she overheard Beth Patterson speculating about Bill being in a new relationship. She wonders if it's true. On the one hand, she's noticed changes in Bill, a renewed youthfulness that wasn't there only months ago, but on the other hand, Beth is known to be overtly jealous and a spiteful gossip, and Libby wouldn't put it past her to have made the entire thing up.

If only there were some way to know for sure . . . Libby bites the edge of her thumb. She's hesitant to ask Bill directly, not until she has something more to go on than conjecture she overheard at the supermarket. She thinks again of the kiss. They're in a good place right now, and Libby doesn't want to risk doing anything to mess that up, to set them back on the path they'd been on before, where she was the nagging wife and Bill was the husband who needed space. If she's wrong about this, Bill might take it as an accusation, an excuse to start pulling away from her again, and she can't have that. Not when they're just finding their way back to each other.

Libby's fingers linger over her keyboard. She hasn't done this in months. Not since Bill first moved out and she was desperate for any crumb of information about what he was doing in all that time and space he'd asked for. She knows it's not right, that logging in to his email account is an invasion of his privacy that he wouldn't take lightly. And yet it's so easy to do, so easy, in fact, that she's logged in to his account before she's even fully thought it through. Bill has always had the same password for everything: BLL123. Bill, Libby, Lucas. All their initials lined up next to one another, right where they belong. It meant something to Libby when she first realized that he hadn't changed it. But maybe, given recent events, it shouldn't have. Maybe he was just being lazy. Either way, the password still works. She's in.

At first, all she finds are coupon offers from various stores, a reminder to renew his real estate license by the end of the year, exchanges with prospective homebuyers. She knew this was a long shot. Who talks to his girlfriend over email? But just as Libby is about to give up and sign out of Bill's account, something catches her eye. An email from an address she doesn't recognize: HeatherBrooks@hmail.com. The subject line: *Forgetting something?* She clicks to open it without a second thought.

```
Hey! Looks like you left your phone at my place
last night. Just wanted to let you know in case
you were looking for it. Guess you'll have to
come back tonight to pick it up . . . ;)
```

Libby feels her stomach plunge, nausea rising into her throat, as the irritating little winking emoticon stares out at her tauntingly. *It's true.* It's hard for Libby to wrap her mind around it. Bill. *Her* Bill. With someone else. It feels impossible, and yet it's so painfully real, written right there in black and white. Bill is dating. A woman named Heather Brooks, with whom he's evidently spent at least one night. Libby's mind immediately begins spinning, catastrophizing. How long has this been going on? Is this woman the reason he'd walked out on Libby so suddenly? Is *she* the reason Libby's family is irreparably broken?

Libby can't believe how foolish she'd been, trusting Bill the way she had. She was only nineteen when they'd met. She'd been too young, too naive, giving herself so freely to him, loving him so completely. Because here he is, casting her aside as casually as one might shuck off an old sweater.

It wasn't supposed to be like this. Not for her, and certainly not for Lucas. Libby knows all too well what it's like to live in a broken home—something she'd never wanted for her own son. She was only nine years old when her parents divorced, her father having decided he was more in love with his secretary than with Libby's mother, but despite her young age, Libby remembers the aftermath with vivid clarity—the strangled sound that escaped her mother's lips the first time they pushed open the door to their new apartment, the one that always smelled of mildew no matter how much they tried to scrub it clean; her mother's bad days, when she couldn't get out of bed, when Libby would creep into her darkened bedroom just to remind herself that her mother was still there, that she wasn't alone. "Don't let this be your life, Libby," her mother had said. "Don't let yourself end up like me." Libby looked at the hollow form of her mother curled up in her bed, her red-rimmed eyes, the sour sheets rumpled around her, and vowed to herself that she wouldn't. She'd never put all her eggs in a basket she wasn't holding.

But that's exactly what she'd done, wasn't it? Thanks to Lily Lane, Libby might be financially independent in a way her mother hadn't been, but Libby understands now what her mother was trying to tell her. It wasn't just about the money. She'd been warning her daughter about the dangers of putting her heart in someone else's hands. How could Bill do this to her? To Lucas?

Something takes hold of Libby in that moment. A desperate need to put a face to the name of the woman who is ruining everything. She has to know who Bill has chosen over their family; she has to see for herself what Heather Brooks has that she, Libby, doesn't.

Thanks to the wonders of the internet, one quick search lands Libby on Heather's public Instagram page. *What did people do before social media?* It's both a blessing and a curse to be able to pull up an image of your husband's lover at the click of a mouse.

Laid out before her is a grid of colorful, pixelated images of Heather Brooks. Tiny squares featuring Heather crossing the finish line of a half marathon, hands raised triumphantly, her dark ponytail swishing behind her; Heather on the bow of a boat, white sails billowing against the azure-blue sky above her head; Heather in front of the Eiffel Tower, a wine-colored beret on her head that would look absurd on Libby but somehow looks annoyingly chic on Heather. Libby clicks on a photo, enlarging it to full size. It's a shot of Heather holding a martini, smiling as she leans against a wood-topped bar. She's Libby's polar opposite. Her hair is dark and sleek-straight where Libby's is a mess of wild curls. Her body curves softly in all the places where Libby's has always been stubbornly flat. She looks at least ten years younger than Libby, without the stretch marks and inevitable wear and tear that comes from carrying a child. In the photo, Heather is looking off to the side, a candid smile frozen on her face. It makes Libby wonder who took the photo, what made her smile that way. And then it makes her imagine Heather smiling at Bill and it's almost too much to take.

Libby tears her eyes from the screen, her breath hitching in her throat as she stifles a sob with the side of her fist. Her gaze falls on the framed wedding photo of her and Bill that's sat on the mantel for as long as they've lived on Hawthorne Lane. She has half a mind to grab it and throw it down now, to stomp on the image of those two smiling people over and over again until the glass shatters, shredding the photo behind it to tatters. But she doesn't. She couldn't. As hurt as she is, that day was still one of the happiest of her life. She can still feel the cool silk of her dress, the flowers woven into her hair. She remembers the warmth of the sun on her shoulders as they exchanged the vows they'd written themselves. They spoke about love at first sight, about fate and how they never would have met if Bill hadn't been late for class that day, cutting across their college quad and running straight into Libby. Neither of them mentioned the baby that would someday be Lucas, the pregnancy she was hiding beneath the layers of her dress, but she loved knowing that he was there with them. This tiny person they'd created together out of love. But now the memory sours, twisting and morphing in her mind into a grotesque facsimile of reality. In a flash, Heather is the one walking down the aisle toward Bill, tears of joy brimming in her round dark eyes. *She* is the one with flowers in her hair. *Hers* are the fingers laced through Bill's as he says, "I do."

A key turns in the lock and Libby slams the top of her laptop down just as Lucas walks into the living room, one of his friends trailing behind him.

"Started to rain. Can Justin and I hang out here instead?"

"Sure. Of course," Libby replies, plastering a hollow smile onto her face. "I just finished working. I was about to head upstairs anyway."

Lucas looks at her curiously as she practically leaps off the couch, but fortunately his mother's awkward fumbling isn't enough to hold his adolescent interest for more than a second. "Cool. Later."

The two boys settle onto the couch and the sound of sportscasters narrating a soccer game fills the house as Libby trots up the stairs.

She gets herself ready for bed, brushing her teeth, washing her face. What the hell was she thinking? If Lucas had caught her internet-stalking his father's girlfriend, it would have been mortifying. He might not know Heather yet, but he could soon. (The very thought makes nausea churn in her stomach once again.) What if Lucas put the pieces together? What if he said something about it to Bill?

Libby slides under her comforter, tucks the corner under her cheek, and turns her back to the cold, empty side of the bed that once belonged to Bill. She can't let herself get carried away like that again.

11

MAGGIE

Benton Avenue

Maggie Tucker's feet ache as she stands outside her front door. It's been a long day, but as she's about to lift her hand to turn the knob, something stops her. She takes a moment, breathing in the thick muggy air. It smells of exhaust and engine oil from the chop shop on the corner. Dean assured her that she'd get used to it, that she'd eventually stop noticing it. But she's lived with him on Benton Avenue for nearly three years now, and she still smells it as strongly as ever. Maggie feels as though she can't escape it. The scent of grease and grime that clings to her clothing, following her wherever she goes. She hates that it's become a part of her. That even when she's working, nannying for the wealthy family on the other side of town—when she's cooking in their beautiful, pristine kitchen or strolling around the cul-de-sac with their polished, well-mannered children—she feels dirty. But this is her home, and she knows that she has to go inside eventually.

Maggie pushes open the door and slips off her work shoes, her feet throbbing as she wiggles her stockinged toes against the threadbare carpeting. Dean is already home. She knows this before she sees him by the stale scent of beer that lingers in the air, by the brown bottles lined up on the tiny kitchen table. She hates that he's been drinking so much. She's learned to gauge his moods by the number of empty bottles in the garbage can, and lately, they've been accumulating more quickly than Maggie would like. Her husband's temperament is a mercurial one. Some days she comes home to find the man she married, that charming smile, his eyes sparkling, so devastatingly handsome as he bounces around the house like a rubber ball, patching a hole in the wall here, fixing a leaking faucet there. But other days, she'll find the curtains drawn, the house dark and dank with the tangy odor of sweat, Dean sprawled on the couch, empty bottles lying on their sides, dropped haphazardly on the carpet beside him.

Today seems to be something of a middle ground: She can tell he's been drinking, but he's not passed out in the living room, and sunlight is doing its best to stream through the windows, which are clouded with the ever-present dirt that has settled on their lives. These are the hardest days, she finds, the days where she doesn't know what to expect.

"Mags?" he calls.

"Yes," she replies. "In here."

She can hear his footsteps as he treads down the narrow hallway, and in a moment he appears in their living room. Maggie watches him curiously, trying to read his mood.

Dean stretches, lifting his arms over his head. His black T-shirt rises with the effort, revealing a strip of his toned stomach, a trail of hair that disappears into the waistband of the jeans that ride low on his hips. They're stained with grease from the mechanic shop he works at, as are the tips of his fingers, the beds of his nails. No matter how hard Dean scrubs, Maggie knows it won't come off. The black stains are a part of him.

"What's for dinner?" he asks.

"I thought I'd cut up some of the leftover chicken from last night. Maybe make some pasta to go with it."

Dean grumbles, but he grabs another beer from the refrigerator without objection and pops the cap off. Maggie watches as it rolls under the table, but Dean makes no effort to retrieve it.

Maggie lifts her sauce pot from the lower cabinet, feeling the waistband of her work pants cutting into the bones of her hips as she bends. She'd like to change, but she knows that she should get Dean's dinner started first. She fills the pot from the tap.

"How was your day?" she asks, her back to Dean.

"You wouldn't believe these people, Mags."

She knows where this is headed. Dean works at an upscale auto shop. He loved it at first, getting to work on cars he'd otherwise only be able to dream of sitting in. But he soon started to resent the people who owned them. He'd once had larger ambitions for himself—owning his own shop, wearing a suit, being the kind of man his customers would see as an equal. But it was a pipe dream for him, something, Maggie has come to suspect, Dean will never accomplish. He's far too foolish with his money, squandering it on booze and gambling. He's no closer to being able to afford his own shop now than he was the day she met him.

She sprinkles some salt into the heating water, encouraging it to boil. She's beginning to get a feel for the turning tides of Dean's mood, sensing that anything she says today will likely be the wrong thing, and so she says nothing. She watches the pot as she waits for him to continue.

"Who the fuck do they think they are, ya know? Had this one guy today, with his fuckin' Porsche, telling me he took pictures of it from every angle before he brought it in, and if I so much as look at his car the wrong way, he's going to know about it."

Maggie nods as she adds the pasta to the now boiling water.

"Don't worry, though," Dean continues. "He got what was coming to him."

He pauses, and Maggie knows he's waiting for her to respond, that he wants to know he has her full attention. She turns to face her husband, watching as a serpentine grin snakes its way across his face.

"What did you do?" she asks, because she knows he wants her to.

"Nothing the fucker didn't deserve. Loosened a spark plug a little. It'll mess with his engine over time. And since this guy knows fuck-all about his fancy car, he probably won't figure it out until he needs some pretty expensive repairs."

"Wow," Maggie says, though the thought makes her feel uneasy. She doesn't know when Dean became this person. Vindictive. Mean. When they first met, he'd been so sweet, so charming.

Maggie had been waiting tables at a diner then. It wasn't a popular place—a greasy spoon where she always seemed to get the worst shifts, late nights bleeding into early mornings. The people who came in were mostly vagrants or street kids who wanted something cheap that would keep their stomachs full. Maggie hardly got any tips, and the pay was abysmal, but it was the only job she'd been able to find. And then one night, Dean walked in, sat himself in her section. She still remembers the way her stomach flipped when she saw him: the dark swoop of his hair, his dazzling smile, his black leather jacket pulled over a white T-shirt.

"Hey," she'd said as she filled his water glass.

"Hey yourself," he'd replied. His gaze was so intense that it made Maggie blush.

He ordered some eggs and toast, and as Maggie attended to the straggle of other late-night customers, she could feel his eyes on her, following her from table to table.

After she cleared his plate and brought him his bill, he asked what time her shift ended.

"Not until one o'clock," she said with a sigh, dreading the long, late hours ahead of her.

Dean nodded, dropped a crumpled twenty-dollar bill onto the table, and popped the collar of his jacket as he slid out of the booth.

Maggie watched with disappointment as he pushed open the glass doors of the diner and disappeared into the darkness. She'd thought that was the last she'd see of him, but when she left the diner that night, he'd been waiting for her in the parking lot, leaning against a vintage-looking motorcycle. His arms were folded over his chest, a cigarette dangling from his lips, and his long legs, crossed at the ankles, ended in dusty black boots. In the soft glow of the streetlights, she marveled at how handsome he was, at his dark lashes, the smooth planes of his face that made him look young and sweet despite the tough exterior. As if he were a boy playing dress-up. Something about it tugged at the strings of Maggie's heart.

He flicked the cigarette away, the red ember burning bright against the cracked black pavement. She should have known then that he was bad news, that he was the kind of man who would break her heart, the kind of man every mother warns her daughters about. Not that it would've stopped her. In that moment, she couldn't believe he was there, choosing her, in her faded pink diner uniform, the scent of fryer grease clinging to her hair.

"Where's your car?" he'd asked.

"I, uh, I walked here." Maggie didn't want to tell him that she didn't have a car. That she couldn't afford one. "I don't live too far."

Dean nodded as though he understood anyway. He held out a helmet toward her. "Want a lift, then?"

Maggie pulled the helmet over her head as she watched him mount the bike in one swift movement, a jean-clad leg swinging over the seat. She climbed on behind him.

"Hold on," he said, revving the engine. Maggie slid her arms around his slim waist, and she pressed close to him, feeling the hardness of his body, breathing in the scent of his worn leather jacket against her cheek. And she knew even then that she was going to fall for him. That there was nothing she could do to stop it.

Dean was wonderful at first. He brought her bunches of daisies every Friday, opened car doors for her when he picked her up for dinner or a movie. She remembers thinking that he was such a gentleman, remembers her disbelief that she'd managed to get so lucky. She wonders now if it was all an act, if he'd ever been that person at all. Dean is quite good at that, at making people believe he's something he's not. Though it's always only a matter of time until his true colors shine through.

"Yeah, but shit like that, it's just not enough," Dean says now, slamming his beer bottle onto the table. Maggie jumps at the sound. It takes her a moment to remember what he's talking about. Work. A Porsche. A loosened spark plug.

"The world is fucked these days. Where pricks like that have more money than they know what to do with, and guys like me who work their asses off can hardly keep a roof over their heads."

Maggie bites her tongue. She says nothing about how much of his money he wastes or how Dean has lost more than one job because he didn't feel like showing up for a shift.

"I'm sick of working my tail off—and for what?" He throws his arms wide, gesturing at the tiny run-down house around them. "For this? Don't you think I—we—deserve more?"

Maggie nods. "Maybe, but what can we do about it?"

"I don't know yet," Dean replies, slowly shaking his head. "But someday soon, I'm going to find a way to move us up in the world, settle the score with those rich fucks across town. I promise you that."

Maggie feels a stirring of dread in the pit of her stomach. She doesn't know what's coming, but she knows it won't end well.

HALLOWEEN NIGHT

Transcript of interview with Doreen Woodrow
October 31, 2024

Detective Olsen: Hello, Ms. Woodrow, my name is Detective Frank Olsen, and I'd like to ask you a few questions about an incident that occurred on your block tonight if that would be all right with you.

Ms. Woodrow: I've lived on Hawthorne Lane for nearly fifty years, Mr. Olsen, and in all my time here, nothing like this has ever happened. The world is changing, I tell you. It wasn't like this back in my day. My late husband, Lenny, would be just sick to his stomach over it if he were still with us. God rest his soul.

Detective Olsen: So you're aware of the occurrence this evening, then, Ms. Woodrow?

Ms. Woodrow: I'm old, not dead. You may not believe it, but I can see perfectly well, thank you very much. Like I wouldn't notice all the police cars outside my own window! A crime scene! On Hawthorne Lane! I didn't think I'd live to see the day. It used to be that you could leave your doors unlocked—you could trust your neighbors that much. But nowadays? Never.

Detective Olsen: I couldn't agree more, Ms. Woodrow. You can't be too careful. Now, given the proximity of your home to the location of the occurrence, I wanted to ask if you saw anything out of the ordinary earlier this evening. Anything at all.

Ms. Woodrow: Well, none of this is ordinary if you ask me. All this commotion over Halloween. What happened to homemade costumes and old-fashioned trick-or-treating? Now we have to have a whole festival? A fireworks display? It's very unordinary indeed. Churchill absolutely abhors it.

Detective Olsen: Churchill?

Ms. Woodrow: He's my cat, of course. Do you like cats?

Detective Olsen: Er, not particularly. More of a dog guy myself.

Ms. Woodrow: That figures.

Detective Olsen: Ma'am, if we could get back to the incident in question—

Ms. Woodrow: Right, yes. Well, I can't say that I saw anything exactly. I was watching my shows at the time, and I heard a ruckus out on the street. People yelling and whatnot. At first I thought it was just part of the ridiculous festival. It gets so loud. But it started to sound like maybe people were arguing. I couldn't make out what they were saying, so I went to the window to see what the trouble was. I couldn't see much of anything by the time I got there, though. I don't move as quickly as I used to. I assumed whoever was out there had left, but I can't be sure. It was quite dark. I just know all that yelling had stopped.

Detective Olsen: Thank you, Ms. Woodrow. That's very helpful. Do you remember about what time this occurred?

Ms. Woodrow: I do. It was around nine o'clock. I remember because of the fireworks. It was just before they began.

Detective Olsen: I appreciate your time, Ms. Woodrow, and if you remember anything else, please give me a call.

Ms. Woodrow: I told them, you know. About the broken streetlight over there by the path to the woods. I called the city council about it no less than four times, if you can believe it. It's been out for weeks! Too dark to see a thing! Even my security cameras can't pick anything up. It's a hazard, I told them. Though I never imagined anything like this would happen.

Detective Olsen: You have security cameras?

Ms. Woodrow: Yes. Lenny had them installed years ago. After an incident involving some kids and toilet paper. I hardly ever look at them, mind you. I used to be able to see who was coming and going out of the woods on that path over there. But with that streetlight out, the damn things are as good as useless. Hey, do you think whoever did this planned it? Maybe they knew about the streetlight too. Lord knows it's been out long enough.

Detective Olsen: Ms. Woodrow, I daresay I think you might have missed your calling as a detective.

SIX WEEKS BEFORE HALLOWEEN

12

AUDREY

Hawthorne Lane

Audrey pulls up to the curb in front of her house, her tires crunching over the pavement. Normally, she'd park in the driveway, but tonight there's a strange car in her usual spot.

Curious, Audrey steps out of her BMW and makes her way up the front walk, inspecting the unfamiliar vehicle—black, sleek, new, paper floor mats still in place—as she passes by. She wonders who it belongs to.

As she reaches for her doorknob, she feels a slight tick of annoyance. She had a long day at the office, putting out fires for *Top Cast*'s upcoming issue, and the last thing she wants is to play hostess to whoever Seth has invited to the house. But, as it seems she was given no choice in the matter, she straightens herself in her heels and pushes open the door.

"Hello?" she calls into the unnervingly quiet house.

"In here," Seth calls back, his voice trailing out of the kitchen.

Audrey's heels click against the hardwood floor as she crosses through the living room to find her husband seated at the counter of their newly renovated kitchen, a glass of deep amber liquid set on the glossy slab of white Carrara marble in front of him. She winces at the ring she knows it will leave behind.

Audrey scans the room, surprised to find him alone. "Whose car is that out front?"

"Huh?" Seth replies. "Oh, it's a loaner. My car is in the shop."

"Again? Didn't you just bring it in for an oil change two weeks ago?"

Seth nods, pulls a draft of his drink. "Sure did. I swear they mess with it on purpose. Tinker with shit just so that you'll have to come back and spend a fortune on repairs. The owner said something about a spark plug and needing to order a part."

"The perils of owning a foreign car, I guess," Audrey jests.

Seth huffs. "Oh, so now you're some sort of car expert?"

Audrey's eyebrows lift in surprise, her arms crossing defensively over her chest. "Excuse me?" She knows that Seth has been a bit . . . surly lately, but if he thinks he's going to speak to her that way, he has another think coming. "Don't—"

"I'm sorry, okay?" Seth is quick to disarm her, slumping over the counter and pushing the heels of his hands against his eyes. "I shouldn't have snapped at you like that. I'm sorry. It's just . . . I don't even know how to say this. But it's done, Audrey. It's over."

"What?" Audrey feels the blood drain from her face, her arms falling limply to her sides. *He knows? About . . . him? How did he find out?* She has no choice now—she's going to have to come clean. "Seth, I—"

"My publisher is dropping me."

Audrey opens her mouth to reply but, stunned by the unexpected turn the conversation has taken, it takes her a moment to find the words. "Jesus, Seth. What happened?"

Seth picks up his drink, rattles the ice in his nearly empty glass. "It's a long story. And I'm going to need a refill first."

He slides off the stool and wobbles slightly as he lands on his feet, using the edge of the counter to steady himself before heading for the bar cart in the living room.

Audrey quickly pulls her phone from the purse on her shoulder and fires off a text:

> Something came up. Can't meet tonight.

A response comes almost immediately.

> What the fuck? You said you could get away tonight. It's been weeks, Audrey.

Audrey's jaw clenches as her fingers angrily jab at the screen.

> Like I said, something came up at home. Not going to work tonight.

She's really getting tired of this, his sense that he's entitled to her time and attention. She doesn't know what gave him the impression that he gets to call the shots here, but she's just about over it.

Audrey hears Seth's shuffling footsteps growing louder as he nears the kitchen. She drops her phone back into her bag.

"Talk to me," she says as she watches Seth arrange himself on a stool, and she takes a seat across from him, her eyes searching his face.

"Evidently, I'm 'canceled.'" He lifts his hands and makes clumsy air quotes on either side of his head as he spits the last word with distaste.

"Canceled?" Audrey's phone buzzes in her bag. She ignores it. "What does that mean?"

"It means," Seth replies, wiping a trail of whiskey from his chin with the cuff of his shirt, "that this delicate new generation thinks my books are *out of touch*." The disgust coils off him like fog lifting from a lake.

"Okay," Audrey hedges, her mind revving into overdrive as she tries to think of a way to spin this. Seth's work is everything to him. This was his dream; the Detective Marlow series is his life's work. As much as Audrey sometimes resented Seth's career, felt like she was jockeying with it for his time and attention, it breaks her heart to see it torn away from him like this. "But they're not your target audience anyway, right? Your books have aways been aimed at an older crowd. So maybe it won't affect sales all that much." Her phone buzzes impatiently and Audrey clenches her hands into fists, her nails digging little crescent moons into her palms. *He needs to stop.*

Seth laughs wryly. "You're not understanding how bad this is. I'm a meme, Audrey. A laughingstock. People are review-bombing my books, leaving one-star reviews everywhere. Calling me washed-up, a middle-aged has-been. And not just on this new book either. It's on all of them. My backlist is tanking too."

"Oh my God..."

"My publisher already cut the cord. My agent says they won't be optioning my next book. It's over, Audrey. I'm finished."

For the third time, Audrey's phone vibrates loudly inside her bag.

"Do you need to get that?" Seth asks, thinly veiled annoyance hovering just beneath the surface.

"It's probably work." She fishes out her phone. "Let me just turn it off."

A series of texts shine out at her defiantly from the screen.

> Later tonight, then
>
> Are you ignoring me?
>
> This is bullshit

This isn't a game, she thinks. *This is my marriage, my life he's messing with.* He's showing absolutely no respect for what's on the line for Audrey. And sure, okay, she hasn't exactly been the picture of marital morality lately, but he's overstepping the bounds.

She wonders if it's because she and Seth don't have kids. If this man thinks her marriage is somehow less valid because she's chosen not to procreate. Audrey sometimes gets the impression that people feel that way. As if she and Seth are just playing house, that their lives, their family of two, couldn't possibly be real, meaningful without children in it. She hears the comments all the time: *Don't you want to experience motherhood? Won't you get bored? Are you sure you aren't going to regret it someday? I couldn't imagine my life without my kids!* As if this were a decision either of them had made lightly. It wasn't. Audrey and Seth agreed very early on that family life wasn't what they wanted. They wanted to be able to travel on a whim; they wanted big careers that they knew would dominate their time and attention. They'd understood that it was just as possible to have a fulfilling marriage without kids as it was to have an empty one with them.

Audrey feels Seth's eyes boring into her as she glares down at the phone in her palm. "It's the office. I'm going to tell them I'm unavailable and that I'll deal with any issues tomorrow." Audrey's thumbs fly over the screen.

Her marriage might not be in the best place right now, but she can't help but feel enraged by those texts, by the utter lack of consideration. She told him she was dealing with a situation at home, and yet he continued to text her. The more she thinks about it, the more it feels like he *wants* her to get caught.

> You know what's bullshit? You not listening to me when I tell you it's not a good time. You need to stop texting me.

Feeling slightly better now that she's taken back the reins, she follows up with another message:

> In fact, I don't think this arrangement is working for me anymore.

Audrey is surprised by how much she means it. When the affair first began, it felt so good to feel wanted again, to feel seen and appreciated. But this isn't feeling very good at all anymore.

Three little dots appear on her phone screen. Audrey knows he's not going to be happy, but she switches her phone off before he can respond. She can't waste her time thinking about his feelings anymore. Not when Seth needs her. When was the last time he needed her?

She looks over at her husband, sipping slowly from his glass. He looks smaller, somehow, folded in on himself, as if he's already given up hope.

Audrey doesn't know what she was thinking. How could she have been so selfish? She made a mistake getting involved with someone else, but it's over now; Seth needs her and she's going to be right here by his side.

13

LIBBY
Hawthorne Lane

Libby tips some kibble into Jasper's metal bowl, where it lands with a clatter. He slowly makes his way over and sniffs at it uninterestedly before looking up at her with round, baleful eyes.

"I know, Jasp," she says. "Blame the vet. He's the one who said you need to be on a diet."

Jasper sits with a *harrumph* as though accepting his fate and slowly begins chewing his new weight-control dog food with little enthusiasm.

She pulls out her phone, checks the time. *Maybe I should go into the shop* . . . It's her day off, but with Lucas at Bill's, it's just too quiet here in her big, empty house. Libby often finds that she doesn't know what to do with herself when she's alone. Free time makes her anxious. *Isn't there something productive I should be doing?*

For so long, there was always something she needed to do, someone she needed to take care of—school lunches to be packed, dry cleaning to be dropped off, shopping to be done, dinners to plan, shifts at Lily Lane to be covered. But now, her family, or what's left of it, doesn't need her quite so much, and she has Erica to share the responsibilities at the store. Libby, for maybe the first time in her adult life, is often alone with herself, and she doesn't have the first clue what to do with that.

She sends a quick text to Erica.

> All okay there? I can come in if you need me.

Erica types back:

> Don't you dare.

Libby smiles to herself. Erica is only five foot one but she is still one of the most intimidating people Libby has ever met. She's curvaceous and loud, the sound of her Colombian accent always filling the store. It was a great decision, hiring her. The customers love her, Libby loves her, and, most important, Erica loves Lily Lane almost as much as Libby does, treating it as if it were her own. She's often shooing Libby off, encouraging her to take some time for herself. "I've got this," she'll say. "Now leave me alone."

Libby knows Erica means well, but she doesn't understand that Libby doesn't *want* time off. She wants to feel needed, useful. Besides, working helps distract her from how very *not* alone Bill is these days.

Libby's fingers stray toward the Instagram icon on her phone screen. It's become an addiction for Libby, checking Heather's account, peering into the Pandora's box she opened when she went searching for Bill's new girlfriend. She navigates to her page now, and Libby finds herself staring at her face again. *Heather.* She clicks on a random photo, a cheerful Heather crossing the finish line of a race, and studies it—the sinew of her strong legs, her taut stomach—as if she hasn't already spent hours memorizing every detail of the curated, smiling grid over the past two weeks, her mind expanding the photos into motion, filling in the gaps between the frames. She's already imagined Bill's mouth on Heather's full, pillowy lips. She's imagined the sound of her laugh: throaty, sexy, unencumbered. She's imagined Bill's fingers tangled in her long, dark hair. She's imagined Heather's body beneath Bill's in the throes of passion, the way Heather, looking up at him, would see the tendons in his shoulders flex, his mouth forming a soft O as he thrusts against her.

Honk.

The sound abruptly halts her spiraling thoughts, yanks her unceremoniously back to reality. It sounds as though it came from just outside her house.

Honk, honk.

Libby slips her phone back into her pocket and makes her way to the front window. Her eyebrows rise nearly to her hairline when she sees the unfamiliar car parked in her driveway, a cherry-red Mustang convertible, engine roaring and exhaust curling up behind it like dragon smoke.

Libby walks outside in a stunned daze.

"Mom!" Lucas shouts from the driver's seat. "Can you believe this?" He sounds like a little boy again, buzzing with excitement, his fingers trailing along the leather-wrapped steering wheel.

"Whose car is this?" Libby croaks with feigned enthusiasm as she approaches the rolled-down window, noticing how Bill, sitting in the passenger seat, doesn't quite meet her eyes.

"Mine!" Lucas is giddy with joy. "Dad bought it for me!"

Libby clenches her teeth, forcing a smile onto her face for the sake of her son. She doesn't want to take this away from him—it's been so long since she's seen him this happy—but it's taking all her self-control not to strangle his father here and now.

"Why don't you go inside so I can talk to Dad for a minute?"

"Yeah, okay," he says, sliding out of the smooth leather driver's seat and pulling her into a quick hug. "And then I'm going to pick up Justin. Wait till he sees me pull up in this!"

He heads toward the house, and Libby gently touches her neck where her son's arm just was. When was the last time he'd been so casually affectionate with her?

She waits until she hears the front door close, until she knows Lucas is inside, and then she rounds on Bill.

"What the hell were you thinking?" she shouts, throwing her hands up in exasperation. She'd spoken to him about this, explained how important it was that they be on the same page about not buying Lucas a car. They'd agreed that Lucas was going to work to save up for it, learn the value of a dollar. And *this* certainly wasn't the car she'd had in mind for their seventeen-year-old son!

Bill's gaze scans the cul-de-sac in a wide arc. "I know you're upset, but let's try not to make a scene for the entire neighborhood."

Right now Libby could care less if her neighbors overhear. She's tired of always holding herself back, considering everyone else's feelings before her own. "How could you do this? There's no way he's keeping this car! He's only seventeen! It's far too expensive, not to mention dangerous!"

"Lib, I know you said you wanted him to save up for his first car, but I have the money and he's my son and—"

"This is exactly what we said we didn't want to do!"

"No, it's what *you* said we didn't want to do." Bill's face hardens. "If I want to buy my kid a car, I'll buy him a car. He's been going through a tough time and I wanted to do this for him. It was my decision to make."

Libby can feel the indignation, the resentment taking hold of her, climbing up her throat. "He's going through a tough time because of *you*! Because of *your* choice! You can't just buy him off and absolve yourself of any guilt you feel over it. And as for it being your decision to make—if you wanted to be a parent, you shouldn't have left your son."

"I didn't leave my son, Libby. I left you. And this is why. The constant arguing. Our marriage was starting to feel like a battlefield. I couldn't take it anymore!"

Tears well in Libby's eyes and she turns away, not wanting to give Bill the satisfaction of seeing how much his words hurt her. But as she does, she sees Lucas standing on the front walk, a backpack slung over one shoulder, car keys dangling from his hand.

"Lucas, I—"

The look on his face tells her that he heard everything.

"Why do you have to be like this, Mom?" he asks, the hurt in his eyes, the hate in his words, like daggers through her heart. "Why do you have to ruin everything?"

Lucas pushes past her, climbs back into his new car. He stares resolutely out the windshield, looking anywhere but at his mother.

"Why don't you get going to Justin's," Bill says as he steps out of the car. "I think your mother and I should finish this discussion inside."

LIBBY PACES THE LENGTH OF her living room. "I just feel like this is something you should have spoken to me about!"

Jasper wanders into the room, his nails click-clacking against the hardwood floor to greet Bill, but at the sound of Libby's shouting, he quickly scuttles back to the kitchen, his tail hanging low between his legs.

"I get it, okay?" Bill says. "Maybe it did warrant a conversation, but, Lib, come on. You know it would just have turned into an argument."

"Not necessarily, we—"

"Libby. Look at me."

Libby pauses her pacing, forcing her eyes to meet Bill's. He's leaning casually against the wall, thumbs looped over the pockets of his jeans.

"We haven't been good at this for a long time, me and you. For the past few years, it feels like all we did was argue."

"That's not fair. Okay, maybe we were going through a bit of a rough patch, but every marriage does. We could have worked through it."

"It was more than a rough patch."

Libby shakes her head. "No, it wasn't, we just—"

"It was for me." Bill's voice is gentle, but his words are resolute. "I wasn't happy anymore. *We* weren't happy anymore. You just didn't want to see it."

Libby is incredulous. She feels all the sadness she's been carrying around, locked tightly inside her chest, giving way to anger.

"You weren't happy? You're not a child, Bill! You can't be *happy* all the time. That's not how marriage works! That's not how *life* works!"

"That's not what I meant."

Libby continues as if she didn't hear him. She's been holding these words back for so long, holding *herself* back for so long. "But I guess it does work like that for you, right? You can just get yourself a girlfriend and move on without a second thought about what it's doing to your family. But, hey, as long as you're happy, I guess!"

"You . . . know?" Bill's arms drop to his sides, his lips parting in surprise. "How?"

"Does it matter?"

"I guess it doesn't. But I wanted to tell you myself, in person. It felt like the right thing to do."

"The right thing to do? *The right thing to do* would have been to work on our marriage instead of throwing it away the second things got tough!" She's shouting now, unrestrained for the first time in as long as she can remember.

"Whoa, Lib, calm down, I—"

"I will absolutely not calm down! I think I've been calm for long enough!"

"We're separated—it's not like I had an affair!"

"Jesus, Bill! You said you just needed some time. I thought we'd work it out, I thought . . ." A defiant tear slides down her cheek and Libby swipes it away angrily with the back of her wrist. *I thought you'd fight for us.*

"Lib." Bill steps toward her, reaches for her hand, but she recoils.

"Don't touch me. I don't need your pity."

"It's not pity, I just . . . I didn't mean to upset you. But I think you should know. Things are getting serious with—"

Libby raises a palm. "Don't you dare say her name in this house." She knows it sounds childish, but she can't bear the thought of hearing another woman's name on his lips in the home they built together.

"Fine." Bill crosses his arms over his chest, distances himself from her once again. "I won't say her name. But it's probably for the best that you know about it now, before she meets Lucas."

"She's not meeting our son." Libby's words carry an edge of warning.

"That's not your call to make." Bill's eyes lock on hers, defiant now. He's drawn a line in the sand, and it feels so unfair. So fundamentally unfair.

"How can you be so selfish? You told me time apart would be good for our marriage, and I tried to give that to you, but what good has it done for us, Bill? Tell me, what good is any of this doing? You threw our marriage, our family, away. And for what? So you could go sow your wild oats like a teenage boy?" She throws her hands up in disgusted frustration. "And now you want to introduce this . . . this . . . *woman* to our son. No. Absolutely not. No."

"You know what? The beauty of being separated is that I don't have to listen to this anymore. I'm going home. We'll finish this conversation another time." He turns and walks away from Libby once again. Because it's so easy for him to do. Because he can come and go from her life, from their family, as it suits him without so much as a second thought. It's unfathomable to her.

Something about the image of his turned back sets her off. It brings back all the pain of the night he left, of all the nights since when she's silently cried herself to sleep. Every day she has to tamp down her broken heart to put a smile on her face, to give him the space he said he needed, to pretend to be okay for Lucas's sake. She has to be the strong one who holds what's left of her family together while he just gets to walk away. She's overcome with it, with the need to *do* something. The need to be seen, really seen, for once.

As if her hand is moving of its own accord, Libby picks up the framed wedding photo on the mantel and hurls it in Bill's direction. It smashes into the front door just as he pulls it closed behind him. Libby watches the glass explode and fall to the ground like shards of scattered ice. In its wake, a deafening silence. Libby is once again alone, left to pick up the broken pieces of her life.

14

GEORGINA
Hawthorne Lane

Georgina pushes the blade of the knife through the skin and watches as her orange falls into neat quarters on its plate. Listening for the sound of the front door opening, she grabs another orange from the fruit bowl to repeat the process. Christina and Sebastian will be home from school any moment, and Georgina always tries to have a healthy snack waiting for them when they arrive. As she fixes a second plate, she's reminded of how little time she has left with both of them at home. Sebastian is a senior now, and in just a few short months they'll be packing his things for college.

The front door opens, and Georgina hears Sebastian's heavy footsteps stomping down the hallway. She used to be able to recognize the sound of everyone's footfalls as they moved through the house, filled it with life: the pitter-patter of Sebastian's running feet, the light tiptoe tread of Christina's. But now Sebastian walks like a man. Like his father. The sound is nearly identical.

He and Colin are close, always going off on their hunting trips, to sporting events. Georgina sometimes feels a pang of jealousy. She and Sebastian have never had the same type of relationship, despite her best efforts. Ever since he was a small boy, he idolized his father, choosing him over his mother. It had been hard for Georgina to watch the way Sebastian's face would light up when Colin came home from a long day at work, the way he'd run and jump into his arms. She'd put so much of herself into raising her son. Everything she had. She'd given up her career ambitions, driven him to every team practice, every doctor's appointment. Georgina was always there. And yet Sebastian has never looked at her the way he does Colin. She supposes it's only natural. It makes perfect sense that a boy would relate more to his father. But his rejection of her still feels like a knife to her heart.

"Hey, sweetie," she says as he strides into the kitchen now. "How was school?"

He grumbles an unintelligible reply as he yanks open the refrigerator door.

"I sliced up some oranges if you're hungry." She holds out the plate to him like a peace offering.

Sebastian eyes it dismissively. "Nah, I'm good." He pulls out a container of leftover chicken piccata from last night's dinner.

"Where's Christina?" Georgina asks. "I thought you'd be walking her home."

Sebastian shrugs. "She got a ride."

"With who?"

"How should I know?" He grabs a fork out of the drawer. "I'm gonna take this up to my room."

"Are you sure you don't want to eat it down here? I could heat it up for you, and—"

"Mom," he barks with an exasperated shake of his head. "Just stop."

Sebastian walks away, and Georgina busies herself packing up the untouched orange slices. She tells herself that he's just a teenage boy, that his disdain for her is only a phase. She wonders if Libby and Lucas have had the same growing pains. Somehow she doubts it. They're so close. Georgina hates to admit it, but seeing them together has always made her jealous. She suspects that this is why her early budding friendship with Libby seemed to wither away after their boys were born. While Georgina was struggling to connect with her son, it seemed to come so easily to Libby and Lucas.

They'd taken their sons to the park together once. Sebastian and Lucas couldn't have been more than four years old at the time, and they'd run around the playground, racing each other down the slide over and over again. Libby and Georgina sat side by side on a wooden bench watching them play while Christina napped in her stroller.

Georgina noticed how Lucas looked back at his mother from time to time as if seeking reassurance, making sure she was still there, waving from the top of the climbing structure. Sebastian hadn't looked for Georgina once. She told herself it was because she was raising a strong, independent little boy, but even then she wondered...

She'd watched as Lucas ran toward the top of the slide, Sebastian racing up behind him. It seemed that they reached the landing at the same time, and both boys tumbled down the slide in a jumble of limbs and bumped heads. Libby and Georgina both sprang up and ran to their children. Libby stroked the back of Lucas's head, whispering reassurances into his ear, while Georgina, tending to the practical, examined Sebastian for injuries. He'd scraped his knee, and his eyes were welling with tears as it started to bleed. Georgina tried to pull him into her arms, but he shoved her away. He yanked the leg of his pants over his injured knee, and angrily wiped away his tears with the back of his hand.

"What a tough little guy," Libby had remarked as Sebastian limped away from them and headed back toward the slide. Lucas had climbed into Libby's lap, his tears slowing as he twirled one of her blond curls around his little finger, comforting himself. What was wrong with Georgina that nothing about her was comforting to her son? That he wanted so little of her?

"Yes," she'd said, "he is." That was the last time they'd gone to the park together.

The sound of a car door closing, Christina's voice calling "Goodbye," brings Georgina back to the moment. Curious, she makes her way to the front of the house and looks out the large picture window just in time to see a little red convertible peeling away down the street, Christina jogging happily up the front walk.

GEORGINA KNOCKS LIGHTLY ON CHRISTINA'S bedroom door, the plate of orange slices in her hand. "Can I come in? I have a snack for you."

"Oh, sure, Mom!" Christina replies. Spying the fruit, she smiles brightly. "Awesome, thanks. I was starving."

Georgina hands her daughter the plate and watches as she nibbles delicately on an orange slice while folding her legs neatly beneath her pleated skirt. Georgina sits on the edge of Christina's bed, and Christina scoots over, making room for her.

She thinks, not for the first time, how different her relationship with her daughter is compared to the one she has with Sebastian. Christina has always demanded so much less of Georgina. She never made her mother work for her affection, and ever since she was a small girl, it seems that she's always done everything she could to make all of their lives easier. If Sebastian was crying over dropping his ice cream cone, Christina would offer to share hers without having to be asked. If Georgina was rushing to get dinner ready, Christina would take it upon herself to set the table. She's the one who never broke curfew, whose school report cards consistently referred to her as "polite and conscientious." While Christina's agreeable nature has certainly made Georgina's life as a parent easier, she hopes she's somehow managed to instill in her daughter the strength she will need to be a woman in this world. She hopes she's raising Christina to be something more than her mother is, to know that she doesn't have to give too much of herself away, that it's okay to prioritize herself. She wants her daughter to know it's not wrong for a woman to take up space in the world, that she can be loud, that she doesn't ever have to compromise who she is, dim her light, to make those around her more comfortable.

"Everything okay?" Christina asks, looking at Georgina curiously as she tucks a lock of her golden-blond hair behind her ear.

"Yes, everything is fine, sweetheart, but I was just wondering . . . who drove you home from school today? I didn't recognize the car." Unlike with her son, Georgina still knows all of Christina's friends, a reserved group of girls who are more focused on making the honor society than tearing through the neighborhood in shiny red sports cars.

Christina blushes, her cheeks turning a sweet cotton-candy pink. "Lucas."

"Lucas Corbin?" Georgina can't keep the look of surprise off her face.

Christina's blush deepens. "Yeah."

Georgina is stunned. For one thing, she had no idea that Christina and Lucas were friends, and for another, she can't imagine Libby buying Lucas such a flashy car. "He got a new car?" Georgina inquires, trying her best to sound casual.

"Uh-huh." Christina adjusts the black frames of her glasses. "His dad bought it for him."

"How nice." Georgina forces a smile onto her face. "Are you two . . . an item?"

Christina's eyes drop, and she looks as if she'd rather melt into the floor than continue the conversation. "No, Mom. Lucas and I are just friends."

"Lucas Corbin drove you home?" Sebastian has appeared in Christina's doorway. He fills the frame, his arms crossed over his chest. For a moment, Georgina is struck by how much he resembles his father these days.

"Yeah," she replies, not meeting her brother's eyes. "So?"

"So that guy is a loser and I don't want you hanging around him."

"Since when do you care who I hang out with?" The words, though bold, are spoken to the floor.

"Since now," Sebastian snarls. "He's two years older than you. What's he doing nosing around my fifteen-year-old sister?"

"First of all, I'll be sixteen in, like, three months. And second, it was just a ride home. Can everyone stop making such a big deal about it?" Christina throws her hands up in exasperation.

"Fine. But stay away from Lucas Corbin," Sebastian retorts before storming down the hall.

"Christina, honey," Georgina starts, "I think Lucas is a nice boy, I really do, but maybe we should talk about—"

"I'm not dating Lucas, okay? He's not even interested in me like that. I'm, like, not even the kind of girl that would be on his radar. We're not exactly in the same crowd at school. And anyway, I know the rules." She rolls her eyes and says, her voice dropping into a lower octave, an imitation of her father's, "I'm too young to date."

"Christina, I'm sure plenty of boys are interested in you, it's just that you're still so young, and—"

"Please, Mom." She gets off the bed and moves across the room to her desk. "I really don't want to talk about this anymore, okay? Besides, I have a ton of homework to do."

Her back to Georgina, Christina opens a textbook and begins flipping through the pages.

Georgina's heart sinks in the silence. She tried, she really did, to create a home for her children that was different from the one she grew up in. And yet, for a moment, it's like she's back there, drowning in the loneliness she'd felt as a little girl.

She sees herself alone in her bedroom, hears the sounds of her parents arguing through the thin walls: "Do you think money grows on trees? Jesus Christ, Joan, look at all this shit! And you got the kid a new coat? How much of my money did you spend on *that*?"

They always spoke about Georgina that way, as if she weren't a person but a burden they'd been reluctant to take on. Rarely did they ever speak *to* her.

"I had to, Gerry. Her teacher called home. Said it was too cold to be sending her in without one. You want CPS showing up at our door?"

"If they did, they'd take one look at the place and have it condemned!" Her father's voice grew to a roar. "Do you think I work like a dog so you can keep collecting your . . . your garbage?"

Their house was full of her mother's "treasures." Bloated boxes of junk, piles of old newspapers that grew larger by the day. They were an oppressive presence, always looming, taunting Georgina with their dust and disorder, threatening to consume her. It made her feel dirty; like her home life was a permanent stain that she was sure everyone around her could see, despite the fact that her mother never let anyone else inside their house. There were no playdates, no birthday parties, no sleepovers with giggling school friends. Her mother's hoarding had all but condemned Georgina to a life of solitude. She'd itched to throw it all away, to scrub and scour every inch of that suffocating house, but she knew her mother would never allow it. She seemed to love her things, her *garbage*, more than her own daughter. And so Georgina did the only thing she could. She weaved between the dusty boxes and teetering piles of garage-sale trinkets, shut herself in her room (which she kept clean with military precision), and did her best to stay out of the way.

Georgina shakes away the memory. Reminds herself that she's not that little girl anymore. But sometimes she worries that a part of her never escaped that place, that her life there damaged her, her ability to connect with other people. Even her own children.

Georgina hasn't been a perfect parent. She knows that. But she hopes they see how hard she's tried to give them more than what she had, to connect with them in a way her parents never did. When they go off into the world, she wonders, will they look back on this home she'd created for them and see the love she'd poured into the home-cooked meals and polished floors? Or will they too remember the silences that she never learned how to break through?

Georgina watches her daughter for a moment more, searching for the right combination of words that will shatter the invisible barrier between them, but they don't come. And so she quietly leaves the bedroom, closing the door softly behind her.

15

HANNAH
Hawthorne Lane

Hannah looks down at her hands, sees the spill of red blood, feels it sliding, warm, between her fingers. Her lungs burn as she gasps for air; she wants to scream but she can't. She can barely breathe. What has she done?

She awakens with a start, her hands grabbing at her throat as she sucks in big gulps of air. *I'm okay. It was just a dream.* She sits up in bed as rain patters on the roof above her head and looks over at Mark, who is still dozing, peacefully unaware, beside her.

Not for the first time, Hannah is struck with the guilt. Over all the things she hasn't told him, about the terrible thing she'd done. She wonders if he could still love her if he knew. Somehow she doubts it.

Mark claims to remember the first time he saw Hannah. He says he knew even then that he would love her. They'd met at the coffee shop in Manhattan where she worked. He was one of the regulars, always ordered the same thing: a hot black coffee with one sugar. He says that Hannah was the reason he came into the shop so often, even though there were plenty of other coffee places near his office to choose from. That when she smiled at him, he knew she was the one, and it had just taken him some time to work up the courage to ask her out. But Hannah remembers it differently. There was no meet-cute moment, no love-at-first-sight Hollywood scene where their eyes met and she just "knew." It felt to her like she gradually awakened to Mark, like one day she looked up and was suddenly aware that he'd always been there, as if she'd known him all along.

Their relationship had progressed in much the same way. After Mark finally asked her to dinner, they were almost never apart again. Their lives blended together so seamlessly that it felt to Hannah like meeting him had been an inevitability. They'd watch television at his apartment, her feet in his lap, and run errands together, Mark carrying her groceries. At times she'd catch him looking at her like he couldn't believe she was real, like he was surprised to find her standing next to him. She knew how he felt. She couldn't pinpoint when she'd fallen in love with Mark; she just knew that she had. She'd never known things could be this simple, that love could be this solid, unassuming thing that grew where you least expected it.

Mark's mother had wanted them to have a big wedding at her country club. She'd wanted to invite all her friends and relatives, to deck out the ballroom with tulle and a five-tiered wedding cake. But that wasn't Hannah and Mark. They'd insisted on a small, private ceremony followed by dinner at a restaurant with only their closest family and friends. Mark wore a black suit, and Hannah wore a plain silk dress in the loveliest shade of cream. Their wedding day was a reflection of exactly how Hannah hoped the rest of their marriage would be: simple and unassuming but full of deep love.

She hadn't planned to lie to Mark, to keep secrets from him. At least not at first. She wanted to tell him, she really did, but she never found the words. She knew once she said them that it would change everything. That once he saw the dark stain of her past, he'd never look at her the same way again. And it killed her to imagine that. The dimming of her in his eyes, Mark's light turning away from her. With him, Hannah was someone new. A better version of herself than she'd been before. And she wanted that so badly. A fresh start. A clean slate. Everyone is guilty of it, aren't they? People hide away their jagged edges, their ugliest thoughts. Show the world the versions of themselves that they wish were real. But, Hannah knows, those small vicious things are part of who you are, whether you like it or not.

Still feeling shaken, Hannah climbs out of bed and heads downstairs to the kitchen to get a glass of water. There's a pile of mail on the counter, a rain-soaked stack of newspapers and bills that Mark must have brought in and then forgotten about. She sorts through it now, gently peeling apart the waterlogged pages. But when she reaches the center of the pile, she sees it. An envelope addressed to *Mr. and Mrs. Wilson* at their old place in the city. She almost throws it away. A voice in her head screams at her not to open it, that once she sees what's inside, there's no turning back. But she has to. She knows that. She has to know what's coming for her if she has any chance of outrunning it.

She slides open the back flap of the envelope and pulls out a single sheet of white paper, a familiar hint of garish red leaking through the page. She unfolds the message with shaking hands.

The ink has started to run, bloody splotches staining the page, but the words are unmistakable:

THIS ISN'T OVER

For a moment Hannah is too stunned to process what she's seeing. This note feels more threatening than the last, like something is bearing down on her, circling the life she's built like a predator.

She hears her mother's voice again, an echo of the past: *It's time to go.*

But no. It feels like such a fragile thing to her, the happiness she's found with Mark. As if it's made of blown glass, beautiful and glittering, delicate in her hands. She knows then that she'll do whatever it takes to protect it.

Hannah crumples the note and shoves it down the garbage disposal. She flicks a switch, and the steely blades begin to spin, grinding the threatening words to a harmless pulp. Hannah no longer has the kind of life she's willing to run from.

As she watches the last traces of it swirling out of sight, she sees something, movement outside her window, that stops her in her tracks. Suddenly Hannah realizes how exposed she is in this big house with its tall windows and open spaces, illuminated as if she's under a spotlight. When she tries to get a better look at the figure outside, all she can see is her own reflection staring back at her, wide-eyed and pale.

She shuts off the overhead lights, throwing her house into darkness. At first, all seems quiet on Hawthorne Lane. Hannah begins to wonder if she imagined it, the figure nothing more than a trick of the light and her jangled nerves getting the best of her. But then she sees it again, someone creeping across her neighbor's lawn. And not just anyone's lawn, Georgina's.

Hannah scampers up the stairs, hoping she'll have a better vantage point from there. She rushes to her bedroom window, presses her hands against the cold glass. Rain pours over the panes in rivers, making the outside world look distorted and blurry.

"Han?" Mark rouses, rubbing the sleep from his eyes. "Everything okay?"

"I thought..." Hannah scans the street, but there's no sign of the figure she'd seen before. "I thought I saw someone outside."

Mark swings his legs over the side of the bed, pushes himself up. He joins her by the window and peers over her shoulder at the dark street below. "I don't see anyone. You sure it was a person? We live out in the 'burbs now. I hear the raccoons are as big as Dobermans."

"Mark, I think I can tell the difference between a raccoon and a human being." She doesn't mean to be sharp with him, but she's shaken and the words come out more pointed than she intended.

He takes her in his arms. "I'm sorry, hun. I didn't mean to make light of the situation. I know you probably had a scare, but this is a good neighborhood. I'm sure it was just someone taking their poodle out for a late-night stroll."

"Yeah..." Hannah replies. "Maybe. But it looked like the guy was on Georgina and Colin's property. Maybe I should let her know? Just in case?"

"Whatever you think is best," Mark tells her as he climbs back into bed. "But like I said, I'm sure it's nothing worth waking the neighbors over."

Hannah walks back to her own side of the bed and sits on the edge with her phone in her hand. She debates whether she should send a text to Georgina. She doesn't want to alarm her; after all, she's not exactly sure what she saw. But something about the idea of a person in the dark lurking on their quiet cul-de-sac has set off alarm bells in her head.

> Hey. Sorry if I'm waking you, but I wanted to let you know that I was looking out the window a few minutes ago and I thought I saw someone outside your house. Just thought you should know.

Three little dots appear on the screen, as if Georgina is composing a reply, but they vanish as quickly as they'd appeared.

16
AUDREY
Hawthorne Lane

Audrey leans back in her seat, her head rocking gently with the movement of the train. It's been a long day, but the new issue of *Top Cast* is finally ready to go to print. This issue had been a challenging one, with a slew of last-minute changes and additions, and that meant a lot of late nights spent in the office. Not that Audrey minded. Her office has always felt like a sanctuary to her. She loves the sleek glass desk, the framed special editions adorning the walls, the way the interns flock to bring her coffee in the mornings (*Is there anything else I can get for you, Ms. Warrington?*), and the way the junior editors jockey for a chance to work with her. She might be overlooked at home, but at *Top Cast,* Audrey is someone who matters.

Besides, work keeps her out of the house, a place that's beginning to feel suffocating. Seth has been moping around in sweatpants for weeks, days-old stubble shadowing his face. At first, Audrey tried to cheer him up, but that only resulted in Seth snapping at her, so she eventually gave up. She sees the way he's been looking at her lately as she dresses for work, pulling one of her many suits from her walk-in closet. She feels his eyes on her as she pushes her feet into her pumps and slings a purse over her shoulder while he skulks aimlessly around the house with nowhere to be. She can't help but feel that her husband resents her, that he can't stand to watch her star on the rise while his sinks. She knows he's going through a hard time, and she wants to be there for him, but it's becoming increasingly difficult.

It's just so infuriatingly unfair. For the past ten years, ever since Seth signed his first major book deal, she's been nothing but supportive of his success. She cheered him on from the sidelines as he toured the country without her, appeared on television talk shows, his face cropping up in all the major newspapers. She didn't mind when he became so famous that he was occasionally stopped for autographs when they were out at dinner; she didn't even mind when he stopped asking her to be the first one to read his early drafts. (Or maybe she'd stopped asking to read them. She can't remember now.) No matter how successful Audrey became in her own right, she was always overshadowed by her husband's accomplishments. It was something they'd both come to accept. But now it was Seth's turn to take a back seat, to watch Audrey soar. And he couldn't do that for her.

Seth isn't the only man in her life who has been testing her limits either. To say that her former lover wasn't exactly thrilled about her calling off their affair would be putting it lightly. He'd texted her, emailed her, left her voicemails demanding that they meet, that they talk about her unilateral decision to end things. He wasn't taking no for an answer, and Audrey was over it. Who did he think she was? Certainly not someone who could be pushed around. But she's held to her convictions, giving him the cold shoulder and ignoring all of his attempts to reach her. Looking back on things now, she can't imagine what she'd ever seen in him. She's hoping that as more time passes, he'll run out of steam, lose interest, and the whole messy affair will just fade into the background. She'd made a mistake, admittedly a pretty big one, but she'd ended it, she'd done the right thing before anyone got hurt. Now she just needs him to see that, needs him to walk away before he ruins both of their lives.

A staticky automated announcement crackles through the train's speakers: "Next stop, Sterling Valley."

AUDREY PUSHES OPEN THE FRONT door of her house, her keys jangling in the lock.

"Hello?" she calls. The house is dark, the air still and heavy. She catches a faint whiff of something sour, and she vaguely wonders if Seth has gotten to the point where he's given up on showering.

"Seth?"

There's no reply. Audrey lets the door close behind her with a thud. She sets her bag on the entry table beside the front door and steps out of her heels. She flexes her toes, stretches the arches of her feet. But when she flicks on the light, she feels as though the air has been stolen from her lungs. She's not alone. There's someone else in the house, his hard eyes fixed on her. She gasps, a sharp intake of air.

"Jesus, Seth," she says, her heart hammering in her chest. "What the hell are you doing sitting in the dark, and why didn't you answer me?"

"I was waiting for you to come home." His words are sharp, pointed things, as though he's been whittling away at them in the dark. "Where were you?"

"At work," Audrey replies, still feeling rattled. She spies the glass on the coffee table, sitting beside a half-empty bottle of bourbon and a scatter of white pills. "What's all this?"

"Just taking the edge off."

"What are those pills, Seth?"

He swipes the glass off the table and takes a swig from it. A small rivulet of liquid leaks down his chin and splashes onto his shirt; a dark gray patch blooms on his chest.

"Left over from my knee surgery a few years back. It was acting up today."

"Seth, I don't know if—"

"Another late night for you, then, huh?" Seth cuts her off, a dizzying change of direction.

Audrey can sense the sarcasm peeling off him in curling tendrils. "Yes. I told you what's been going on with the new issue, but—"

"Hmm," he grumbles. "Right, your all-important job running puff pieces on celebrity gossip and the latest makeup trends."

Audrey feels a spike of rage pierce through her at the insult, but she forces herself to shove it down. Seth has never spoken about her job that way, even if she's secretly always suspected that he thought her work was beneath him. And there's something so pathetic about the sight of him right now: his stained shirt, his thinning hair uncombed, his unshaven face. She decides to let it pass. Whereas once they would have argued as passionately as they did everything else—glasses thrown, insults slung—it now feels like all the energy has been drained from their marriage. She wonders when they'd stopped fighting for each other and simply given up. "I know you're going through something right now, but that doesn't give you the right to speak to me that way. There's no need to be condescending."

Seth scoffs disgustedly as he takes another pull from his glass.

Audrey crosses her arms over her chest. "Well, since you're obviously in no state to have a conversation, I think I'll just go upstairs and get changed." She turns on her heel, her long, dark hair fanning out behind her.

"Something came for you."

Audrey hears his words slink over her shoulder.

"In the kitchen," he mutters into his glass.

A wave of dizziness washes over her. "What is it?"

"Why don't you go see for yourself?"

She hates this, hates feeling like she's walking into a trap, like she's powerless to stop whatever will happen next. And yet she has no choice but to go. She feels Seth's hard, scrutinizing eyes following her as she pads out of the room and into the kitchen.

There, on her new white marble counter, sits a bouquet of blood-red roses tied with a black satin ribbon. Audrey lifts the bundle into her arms as cautiously as if it were a bomb. She searches for a card, though a part of her knows she won't find one. *He* must have sent them. Not as a romantic gesture but as a warning that he won't be ignored. A shot fired to remind her how easily he can overturn her life. Audrey's jaw tenses; the musky scent of the roses is heavy and cloying in her nose. *How dare he.*

"No card, huh?" Seth asks.

Audrey whirls around to find him leaning against the entryway to the kitchen, arms folded over his chest. "Uh, no. They're not from you?"

Seth's scowl deepens.

"They're probably from Arlene, then," Audrey says, pivoting.

"Your boss at *Top Cast* sent you two dozen red roses?" He raises a skeptical eyebrow.

"Had to have been. For all the extra hours I've been putting in. I can't imagine who else would have sent them."

"Really? No one else comes to mind? No one at all?"

Audrey's fingers tighten around the bundled stems. She feels a thorn dig into the pad of her ring finger, a drop of warm blood sliding over her skin. "I don't know what you're getting at. But look, I'll throw them out if they're offensive to you for some reason."

Audrey can see the moment the fight drains out of her husband, the anger he'd been clinging to like a life raft deflating beneath him, leaving him floundering in an endless expanse of hopelessness.

"I asked around, by the way." His voice comes out heavy, defeated. "The tie clip doesn't belong to anyone I know."

Audrey opens her mouth and then closes it again. She wants to argue, to bury her indiscretion under an insurmountable mountain of lies, but she finds that she can't bring herself to do it. She hardly recognizes this man standing before her. In just a few weeks, her husband has withered to a smaller, less substantial version of himself. The larger-than-life Seth Warrington pictured on the inside of his book jackets, the one with the cocky smile standing before a wall of his own books, is gone. This version of him looks so much more ... human. Like someone she could break as easily as blowing dust from her palm.

"I'm going to take these outside," she says, unable to meet his eye.

AUDREY CARRIES THE ROSES INTO her front yard. She holds them by the stems, letting them dangle upside down, dropping petals in a meandering trail as she crosses her lawn.

She opens the lid of the garbage can that sits politely at the curb in front of her house. It's garbage day tomorrow, and she can't be rid of these damn things soon enough. She drops the roses in, lets them fall atop the bundled bags of coffee grounds and greasy banana peels. She imagines them being picked up tomorrow, the beautiful, delicate blooms being chewed up by the metal jaws of the trash compactor. *Good.* He never should have sent them to her house.

She slams the lid of the garbage can, ridding herself of them, ridding herself of *him,* of his obtrusive presence in her house, in her marriage.

She jumps when she sees the figure standing just outside the amber glow cast by the streetlight across the lane. She'd thought she was alone out here. It's a warm September night, but the sight of this man, standing so still, watching her in the dark, sends a chill shivering down her spine.

"Hello?" she calls, her quaking voice betraying her nerves.

He steps into the light then. Audrey takes in his familiar form, the tall stature, the broad shoulders, the golden-blond hair. *Sebastian Pembrook.*

He waves as he walks casually down the street, as though he hadn't been watching her at all.

"Have a good night, Mrs. Warrington," he calls.

17
LIBBY
Hawthorne Lane

Libby looks down at her phone, which fills the dark interior of her car with a blue-white glow. She slouches in her seat as her thumb scrolls over the screen. *Heather Brooks.* Her face is all Libby can see anymore. It haunts her at work, in the shower, while she's stopped at red lights. Heather has become like a ghost that's always hovering in the periphery of Libby's mind. Ever since her argument with Bill, she's been replaying his words in her head like lyrics from a scratched record: *Things are getting serious.*

She clicks on Heather's most recent post, a photo uploaded three days ago, and studies the image that fills her screen: a key ring dangling from Heather's long manicured fingers with a caption reading *Key to his heart <3*. (The woman's overuse of emoticons seems to be her only flaw, as far as Libby can tell.)

Libby wonders what the other woman thinks of her. She wonders if she thinks of her at all. Is Heather aware that she's the antagonist in Libby's story, the one who swooped in and carried away all the broken pieces of her marriage and reassembled them for herself? Probably not. She imagines the lines Bill would have fed his young, gullible new girlfriend. She's sure they were something clichéd and middle-aged. *We were just too young when we got married* and *My wife never really understood me, not like you do, babe.* Something that would make Heather want to fall into his arms, kiss the pain away. Libby shudders at the thought.

She looks again at the photo of the key, a blurry brick building in the background. It's Bill's town house. She recognized it instantly from all the times she's dropped Lucas at that very building, but she couldn't believe Bill would really ask this woman to move in with him. How could he possibly be that serious about her? Libby can't even imagine herself kissing another man, never mind *living* with one. She pictures their things side by side: Heather's clothes hanging in the closet next to Bill's, their shirtsleeves touching, her shoes beside his in the entryway, her pink toothbrush sharing a cup with Bill's blue one. Something about the intimacy of it, of all the simple, inconsequential things that add up to a life together, causes an aching pain in Libby's chest. She's mourning, she realizes. As if her marriage had been a person, its own living, breathing entity, a life created by her and Bill, as real as Lucas. She can't understand how he could so callously snuff out this precious thing they'd made.

It's possible that Libby is wrong. She doesn't mean to get ahead of herself. Maybe Bill just gave Heather a spare key for emergencies, and the girl took to social media to make it look like something more. Maybe Libby overreacted to the photo of the key; maybe she's making a mountain out of a molehill. Or maybe it's exactly what it looks like . . .

That's why she's driven here tonight. She was home earlier, all alone, Lucas having stayed over at Justin's house, letting her imagination run wild, and eventually she couldn't take it anymore. The not knowing. She's grown so accustomed to knowing everything about Bill. She knows his favorite brand of socks, that he never eats the last bite of a banana, and that sometimes his left knee hurts when it rains, a holdover from a car accident he'd been involved in years ago. And now they weren't even speaking to each other. They hadn't exchanged one single word since their argument. Libby hated the idea that she didn't know this most basic thing about him now—if he was living with someone new. It was a glaring reminder of how much of him she was losing. She told herself that if she just *knew,* she could learn to live with it. Anything had to be better than dwelling on the *maybe*s and *what-if*s. And so Libby grabbed her keys, slid her feet into a pair of sneakers, drove across town, and parked outside Bill's town house, ready to find out the truth one way or another.

But now that she's here, the insanity of the situation is dawning on her. She knows she has absolutely no business being here. And yet... and yet, she can't help but stare up at Bill's window, waiting to catch sight of something she's not sure she wants to see.

Libby bites at the skin on the edge of her thumb. It frightens her a little, the sense that she's losing control. She wishes she were a different kind of person. She wishes she didn't feel things as intensely as she does; she wishes she could focus her thoughts on anything but Bill and Heather. But she can't. No matter what she does, her mind always finds its way back to the other woman. Libby hopes that if she sees for herself that Bill has chosen Heather, that he's really and truly moved on from their marriage, it will set her free, maybe allow her to do the same. But so far, all Libby has seen is the glowing lights of his living room, the occasional flicker of a nearby television.

She shifts in her seat, her lower back aching as she does. It's just another reminder that she's getting old. That she's no longer the fun, youthful version of herself she was when she first met Bill. That she's not Heather.

Maybe she should just go home. It was a mistake to come here in the first place. What if Bill happens to look through the window and spots her car? Libby feels a clawing heat rising up her neck at the thought. She really needs to get herself under control.

She turns the key in the ignition, and her Chevy Traverse rumbles to life beneath her. She casts one last look at Bill's window as she grips the gearshift, and that's when something catches her eye. The flickering lights of the television suddenly stop. Libby takes her hand off the shifter and sits up taller in the driver's seat. She watches the window, waiting, her breath held in her throat. She watches as Bill walks in front of the glass, stretching, his arms lifted over his head, and she feels a tiny thrill that something is finally happening. With the lights on inside his house, she can see him only in silhouette, but it doesn't matter. She'd know her husband anywhere. And then she sees *her*. A woman, petite and slim, stepping into the light.

Libby watches as her husband, the love of her life, wraps his arms around another woman. She watches as he kisses her, his hand sliding up the back of her head, his fingers tangling in her hair. It looks so familiar that Libby lifts her hand, touches the back of her own head. She can almost feel Bill's fingers there, the way he'd bury them in her curls. And then she watches as he lifts the woman into the air, her shapely legs wrapping around his waist, and Libby feels something inside her changing. The soft vulnerability of her broken heart hardening into a granite anger. Libby feels this new thing flooding through her veins like fire. She lets it wash over her, basks in the warmth of it. She lets the rage fill her, burning away the sadness that has weighed her down for the past nine months, reducing it to smoldering ash.

Libby doesn't know how she's supposed to contain it, this roaring, destructive thing that now sits in her chest like a ball of fire, and for the first time in her life, she doesn't know that she wants to. For as long as she can remember, Libby has bent and contorted herself to fit the needs of others, especially her husband. She held herself back, made herself smaller, shrank from conflict, and put everyone before herself. And where has that gotten her? Here. That's where. Alone in her car in the middle of the night, watching her husband grope her replacement. No, Libby is done being a doormat. She's done standing idly by and watching some other woman live the life that was supposed to be hers.

18

MAGGIE
Benton Avenue

Dean paces the length of the living room like a tiger in a cage, and Maggie watches him, her eyes cautiously tracking his movements.

"Fuck that guy!" he shouts for the umpteenth time.

Maggie winces at the rage in his voice.

"Motherfucker got me fired over a damn spark plug! Like he couldn't afford the repairs, like it wasn't pocket change to him. And Ernie just believed him that I'd messed with his car, that I'd fucked up his engine on purpose! Let me go like that." Dean snaps his fingers, the pop of it cracking through the silent house.

Maggie sits anxiously on the edge of the couch, not daring to make a sound.

"It's such bullshit," he hisses.

Maggie wishes he wouldn't use that kind of language. He never did when they first got together, but it feels like everything that comes out of Dean's mouth lately is foul. She finds it hard to see the man she loved in him anymore. She once thought him so beautiful, but now everything about him is hard for Maggie to look at. It's like one of those optical illusions she'd seen in a book as a child, an image of two angels that shows the devil in the negative spaces. And once you see it there, it's all you can see.

"I'm sorry," Maggie says, because she doesn't know what else to say, but she knows that she has to say *something,* and pointing out that Dean brought this on himself is out of the question.

"You're sorry," Dean spits. "Lot of good that does."

He digs into his pocket, pulls out a small clear bag of white powder, and shakes some out onto the coffee table. Maggie watches as he leans over and inhales it into his nose in one quick motion.

Maggie's hands quake nervously in her lap as she watches him, the tip of his nose twitching, his pupils dilating as the high hits, a trace of cocaine still dusting his nostrils.

She hadn't known about the drugs. Not at first. He'd hidden it so well; until he stopped caring what Maggie thought.

"I needed that job," Dean mutters more to himself than to Maggie.

"It'll be okay. You'll find another job. I'm sure of it," Maggie tells him, even though she's not certain she believes it. The bills have been piling up in their mailbox, and debt collectors hound them over the phone. Her income alone won't stretch far enough to keep them afloat.

Dean huffs. "Sure. Let's say I get another job tomorrow. It's just going to be the same shit in another place. How the fuck is anyone supposed to get ahead? How is it that people like us—me and you—we're always in the red?"

Maggie blinks at him, uncertain how to respond. She can't mention that Dean squanders any money they manage to save, letting it run through his fingers like water. The drinking, the drugs, the gambling.

Dean continues, the words leaping manically off his tongue, without waiting for her response. "I work my ass off and I have nothing to show for it."

Maggie nods agreeably. Dean gets like this when he's high, he hyper-fixates on a topic, and Maggie knows there's nothing she can do but wait it out.

"Meanwhile, that rich prick with his Porsche—"

The doorbell rings and Dean stops his pacing, looks in the direction of the front door. "That'll be Mike. I asked him to come by."

Maggie does her best to hide the grimace that edges onto her face.

Evidently, she isn't successful. "Don't make that face," Dean chides her. "I don't know what you have against Mike, but he's been my best friend since we were kids. You're going to have to get over it."

"Sorry," Maggie says, her eyes dropping to her shoes.

Dean crosses the tiny living room, pulls open the door.

Mike Salter strides into the house, not bothering to wipe his dirt-coated work boots on the mat Maggie has laid out.

Something about Mike has always made Maggie uneasy. She's not sure if it's the shark-like look of his dark, almond-shaped eyes, the smooth, slippery way he talks, or the fact that her husband seems, inexplicably, to hang on his every word. Mostly, she suspects, it's the leering way he looks at her, like he's imagining what's under her clothes.

"Hey, Mags," he says with a nod and a wink that makes Maggie inwardly cringe.

"Hi, Mike."

"Let's talk out back," Dean says. He leads Mike through the kitchen, grabbing a few cold beers from the fridge on the way.

Maggie feels a gust of relief pass over her when she hears the kitchen door close with a metallic clatter.

With a sigh, she takes inventory of the mess in her house—the muddy footprints tracking across the floor, the pile of dishes Dean has left waiting for her in the sink, the food wrappers and crushed cans he let accumulate on the kitchen table while she was at work. She'd better get a start on straightening up.

Maggie pulls a garbage bag out from under the kitchen sink, shakes it open with a jerk, and begins to stuff the remnants of Dean's lunch into it. *How did this become my life? How have I let things get this far?* It happened so slowly, Dean taking the reins of her life, that she hadn't noticed until it was too late, until he was choking her with them. Maybe it was because she'd been so young when they'd met. She was only eighteen, so gullible and impressionable. Dean probably sensed it on her, how eager she was to believe the promise he'd offered of a better life. It had been such a pretty lie.

Maggie risks a glance out the kitchen window, watches the two men standing on the cracked pavement of the driveway drinking long-necked beers from brown glass bottles. They're congregated around Dean's bike, his pride and joy, Mike bending down to inspect the work Dean has done on it. She wonders if Dean's told Mike about losing his job, if maybe this time with his friend will improve his mood somewhat.

Maggie had a friend like that once. Someone she could call when life got tough. It still hurts Maggie to think about Sam, the one friend she had in the before. (That's how she's come to think of her life, divided into Before Dean and After Dean.) They'd been neighbors as children, when Maggie was so painfully shy that she didn't have any friends her own age. She still remembers the way she'd sit inside staring out the window of the tiny, ground-level apartment she lived in, watching the other kids run and laugh, watching the world pass her by. Until one day, Sam rang her doorbell.

"Wanna play?" he'd said.

Maggie blinked at him and looked back at her mother, who was hovering in the doorway to the kitchen.

Go on, her mother mouthed, making a shooing motion with the wooden spoon in her hand.

"Come on," Sam said, taking a wordless Maggie by the hand. "Let's go to the park."

They were inseparable after that, Sam-and-Maggie, a package deal. And Maggie found that she liked it, belonging to someone.

Maggie shakes her head. There's no point in dwelling on it now. Dean drove Sam away a long time ago. He took away the one truly good person in her life.

She collects the cans from the kitchen table, sweeps them into the bag in her hands, and looks out the window. The atmosphere around the two men seems to have shifted. Maggie can't make out what they're saying, but they're deep in conversation, stone-faced and serious. She watches as Mike explains something to Dean, his hands slicing through the air to punctuate his speech. Dean casts a furtive glance toward the window, and his eyes briefly meet Maggie's before she turns away.

It's none of my business, she tells herself, setting down the garbage bag and turning her attention to the dishes.

IT'S AFTER DUSK BY THE time Dean comes back inside, bringing the earthy smell of the outdoors with him.

"Maggie?" he calls.

She's just finished cleaning and is stowing the mop away in the tiny broom closet at the front of the house. "In here," she replies as she nudges the closet door closed.

Dean strolls in, tracking fresh boot prints onto the floor, but Maggie says nothing. He looks different, less intense than he did earlier, and she's grateful for the change. As much as she dislikes Mike, maybe his coming here tonight really did do Dean some good.

"I've found a way to solve all our problems." He smiles, sharp and cutting.

"What do you mean?" Maggie feels a stirring of dread, like the scent of an impending storm.

"Mike offered me a business opportunity."

"What kind of business opportunity?" Maggie doesn't know what Mike does for a living, but she's always gotten the impression that it's best if she doesn't ask—she might not like the answer.

"The kind that's going to finally move us up in the world. That's going to have the rich fucks across town kissing up to *me* for once."

"Dean," Maggie manages to say past the lump that's formed in her throat, the storm drawing nearer. "I'm not sure what this is about, but it sounds like something that could maybe get you into trouble. I don't think—"

Dean steps forward, grabbing her throat so quickly that Maggie doesn't have time to react. "That's right. You *don't* think."

Maggie feels her airway closing as his fingers tighten on her neck.

"I don't need you second-guessing me. I've already thought about it, and this is what I'm going to do. Got it?"

Dean releases her, and Maggie gasps for air. "Okay," she says, her voice raw and hoarse. "Okay."

HALLOWEEN NIGHT

Sterling Valley Community Board

Forum: Neighborhood Happenings
10/31/2024

Poster: Anonymous member
   Does anyone know what's going on over on Hawthorne Lane? We skipped the fall festival this year because my son has the flu (what's the point of getting a flu shot if they still get sick?!?), but I saw a bunch of police cars and an ambulance heading that way.

> Reply: Jeff Scarlotta
> What's with all these anonymous posts lately? This feature is so overused!
>
> Reply: Piper Grow
> I don't know about what happened at the festival (we never go. Too many processed snacks), but my daughter had the flu last year and we treated it at home with elderberry syrup. Works better than any prescription medication!
>
> Reply: Lauren Arca
> I was there. Someone was killed! The police are calling it a homicide. On Hawthorne Lane, of all places, can you believe it? I don't know what this town is coming to . . .

Reply: Original poster
A MURDER?!? So glad we didn't go! I never thought I'd say this, but thank God for the flu!

Reply: Beth Patterson
You mean—gasp—life isn't perfect over on Hawthorne Lane after all? The grass isn't always greener, people! I've been saying it for years! They all walk around like they're breathing rarefied air up there on Hawthorne Lane, but this just goes to show you that they're even more messed up than the rest of us!

Reply: Jeff Scarlotta
More money, more problems!

Poster: Anonymous member
Update, everyone: My sister's boyfriend's cousin works at the police station, and he said that they just made an arrest.

ONE MONTH BEFORE HALLOWEEN

19

LIBBY

Hawthorne Lane

"I'm so glad we could all get together," Georgina says, daintily dotting her lips with a cloth napkin. It comes away with traces of her red lipstick clinging to it. "I know we don't usually do this sort of thing, but I thought it would be nice."

"Well, I've never been one to say no to a mimosa," Audrey chimes in.

Hannah smiles politely. "I'm glad we're doing this too. I thought it would be hard being the newcomer in town, but you ladies have made me feel right at home."

"To the ladies of Hawthorne Lane," Audrey says, raising her glass in a toast. She lifts her phone in her other hand and snaps a photo as all of their glasses clink above the table.

As her friends sip their mimosas, Libby looks down at her own phone, hidden in her purse. There's a new notification waiting for her from the dating site. She reaches for it, her fingers twitching over the phone's screen as she debates whether she should open it now. But maybe that would make her come across as too eager? Too desperate? Too much of a pathetic, middle-aged, soon-to-be divorcée?

She suppresses a sigh as she drops the phone back into her bag, snaps it shut. How do people date at her age? Libby already finds it exhausting and she's been on the dating site for only about a week now.

She was jittery with nerves as she signed up for it. It was the kind that you have to pay for and then fill out a questionnaire that asks you about everything from your star sign to your favorite sports team. She'd hated every second of it. But Bill was moving on, so she thought maybe it was time that she try to do the same.

Libby thought this kind of site would give her the best chance of finding someone who wanted the same things she did. Someone she might go to dinner with from time to time and who would never send her an unsolicited photo of his . . . nether region. She'd heard the horror stories from some of her single friends. About the types of men who swam in the murky waters of the later-in-life dating pool. They'd either never been married, which to Libby was a red flag (Didn't they know how to commit? Were they serial daters, self-proclaimed perpetual bachelors?), or they'd been married and it didn't work out. Another potential red flag. (What happened the first time around? Was it something they'd done that ended the marriage?) Libby knew she was being hypercritical. After all, wasn't she in the same boat? But she just couldn't help but feel bitter about the whole thing. At thirty-eight years old, Libby wasn't supposed to be here. This wasn't supposed to be her life. She cursed Bill under her breath as she typed in her credit card number to pay for a service to help her meet his replacement. Libby didn't *want* to replace him.

But now he has Heather. They're living together. Libby is certain of it. She's not proud of it, but she's driven past his town house more times than was strictly necessary, and she's always there, her little red Fiat parked infuriatingly in his driveway. Bill is *dating*.

And now here's Libby, with her photo cropped into a little square, her life summed up in a few scripted lines, and a message from a strange man waiting on her phone.

It was one thing to fill out the profile, to put herself out there into the void of the internet, but it's another thing entirely to actually *talk* to someone. How is she supposed to do this? Bill was the only man Libby had ever seriously dated, and she'd managed to meet him only because he literally ran into her. She pictures herself on a date now. She can see the setting: a white tablecloth, leather-bound menus, dim lighting, maybe a flickering candle. But when she looks up at the man sitting across from her, the only face she can envision is Bill's. He's been all Libby has known for so long now that she worries she won't know how to start over. What would she talk about with someone who doesn't already know everything about her?

She takes a long pull of her mimosa, cringing as the bubbles tickle her nose. She's mad that she even has to think about these things. God, is she mad. Her anger has been hovering under the surface for the past two weeks, ever since the first time she saw Bill and Heather through his living-room window. She feels as though it's been building, gaining momentum, bursting out of her at the most inconvenient times. She snapped at Lucas yesterday for leaving his muddy cleats in the front hall, and the day before she'd been short with a customer who complained that she didn't have the specific type of orchid his wife preferred. Didn't he have any real problems to worry about? She's trying to keep it together, she really is, but inside it feels like she's being slowly eaten alive.

"Lib?" It's Georgina's voice, and it snaps Libby out of her reverie.

Georgina is a vision in shades of white today, her red hair shining in the sunlight that streams in through the café window. She looks so put together. She's *always* so put together. It's part of the reason, Libby suspects, that their early friendship burned out. They were two totally different people. Georgina was, well, *Georgina*. And Libby was always one misstep away from falling apart. "Sorry, lost in thought there for a moment. What were you saying?"

"I was just asking if you're going to the PTA goodwill auction next week."

Libby groans. "I'd forgotten about that. But yes, I'm going. They're raffling off a gift basket from Lily Lane."

"Wonderful!" Georgina clasps her manicured hands together in approval, the diamond bracelet on her wrist catching the sunlight. "I just extended an invitation to Hannah and Mark as well. Colin's firm sponsored a table, so there are plenty of extra seats. Audrey, I do wish you and Seth would join us."

Libby glances in Audrey's direction. She suspects there is nothing Audrey would hate more than crowding into the high school gym with a pack of PTA moms. She tries to picture her there, Audrey, her hips wrapped in designer jeans, her Hermès purse tucked under her arm, standing under the paper streamers. She can't quite conjure the image.

"Appreciate the invitation and all, but that's a hard pass for me," Audrey replies, adjusting the oversize black sunglasses that are perched atop her head. "And Seth will be out of town anyway."

"Is he on another book tour?" Libby asks. "I thought I saw somewhere that he recently had a new book come out."

"No, not on tour," Audrey replies, her gaze shifting across the room as she smooths a lock of her thick dark hair. "Just a meeting with his agent."

Hannah props her chin in her palm, her elbow resting on the white linen tablecloth. "I find it so impressive that he's a published author. He must be so proud."

Audrey shifts her attention to her drink, rolling the glass stem between her fingers. "Yup."

It seems to Libby that Audrey would prefer to talk about anything but her husband. She briefly wonders why, but then again, Libby isn't too keen to bring up the topic of her own marriage, so she's not exactly in a position to judge. "So," she starts, diverting the conversation into less troubling waters as she turns toward Georgina, "I've noticed that Lucas and Christina have been hanging out lately."

Georgina lifts one of her perfectly sculpted eyebrows. "Have they? I did see that he gave her a ride home from school once. That's quite a car Lucas is driving these days, by the way."

That damn car. Libby feels the dark tides of her anger rising again. Every time she sees it sitting smugly in her driveway, she's reminded of Bill's utter disregard for her feelings on the matter. And then she remembers the argument they'd had afterward. His pointed words, the broken frame.

Libby presses her lips into a smile now as she replies to Georgina. "He can thank his father for that one. Anyway, I think it's nice that he and Christina are getting closer."

"What do you mean?" Georgina asks, a noticeable edge in her tone. She spins the bracelet on her wrist, and Libby can't help but wonder what something like that cost. Probably almost as much as

Lucas's new car. While it's no secret that they all live pretty comfortably, as they'd have to in order to afford houses on Hawthorne Lane, Colin and Georgina seem to be, as far as Libby can tell, in a different stratosphere than their neighbors.

"Is it more than just the ride home?" Georgina continues, her focus locked on Libby.

Libby is surprised by the intensity of Georgina's inquiry. "I don't know, I just saw them out for a walk the other day. They went down the path through the woods. I thought it was sweet." She catches sight of Audrey watching the exchange across the table, both eyebrows raised, and Hannah pretending to be very interested in pushing the crust of her avocado toast around her plate.

"I don't know . . ." Georgina hedges, her polished red fingernails tapping on the tablecloth. "Maybe it's different when you have girls, but I'm not sure I like the idea of that, them being alone together."

"And why would that be?" Libby snaps, her hands balling into fists in her lap. She feels the familiar flutter of fury. "They've known each other since they were children, Georgina. And it was only a walk. I don't know what you're trying to suggest about my son, but—"

"Nothing," Georgina is quick to say, her hand reaching for Libby's over the table. "Nothing at all. Forget I even mentioned it."

Libby allows Georgina's cold, elegant fingers to wrap around her hand, but she wishes she could yank it away. Of course Georgina—perfect, frigid, holier-than-thou Georgina—would think that Lucas isn't good enough for her precious daughter. A small voice in the back of her head suggests that her rage might be misplaced, but she feels it just the same. She feels as though there's a dam inside her, fit to break. She's been holding back so much for so long—Bill leaving, the incident with the car, Heather, Lucas's newfound disdain for her—that it's only a matter of time until she explodes.

20

MAGGIE
Benton Avenue

Maggie pushes the stroller along the smooth pavement of the sidewalk on Main Street. From under the sunshade, she hears baby Lila babbling to herself, swatting playfully at the colorful toys that dangle from the awning. She smiles and looks down at Carter, who trots happily by her side licking at a lollipop, one shoe untied, the laces trailing behind him. Maggie loves the children she nannies for as fiercely as if they were her own.

They pause outside a café, one Maggie couldn't even afford a slice of toast in, so that she can attend to Carter's laces. She ties them into a tight double knot and then stands, rocks the stroller back and forth as Lila calmly drifts toward sleep inside. As she does, Maggie gazes longingly through the café window at the fancy mommies clinking fizzing cocktails over a table laden with pastries. She marvels at how flawless and happy they look, how glamorous their lives are. All of them made up, designer bags casually draped over the backs of chairs, diamonds glistening at their wrists, twinkling on their manicured fingers. One of them tilts her head back in laughter, her vivid red, salon-styled hair spilling down her back. And then, just beside her, Maggie catches her own reflection in the glass, her mousy brown hair, the misshapen sweater she'd bought from a secondhand shop, and she turns away, ashamed that she'd almost been caught staring.

The women hadn't actually noticed her, of course. Maggie knows she's invisible to people like them. Even pushing a stroller though their town, she can't pass for one of the mothers. She's nothing more than the hired help, part of the seamless backdrop of their lives, one of the silently grinding gears that makes it all possible. But sometimes she likes to pretend. That Lila is her little girl. That the UPPA-Baby stroller, which costs more than her car, belongs to her. She allows herself to linger on that thought, turning it over in her mind. She considers the way her heart trills when Carter accidentally calls her Mommy, the longing she feels deep in her belly when he slips his small, warm hand into hers.

She can't bring children into the home she shares with Dean. That sad, desperate space is no place for a child. But that won't be her life forever. Maggie knows that now. She doesn't know what trouble Dean's new "business venture" with Mike will bring, the details of which he's spoken very little of these past weeks, but she knows that whatever it is, it will not end well. She's had to be careful not to tip him off. She can't let Dean know that something has changed in her, that she's readying herself to leave him. If he found out... well, Maggie doesn't even want to think about what he'd do. But she finds that she likes this, having a secret that is all her own.

She feels a pleasant warmth spreading through her at the thought of the old jam jar hidden behind the shoeboxes in the back corner of her closet that has quickly been filling up with cash. She'd asked the Sullivans if they could start paying her that way, in cash rather than her weekly check. It makes it easier for Maggie to skim a few dollars and cents off the top before she has to hand her earnings over to Dean. She hadn't explained this to Ms. Sullivan, of course. She wouldn't want Ms. Sullivan, in her big house with her nice clothes, to think less of Maggie. Ms. Sullivan is not the type of woman who would find herself needing to hide dollar bills from her husband in a jam jar. But it seemed she didn't have to explain. Ms. Sullivan had torn up Maggie's check and reached into her purse without saying a word, the pity in her eyes enough for Maggie to know that she understood. Maggie had felt so ashamed, but she took the cash anyway, stuffing it into the pocket of her jeans, her eyes on the ground as she mumbled her thanks. It had been a humiliating experience, but it had to be done. Maggie has to stick to her plan.

"Are we going home now?" Carter asks, pulling Maggie from her thoughts. He looks up at her with wide, innocent eyes.

"Yes," she replies, turning the stroller in the direction of the safe, quiet cul-de-sac. "Let's go."

She looks back at the café one last time. *Maybe someday,* she thinks.

21

GEORGINA
Hawthorne Lane

"Hannah! Mark! Over here!" Georgina calls, the gold bangles on her wrist jangling as she waves across the Sterling Valley High School gym. It's crowded tonight, the annual goodwill auction being one of the larger community events. Fairy lights have been hung from the ceiling, and tables draped in white and navy blue—the school's colors—line the space. At the center of the room is a long row of tables crowded with numbered baskets, each brimming with goods donated from local businesses to be raffled off in a silent auction. This year, the funds will be put toward building new playing fields for the high school. The school's new principal, a former college football player, had practically insisted on the upgrade. He'd reminded parents of the importance of Sterling Valley remaining a top-tier district, a name that will continue to stand out to the competitive Ivy League colleges.

Georgina sees recognition crest over Hannah's face as she spots Georgina in the crowd, and she picks her way through the throngs of people, leading Mark by the hand. Georgina has taken quite a liking to the younger woman. Hannah feels like a breath of fresh air in this town—she's real, genuine. With her, there's no undercurrent of competition the way there is among so many of the Sterling Valley mothers, who Georgina knows smile to her face but will cut her down the second her back is turned. When she's talking to Hannah, Georgina never gets the impression that she's biding her time, waiting for her turn to speak; she never feels judged or scrutinized. Hannah simply listens in that quiet, thoughtful way of hers. She hopes she never loses that, that this place doesn't change her.

"Hi, Georgina," Hannah says as she reaches the table. "I love your dress."

"Thank you." She'd chosen a fitted sheath dress in emerald green because Colin had once mentioned that it complemented the red of her hair.

Hannah and Mark make the rounds, hugs and handshakes offered to Colin and Libby, who are already seated.

Things have been tense with Libby since they went out for brunch last week. Georgina worries that she might have accidentally offended her when she mentioned that she wasn't keen on the idea of Christina and Lucas spending time alone together. She hadn't meant it as a personal affront to Libby's son—Georgina doesn't like the idea of her fifteen-year-old daughter wandering off into the woods with *any* boy. Georgina might be forty, but she's not too old to remember what it was like to be a teenage girl. To want things you don't understand, to be worried about how to say no to the things you don't.

As they all take their seats, Georgina senses a strange charge crackling over the table. She knows that Libby is probably still upset with her, but even Hannah doesn't seem like herself tonight. She's fidgeting in her seat, smoothing her napkin on her lap over and over again.

"I had a chance to play that golf course you recommended," Mark tells Colin.

Colin smiles delightedly. "What did you think?"

The two men are quickly lost in conversation about fairways and putting greens, and Georgina looks over at her friends. Libby has her nose buried in her phone, and Hannah is looking out over the crowd, her gaze distant and unfocused. She hates that they both seem so unhappy.

Georgina is reminded once again of her childhood home. All of them—Georgina, her parents—miserable in their own ways, orbiting one another in concentric circles beneath the same roof.

When Georgina left for culinary school, she'd promised herself she would never set foot in that house again. But Colin had insisted. He said they should deliver the news of their engagement in person. He felt it was the proper thing to do.

Georgina looked at Colin then, the handsome young lawyer who'd just asked her to spend the rest of her life by his side, and felt her excitement over their impending nuptials fade. She hated the thought of him in that house, surrounded by the dust and the dirt—the sagging cardboard boxes, the half-finished renovations her father would start but could never afford to complete. He would see her differently then. She could no longer project the image of herself she so desperately wanted him to see, the ambitious culinary student, the proper lady with the impeccable manners that had impressed his mother so much. Now she'd just be the girl who'd come from that sad, awful place. A girl pretending to be more than she was.

As they stood on the doorstep, hand in hand, a box of pastries tucked under Colin's arm, Georgina braced herself for disaster. Colin didn't understand. Her family wasn't like his, loud and excitable, his mother calling all of their distant relatives to share the happy news of Colin's engagement the moment she saw the ring on Georgina's finger. Georgina's parents had always been, at best, coolly indifferent toward her, and she expected that news of her engagement would be met with much of the same. But she'd been wrong. As Colin introduced himself, lifted Georgina's hand to show her parents the two-carat ring that sparkled on her slim finger, her father clapped him on the back, and her mother hugged him, wishing them both the best of luck. Who were those smiling, laughing people? She hardly recognized her own parents.

They'd stayed for coffee, Colin politely ignoring the piles of junk that seemed to have multiplied since Georgina's departure, and shared the pastries Colin had brought from the nice bakery across town. It was the happiest she'd ever remembered being inside her parents' house. It was the first time they'd ever looked at her like they were proud.

As they gathered their things to leave, coffee cups soaking in the sink, Georgina's mother grabbed her, her bony fingers encircling

Georgina's arm. "He's going places," she'd whispered in her ear, her voice suddenly nasty and pinched. "You better not screw this up."

Georgina had wanted to yell, she'd wanted to scream, she'd wanted to remind her mother that she was putting herself through culinary school, that she was going places too. But being back in that house had made her revert to the girl she once was. The girl who'd learned to stay quiet, to make herself so small that she wouldn't be noticed. And so she'd just nodded.

As much as she hated to admit it, a part of Georgina knew that her mother was right. With Colin and the illustrious legal career ahead of him, she could have a different kind of life. The kind of life where she wouldn't have to clip coupons to go to the grocery store, where she'd never have to decide whether to pay the water bill or the electric bill that month, where her children would never have to feel like they were a burden. She'd wanted that so badly that it felt like an ache in her chest. To have a family of her own, to create a home for them that didn't feel as gray and hopeless and suffocating as the one she'd always known. There would be home-cooked meals in a clean kitchen; there would be a garden full of life and color; her kids would always know how much they were loved and wanted. They would go to the best schools, the kinds that would open doors for them. Her children would have all the opportunities that Georgina didn't. She was going to do things differently, and she couldn't deny that marrying Colin was going to help her get there.

"How about a round of drinks?" Colin asks now.

"I'll get them," Georgina is quick to offer, happy for the distraction.

"Do you need a hand?" Mark asks, already pushing his chair away from the table.

"No, I've got it," she assures him. "I have to finish putting in my tickets for the silent auction anyway. But thank you. You two carry on discussing nine irons or what have you."

Mark laughs as he adjusts his glasses. "Oh, if we must."

On the outside, he and Hannah seem a strange pairing. There's the age difference, for one thing, and her looks, which far outshine his, for another, but Georgina sees why they work so well together.

She notices the way Mark casually rests his hand on Hannah's knee, even while he's talking to Colin, the way he looks at her while she's speaking, like every word that comes out of her mouth is the most interesting thing that's ever been said. They make their own kind of sense.

"Last call before the silent auction begins!" one of the volunteers announces into a microphone.

Georgina stands from the table and makes her way to the display in the center of the gymnasium. She looks at each basket as she passes, but she already knows she's going to put all of her tickets toward the one from Lily Lane. Georgina sighs as she drops her tickets into the box in front of Libby's basket. She knows Libby is going through a difficult time as she navigates her separation from Bill. She suspects this is part of the reason she got so angry at Georgina's comment over brunch. Georgina, of course, knows that Bill moved out of their house—it's hard not to notice when a U-Haul truck pulls into your neighbor's driveway—but she finds herself wishing that she and Libby were closer. That Libby felt like she could talk about these kinds of things, that they both didn't feel the need to keep up pretenses, to cover everything with a smile.

"Well, hello, Georgina." Beth Patterson sidles up next to her.

Georgina smiles politely. "Hi, Beth. How are you?"

"Good, good. And you? How are the plans for the fall festival going? We're all really looking forward to it."

"Oh, it's all coming together nicely. I have a few vendors lined up to hand out treats to the little ones, and I'm just waiting on the permits for the fireworks display."

"A fireworks display! How fun!" Beth exclaims with what feels to Georgina like a put-on level of enthusiasm.

"Ah, Ms. Pembrook!" It's Principal Skinner. He approaches them and slings his arm over Georgina's shoulder. "Just the woman I was hoping to find!"

Georgina's face burns as she sees the scandalized grin crack across Beth's face, her eyes glittering.

"I suppose I'll just leave you two to it, then," Beth says. She slinks off toward the other mothers, who are already looking in Georgina's direction, their whispers rolling in like fog, swirling around Georgina. The new principal's slight southern drawl, laid-back demeanor, and larger-than-life presence has made him a favorite topic of discussion among the women in town.

"You said you were looking for me?" Georgina asks, trying to think of a way to politely extricate herself from beneath Principal Skinner's arm.

"Yes, indeed I was." He smiles down at her, all dashing southern charm. "I wanted to thank you for your generosity this evening. The donation you and Mr. Pembrook made will go a long way toward funding the new athletic fields."

"Oh," Georgina says, her eyes flitting back to her table, to her husband. "You're very welcome, but it was actually Colin's—"

"Please," he says, his arm still draped casually around Georgina's neck. "Let me introduce you to some of..."

He's still speaking but Georgina is no longer listening. All she can focus on is the weight of his arm around her shoulders, the closeness of his body to hers. She feels herself begin to sweat, her dress sticking to her skin, her feet sliding in her heels.

And then Colin is there, his hand outstretched toward Principal Skinner.

"Colin Pembrook," he says by way of greeting.

"Arnold Skinner." Principal Skinner takes Colin's hand in his larger one, pumps it up and down in an exaggerated motion. "I was just thanking your wife for your family's generosity this evening."

Colin smiles in that handsome, charismatic way of his, but Georgina can see through it. She can see the frost in his blue eyes, the darkness behind his bright white teeth.

"Of course," Colin replies coolly. "You're very welcome. Now, if you don't mind, might I steal my wife for a moment?"

Principal Skinner laughs affably as he steps away from Georgina. "Of course, of course. Y'all enjoy the rest of the evening now."

As Principal Skinner disappears back into the crowd, Colin leans close to Georgina's ear. "Let's get some fresh air, shall we?" He laces his fingers through hers.

Georgina knows how it looks to everyone else. She knows that tomorrow all the other mothers will be talking about how lucky she is. How her handsome, successful husband took time out of his busy schedule to join her at a school event when so many of theirs hadn't, how sweet and romantic Colin is, the way he still holds Georgina's hand in a crowd. But they don't see how he squeezes her fingers so tightly that the band of her wedding ring digs into her skin, how, more than anything, she wishes he'd just let her go.

22

HANNAH
Hawthorne Lane

"Did you win?" Mark asks.

Hannah blinks. "Huh?"

"I asked if you won the raffle." He nods toward the ticket in her hand, and Hannah realizes she's been staring at it.

"No," she says with a small shake of her head. "I didn't."

Mark looks at her curiously, his brow furrowing slightly, as if Hannah is a puzzle he's trying to solve. "Are you all right?"

"Yup," Hannah says a touch too brightly. "I'm fine."

Mark opens his mouth as if to question her further, but then closes it again. They've been having a version of this same conversation for two weeks now, ever since Hannah opened the latest message—*This isn't over*—and every time her answer has been the same: Everything is fine. Hannah is fine. There's nothing bothering her at all. She knows Mark doesn't believe her, but they seem to have reached something of a stalemate.

"I wonder what's keeping Georgina," Libby says, setting her phone aside for the first time all night.

Libby has been quiet for most of the evening. More so than usual, Hannah thinks. But then again, she doesn't know the other woman that well. Maybe she's always this connected to her phone. Hannah knows that Libby has a company to run, and perhaps it's keeping her busy tonight, but she suspects it's something else. Something that has her occasionally smiling down at the screen in her palm.

"Yeah," Mark agrees. "She and Colin never did come back with those drinks."

"Probably cornered by a pack of PTA moms," Libby replies. "They can be pretty aggressive on their home turf."

Mark laughs, that deep, open laugh of his, and Hannah is nearly broken with it. With the love she feels for her husband and the knowledge that she might soon lose him.

She closes her eyes, wincing at the unexpected stab of guilt. She sees herself then, so clearly it's as if she's back there: her hair fanning out behind her, caught in the wind, her shoes hitting the pavement so hard that she can feel the impact reverberating in her shins. And then there's the blood. Always the blood. So much of it that she feels it sticky and warm between her fingers, the dark bloom of it soaking through her shirt. *What have I done?* she thinks. *What have I done?*

Hannah opens her eyes with a jolt, suddenly feeling lightheaded. These episodes have been happening more and more frequently, images of the past bursting into her mind when she least expects them, so vivid, so real, that they take her breath away.

She feels Mark's eyes on her again, and she stands from the table, wobbling slightly in her heels.

"Are you sure you're okay?" he asks, his eyes searching Hannah's for a truth he must know he won't find.

"Fine," she says again. "I'm fine." She sees something dim in her husband's eyes as he absorbs her latest lie, and it's so painful that she has to turn away from it. "I'm just going to get some air."

Mark is everything good, everything right in Hannah's life. Her clean slate. She hates the thought of her past contaminating it, spreading its poison, corroding the life they've built until it crumbles. There has to be something she can do. Something to stop what she knows is coming.

But sometimes it's impossible. Sometimes reality catches up to you, a storm you can't outrun, no matter how hard you try. Another vision of the past breaks through as she stumbles through the gym, but this time Hannah isn't running. She sees herself as a little girl, knees tucked to her chest, arms wrapped around herself protectively, her spine digging painfully into the back of the small plastic chair in the hospital waiting room. And yet she didn't move. She sat perfectly still, counted the butterflies painted on the wall: four purple, two blue, three pink. She hadn't spoken, not one single word, for what felt to Hannah like hours. Though it could have been days, even weeks, and she wouldn't have known. She was vaguely aware of other people coming and going, some who talked to her, some who talked about her in concerned whispers, using words like *mother* and *passed away* and *child protective services*. But Hannah couldn't bring herself to respond. She couldn't even bring herself to move. She just stared at those butterflies, imagining she could shrink herself down until she was small enough to ride one, that it could take her far away from this place with its strange antiseptic smell and evil things like cancer. Hannah hadn't even known her mother was sick, and then, in what felt like a heartbeat, she was gone. She simply couldn't imagine a world without her mother in it, so she didn't. If she didn't move, if she didn't speak, maybe time would forget about her; maybe it would march by without her and she wouldn't have to face whatever came next.

Hannah doesn't know how long she sat there like that before the lady came. The one that had the lanyard around her neck, a plastic ID card dangling from the end, who said that she was there to help Hannah. Didn't she know that no one could help Hannah?

The lady squatted down in front of her. She had kind eyes, but Hannah still turned away from them.

"I'm sorry about your mother," the woman said, her voice gentle and coaxing. Hannah did not reply.

"Do you have another grown-up at home?" The woman waited, seemingly comfortable in Hannah's silence. Slowly, Hannah shook her head.

"What about your dad?"

And for the first time since her world had ended, Hannah spoke, using the words her mother had taught her: "I don't have one."

Hannah shakes the memory away. If someone found out what she'd done, the lies she'd told, the life that she's built here with Mark will be over. She'll be as alone as that little girl.

Hannah pushes open the doors leading to the school's courtyard. There's a bubbling fountain in the center, string lights hung like a canopy. There were a few people out here earlier in the evening, but it's grown colder and they've gone inside. September is a strange, transitive month, Hannah thinks, where the days still cling to the warmth of summer but at night the autumn chill slinks in on catlike feet. She's happy to be alone out here, out of the crowd for a moment while she regains her composure.

She leans against the rough brick of the building, exhaling deeply. That's when she hears the voices, realizes she's not alone after all. There are people around the corner of the building, just out of sight. She can't make out all of the words, but one seems to be a man, and he sounds angry. Hannah pauses, holding her breath while she listens.

"Embarrassment... no respect..."

The voice sounds familiar, but Hannah can't quite place it. And then she hears the second voice.

"I'm sorry."

This one is much smaller, and there's a slight tremor of fear in it. This one Hannah recognizes immediately. *Georgina.*

Before she has time to think it through, Hannah starts walking, following the sound of Georgina's voice.

She rounds the corner just in time to see Colin grab his wife by the wrist, his knuckles white as he holds her arm at a painful angle.

"Is everything okay?" Hannah asks, her tone uncharacteristically bold as her voice echoes through the empty courtyard.

Colin releases Georgina's arm. "Everything is just fine," he replies, that dazzling smile pinned to his lips.

It's disorienting for Hannah, how quickly he's transformed himself into someone shiny and new. It makes her question what she just saw. Maybe she'd been mistaken... but then she looks at Georgina, sees the fear in her eyes, and she knows.

"I was asking Georgina." Hannah is surprised by her own brazenness as she stands her ground, her arms folding over her chest as she braces herself against the cold.

"We're okay," Georgina says, her perfect smile back in place even as she rubs her wrist, which is red and raw. "We'll be inside in just a moment."

Hannah doesn't want to move, doesn't want to leave Georgina

alone out here with Colin. But Georgina gives her the smallest nod, the look in her eyes pleading with Hannah to walk away before she makes things worse.

"All—all right, then," Hannah says, and she turns to go, feeling entirely unsure of whether she's doing the right thing.

23

AUDREY
Hawthorne Lane

Audrey curls up on her living-room couch with a bowl of air-popped popcorn and a glass of pinot noir. She flicks through Netflix looking for a rom-com, the kind of thing Seth never wants to watch with her, as she sips her wine. Seth, thankfully, was asked to speak at a creative writing conference at the University of Rhode Island, which means he's out of town overnight, and Audrey has the house to herself. She's hopeful that the conference will give Seth the boost of confidence he needs, and she's grateful for the time alone it's afforded her. For the first time in weeks, she feels like she can breathe.

Lately, it's been impossible to find a moment of peace. Seth is always here, always watching her. It's gotten worse since those damn roses arrived on her doorstep. She feels like his eyes are always on her now, as if he's just waiting for her to slip up. She's constantly walking on eggshells in her own home. And Audrey is supposed to love this house. She designed every inch of it, from the white upholstery of the couch to the coffered ceilings. She'd taken her time selecting the Schumacher wallpaper in the hall bathroom, the slab of marble for the kitchen island with just the right amount of veining, and the perfect shade of snowfall-white paint for the primary bedroom. The house was meant to feel like an extension of her, brick-and-mortar evidence of her and Seth's success. Not a prison that she can't wait to escape from every morning.

Audrey clicks through the movie selections, finally settling on

Sleepless in Seattle. She's seen it a thousand times, but it's one of those movies that brings her right back to her childhood. To being curled up on her mother's floral-print sofa, eating popcorn (the real, full-fat kind) and drinking cherry soda. She'd loved those nights when her father was working a late shift and it was just Audrey and her mom. Both of her parents worked so much—her father as a security guard at the local hospital, and her mother as a receptionist at a dental practice during the day, a waitress at a local diner on odd nights—so between that and having to share their attention with her two older sisters, Audrey rarely had time alone with either of them. It made her appreciate their movie nights all the more, bringing out the big metal bowl and filling it to the brim with buttery popcorn mixed with handfuls of M&M's. Her sisters couldn't stand rom-coms. They'd make mock gagging noises, teasing Audrey and her mom as they cried at the same scenes no matter how many times they watched them. But Audrey didn't care. Those nights belonged only to her and her mom.

It's been a long time since Audrey thought of her once-cherished movie nights, since she'd even called her mother. She makes a mental note to reach out to her parents soon, to invite them to the house. They haven't seen the new renovations yet, but she can already imagine their reactions: her mother standing nervously with her purse in her hands as if afraid to touch anything in the house, her father unreservedly asking how much they'd spent on the new Wolf cooking range. They don't understand Audrey's life choices, her focus on her career, buying this big house and not filling it with children. Their silent disapproval has driven a wedge between Audrey and her parents over the years. And her sisters are no better.

Audrey had never been close with her older sisters, Camila and Isabella. She always felt like she didn't fit in, a useless third wheel among her own siblings. Her sisters are only two years apart in age, while Audrey is the youngest by five years. That meant that her sisters experienced high school together, shared friends and inside jokes, and Audrey was always too young to join in, was cast aside, ignored. It also meant that she'd never owned a single thing that hadn't belonged to her sisters first—clothes, bicycles, even her shoes always passed through Camila and Isabella before they made their way, worn and mended, to Audrey.

The money, hers and Seth's, changed everything. Now she has shiny new things, things her sisters could only dream of. Like this house, her wardrobe. Luxuries that Audrey earned and that belong only to her.

Her parents don't understand her lifestyle, and her sisters resent it. Audrey suspects that they all thought she'd eventually change her mind, that one day her priorities would shift. They'd expected her to follow in her sisters' footsteps, pop out a couple of kids and give over her beautiful living room to the chaos of bright plastic toys and pack-and-plays. But she never has, and the older she gets, the clearer it's becoming to them all that she never will.

There's nothing wrong with the way her sisters live. Audrey doesn't look down on them, as they probably assume, but it's simply not the life she's chosen for herself. And she gets to choose now. She no longer has to take their hand-me-downs. She just wishes her family could accept that.

Last Thanksgiving had been particularly brutal. Camila, Audrey's oldest sister, had hosted it in her tiny one-story ranch on Long Island.

Audrey was already overwhelmed by the time she and Seth pushed open the front door. Kids, Audrey's nieces and nephews, were tearing around the small house in paper turkey hats, her dad was in front of the TV watching football at maximum volume, and Audrey could hear Camila barking orders at their mother and Isabella from the kitchen. It was warm in the house, so warm that Audrey was already regretting the cashmere sweater she'd worn, and the smell of the cooking food—fatty meat, butter-soaked vegetables, pan-fried bacon—felt like an assault. She could feel a headache blooming behind her eyes.

It hadn't helped that she and Seth had argued in the car on the way there. She'd been snappy with him because they were running late. She hated being late to anything, especially to Camila's house. She was already anticipating the comments her family would make, and arriving late would just give them one more thing to criticize. But this one might have been avoidable if Seth hadn't spent so much time on his damn phone instead of getting ready when she'd asked him to.

"Is it really that big of a deal?" he'd said as he slid on a pair of Ferragamo loafers. "You hate going to your sister's house. And the later we arrive, the less time we have to spend there."

He could be so clueless sometimes. And so they were late, and they'd argued, and Audrey felt like a rubber band about to snap.

"Oh, look who decided to grace us with her presence," Camila trilled as she stepped out of the kitchen, her hair tied up into a messy bun on top of her head, a spatula in her hand. It was obvious that she'd been cooking all day. Flour dusted her misshapen black T-shirt, and sweat slicked her hairline.

"Hi, Camila," Audrey said with a wave, the heels of her Stuart Weitzman boots sinking into the wall-to-wall carpeting.

They weren't off to a great start. And it only got worse when they finally sat down to eat and Seth handed Camila's husband, Ted, the bottle of champagne he'd brought for the occasion.

"Dom, huh?" Ted announced to the table in that loud, brash way of his as he inspected the label. "That's some good shit."

Audrey wanted to crawl under the table. The selection was a mistake, but Seth had insisted: "Who doesn't appreciate good champagne?" His heart was in the right place, but Audrey knew that the gift was all wrong.

Camila's lips curled into something between a smile and a sneer. "Well, excuse us!" she tutted sarcastically, drawing out her vowels. "I didn't realize we were hosting royalty today."

Audrey sat at the other end of the folding table that had been set up in Camila's living room to seat them all. It was laid with an assortment of mismatched plates and paper napkins. "It's just some champagne, Camila," she retorted through gritted teeth. "No need to make a big deal out of it."

"Well, Princess Audrey, to some of us, it's a mortgage payment."

Seth looked confused, his eyes flitting between Audrey and Camila as their spiked words flew over the table. "Would you have preferred wine?" he asked with a chuckle, an awkward attempt to lighten the mood.

Isabella looked amused, both eyebrows raised, arms folded over her chest like a spectator at a tennis match as she watched Audrey and Camila stare each other down. Meanwhile, Audrey's parents eagerly held up their champagne glasses to Ted as though they were about to receive a taste from the fountain of youth. The entire ordeal had been horribly mortifying.

The rest of the night had been filled with subtle barbs from Camila: "Is that a new bag? Chanel! Must be nice!" "Kids, be careful not to spill on Aunt Audrey's fancy sweater, Lord knows we can't afford to replace it!"

She and Seth decided to celebrate Christmas in Bali. Sometimes it's just easier for her to keep her distance from her family. They all act like Audrey thinks she's above them, but she doesn't. They act like everything she has magically fell into her lap, but it didn't. She just wishes they could acknowledge that she's worked hard for and deserves this life she has.

The movie starts to play and Audrey pulls a throw blanket over her lap, settling into the couch. On the screen, Tom Hanks catches a passing glimpse of Meg Ryan in an airport terminal, and Audrey sighs. She once thought her life would be like that. That she and Seth had the kind of love people make movies about. And, she supposes, they do, except it's turning out to be more like *A Bold Affair* than *Sleepless in Seattle*.

At least her former lover has been quiet lately. Although Audrey suspects he still lurks on her Instagram account—she'd made it public for that very reason. Let him see the photo she'd posted of herself and her neighbors at brunch, all their glasses clinking over the table—*Brunch with the ladies in our favorite spot!* Let him see that he hasn't gotten to her, that he hasn't won.

The doorbell rings, echoing through Audrey's empty house. She pauses the movie, freezing in place along with the actors on the screen, one hand gripping her wineglass, the other holding the remote in midair. Was she hearing things? She glances at the time on her phone screen. It's nearly eleven o'clock. Who the hell would be at her door at this time of night? And then the bell rings again, and she knows for sure. Someone is here.

Audrey tosses her blanket aside, sets her wineglass on the table in front of her. Could it be one of her neighbors? They'd been out earlier at a school charity thing she hadn't wanted to attend, but she's certain that would have ended by now. How late do those things typically go? Or maybe there's been an emergency of some sort? But even as she thinks it, the bubbling dread that churns in her stomach tells her that she's wrong. That she knows *exactly* who is on the other side of that door, and it's the last person she wants to see.

The bell rings for a third time, and is Audrey imaging things, or does it sound more angry, insistent this time? "Coming," she calls just to stop the ringing.

She pulls open the door just a crack. Just wide enough to catch a glimpse of a man's leather shoe, the cuff of a French sleeve. She can smell his cologne, the one that she once loved to find on her sheets after he'd gone, inhaling it deeply into her lungs before she had to wash it away. But now the scent causes something sour to rise into the back of her throat.

His hand shoots out, and his palm flattens against Audrey's front door as he pushes it forcefully. She leaps back and it swings wide, bouncing on its hinges.

"Hello, my darling," he slurs.

She can tell he's been drinking. His movements, usually so elegant and intentional, are clumsy, cloddish. For the first time, she finds him repulsive.

"Why have you been ignoring me?" he asks, brazenly attempting to walk into her house as if he has a right to be there, as if he doesn't need her permission to trample through her life.

She lifts an arm, grabs onto the doorjamb to bar his way. "You can't be here."

Colin Pembrook's blue eyes turn to frost, his handsome face hardening into a grotesque mask of rage.

Audrey's grip tightens. She shouldn't have posted that photo. Baited him with the image of Audrey seated across the table from his wife at brunch. She'd wanted him to understand that if he was going to meddle in her marriage, she was capable of doing the same. He sent her a warning with the roses, and Audrey had fired back with a warning of her own. *See how close I can get to blowing up your life too?* But she sees now that the photo was a step too far. She shouldn't have provoked him.

"I don't know if you've noticed," Colin says, his words slow and measured, "but I can do whatever the hell I'd like." He smiles then, a twisted, taunting grin that feels like a shot of ice in Audrey's veins.

She slams the door in his face and slides the dead bolt into place.

24
MAGGIE
Benton Avenue

"There you are," Dean exclaims impatiently the instant Maggie walks through their front door.

She startles, the doorknob still clutched in her hand. "Hi," she says, watching Dean uneasily as she steps inside.

In the center of the living room, the cracked leather couch sags sadly, and the coats on the rack hang like the ghosts of the life she thought she'd have here. Maggie wonders how many more times she'll have to do this, how many more times she'll have to come home to this gray and lifeless place. A few more weeks, maybe. Just a couple more paychecks until the jam jar will be full. Maybe then she could afford an apartment of her own. It wouldn't be anything fancy, but it would be hers. Maggie imagines vases of hand-picked flowers; she imagines painting the walls a sunny yellow; she imagines a single bed topped with a clean white quilt in a small but tidy room. She could be happy, she thinks, on her own.

"I have a job for you," he says, cracking his knuckles.

"A . . . j-job?" Maggie stammers. "What kind of job?"

"One easy enough that even you should be able to manage it."

Maggie is confused. Dean has been out of work for weeks, and all he's been talking about is how he's on the verge of coming into some money, but as with most things in Dean's life, his grand ambitions have yet to come to fruition. As far as Maggie can tell, Dean has done very little to pursue whatever business deal Mike had offered him, and Maggie has been grateful for that.

"All you need to do," Dean explains, "is deliver a package to an address across town."

"A package?"

He scowls. "Yes, Maggie. A package. You know what that is, don't you?"

"I do, but why do you need me to drop it off for you?"

"Because," Dean starts, exasperation lacing his tone as though Maggie had already missed something important, "you'll look far less suspicious than me in that part of town. You know, since you already work there and all."

Maggie opens her mouth to object, but Dean presses on before she has a chance to respond. "Just take this package"—he shoves a parcel wrapped in brown paper into her hands—"and bring it to the address I give you. Leave it exactly where I tell you to. That's all you need to do. Nice and simple."

"What's in it?" Maggie asks.

Dean shakes his head. "That's none of your concern. Just drop it off and come straight back here. Do you understand? Do you think you can handle that?"

"I—I guess," Maggie replies, weighing the package in her hands. She notes the muscle twitching in Dean's clenched jaw, the firm set of his glare, and knows that she has no choice.

MAGGIE LOOKS DOWN AT THE slip of paper Dean had handed her, then back up at the grand colonial home sitting in front of her. The porch lights are on, casting a warm pool of light onto the rounded bend of sidewalk. This is definitely the right address, but what could Dean possibly need her to deliver here?

Maggie shifts her car into park and reaches for the handle, but something gives her pause. She knows this block. The family she works for lives only a few houses down the road, and yet she doesn't know who lives here, in this big, fancy house. She wonders what business dealings someone who lives in a house like this might have with Dean, of all people. She can't picture him here, in his leather jacket, the roar of his motorcycle echoing around the quiet cul-de-sac. Something doesn't feel right to her. Maggie knows she's not supposed to, but she looks down at the bundle resting in her lap and slides her thumbnail under the corner of the paper wrapping. She inspects the tiny opening she's made, shifting the package this way and that in the dim light, but she's unable to determine the contents. Maggie bites her lower lip. If she does this, if she opens the package, sees what's inside, there will be no going back. She knows that. She'll no longer be able to pretend that she doesn't know what Dean has gotten himself involved in.

But it's not just Dean, is it? *Maggie* is the one sitting in this car, idling in the shadows between the streetlights. *She* is the one who is expected to take the risk of stepping out into the dark night and leaving this unknown package in the hiding spot Dean has directed her to. Whatever Dean is up to, he's dragged Maggie into it too. And she deserves to know what he's gotten her involved in. Swallowing hard, Maggie unwraps the parcel.

In her hands is a bundle of tiny bags, some filled with a familiar white powder, others unmarked pills. *Drugs.* Dean is dealing drugs. A lot of them, by the looks of things. A small voice in the back of Maggie's mind reminds her that she already knew this. That she would have seen the truth if only she'd wanted to see it sooner. But she pushes it aside. She needs to do something. She's sitting in her car mere yards away from where her employers live with enough drugs to send her to prison for a very long time.

Maggie shifts her car into drive; turns out of the familiar cul-de-sac. She can't do this. She can't bring this poison onto the block where Lila and Carter live, to the neighborhood where they visit the playground and go for ice cream.

Maggie drives down Main Street with its cafés, its florist shops and bakeries. She stops at a red light, and out of the corner of her eye, she watches a police car pull up silently beside her. Maggie feels her palms slick with sweat on the steering wheel, her heart thudding violently in her chest. She looks straight ahead, willing her eyes not to slide down to the package on the passenger seat beside her. She could be arrested. Her freedom, the little apartment, the sunny-yellow walls, had been so close, but now the image starts to melt before her eyes, a snowflake held in her palm.

After what feels like an eternity, the light turns green. The police cruiser pulls ahead of Maggie's car, turns down a side street a little farther down the road. Maggie's shoulders sag with relief, but she's not out of the woods yet. She can't take the risk of driving around with drugs in her car, and she can't go home to Dean and tell him that she didn't make the delivery. There's no way out of this.

But maybe . . . Maggie turns off Main Street and drives through winding side roads until she no longer recognizes the street names. On a lonely stretch of pavement, she comes across an abandoned gas station and quickly pulls into the dark parking lot. Heart racing, she gets out and scans the area cautiously until she's certain that no one is around, then she creeps through the deserted lot toward a long-forgotten dumpster rusting in the far corner. She stashes the drugs behind it, covers them with a mound of fallen leaves. She'll tell Dean that she left the drugs exactly where he'd instructed. And if something goes wrong, she can always come back here and get them. Dean will never have to know.

HALLOWEEN NIGHT

Transcript of interview with Tony Russo
October 31, 2024

Mr. Russo: Am I under arrest?

Detective Olsen: No, not at this time. We've brought you down here to ask you a few questions about an incident that happened up on Hawthorne Lane earlier this evening.

Mr. Russo: I heard about it, but I had nothing to do with all that.

Detective Olsen: See, the thing is, we found your fingerprints near the crime scene.

Mr. Russo: Well, yeah, I'm the gardener for the whole damn block. My fingerprints are probably all over the place.

Detective Olsen: Would that include on a beer bottle in the woods? Right next to a dead body? Does that fall within your job description?

Mr. Russo: Yeah. I mean, no. I—do I need a lawyer?

Detective Olsen: That's entirely up to you, Mr. Russo. But as I said, at this point we're just having a friendly little chat. It's your decision if you'd like to make it something more than that.

Mr. Russo: Is this because of my prior . . . incident?

Detective Olsen: The thought did cross my mind. I find it very interesting that you were previously arrested in those very woods and now your fingerprints turn up a few feet from my victim.

Mr. Russo: No, no, no. You've got it all wrong. Look, sometimes I go out to those woods for a drink. My wife, she can be kind of a hard-ass. Always on me about how much I'm drinking. So sometimes, if I finish my work early, I go out there and have a cold beer by myself, just to unwind before going home. That's how the whole thing with the . . . you know . . . happened.

Detective Olsen: You mean your arrest for indecent exposure? Wherein you exposed yourself to several minors?

Mr. Russo: That's what I'm saying! It wasn't like that! I was in the woods having a beer. I had to take a leak. It was dark. I thought I was alone. I had no idea those kids were going to come walking out of the woods. I'm not some kind of pervert. I wasn't trying to show my junk to a bunch of teenage boys.

Detective Olsen: I see. And were you doing that earlier tonight? Having a beer in the woods by yourself?

Mr. Russo: No, I wasn't anywhere near Hawthorne Lane tonight. I swear. I was at home with my wife and kids. You can ask her. The bottle you found, it must have been an old one.

Detective Olsen: Your wife, huh? Not generally the strongest alibi, in my experience. Are you telling me that if I ask around—and I will—no one is going to tell me that they saw you at the fall festival tonight?

Mr. Russo: No chance. I wasn't there. And no one up there ever notices me anyway. I'm just the hired help. But listen, you're way off base here. I'm not the one you should be looking at.

Detective Olsen: What does that mean exactly?

Mr. Russo: It means that if someone over there bit the dust, there are at least fifty good reasons why. Those people up there in those big, fancy houses, they got problems like you wouldn't believe. It's not all as pretty as it looks. Like I said, no one notices me, so I just go about my business. But I see things, you know? Stuff they'd probably rather I didn't.

Detective Olsen: Like what?

Mr. Russo: Do you know Seth Warrington?

Detective Olsen: He's one of the residents, right?

Mr. Russo: Yeah. He's some kind of writer or something. I looked him up recently. Turns out his career is in the crapper. I read that he was asked to leave some fancy college talk he was giving in Rhode Island a few weeks back because he was all kinds of messed up. Guy must be going through the wringer.

Detective Olsen: And?

Mr. Russo: And did you know that he tried to off himself?

Detective Olsen: As in commit suicide?

Mr. Russo: Exactly. Suicide. I was up at their house to spray for the mosquitoes. With the woods around, the bugs can get pretty bad. But I gotta tell the residents before I spray. Make sure they keep pets and stuff indoors for thirty minutes after. Anyway, I knocked on the Warringtons' door and there was no answer. Figured no one was home. Then, just as I was about to start spraying, I heard a car running in the garage. The closed garage. I pulled the door open, thinking maybe there was some kind of emergency, and there he was. Just sitting in his car.

Detective Olsen: And you're sure he was attempting to take his own life?

Mr. Russo: Sure as I can be. He jumped up when he saw me, told me it had been an accident, that he was just making a quick phone call and had forgotten to open the door first. But I didn't see any phone. When I'd opened that garage door, he was just sitting there, perfectly still, staring out the windshield. And on the passenger seat, there were all these pills. I don't know what they were, but I assumed he either took some or was planning to. He was pretty out of it, now that I think about it. But maybe that was just from the fumes. Who knows.

Detective Olsen: Did Mr. Warrington say anything else to you?

Mr. Russo: Yeah: "Don't tell my wife."

ONE WEEK BEFORE HALLOWEEN

25

HANNAH

Hawthorne Lane

Hannah pulls to a stop in front of her house. The curtains she'd chosen are now hanging inside the windows; the doormat Mark picked out at the garden center, HOME SWEET HOME in looping cursive, is lying in front of the door; and the mums Libby recommended for the planters on the porch are blooming in shades of deep purple, burnt orange, and saffron yellow. This is Hannah's home, and yet she's afraid to let herself believe that it won't all be snatched away from her in the blink of an eye.

She waits before turning into the driveway to let a woman about her age with a stroller pass by, a little boy trotting beside her. Hannah has seen the woman before. From what she understands, she's a nanny for the family at the end of the block. Hannah smiles politely, lifts a hand in greeting. But the other woman's eyes hardly meet hers before she hurries away. Hannah considers the sleek Mercedes rumbling beneath her, the big house in front of her, the flawless diamond glittering on her finger, and imagines how she looks to the other woman, wonders if she realizes that they aren't as different as it might appear.

Hannah edges into her driveway and steps out of the car, hefting her canvas tote bag onto her shoulder as she closes the door. The bag is weighed down with books she borrowed from the children's room at Sterling Valley Library, and she feels them bumping against her hip as she walks toward her house. She wants to get a head start on planning next month's activities. Although Hannah is only an assistant in the children's room, the head librarian asked for her input on upcoming events for the kids, and she was happy to help.

"You have a knack for this, you know," her boss had said, and Hannah beamed with pride, her cheeks rising like two round apples high on her face.

Hannah loves her job and the children she works with. She likes the quiet kids who curl up with books in the library's nooks and crannies; she likes the loud ones who bounce in their seats and can't help but exclaim in excitement when the read-aloud story takes an unexpected turn; she likes the ones who come in wearing superhero capes or sparkly tutus because they know that they can be anyone they want to be inside the library walls. She wonders which of them her own future children, hers and Mark's, will be like.

A pang of longing, regret, strikes her then, a physical stabbing pain in the center of her chest. She thinks of the texts she sometimes gets from Mark, baby names he thought of, photos of tiny blue booties and pink satin bows that he saw in shop windows. Hannah wants to start a family with him more desperately than she can put into words. It was the whole reason they bought this house on Hawthorne Lane with all of its empty bedrooms waiting to be filled. But how can she even consider a child now, with the past closing in on her like an ominous storm brewing on the horizon?

Liar. This isn't over. The notes have unsettled Hannah to the point where she can't sleep—the past revisits her every time she closes her eyes. But what do they mean? Is it possible that someone knows what she did? Hannah is used to living a life where she's constantly having to look over her shoulder. Her mother taught her the importance of vigilance from a young age. But these notes—this feels different. She finds that the vague, cryptic threats from a distant, faceless enemy are much more frightening than the devil she's always known.

Hannah digs her house keys from her bag and absently reaches into the mailbox as she does every day when she gets home from work, lost in her own thoughts. But today, all she's met with is cold metal at her fingertips. It's empty.

That's strange. She looks out over the cul-de-sac, at the other houses, mailboxes brimming with catalogs and flyers. And then a thought occurs to her. A memory of her first night on Hawthorne Lane, when Doug, the mailman, had accidentally delivered Georgina's mail to Hannah's address. Perhaps he's mixed up their house numbers again, given Georgina Hannah's mail this time.

She lifts one hand, uses it to shield her eyes from the sun like a visor as she looks across the street. Georgina is outside, tending to her garden beds. Hannah hasn't seen Georgina since the PTA auction two weeks ago, and she's gotten the impression that the other woman is avoiding her. She sent a text asking Georgina to grab a cup of coffee in town but she got no response, and their paths conveniently haven't crossed at all since. But checking for her mail would be a perfect excuse for Hannah to go over there.

Hannah bites at the cuticle on the edge of her thumb as she considers the idea. She understands that Georgina is probably embarrassed by what Hannah witnessed at the auction, and maybe she should just leave her alone, but despite everything Hannah is dealing with in her own life, she hasn't been able to get it out of her head, that image of Colin with his fist clamped around his wife's wrist, the look of twisted rage on his face. It strikes her as deeply unfair—Georgina shouldn't have to hide and feel ashamed over her husband's behavior. *She's* not the one who did anything wrong. Hannah makes up her mind and drops her keys back into her purse.

She strides across the street and up Georgina's front walk.

"Hey!" she says sunnily.

Georgina startles, her knees in the dirt, one hand gripping a spade. "Oh, Hannah, hi! I didn't even hear you coming. I guess I was in my own little world for a moment there." She smiles brightly from beneath her wide-brimmed hat. "How have you been?"

"Er, I'm . . . I'm good," Hannah stutters. She's thrown off by Georgina's cheerfulness, her practiced, flawless smile. "I just came by to see if you'd gotten my mail by mistake. It seems Doug is at it again."

"As a matter of fact, I did." Georgina chuckles. "I was going to run it over to your mailbox as soon as I finished here." She reaches deep into the pocket of her apron, pulls out a bundle of envelopes, and hands them to Hannah.

"Thank you, I appreciate it!" Hannah shifts her weight on her feet. "I've actually been hoping to run into you . . ."

"You texted." Georgina presses a gloved palm to her forehead. "I completely forgot to answer. My apologies, Hannah. I was feeling a bit under the weather this week, and it must have slipped my mind."

"Oh, I'm sorry to hear that." Hannah flounders to find the words to respond to the obvious lie. "I hope you're feeling better now."

"I am," Georgina replies, nodding. She stands up, takes off her gardening gloves, and brushes the granules of soil from her knees. "Thank you."

As she lowers her head and tucks her gloves into the pocket of her apron, her face catches the light for the first time, and Hannah sees it. The slight discoloration beneath Georgina's right eye, just above her cheekbone. It's been expertly covered with makeup, as though Georgina knew exactly what combination of hues to use to conceal a bruise, but Hannah recognizes it right away.

In a flash, she's back in the house where she grew up, the first place she remembers calling home. The only one where they'd lived with her father. Hannah remembers that place only in fragments, like a film she'd once watched and mostly forgotten. She remembers the way the kitchen always smelled of cooking oil and the bright pink of the roses her mother had painted on her bedroom wall, the way her fingers would trace the curling vines in the moonlight as she lay in bed, and she remembers the booming sound of her father's voice when he thought she was asleep: "Shut the hell up, Julie!" She remembers the crack of his fist against plaster, the sound of shattering glass, and the bruises on her mother's body. Red welts that would bloom into deep purple blemishes that Hannah couldn't stand to look at. "I bumped my head on a cabinet door," her mother would say, laughing at her own clumsiness, or "I tripped on the stairs. Mommy can be so silly sometimes." But Hannah, even at seven years old, could tell she was lying.

Her father became this frightening thing in her mind, a

shape-shifter that turned into a lurching monster at night, all bellowing roars and sharp teeth on the other side of her closed bedroom door. She'd squeeze her eyes shut, wishing she was bigger, stronger. She imagined herself facing him in his monstrous form. In these visions she was always brave like the cartoon superheroes she saw on television—she was a hero. But in the harsh light of reality, Hannah was none of those things. She was just a little girl cowering in her bed, desperately wishing to be more than she was.

Until the night everything changed. Hannah's mother crept into her room before dawn. She was holding her side, which would later be covered in bruises that stretched across her skin and looked to Hannah like watercolor paint on canvas.

"Get up, baby," she'd whispered. "We have to go."

Hannah sat up in her thin cotton nightgown, rubbing the sleep from her eyes. Her mother was already stuffing Hannah's clothes and her favorite soft toys into a big black garbage bag. "Where are we going?" she'd asked.

Hannah's mother paused, knelt by Hannah's bedside. "We have to get out of here, baby. Your daddy, he . . ." Her voice faltered, as if even then she felt the pull to make excuses for him.

"Turns into a monster," Hannah filled in for her. It was the first time either of them had spoken about the things her father did, the kind of man he was. But Hannah hadn't needed her mother to say the words. She already knew.

Her mother swallowed hard, and when she spoke again, her voice was strained. "Yes, baby. He does. And I don't want that for you. Do you understand? I don't want my little girl to grow up around a man like that. It's no good for you, and so we have to go. Right now. Before he wakes up."

Hannah nodded and silently helped her mother finish packing. They worked in tandem, as if they'd already planned for this day, already decided what would stay and what would go. And then they'd left. They drove off in the dead of night with everything they cared about packed into one small car.

"We can never look back," her mother said, her eyes meeting

Hannah's in the rearview mirror. "I need to hear you say it, baby: We can never look back."

Hannah rested her head against the cool glass of the window by her side and repeated the vow she'd later break. "We can never look back."

"Georgina," Hannah says now. "You can talk to me." *You don't have to face this alone.*

"I appreciate that, but there's nothing to talk about." Georgina busies herself gathering her gardening supplies.

Hannah reaches out, touches her lightly on the arm. She feels the other woman bristle at the contact. "I understand. More than you know."

Georgina pauses, considers Hannah, her green eyes searching Hannah's blue ones. And Hannah waits, her breath held. For a moment it feels so real, as if Georgina is reading all the words Hannah hasn't yet brought herself to say, as if the broken thing in Georgina sees its own reflection in Hannah's eyes: *I recognize you.* And then it's gone. The false brightness is back, and Georgina smiles that perfect smile of hers.

"I'm afraid I don't know what you're talking about."

"Georgina, please," Hannah tries again. "What happened the other night—"

"Nothing happened the other night," Georgina insists.

"But your face . . ." Hannah's hand rises to her own cheek, traces the crest of her cheekbone.

"I walked into a door," Georgina says with a self-deprecating chuckle. "I can be so clumsy sometimes."

The hollow excuse sounds so familiar to Hannah's ears that it's like hearing her mother again, feeling the same searing indignation she had as a child. It wasn't fair what her father had done to her, what he'd done to them, relegating them to a life of fear, living out of her mother's car, always looking over their shoulders. Hannah hated him for it so fully that it felt like it could consume her. If only there were something more she could have done . . .

We can never look back.

Except Hannah did. At first, only in her mind. She imagined herself going back there, creeping into the house she'd once called home, and finding her father passed out on the couch, his terrycloth robe gaping open to reveal the pale, flabby skin of his chest, a scene she'd witnessed so many times that she could almost smell the rank scent of sour beer on his breath, hear the sputtering snore that rattled in his chest. She pictured herself picking up one of the lumpy couch pillows and holding it over his face with her small hands until the noise stopped—

"Ahem." The sound of throat-clearing snaps Hannah back into the present. She looks up to find what must be Georgina's son, the spitting image of his father, standing on a balcony one story above their heads. He's leaning casually over the railing, watching the exchange between the two women with a curious expression on his face.

"I appreciate you checking on me," Georgina says to Hannah, "but I'm feeling much better now, and I really should go inside and get started on dinner."

"I—" Hannah begins, but Georgina has already turned away from her.

Hannah watches as she hurries up her front walk and closes herself behind the door of her picture-perfect house.

HANNAH SLOWLY MAKES HER WAY back to her own house, her mind still reeling from her interaction with Georgina. It's like she's a prisoner in her own home. Hannah knows that she should mind her own business, that she has enough to worry about right now without taking on someone else's problems, but she also knows that she won't be able to. That now that she's aware of what's going on behind Georgina's closed doors, she won't be able to ignore it. She's not a frightened, powerless little girl anymore.

She looks down at the envelopes in her hand, rumpled from her grip. She hadn't realized how tightly she'd been holding them. And then she sees one that stands out from the others. A cream-colored mailer, sealed with a scrap of clear tape.

Hannah's hands feel numb as she pulls it from the pile, lets the rest of the mail drop, fluttering, onto the smooth black asphalt of her driveway. She slides out the note, and this time the message is crystal clear: *Murderer.*

There's no denying it anymore. Someone, somewhere, knows exactly what Hannah is.

26

LIBBY

Hawthorne Lane

Ping.

Libby hears the notification from her phone as she helps her customer, an older gentleman who is looking for a bouquet for a new "lady friend" he'd met at the retirement village. It's sweet, Libby thinks, the way he carefully considers each type of flower, taking his time to select the best ones.

"Let's add some irises," he says. "The blue will match her eyes."

Libby wants to ask him if he was married before, if his ability to find love again took him by surprise, if the moving on ever became easier, but she doesn't. Instead, she chooses the most vibrant irises in the bunch and adds them to a bundle of white roses that she knows will make the color pop.

"Yes, yes, that's perfect," the man says as he shuffles toward the register.

Ping. Libby's phone chimes again. She usually puts it on silent while she's working, but it has been a busy morning and she forgot about it entirely in the pocket of her apron.

Erica rings up the customer while Libby clips the stems of his blooms, wraps the bouquet in a sheet of brown paper, and ties it with a simple white bow. She smiles down at the finished product. It's perfect.

Libby loves her job, loves this place. Sometimes she wonders where she'd be without it.

This, owning a flower shop, hadn't been the plan. The plan was to pursue a career in finance, a field that promised a steady, reliable career path that would ensure she'd never be left struggling, like her mother had been, to afford the rent on an apartment that smelled of mildew. Libby would have been good at it too. When she was in school, her professors often called her ideas brilliant and her contributions to the class discussions intuitive. She saw a promising future stretched out before her like a road paved in gold.

But then, just before her college graduation, Libby unexpectedly found herself pregnant. As she looked down at the pink plus sign on the little plastic stick in her hand, she could see that road, the path of her life, forking, splitting. At the end of one path, there was Libby standing in a boardroom, power suits and accolades, the kind of life she'd always envisioned for herself; at the end of the other, school parties, rickety Popsicle-stick crafts, sandwiches tucked into little plastic bags, all the small things that would make up her son's childhood. For nine months she'd stood at the turning point, frozen. She wanted children, always knew she'd be a mother one day. But not yet. It was too soon. There was still so much she'd planned to do. She told herself that she could have both, that she could do it all. The thing all women were meant to want. But how? Even then, Libby understood that motherhood was going to demand sacrifices of her. That she would never again be wholly one thing. For the rest of her life, she would be a woman divided.

But then Lucas was born. As she held him in her arms for the first time, looked down into his impossibly tiny face, traced the curve of his perfect seashell ears, the decision suddenly became an easy one. She couldn't imagine leaving him in someone else's arms each morning while she fought and clawed her way up a corporate ladder. Who could ever love him like she did? Who would care for him the way she would? Libby no longer cared about what she was giving up; all that mattered was what she had gained.

And so Libby tackled motherhood with vigor. She signed up for every mommy-and-me class, read all the parenting books, attended every preschool class party. Her involvement in Lucas's childhood felt like the most important thing she'd ever done. She didn't miss the lofty discussions or economic analyses of her college days; she didn't find herself wishing for a wardrobe full of pencil skirts and silk blouses, daily train rides into a noisy city. Giving up her career aspirations didn't feel sacrificial to Libby, not in the way she'd thought it would. She simply wasn't that person anymore. Not since she became a mother—motherhood had changed her. Completely. Irrevocably. The love she felt for her son was all-consuming, her devotion to him filling all the space inside her.

Until it didn't. Until the tiny baby that consumed her every waking hour started to demand just a little less of her, until she found herself only half engaged as she played blocks on the floor beside him, until she caught herself watching the clock that seemed to move impossibly slowly during the endless afternoon hours. The guilt she felt over this was debilitating. There was nothing more important than her son. And she was so fortunate to be able to be present for him in the way she was. And so, why? Why did it still feel like something was missing? Why did she find herself wanting more?

Libby wished she had someone to talk to about these things. Bill wouldn't get it. Parenthood hadn't demanded the same sacrifices of him that it had of her; he had stepped, smoothly, into his father's shoes, taking over the family business. His life looked more or less the same way it would have had Lucas never been born. What Libby needed was someone who understood, who wouldn't meet her with the usual hollow platitudes: *They're only little once—enjoy every moment!* and *A mother's life isn't her own; everything we do is for our children.* As if she were expected to continually sacrifice herself on the altar of motherhood and never dare to want anything more for herself. As if by the act of procreating, a woman was required to endlessly give pieces of herself away until nothing remained. Libby had considered talking to Georgina. They'd formed something of a friendship during their pregnancies. But no, Georgina couldn't possibly understand this restlessness Libby was grappling with. She thought of Georgina, with her chic outfits and styled hair, pushing her designer stroller through the neighborhood. She thought of Sebastian in his tidy seersucker overalls, his neatly combed hair; she thought of the jars of organic baby food that Georgina made for Christina, her beautiful baby girl that Libby couldn't bring herself to look at without a crushing sense of loss and longing, of jealousy so unwieldy that it forced her to keep her distance. Georgina had transitioned to motherhood as seamlessly as the seasons changed. She seemed so content, so sure of who she was and what she was meant to be doing, as if motherhood had fulfilled something in her that had previously been empty. How could Libby possibly explain that as much as she loved her son, it wasn't enough for her? That she wanted, *needed,* something of her own before she lost herself entirely?

And then one day, as she was taking Lucas to story time at the library, she saw an advertisement for a floral-arranging class posted on the bulletin board.

"Making bouquets and stuff?" Bill asked, eyebrows raised in surprise when she first mentioned it. "I didn't know you were into that."

Libby hadn't known either. All she knew was that it felt exciting to her, like it could be something for *her,* outside of being a wife and a mother, something she could love.

And she did. That one class soon became many. At first, Libby simply enjoyed how relaxing it was, trimming, bundling, creating something beautiful. She liked learning about the different types of flowers, experimenting with new arrangements. But later, she could feel her mind stretching and growing, old wheels beginning to turn once more when she considered the business it could someday become. She felt a small piece of her old self returning, the version of her she'd been before motherhood, as she created a business plan, calculated start-up costs and overhead expenses. The idea filled Libby with a renewed sense of purpose, of value. And when the time was right, she'd made it a reality and opened Lily Lane.

Libby hands the gentleman his purchase, the paper wrapping crinkling as he takes it in his arms, and she looks around her store. At the colorful displays, the hanging wreaths, the shop window bursting with autumn blooms. She'd done this. All of it. She created this with her own two hands.

She and Lily Lane have been through so much together over the years. This place was there for her when she'd dropped Lucas off at kindergarten, holding back her tears as he let go of her hand and walked through the front doors all by himself; it was a sanctuary for her when she and Bill had tried and failed for a second child, a place she could come to work through the heartbreak of each negative pregnancy test, the babies that weren't meant to be; it was there to support them when Bill got into that car accident years back and was unexpectedly out of work for three months, and now it's here for her when he no longer wants to be.

"Good luck on your date," Libby says as cheerily as she's able as her customer shuffles toward the door.

"Thanks, but I won't be needing it," he replies with a wink and a tip of his driver's cap.

"Well, *that's* a disturbing visual," Erica mutters as the shop door closes.

"I'm not sure I'll ever be able to get it out of my head," Libby replies with a mock shudder, surreptitiously trying to sneak a look at her phone.

"Who's been texting you all morning?" Erica asks, one eyebrow raised.

Libby drops the phone back into the pocket of her apron, messages still unread. "Oh, uh, just Lucas letting me know his plans for the afternoon." She blushes despite herself. She's never been a very good liar.

"Right," Erica replies, stretching the vowels sarcastically, "of course. It's Lucas who has you in such a suspiciously good mood lately." But mercifully, she doesn't press the issue. "How did his math test go yesterday?" she asks. "I know you said he was nervous about it."

Libby exhales in relief, happy to move to a safer topic. "He aced it."

"Some kid you've got there, Lib. A varsity athlete *and* straight As. It's impressive."

"I know. Sometimes I can't believe how lucky I got with him."

"Lucky?" Erica huffs as she bundles the cut stems on the workbench and points them at Libby. "You never give yourself enough credit. Do you realize that? Luck has nothing to do with it. Lucas is a great kid because he was raised by a great mom."

Libby feels a lump forming in her throat as she watches Erica finish wiping down her station. She hadn't realized until this very moment how much she needed to hear those words. She *has* been a good mother to Lucas. Or at least, she's tried to be.

It wasn't always easy, running Lily Lane and raising her son. After she opened the shop, she finally felt like she had it all: a family, motherhood, a job that made her feel personally and professionally fulfilled. Though it often felt like she had two cups, work and home, and she had to be deliberate about how she poured her time and attention into them, giving each what they needed at any given moment without allowing the other one to run dry. But at the end of the day, Lucas had always been her priority.

Libby might not have been the type of mother who was known for her homemade cookies at the school bake sale, but she was there for her son when it mattered. She'd closed the shop early, without hesitation, whenever the school nurse called, and she'd organized her shifts around Lucas's soccer schedule so that she never missed a game. She knew how much it meant to him to have her there in the stands, even when he became too cool to admit it. She could see it in the way he'd always search for her face in the crowd after he scored a goal, pride in his eyes, and the way he'd dissect the game in the car on the way home, chatting animatedly to Libby as he recounted each save, every offensive maneuver.

She and Lucas might be going through a tough stage right now, but she hopes he knows that he's always been the most important thing in her life. She hopes he knows she did her best.

"You okay?" Erica asks, watching Libby suspiciously.

"Yes. I'm fine. Just . . . thank you. You know, for everything. For what you do around here, and for being such great a friend to me."

"Oh, no, you don't," Erica replies, waving Libby off. "Don't go getting all sentimental on me now."

Libby laughs, though she still feels like she could cry. And then her phone pings again.

"Do you need to answer *Lucas*?" Erica asks, a knowing smile playing on her lips. Libby should have known that Erica wouldn't let this go so easily. She can imagine her reaction if she were to tell her the truth: that she's been chatting with a man named Peter, whom she met on the dating site. Erica would be elated, wanting to see a photo, scouring his profile.

Erica has been fiercely loyal to Libby since she hired her but even more so since Bill left.

"I never liked him," she'd declared, folding her arms over her chest, when Libby told her that she and Bill were taking some time apart. "He's a goddamn idiot, that's what he is," she'd added, her consonants clipped. (Her accent is always more noticeable when she's angry.)

Libby is thankful to have Erica in her corner, but she's not sure she wants to unleash her on Peter just yet. It still feels so new. Tenuous.

"How about I grab us some lunch from that café you like?" Libby offers, eager to change the subject. "My treat."

"Oh, Green Fare?" Erica essentially moans. "That sounds amazing. Have I told you lately that you're the best boss ever?"

"Yes, and I never get tired of hearing it." Libby unties her apron and shrugs the strap of her purse over her shoulder.

IT'S A BEAUTIFUL FALL DAY outside, sunny and golden in the way only autumn afternoons can be, and Libby walks slowly down Main Street, enjoying the crisp breeze, the smell of the dry leaves that have gathered in windswept piles along the curb. Now that she's alone, she pulls her phone out of her pocket, eager to read Peter's latest messages.

They've been chatting for a few weeks now, which is more than she can say for anyone else who'd messaged her through the site, most of whom had sent her aggressive advances that she'd quickly turned down. But Peter was different. At first, he'd seemed nice enough, if a little bland. They'd exchanged a few harmless messages—comments on the weather, their favorite artists, classic movies. But lately Libby has noticed that their conversations have taken a turn. They've gone from making small talk to discussing things that really matter: his job as a mortgage broker, her store, their families. Conversations that span days and weeks as they slowly, cautiously get to know each other.

Peter has written now:

> Just thinking about you. I hope you're having a good day!

Libby smiles to herself as she types out a reply:

> It's been busy, but good! Yours?

He replies almost immediately:

> Better now that I'm talking to you ;)

Libby's smile widens. How nice it is to know that someone is thinking of her.

She was surprised to discover just how much she liked seeing a familiar name on her phone screen, how much she missed having someone, *anyone,* ask her about her day. Peter isn't her usual type—his rectangular glasses and combed-over hair are nothing like Bill's athletic build and charming smile, though Libby supposes he's cute in a nerdy sort of way. But above all, talking to Peter has been a good distraction. She realizes now that Erica was right—she *has* been in a better mood lately. Less of that burning anger she'd felt when she first learned about Bill and Heather. She's found herself checking Heather's Instagram page less often since she and Peter started exchanging messages too. And she recognizes that this is a good thing. All it was doing was making her more bitter.

When Libby reaches Green Fare, it's packed, a line snaking from the small café to the sidewalk. Personally, Libby can't understand why Erica loves this place so much, but judging by the dozens of people waiting for their lunchtime wheatgrass smoothies and kale salads, she's in the minority on that one. Libby studies the menu board hanging over the registers. What the hell is in a protein wrap? Next time, she's definitely choosing a different lunch spot. Someplace where the word *keto* is nowhere on the menu.

She pulls out her phone again, considering sending another message to Peter while she waits, but she finds that he's already typing, three little dots pulsing on her screen. She feels a quiver in her stomach as she always does when waiting for Peter's next message, bracing herself for what she suspects is coming soon.

Peter hasn't asked her to meet in person yet, but it's only a matter of time, right? That's what these sites are for. And yet, as much as she's enjoyed his messages, she's not sure she's ready for that. With what they're doing here, texting, slowly opening up to each other in measured steps, she feels like she's in control, like she hasn't committed to anything yet. But as soon as she meets Peter, as soon as he becomes a real flesh-and-blood person in her life, things are bound to get more complicated. Is she ready for complicated?

The three little dots disappear from the screen and Libby sighs, dropping her phone back into her purse. She'll cross that bridge when she comes to it. For now, it's just nice to feel a little less alone in the world, even if her connection with Peter is confined to the little rectangle of her phone. At the very least, it keeps her from dwelling too much on thoughts of Bill and—

"Heather! Order for Heather!"

Libby's head snaps up at the sound of the name and she sees one of the staff members holding up a large green smoothie. "Pickup for Heather!"

Libby frantically scans the room. *Heather is a fairly common name, right?* There's no reason to think that it's *Bill's* Heather. What are the chances of—

But then she's there. Heather. As if she'd stepped out of the pixelated images Libby has lost so many hours staring at and into vivid, three-dimensional reality. Libby watches her walk up to the pickup counter and collect her drink, smiling at the worker who made it for her.

Libby wanders off the line, her eyes fixed on Heather, as if she's been lulled into a trance by her presence. She watches as Heather places the straw between her lips, slick with a coat of cherry-red lipstick, and pulls a deep sip. There's something so suggestive about the gesture, about the way she moves, about the sway of her ultra-trendy cape jacket as she heads for the door.

Libby follows her, picking her way through the crowd. She watches how the other woman walks, her cognac leather boots taking long strides down the sidewalk, her long, sleek, black hair shining in the afternoon sun.

Until now, Libby had only ever seen Heather through her computer screen or as a shadowy silhouette through Bill's window. But now she's so close that Libby could close the gap between them with a few hurried steps; she can smell the sugary-sweet scent of her perfume carried on the gentle autumn breeze. She's *real*. Heather is real, and Libby is transfixed by the sight of her, overwhelmed by the reality of her.

Heather stops as she reaches a crosswalk, flicks a glossy sheet of hair over her shoulder in one graceful movement, and waits patiently for the light to change. That's when Libby feels it. The Band-Aid Peter had been acting as suddenly ripped from her skin, exposing the raw open wound beneath. What does it matter that she's been chatting to some random man from the internet when Bill has *her*? This woman, with her youthful beauty and sultry smile, has taken everything from Libby. And now she's standing here, ten feet away, wholly and completely unbothered, drinking a fucking smoothie in the afternoon sun like all is right in the world.

Libby clenches her teeth, her molars grinding together painfully. The image comes to her then in a flash. It's not a conscious thought, something she's considered and decided upon; it comes to her at once as though it sprang fully formed from the darkest corner of her mind: She imagines herself walking up behind Heather. She imagines stretching out her arms, her palms slabbed against the wool of that stupid coat, and she imagines pushing the other woman into traffic. She can hear the crunch of bone, smell the scent of burning rubber; all of her problems disappearing in an instant—

Ping.

Libby's phone chirps, and it releases her from whatever spell she'd been under like a cold shot of reality injected straight into her veins.

Where did that come from? she thinks as she checks the screen with trembling fingers. *I'm not that person. I can't be that person.*

> I'd really like to meet you, Libby. Even if it's just for a cup of coffee. If you're ready?

Libby stares down at the phone, frightened of the darkness that just took hold of her. The truth is that she doesn't know if she's ready to put herself out there, but maybe it's what she needs to do. This unhealthy obsession with Heather has to stop. Libby doesn't like the person it's turning her into, someone capable of such terrible, violent thoughts. That's not Libby. Or at least, it's not who she wants to be. She wants to be the idyllic, uncomplicated version of herself that Peter sees; she wants the clean slate he's written her story on. But in order to do that, she needs to stop wallowing in the anger and pain of her past with Bill; she needs to find a way to let it go, to move forward. Maybe forcing herself to take this step with Peter is the way to do that. Even though it scares her, maybe it's the very thing that will save her.

> Yes. I'm ready.

27

MAGGIE
Benton Avenue

"Where the fuck is my money, Dean?"

Maggie has never seen Mike like this before, his nostrils flaring, his teeth clenched as he glowers down at Dean.

"I don't know what you mean, man," Dean replies.

"See, the thing is," Mike snarls, his hands gripping the edge of Maggie's kitchen table so tightly that his knuckles blanch, "people don't tend to pay when they don't get their product. And so I'm going to ask you again—where the fuck is my money?"

"We made the drop," Dean insists. "Just like you said."

"We?"

"Yeah. I mean, Maggie was the one who drove it out there but—"

"You sent *Maggie* to do *your* job?" Mike slams his fist down on the table so hard that it makes the rows of empty bottles jump. One of them teeters a moment before crashing to the floor and shattering at Maggie's feet.

Both men look at her now. She stands straight-backed and rigid, afraid to so much as breathe as she stares at the shards of broken glass, at the jagged pieces reflecting the dull overhead light. She can't bring herself to meet their eyes.

"And did you do it, Maggie?" Mike asks her.

Maggie opens her mouth to reply, but all that comes out is a tiny strangled cry. She swallows hard and tries again. "Yes," she manages to squeak out this time.

Mike shakes his head, sets his sights on Dean again. "Well, something went wrong, and I'm holding *you* responsible. You have one week. One week to get me either my drugs or my money. The choice is yours, but if you don't have one or the other by the time I come back here, we're going to have a problem." Mike curls and uncurls his fingers at his side.

Maggie watches the muscles in his forearm flex beneath his skin. She wonders what a man like Mike is capable of. It feels as though her insides have turned to liquid.

"It doesn't have to be like this," Dean replies. "We've been friends since we were five years old, we're business partners, I'm sure we can—"

"We are *not* partners," Mike snaps. "You work for me. And I'm not the top of the food chain either. The guys I answer to . . . they aren't gonna care how long we've been friends. *I* have to pay up, which means *you* have to pay up. That's the only way this is going to go down."

"I told you," Dean insists, a wheedling tone edging between his words. Maggie can tell he's scared now, and this, more than anything, frightens her. "I don't have the package anymore, and I definitely don't have that kind of money."

"Then you'd better find a way to get it," Mike growls. "Fast."

He storms out of their kitchen, and the aluminum door rattles on its hinges behind him.

Dean collapses into a chair, drops his head into his hands.

Maggie slowly backs out of the room and collects her keys from the ring. She has to get those drugs back. Why did she ever think she'd get away with this? She'd just been so panicked, she wasn't thinking straight. And when she came home empty-handed, Dean looking at her expectantly, she'd been too afraid to tell him anything other than what he wanted to hear. And so she'd lied, let him believe that she'd done as she was told.

MAGGIE'S HANDS FUMBLE WITH HER KEY. They're shaking so badly that she can't manage to slide it into the lock on her car door.

Suddenly a shadow looms over her shoulder, large and menacing, blocking what's left of the fading evening sun. "Going somewhere?"

Startled, Maggie drops the key. It lands on the dry dirt at her feet, sending up a small puff of dust.

Mike bends down and retrieves it for her. "I think you lost something."

She can't be sure if he's talking about the key or if he's somehow figured out what she did.

"Th-thanks," Maggie stammers, teeth chattering. Mike presses the key, warm, into her palm.

"Listen," he says as calmly as if he were talking to a small child, "I don't know what happened here, but Dean roped you into something he shouldn't have." His eyes search her face before dragging slowly down the length of her body.

Maggie feels a shudder roll through her.

Mike reaches out a rough, callused hand, gently sweeps it along her cheekbone, and tucks a lock of her limp brown hair behind her ear.

"Dean and I have been friends a long time, but he's never deserved you."

Maggie is too frightened to agree, too frightened to move. Her skin feels like it's burning where Mike's fingers were, but still she says nothing.

"What if..." Mike continues, drawing closer to her now. "What if I found a way to leave your name out of all of this? Would you like that?"

He trails the back of his hand over the curve of her neck, his touch featherlight. It sends a wave of chills coursing through Maggie's body, and she jumps away from him, presses herself against the cold metal of her car, her heart firing rapidly in her chest.

Mike narrows his oil-black eyes at her, her rejection kindling anger. "Have it your way," he spits. "This is *both* of your problems now. And you're going to pay up. One way or another."

Maggie clambers into the car and pulls the door shut behind her. She jams the key into the ignition and peels out of the driveway, her foot quaking on the accelerator. As she looks into her rearview mirror, she finds that he's still standing there, watching her in the cloud of dust she'd left behind.

MAGGIE DRIVES SLOWLY DOWN MAIN STREET, trying to retrace her steps on that awful night. She knows it's the only way she'll be able to find the old gas station again. She'd been lost then, in an unfamiliar part of town.

On the sidewalk, two teenagers whiz by on bicycles. A boy and a girl, the girl's hair fanning out behind her as she rides. It's like seeing a memory broadcast over reality, Maggie and Sam at that age. Tears well in Maggie's eyes at the thought of her old friend. What would he think of her if he could see her now? Why hadn't she just listened to him when she had the chance? He'd tried to warn her about Dean, but she'd been too stubborn to listen.

Sam and Dean met only once. At a bar Dean had chosen. The kind of place where beer was served in frothy pint glasses, and the paper menus were slipped into sticky plastic sleeves. It was shortly after Maggie and Dean had started dating, and she found that she was nervous. Sam and Dean were the two most important men, the two most important *people,* in her life, and she was desperate for them to like each other.

When Sam walked into the bar, Maggie felt her heart crack wide open. It had been months since they'd seen each other, and she hadn't realized how much she missed him. He wore worn, dark-washed jeans and a button-down flannel shirt, and he had something of a beard that Maggie had never seen before. She stood from the table, a huge smile on her face as she waved him over. She felt Dean bristle next to her, his eyes sharp and appraising on the other man. It hadn't occurred to her that Dean might be jealous of Sam. She'd never really thought of Sam in that way. He'd always just been Sam. Her Sam. More like a brother to her than anything else. A brother who was now standing beside the table, casting a large shadow across Dean's face.

Sam offered Dean a hand and they shook, nodding at each other coolly, and then Sam wrapped Maggie in a hug, lifting her off her feet and spinning her around. "I've missed you, Mags."

They sat at a small, round table, Maggie positioned between the two men. She felt like she was playing Ping-Pong all night, her attention swiveling from Dean to Sam and back as she tried to engage them both in conversation. The atmosphere was tense, the men appraising each other like boxers in a ring.

"So what do you do for a living?" Sam eventually asked Dean. It seemed to Maggie that, thus far, they'd both gone out of their way to avoid speaking to each other directly.

"I work on cars."

"Oh, that's cool."

"Yeah, I hear you know a thing or two about cars." Dean grinned maliciously.

Sam raised one eyebrow, folding his arms over his chest, and Maggie coughed, nearly choking on her soda. Why had she told Dean about Sam's past? She'd never dreamed he would bring it up like this. And besides, what happened hadn't been Sam's fault. He was with a group of friends at a party; they'd had too much to drink, someone had stolen a car and they'd taken it for a joyride. Sam hadn't been the one driving, but in the end they'd left him holding the bag. He'd been arrested. Maggie knew that was one of the lowest points of Sam's life. And he'd worked so hard to turn things around since then, now running a successful furniture-restoration company that he'd built from the ground up. She couldn't believe Dean had taken this opportunity to throw Sam's past in his face. She'd told him that in confidence.

Sam nodded as if accepting a challenge. "Okay, man. I see how it is."

When the check came, Maggie was relieved. The night hadn't gone at all as she'd hoped. Sam and Dean could barely stand to look at each other.

Both men reached for the check at the same time.

"I've got it," Sam said, standing and sliding his wallet from his pocket.

Dean's lips curled. "I can pay for dinner for *my* girl."

"Didn't say you couldn't, man," Sam replied breezily, tossing more than his share of cash onto the table. "I think it's time I get going."

"Good idea," Dean snarled. He turned to Maggie. "I'm going to go settle up at the bar."

Sam watched Dean walk away and then his eyes fell on Maggie. "Mags, are you sure about this guy?"

"Listen, Dean was out of line with that car comment. He never should have brought that up, but—"

Sam huffed.

"I think he's just intimidated by you. He's not usually like this."

"If you say so." Sam's gaze drifted to the back of Dean's head. "It's just . . . I don't know. There's something off about him. Something I don't trust."

Maggie felt herself growing defensive. "I'm just asking you to give him another chance. I think if you two get to know each other—"

"I don't think I want to know him."

Maggie crossed her arms over her chest. She wasn't ready to hear what Sam was trying to tell her. Not yet. At that time, Dean had still seemed like the answer to all her prayers, the thing that was going to save her from the grim outlook of her life. "Well, he makes me happy. I'm *happy*, Sam. For the first time in God only knows how long. Dean is a part of my life now, and if you can't accept that, if you're telling me you're not even going to make an effort because of one stupid comment, then . . . then I don't know how this friendship is supposed to work."

"Wow. Okay." He kissed her on the cheek, his lips lingering a touch too long on her skin. "It was good to see you, Maggie." And then he turned and walked away.

That was the last time Maggie had spoken to her closest friend. She tried calling him the next morning, feeling bad about the way they'd left things, but Sam didn't answer. And he never called her back.

By the time Maggie realized that Sam had been right about Dean, far too much time had passed. She'd already lost him.

Now, finally, Maggie spots a familiar stretch of road, sees the abandoned gas station. She pulls into the lot, just as she'd done before, and sighs with relief. She never thought she'd be so happy to see a rusty dumpster.

She rushes out of the car, the engine clicking idly in the silent night, falls to her knees beside the dumpster, and shoves away the pile of fallen leaves that had accumulated behind it with both hands. But the only thing beneath is stained black asphalt, the lingering scent of decay. The drugs are gone.

28
AUDREY
Hawthorne Lane

Buzz. Audrey hears her phone vibrating, facedown on her desk, and the sound makes her jump. *This has to stop.* She's been so on edge since Colin's unexpected appearance at her front door that every little thing startles her these days. She hates that he has this type of control over her life, that one unannounced visit from him has sent her into a tailspin. After all, Audrey recognizes that this was exactly what he'd intended. Colin holds all the cards right now and he knows it. But as much as Audrey doesn't want to play into his hand, she can't help but feel like she's unraveling. Things have been quiet since she slammed her door in his sneering, arrogant face. Of course it helps that she'd blocked his number, but she knows that she hasn't heard the last of him yet. A man like Colin Pembrook won't let her have the last word.

She flips over her phone, bracing herself for whatever might be waiting for her.

> Still planning to be home on time tonight?

Audrey's initial reaction is frustration. Seth is constantly checking on her whenever she's out of the house these days. Her phone has become like a leash that he tugs on whenever she strays even slightly out of his sight. She already told him she'd be home at her regular time tonight, and this text is simply a reminder of how little he trusts her.

But the frustration is quickly replaced by guilt and then resignation. She brought this on herself. She brought it on both of them.

Audrey pictures what Seth probably looks like right now: slouched on the couch, his unshaven face a ghostly white from the glare of the phone in his hands as he sits in their darkened living room, curtains drawn, his T-shirt rumpled, the collar loose and misshapen. His gloom seems to fill the house lately, seeping through the walls, curling under doorways like a dense fog. It's suffocating them both.

Seth has had setbacks in his career before—every writer has—but Audrey has never seen him like this. He's not writing, he barely leaves the house, and he's angry all the time. So angry. At Audrey, at his publisher, at his fans, who he feels betrayed him. She doesn't know how long he can go on like this. She's afraid that he's going to snap, that he'll do something he won't be able to take back.

He'd shown some signs of improvement when he was asked to give that lecture at the University of Rhode Island, but after he got back, he seemed worse. What's most concerning to Audrey is his refusal to talk about what happened there.

She'd suggested that he see a therapist, that he talk to someone if he wasn't going to talk to her, but he rejected that idea as well.

"What's the point?" he'd said, his eyes narrowing on Audrey. "It's not like sitting in a room and talking about my feelings is going to bring back what I lost."

Audrey wasn't sure if they were talking about his career or their marriage. The two things have blended and merged for Seth, the collective loss of the life he once had, the whole of it greater than the sum of its parts.

She picks up her phone; her plum-colored nails tap at the screen.

> Yes, I'll be home at my regular time. And I'll pick up the pasta dish you like from Gino's on my way.

She pauses, and then she sends another message.

> Love you.

It's how they've always ended their conversations. Even after the words started to lose their meaning. Seth seems to be typing a response, three little dots appearing on the screen, but then they disappear.

Audrey hadn't expected him to say it back. He hasn't since the day Colin's roses landed unceremoniously on their doorstep. Seth is hurting, she knows that. And if he were to find out about her affair with Colin now, it would only make things worse. It's *Colin Pembrook*. Colin, with his high-powered career and enviable good looks. Colin, whom Seth already thought of as insufferably arrogant. For some reason (it feels inexplicable to her now), Audrey had chosen *that* man. And that might be enough to push Seth over the edge.

Audrey collects her things and drops her phone into her bag before looping it over her shoulder. She's going to have to hurry if she wants to make her usual train back to Sterling Valley. If she misses it, it's going to raise Seth's suspicions. She wonders how long it's going to be like this, how many days in a row she's going to have to prove herself, to show up exactly when and where she says she will, before Seth will start to trust her again. It's amazing, she thinks, how easily trust can be broken but how difficult it is to mend the shattered pieces.

She steps into the elevator, directs it to the lobby. A part of her suspects that she and Seth won't survive this, that even if Seth never finds out the truth about Colin, that the suggestion of infidelity, that whisper of distrust, is enough to break them beyond repair. But maybe they'd been broken long before that. So much so that there was room for Colin to squeeze himself between them.

Audrey never planned on having an affair. In fact, all she'd planned to do the night it all began was work. She'd been in a martini bar in Manhattan wearing her favorite fitted sheath dress, a notepad on the table in front of her, waiting to meet with an artist, a flighty musician who'd given her junior staff the slip, for an interview. When her phone buzzed with a text, she knew, without even looking at the screen, that he was standing her up. Audrey was gathering her things to leave, already calculating when she might be able to reschedule, when the waiter brought her a drink, courtesy of the gentleman at the bar. She looked up to see Colin, her undeniably attractive neighbor, his own glass raised to her in a toast. Audrey slipped her notebook into her bag, pulled up a stool beside Colin. It was only polite, after all.

Several martinis later, they'd stumbled out onto the city street, the sidewalk lit by streetlights and jewel-toned neon signs. Colin raised one hand in the air in an attempt to hail a cab, but none stopped.

"I usually have better luck than this," he'd joked as the fourth taxi whizzed by them.

Audrey smiled and shivered in her sleeveless dress, the night air prickling her skin. "It's fine."

"You're freezing." Colin immediately took off his suit jacket and draped it gently over Audrey's shoulders. "Better?"

She looked up at him, surrounded by the smell of his cologne, the warmth of his body enveloping her. They stood so close that she could feel the electric charge running between them, and she saw something in his eyes: a burning desire she hadn't seen from her own husband in so very long.

"You're so beautiful," he breathed, one hand running the length of her hair.

Audrey felt a warm glow pulsing inside her, pieces of herself that had long lain dormant waking. When was the last time Seth had wanted her this way? When was the last time he'd really seen her?

Colin's hand grazed her cheek and came to rest under her chin. He tilted her face up toward his.

She knew he was going to kiss her then and that once he did, there would be no turning back. But Audrey didn't pull away; she allowed herself to be carried away in the rush of it, in the feeling of being wanted, desired, as Colin's warm lips closed over hers. It was the beginning of the end.

The elevator doors slide open, and Audrey steps out. She glides through the airy lobby of *Top Cast,* pushes open the heavy glass doors, and steps out onto the city sidewalk.

Suddenly, a figure dressed in all black jumps out and knocks her backward. Audrey gasps in alarm, her body going rigid with fear. It takes her a moment to realize what it is: a teenage boy in a Ghostface mask, the eyes wells of black, the mouth pulled into a demented, elongated scream. The boy laughs and tears down the street, his black robes twisting in the breeze behind him. Audrey swallows hard before she starts walking again, willing her heart to stop jackhammering against her ribs.

She forgot that it's nearly Halloween. Soon her street will be overrun with families, children skittering through the cul-de-sac, sugary treats plunking in their orange plastic buckets. She reminds herself to pick up more candy. They ran out early last year, which was considered a cardinal sin on Hawthorne Lane.

Audrey turns around the corner of her building, picking up her pace as she heads toward Forty-Second Street and Grand Central Station.

That's when she sees him, leaning against the building, *her* building, as if he belongs here. Colin, in a charcoal-gray suit, his shoulder resting comfortably against the glass facade, his arms folded, his legs crossed casually at the ankles. He smiles at her, that dazzling smile that had once lured her in like a mariner following a Siren's song to a watery grave.

"Fancy meeting you here," he says as he saunters toward her.

"I work here," she grumbles. "As I'm sure you know. Now, if you'll excuse me, I have a train to catch."

She breezes past him, her chin held high, though inside she's trembling.

Colin matches her pace, easily striding beside her on his long legs. "Can't even spare a moment then for an *old friend?*"

He sounds so smug, so tauntingly infuriating, that Audrey's hands curl into fists at her side. She feels her nails digging into the soft pads of her palms.

"We're not *friends,*" she spits. "We were never *friends.* And whatever this is that you think you're doing, it needs to stop. Now. You have no right to show up here and—"

He grabs her arm before she even realizes what's happening and yanks her into a narrow alleyway between two buildings. Audrey feels her feet go out from under her, smells the heavy-sweet stench of the nearby dumpsters, sees the butts of discarded cigarettes littering the pavement, and something snaps inside her. Suddenly she's thrashing, desperate to get away, but Colin's grip only tightens as he digs deeper into the muscles of her upper arm. She knows it's going to bruise, leaving her with a branding in the shape of his fingers that she won't be able to scrub away.

"That's enough," he says, a booming command.

Audrey stops, her breath a rapid staccato. She feels like an animal in a snare, desperate to run but aware that struggling will only make it worse.

She's never seen this side of Colin before. She'd caught a passing glimpse of it at her front door, but not like this. It's like she's finally seeing him, the real him, standing before her, exposed for the first time. She can't believe she'd ever been taken in by it, that the shine of his handsome appearance had been enough to hide the dark rot beneath it.

"That's my girl," he says as one hand slides up her body and cups her face. He trails his thumb along Audrey's lower lip, and she feels her stomach turn over.

She should fight, she thinks. She should be doing something, anything except standing here and letting this happen. But her body isn't moving. Why isn't she moving?

He runs the back of his hand along the length of her hair now, slowly, as if memorizing the feel of it against his skin. "Isn't it much easier when you do as you're told?"

Audrey opens her mouth, her lips trembling, but no sound comes out. She feels as though she's paralyzed.

Colin's hand comes to rest beneath her chin; he tips her face up toward his, forcing her to look at him. "I asked you a question," he says, gently now, almost tenderly, unfazed in the face of her terror. "Aren't things easier when you do as you're told?"

"I—" Audrey's voice comes to her in a small squeak as she forces the sound past the hard lump that's formed in her throat. "Yes."

Colin smiles, a twisted grin of satisfaction at her response. "Good girl," he says as he brings his mouth to meet hers, his fingers circling her throat.

Audrey wants to shove him away. She wants to cry, she wants to break, she wants to shatter into one million pieces at his feet. But a small voice in the back of her head hisses a reminder of the truth she isn't ready to face: She brought this on herself. Maybe this is what she deserves, her penance for the pain she'd caused Seth.

Colin kisses her deeply, his tongue forcing its way past her teeth, and she feels her body softening, her survival instincts kicking in. *I just need to get through this,* she thinks. *I need to give him what he wants so that he'll let me go.* She doesn't know this man in the alley, the one who has her back pressed against the rough brick of a filthy wall. This isn't the same man who'd made love to her, who'd explored her body, who'd relished in discovering all the little ways that he could bring her pleasure. This man is dangerous, unpredictable.

"Go on, then," Colin says as his lips leave hers. "Go and make your train. We don't want to keep Seth waiting, now, do we?"

Audrey shakes her head, her hair a wild tangle against the brick wall.

"And next time I call, you'll pick up the phone. Understood?"

Audrey finds herself nodding, and she hates herself for it. But she needs to buy some time. She needs to figure a way out of this mess, because she's realizing now that one of them might not make it out of this affair alive.

29

GEORGINA
Hawthorne Lane

Georgina adjusts the knife and fork beside her plate, nudging them into neat parallel lines, before checking her watch again.

Sebastian is nearly half an hour late now. Across the table, Christina is on her phone, texting or playing some sort of game, Georgina isn't sure. She normally doesn't allow cell phones at the dinner table, but Christina has been made to wait on her brother, who may or may not decide to grace them with his presence, so she's letting it slide tonight.

Georgina called Sebastian earlier and left him a message reminding him of what time he was expected home for dinner, but he hadn't responded, nor has he bothered to come home on time. Colin has always stressed the importance of their children being served homemade meals, family dinners. Though the same rules have never applied to Colin, Sebastian is certainly aware that they still apply to him. It frustrates Georgina to no end that he continues to flout them.

"You might as well start eating," she tells Christina.

Her daughter looks up from her phone, blinking at Georgina from behind the lenses of her glasses as though her mother had just spoken a foreign language.

"Go on," Georgina adds. "No sense in letting it get cold."

Christina sets down her phone and begins to serve herself a portion of Georgina's roasted asparagus.

"So how was school today?" Georgina asks across the near-empty dining room.

"Er, fine," Christina replies. "I had an English test. It was easy, though."

"That's great," Georgina says, nodding her approval.

"I actually wanted to talk to you about something." Christina sets her fork down, stealing a quick glance at her darkened phone screen.

Georgina forces herself not to react. Not to let her face betray the fact that she already knows about Lucas, knows that Christina has secretly been spending time with him. She'd been waiting for her daughter to open up to her about this new relationship, and this seems like the perfect time to have that conversation, while it's just the two of them. Georgina is glad that Christina feels comfortable coming to her with such things, that she's built a strong enough foundation for their relationship that they can talk like this.

"I'm thinking of applying to UCLA next year."

"What? California?" This isn't at all what Georgina was expecting. "But you'll only be a junior! You still need to finish high school!"

"There's an exchange program," Christina says, her eyes on her plate. She picks up her fork and pushes a stalk of asparagus around the edge. "I'd do my senior year in California, get a head start on college courses."

"Honey, I don't know . . ." Georgina thinks of her daughter all alone on the other side of the country, and then she thinks about how Colin would react to this request. He'd never allow it. "You're so young to be so far from home."

"It would be a long shot that I'd even get in, but there's a fellowship I could apply for." The words bound eagerly from Christina's mouth now, as if they're competing to be heard. "My English teacher said that he'd help me with my application, and he thinks that I could have a real chance and—"

"No." It comes out more forcefully than Georgina intended, and Christina falls silent, her eyes round in surprise. Georgina feels terrible. She could hear in Christina's voice how excited she is about this opportunity, how important this is to her, but there's no sense in giving her false hope. Even if Georgina were to agree to it, she'd never be able to get Colin on board. "I'm sorry, but I don't think it's a good idea."

"But I didn't even tell you about the program. Maybe I could—"

The front door swings open, the sound of it interrupting the moment.

"Sebastian?" Georgina calls as she stands from the table. Christina looks at her, a mixture of disappointment and resignation heavy in her pretty green eyes. Georgina's heart contracts in her chest. Her daughter is so young to have her dreams snatched away from her, but she doesn't know how to help her.

"We can talk more about this another time, okay? I promise." She wishes that Christina would understand that Georgina isn't trying to hurt her, she's trying to protect her, to let her down more gently than her father would.

"Yeah," Christina says with a sigh. "Fine." She slouches in her seat.

Sebastian saunters into the dining room. "I'm home. You can stop calling me now."

Georgina releases a heavy sigh, folding her arms over her chest. "Do you have any idea what time it is?"

"No." Sebastian shrugs. "Not really."

"You were supposed to be home for dinner."

"Well, I wasn't."

"I can see that," Georgina snaps.

Sebastian rolls his eyes as if his mother is nothing more than a bothersome gnat. "I had dinner out anyway."

"Out?"

"Yes," Sebastian sneers. "Out. As in outside of this house, as in with my friends and not my *mother*." He spits this last word as though it's unpalatable to his tongue.

"That's incredibly disrespectful, Sebastian. You can't speak to—"

"Mom!" he shouts.

From the corner of her eye, Georgina sees Christina jump in her seat.

"It was one fucking dinner, okay?" Sebastian's palm comes down so hard on the table that the china rattles. "Get off my fucking back about it!"

Georgina stares, open-mouthed, at her son. At this nearly grown man standing before her with such disdain in his eyes. When had he become so angry? When did he start to hate her this much?

"What exactly is going on here?"

Everyone in the room turns at the same time to face Colin, who stands menacingly in the entryway to the dining room.

"Well?" he demands.

No one dares to speak.

"Sebastian," he barks. "Outside. Now."

GEORGINA PACES THE FLOOR OF her bedroom. She'd come up here earlier after Colin pulled Sebastian outside, hoping that if she cracked open the window above the yard, she might be able to catch a snippet of their conversation. She hoped Colin would take a firm hand with Sebastian for once, that he'd rein their son in where she'd clearly lost control. Georgina couldn't make out much of what was said but she distinctly heard the sound of laughter floating toward her.

As she waits for Colin to come upstairs to change, she busies herself by fluffing the pillows, smoothing the duvet, reorganizing the books on his nightstand so that the corners align just so. It's what she does when she's anxious: She cleans. It brings her some comfort to take control of her surroundings, to bring order to what she can. Georgina recognizes that this is likely a by-product of growing up in the relentless chaos of her mother's hoarding, feeling ashamed of the dust and the dirt but being powerless to change it. Though, Georgina supposes, she could certainly have developed worse habits.

She hears the heavy thud of Colin's footsteps ascending the stairs, and in moments he is pushing open the bedroom door. Georgina looks at him expectantly, waiting for him to recount the details of his discussion with Sebastian, but he says nothing as he pulls on the knot of his tie, loosening it around his neck. Normally she'd take Colin's lead, wait for him to talk, but he looks, Georgina thinks, surprisingly calm, given the circumstances. Perhaps she could just ask . . .

"How did it go?"

"Huh?" Colin works at his cuff link. "Oh, fine. It's been sorted out."

"So you spoke to Sebastian about his behavior?" She can't stop thinking about the laughter she overheard. She imagines the two of them outside sharing a joke, doling out pats on the back. She wonders if the tone would have been so jovial if it was *Christina's* behavior in question. She doubts it. Colin has always been far too indulgent with Sebastian.

Colin's hand stills on his cuff, and Georgina freezes. He looks at her, his eyes as cold as ice. "I told you I handled it."

"Sorry," she says, wringing her hands nervously.

"And stop fidgeting like that. You're like a damn child."

Georgina forces her hands to her sides, and as she does, her diamond bracelet catches on the fabric of her dress. She feels the compulsion to fix it, so strong that it's a physical itch that won't be satisfied until she can correct the flaw, but she doesn't. She makes herself stand there and ignore the imperfection.

"So how was your day?" Colin asks, his voice suddenly honey-sweet.

The unexpected change of direction is dizzying, and Georgina finds herself at a loss to remember what exactly she'd done all day. "G-good," she stutters.

"G-good?" he parrots. "Any specifics?"

"Well, I did some gardening, I picked up your dry cleaning..." She counts the tasks off on her fingers as she goes back through her day, wondering why he's suddenly so interested in how she spent her time. Colin rarely asks about the banality of Georgina's day-to-day activities. There must be a right answer here, something specific he's fishing for, but she can't imagine what it is. "Oh, I also finalized some of the details for the fall festival. I checked in with all the vendors, and the permit for the fireworks show came in, so—"

"Did you have any company at the house?"

"Company?"

"Yes. You know what that means, don't you? Was anyone here at the house? Someone who doesn't live here?"

"No..." She didn't have any company today, so she's not sure what Colin is getting at, but she knows her husband, and she knows there must be a reason he's asking.

"Well, that's interesting," he says, his finger tapping on his chin performatively. "Because Sebastian told me that you did." Something changes in him then, as if a cold front has swept across his handsome face, turning it to something ugly and hard.

"I don't know what—"

Colin raises his palm, halting her words. "Before you dig any deeper into your lie, I want you to think." He draws closer so that he's towering over her and taps her on the temple with one long outstretched finger. "Think really hard with that little brain of yours. Did anyone come by today, anyone at all, who had no business being here?"

Suddenly it dawns on her. *Hannah*. He's talking about Hannah. "Oh, right!" she says, a forced lightness to her tone. "Hannah Wilson dropped by while I was gardening this afternoon. It must have slipped my mind."

"Slipped your mind, huh? And what exactly did *Hannah* want?" Her name falls heavily from his tongue like curdled milk.

"She came to collect her mail. Doug mixed up our addresses again, and we just chatted outside in front of the house for a moment. That was all." Georgina offers her husband a weak smile.

Colin grabs her chin, presses his thumb into the soft spot beneath Georgina's jaw, and angles her face upward. He examines her the way one might a horse at auction, searching her face for traces of the lie, or maybe he's looking to see how well she managed to hide her bruised cheekbone from gossiping neighbors.

His eyes narrow. "And what did you tell her?"

"Nothing," Georgina assures him.

Colin's gaze lingers on the swelling beneath Georgina's right eye.

He's usually smarter than that. Colin generally retains enough self-control not to leave a mark on his wife—not where anyone might see it, at least. But he'd been so angry on the night of the auction, especially after Hannah had made a surprise appearance in the courtyard at a rather inopportune moment. He'd had quite a bit to drink after that, surely thinking about the toll this might take on his reputation, and he'd lost his usual measure of restraint once they'd gotten home.

Georgina swallows hard, praying that he believes her. The last thing she needs is for Hannah to be caught in the crosshairs of her marriage. It's bad enough that Georgina got herself here, never mind someone else.

Colin hadn't always been like this. At first, he'd seemed like a dream come true. This handsome, successful man who whisked her away from a home she couldn't wait to escape. They were happy for a time, or at least Georgina thought they were. Until the abuse started. It happened so gradually—a harsh word here, an insult there—that Georgina hadn't seen what was coming. She was like the frog in the pot, the one who didn't notice the temperature slowly rising until it was too late to jump.

Colin lets go of Georgina's face, and his lips curl in disgust. "Seems to me like Hannah needs to learn to mind her own fucking business."

"I'm . . . I'm sorry I didn't tell you about it," Georgina stammers, eager to divert the focus away from Hannah and back to herself. Colin is *her* problem, her cross to bear.

Colin's hand reaches out for her so quickly that Georgina can't react before he grabs a fistful of her hair. Colin loves her long, distinctive red hair. He says it was the first thing he'd noticed about her when they met, the thing that drew him to her across the crowded bar where she'd been out celebrating with some friends from culinary school. Since then, she's thought about cutting it off so many times. She knows he'd be furious, but she imagines herself sitting in the chair at the salon watching it fall away in chunks, collecting in a coppery puddle around her feet.

Colin yanks her head backward so that Georgina's throat is bared to him. She marvels at how her life has come to this, how she finds herself wishing he'd just hit her already. Get it over with. One quick slap, and Georgina could watch the anger drain right out of him. It's like a compulsion, his need to be cruel to her. An addict who just needs his next fix.

Georgina presses her arms to her sides, willing herself to be still.

As she does, she feels her diamond bracelet pressing into her wrist. She's always conscious of it, a shackle made of gold and precious stones. It was one of Colin's gifts, the kind he always gives her after a particularly brutal fight when he's taken things too far. Colin likes to see her wear the jewelry he buys her. Exquisite, expensive things. At first she thought they were signs of his remorse, but now she knows he's not capable of such feelings. Now she can't be sure whether he forces her to wear them because he thinks she should be grateful for his generosity or because he likes to see the reminder of her humiliation.

"You know I don't like it when you lie to me," Colin says, a whispered hiss that rings sour in her ear.

She feels his warm breath against her skin, and she squeezes her eyes shut, wishing she were somewhere else, anywhere but here. Her mind takes her, unbidden, to the first time Colin hurt her. Sebastian was so young then. He wasn't sleeping through the night and Georgina felt as though she might die from the exhaustion. She wished she had the kind of mother who would fly up to New York to help her, to teach her how to do this. She wished that she had *anyone* who could help her. She loved her son, but she didn't know how to do this. She didn't know how to cope with the unexpected depression that haunted her after his birth. Weren't new mothers meant to be blissfully in love, humming lullabies in rosy nurseries as they rocked chubby infants in their arms? What was wrong with Georgina that she always felt like she wanted to cry? That there were days where she couldn't even find the strength to shower? That when Sebastian would squall and scream for hours, she didn't have the motherly instincts to know how to soothe him? She felt like she was lost in it, drowning in the isolated gray days that stretched into long, sleepless nights.

Colin had been of little help. He was in the running for junior partnership at his firm that year, and he'd essentially been living at the office. Georgina could tell how stressed he was. She could feel him changing—the way he'd snap at her over the smallest things, the way he'd come home from work and drop his briefcase at the door and immediately trudge upstairs, hardly stopping to acknowledge Georgina or the crying baby on her hip. Georgina knew Colin's job was a demanding one, but she'd needed his help. Couldn't he see that she needed him? Couldn't he see how lonely she was?

Georgina remembers the night it all changed, the night she realized just how alone she really was. Sebastian had woken in the dark, early hours of the morning and Georgina could hear him crying, that high-pitched scream that seemed to punctuate her every moment. She cringed. She knew she should go to him, but she was so tired. So very tired. When was the last time she'd slept through the night? Maybe she'd feel better, more like herself again, if she could just *sleep*. She rolled over, pulling her pillow over her head, blocking out the noise.

Colin grabbed her shoulder, shaking her awake. "The baby is crying."

"Huh?" Georgina pulled the pillow away. She must have managed to doze off.

"The baby. He's crying," Colin repeated, irritated now. "Don't you hear him?"

"I need to sleep, Colin," she insisted. "I'm tired all of the time and—"

"*I* need to sleep," he barked. "You're tired? You're home all day long! *I* have a client meeting in the morning, and I can't be up listening to this all night!"

"So go put him back to sleep!" She rolled over, indignant. Sebastian was Colin's son too. *He* could get up with him for once.

Colin yanked the comforter off Georgina's body, and the rush of cool air pimpled her skin. "What kind of mother are you? You're just going to sleep while your baby cries for you?"

Georgina sat up, her eyes flashing with anger as she glowered at her husband in the dark. "Maybe I am!"

Suddenly his open palm collided with her cheek. He'd *hit* her. Colin had *hit* her. They both sat there in the dark, stunned into silence for a moment while the realization washed over her.

"I'm . . . oh God, Georgina, I'm so sorry." He pulled her to his chest.

Georgina sat rigidly in his arms, trying to make sense of what had just happened. This wasn't Colin. Sure, he could be moody at times, but he'd never been violent before. He wasn't a monster. He was Colin, the man she loved, the man everyone was always telling her she was so lucky to have. And she *was* lucky... wasn't she?

Colin cried, his warm tears soaking through the thin cotton of her nightgown, and the feeling of it on her skin brought her out of the state of shock she'd been in.

She wrapped her arms around him, consoling him, though she wasn't sure why.

"I've just been so stressed at work," he said, sobbing. "And with the baby waking us up every night, I—I don't know what came over me. I'm not that person, Georgina. Please tell me you know I'm not that person."

He looked at her, his eyes glittering with tears, silently pleading with her to forgive him. Georgina had never seen Colin like this before, vulnerable, afraid. He was giving her a rare glimpse of who he was behind the strong facade he always maintained.

"I know," she said, her hand rubbing circles on his back.

"I can't lose you," he whispered, his voice cracking with remorse.

"We're going to be okay," she said, as if speaking it aloud could will it into truth. What Colin did... it had been an accident. They were both sleep-deprived, dealing with the stress of being new parents. She knew her husband—he wasn't a bad person. He'd just made a mistake.

Georgina silenced the little voice in the back of her head that told her that this wasn't normal. That mistakes like those should never happen. What would she do if that voice was right? If she'd made a mistake in giving up everything to marry Colin?

She listened to the sound of her infant son's plaintive cries. He needed her. And she couldn't do this on her own. Most of the time she felt like she could hardly make it through the day, so how was she supposed to start over? How would she provide for her son with no career, no support, no one she could turn to? She couldn't. She had to believe that Colin was telling her the truth, that it would never happen again.

"I'm going to make this right," Colin swore, clinging to Georgina's arm as she got up to tend to their son, and she'd wanted more than anything to believe him.

The next day, he came home with a gold necklace.

"Get undressed," he demands now. No sign of the remorse he once felt at the pain he caused her. It seemed to get easier for him over time, his outbursts more frequent, his apologies less sincere until eventually they'd stopped altogether.

Georgina complies, her eyes avoiding his, her face burning with shame as she unbuttons her blouse, lets her skirt drop to the floor. She can't look at her husband, doesn't want to see how much he's come to take pleasure in her shame.

Georgina wonders whether something happened with his latest mistress. It's been so long since Colin looked at her in this way. Yes, Georgina knows about Colin's many affairs. But they're of no consequence to her. It was only a matter of time before whoever this person was saw his true colors. And good for her for getting away while she could. Georgina is just biding her time until she can do the same.

She'd tried leaving him once before. It was after Christina was born, when she realized she couldn't blame the stress of Colin's job for the darkness in him. He hadn't laid a hand on her in almost a year, since before she'd gotten pregnant for the second time, and that was just long enough to allow her to convince herself that it wouldn't happen again. Until it did. She can't recall now what pushed him over the edge that day, why he'd struck her in their kitchen while Christina napped in her crib and Sebastian played on the floor of the living room, pushing metal cars across the carpet. But she remembers the way he'd looked at her afterward, the way she no longer saw guilt in his eyes but disgust. She remembers the way Sebastian had stopped playing, the way he looked, curiously, at his mother, as if waiting for her to show him how to react. She'd smiled at Sebastian, assured him that Mommy was okay, that he should go back to his cars, but she knew then that she'd have to leave.

That night, she waited until Colin fell asleep and then carried her two beautiful sleeping babies into the car and strapped them securely into their car seats. She didn't have a plan, she didn't know where she was going, but she knew she couldn't raise them in that house. Not with him. He was going to ruin them, her perfect, innocent babies.

Georgina closed the passenger doors as quietly as she could, but when she turned around to get into the car, Colin was standing in their driveway, his eyes glinting menacingly in the moonlight.

"Going somewhere?"

"I can't live like this, Colin," she'd said, a slight tremor in her voice at the sight of him.

"And what is your plan, exactly? You have no job, no money of your own, no friends, nowhere to go." He smiled then, his teeth a flash of white in the dark, and Georgina had never hated him more. It was the first time she'd realized that he'd done this on purpose, that he'd trapped her. He'd built her a gilded cage and she'd naively walked right into it.

"I'd rather live on the streets than with you."

"You're certainly welcome to do that," Colin said calmly. "But you aren't taking my children with you. If you leave, I can promise you that you'll never see them again. I'm a lawyer, remember? A partner at one of the biggest firms in the country. I know every judge in this county and the next, and every single one of them loves me."

Georgina could picture it, Colin laughing in the courtroom, charming the judges he practiced in front of like he did everyone else.

"There's not a chance in hell that you walk away with these kids," he continued. "So just know that if you leave, you're leaving them behind."

Georgina knew he was telling the truth. Colin would fight tooth and nail to keep her children away from her. Not because he wanted them but because he didn't want her to have them. That would be her punishment for daring to walk away from him. She could fight back, she could try, but he would win. He always did.

"You can't give them the kind of life that I can," Colin added as if reading her mind. He had so much while she had so little. "Look at all of this." He swept his arm across the view of their beautiful house, their quiet cul-de-sac. "It's everything you ever wanted for them, isn't it? So much more than you ever had. Are you going to take that away from them?"

Georgina looked through the car window at her peaceful, sleeping babies, at their tiny, innocent faces. If she left Colin, she'd risk leaving them with *him*. Who would protect them then?

"And if you do," Colin said with a sneer, "if you leave me, if you leave these kids, I'll never let them forget it. I'll make sure they know exactly what kind of mother you were."

Georgina opened the car door and lifted Christina from her car seat. Her infant daughter curled into a tiny ball, her breath soft on Georgina's neck as she held her close. Georgina imagined the things Colin would tell her as she grew older, the lies he'd feed her, poisoning her against her mother. She knew then that there was no escape.

Georgina would have given it all up. The nice neighborhood. The big house. The money, the comfort, the status. None of it was worth the price she was paying. But she'd never risk losing her children.

"You belong to me," Colin says now, his eyes like burning coals raking over her exposed skin. "And you will not lie to me again."

"I'm s-sorry," Georgina says, her words as broken as she is.

"Well, luckily for you, I know exactly how you can make it up to me." Colin reaches for his belt, the metal buckle jangling as he unfastens it.

30

MAGGIE
Benton Avenue

Maggie feels numb as she walks through her front door, then pushes it closed with a creak that seems to echo through the small house. *The drugs are gone.* She lost them. Whatever happens next is going to be all her fault.

A part of her wants to tell Dean the truth. To get it over with quickly, come clean and plead for his forgiveness. But a larger part of her is afraid of how he'll react.

She pads into the bedroom silently, like a ghost moving through her own home, and finds Dean pacing the floors, his hands running through his thick dark hair over and over again.

He stops immediately when he sees her, zeroing in on her with laser focus. "Where the hell have you been?"

"I had to run some errands," she lies. She sees then that his pupils are dilated to the size of dinner plates. It's like looking into two endless black voids. Maggie finds it unnerving.

"You had to run errands now? When we're in the middle of a fucking shitstorm?" He doesn't wait for Maggie's reply, just barrels ahead, the words leaping manically from his tongue. "It doesn't matter. I figured out how to solve our little problem. I came up with a plan and it's fucking brilliant."

"A plan?"

"Yeah. See, next week is Halloween!"

"I know, but—"

He's excited now, almost salivating at the thought of it. "We're gonna hit the houses on the other side of town. And Halloween is the perfect time to do it. Everyone will be out of their houses trick-or-treating and shit, and we'll have the perfect cover to be walking around the neighborhood ringing doorbells. See? I told you it's brilliant."

"You want to rob people's houses? Dean, we—"

"Those rich fuckers uptown have had this coming for a long time. Haven't I been saying that? Didn't I tell you I'd find a way to settle the score?" Beads of sweat gather at his hairline as he pounds his fist into his palm. "And I did it. I figured out how to get back at those pricks and find the money we need to get us out of this shit with Mike at the same time." He smiles, a contorted grin that elicits a spasm of fear in Maggie's chest.

"Okay," she says. Because she knows there's no use arguing with him when he's like this. He's already fixated on the idea. She'll just have to wait for him to sober up to try to talk some sense into him. She thinks of the jam jar, so full now that it's getting difficult to screw on the lid. Soon this won't have to be her life anymore. Soon she'll be free.

Dean grinds his teeth, his jaw rocking. "What about those people you work for?"

"What about them?"

"They live up on that fancy cul-de-sac, the one with all the big houses. They have anything worth taking?"

Maggie swallows hard. "No, they—"

"I'm sure they do," Dean continues, nodding as the idea spreads in his mind like poison. "Jewelry and shit they wouldn't even miss."

Maggie shakes her head vigorously. She can't let him rob the Sullivans. They've always treated her so well, and their house feels like a sanctuary to her, more of a home than the one she lives in. She hates the thought of Dean invading their nice, clean space, dirtying it, taking things that his fingers have no business touching. She imagines him picking up one of baby Lila's teddy bears, his stained nails digging into the soft plush, and it makes her feel queasy.

"No," she says. "You can't."

Dean rounds on her, his eyes flashing with rage. "I *can't*? And exactly why can't I, Maggie?"

Dean takes a step toward her, and Maggie feels her teeth start to chatter in her skull. "They have . . . cameras," she tries feebly.

"And you'll know how to get around them."

"But we could get caught, and—"

"And you work in their house. If they find you there, you just say you left your keys behind or something."

"No, I—"

She could call the police, give them an anonymous tip. That's possible, isn't it? But what if Dean were to find out it was her?

"You what, Maggie? Because, honestly, I'd love to fucking know how we got into this mess in the first place."

Maggie can sense the tide of Dean's high turning, the early manic euphoria giving way to aggression, paranoia.

"Did you take the stash for yourself? Maybe you thought you could cut me out of the deal, do this on your own."

"Dean, no. Of course not. I wouldn't." She backs away from him, small tentative steps.

"Well, I think you would. First the product goes missing on your watch and now you're telling me that you don't want me saving both our fucking necks. Like you're more worried about the rich assholes you work for than you are about me. They don't care about you. You know that, don't you? You're just the hired help."

"It's not that."

"Then tell me what it is, Maggie. Because I know you're lying to me. And if you don't tell me the truth right now, maybe I'll just have to go over there tonight."

Maggie imagines little Carter waking up in the middle of the night, how terrified he would be to find Dean ransacking his beautiful, peaceful home. She imagines Lila crying and Dean, in a coke-fueled rage, shaking her to shut her up. She imagines the look of horror on Ms. Sullivan's face when she learns that Maggie brought this monster to their doorstep. This is all Maggie's fault.

"I—I lost them. The drugs." The truth spills out of her before she can stop it. "There was a cop, and I panicked, so I stashed them behind a dumpster, but when I went back to get them, they were gone, and I'm so sorry, I never meant—"

Dean's fist collides with her ribs, knocking the wind from her lungs. Maggie doubles over, her arms wrapping around her body protectively, but Dean's knee slams into the underside of her chin. Maggie feels her jaw snap shut, tastes the warm blood filling her mouth.

She falls to the floor and curls into a ball while Dean kicks her over and over again, the toe of his boot repeatedly crashing into her ribs, her spine, the back of her skull. Maggie whimpers with pain as his foot finds her kidney and she's overcome with nausea.

She doesn't plead with him to stop. She knows by now that begging will only prolong her suffering. Instead, she covers her face, protecting herself where she can, until her husband grows tired of hurting her.

Dean is out of breath when he's finally through, panting as he bends over, bracing his hands on his knees to glare down at Maggie, bloodied on the floor at his feet.

"Look at me," he demands.

Maggie turns her head with great effort, her vision unfocused, blood and tears stinging her eyes as she looks up into Dean's glowering face. *How can I ever have thought he was beautiful?*

"You will never lie to me again," he says, the words curling out from between his clenched teeth. "Now, is there anything else you'd like to tell me?"

"I'm . . . leaving you," Maggie manages, her voice nothing more than a breathy whisper but there nonetheless. She hates that it took her so long to find it that she barely has one left to use.

Dean turns. He rummages through a drawer for a moment, then pulls something from it, holding it out for Maggie to see.

Maggie blinks slowly, fighting for consciousness as her mind struggles to process what Dean is holding: an empty jam jar.

A rictus grin creaks slowly across his face like cracking ice. "You have nowhere to go."

HALLOWEEN NIGHT

Transcript of anonymous call
October 31, 2024

Anonymous caller: Uh, hi, I wanted to report something that I saw on Hawthorne Lane? I, uh, I don't know if it has anything to do with what happened there tonight, but I thought maybe I should call just in case.

Detective Olsen: May I ask who this is?

Anonymous caller: I'd rather not say, if that's okay?

Detective Olsen: All right. Let's just start by you telling me what you saw. Any information is helpful in a case like this.

Anonymous caller: There was this man wandering around the block. And he just, I don't know, something felt off about him. For one thing, he was alone. No family or kids or anything. That's what caught my attention at first. And the fact that I didn't recognize him from the neighborhood. He was just walking around slowly, looking at all the houses like he was casing them or something. He just seemed very suspicious to me.

Detective Olsen: Can you describe what this man looked like?

Anonymous caller: Good-looking guy, in his thirties, maybe.

Detective Olsen: That's very helpful, thank you. Now, if you're comfortable giving me your name, we could—

Call ended

TWO DAYS
BEFORE
HALLOWEEN

31
LIBBY
Hawthorne Lane

Libby's side aches as she picks up the cloth napkin in her lap, dabs at the corners of her eyes. She can't remember the last time she laughed like this. The last time she felt so light.

"You don't know how much I needed that," she tells Peter.

He beams at her over the table, the rounded tops of his cheeks rising to meet the frames of his glasses. "Happy to be of service," he replies.

Libby can tell that he means it too. That he's happy simply because he made her happy. Maybe she was wrong, maybe this dating thing doesn't have to be complicated at all. She'd made it out to be this looming, frightening obstacle in her head, but in reality, it's rather nice to be sitting here in this quaint little restaurant with such pleasant company. The problem, she realizes, is that she was looking at this all wrong—she'd looked at dating someone new as the end of a chapter of her life, the final nail in the coffin of her dying marriage, but she sees now that it's not an end, it's a beginning. The beginning of something that feels as airy and unencumbered as champagne bubbles.

"It still feels so strange to be sitting here with you, live and in person," she tells him, spinning the stem of her wineglass between her fingers. He looks different outside of the pixelated square she's used to looking at on his dating profile, better somehow. She'd come to associate him with that one static image, the parameters of him rigid and unchanging. But here, in person, he's so much more. There's a brightness to him, a realness that even the best camera can't capture.

"I know what you mean," he replies. "But at the same time, it kind of *isn't* strange, if that makes sense? Maybe it's because we've already been talking for a while, but I don't know, sitting here with you, it doesn't feel like a first date. It feels like we're old friends."

"Friends, then?" Libby smiles playfully. "Is that the direction we're going in?"

Even in the soft glow of the candlelight between them, Libby can see him blush.

Peter adjusts his glasses. "Er, no. At least I hope not. Gosh, I'm really awful at this, aren't I?" He laughs, and it flows as easily from his mouth as water in a brook. "What I meant to say is that even though we've just met, I feel like I've known you all my life."

He looks at Libby, the light from the candle dancing playfully across his features, and it causes something to stir in her. A feeling that has long lain dormant. He really *is* quite attractive. It was hard to see it at first, behind the rather dated way he styles his hair, the thick rims of his glasses—Peter isn't the type to fuss over his appearance—but sitting across from him now, it's all she sees. "I know exactly what you mean."

There's a silence then, but for once, Libby doesn't rush to fill it. She finds that she's comfortable here, that she can exist in the gaps between their words.

"I'm glad we did this," Peter says. "I was pretty nervous about tonight."

"Were you?" Libby hadn't considered that, that Peter might have been feeling the same way she was about meeting. He seemed so confident, so sure, in his messages.

"Well." He drums his fingers on the tablecloth. "To be honest, this is the first date I've been on in . . . hell, I don't even know. Years."

"Me too," Libby admits, her voice small.

"I was afraid I'd forgotten how to do this. That it would be awkward and I'd make a fool of myself trying to impress you."

Libby's fingers rise to her lips, covering the smile that's crept onto her face. "I was feeling exactly the same way."

Peter laughs, and Libby finds that she loves the sound of it. "And just look at us now. This isn't even the *slightest* bit awkward."

Libby's smile grows wider. "Not in the least. But seriously, though, I didn't realize that this was your first time on a date since... since your..."

"You can say *divorce,* Libby, it's not a curse word." He chuckles. "And, yes, it is. I know we talked a little bit about this in our messages, but I was married for a long time. And when it ended, I wasn't sure that I'd ever be ready to move on."

"What changed?" Libby asks. Maybe it's strange, asking Peter's advice about how to move on from her own marriage while she sits here across the table from him on their first date, but somehow she feels like he understands.

"I'm not sure, to be honest with you. I think one day I just got tired of being alone, you know? And I realized that the longer I waited to put myself out there, the harder it was going to be to do it. So I signed up for a few dating sites. I never really seemed to connect with anyone, though. If I'm being frank, I'm not sure my heart was in it before. I was sort of just going through the motions, edging into the whole dating thing slowly. But then you popped up as a match, and, I don't know, something just felt different this time. I wanted to know you."

Libby feels a warm flush spread across her cheeks. Maybe this really could work. Or maybe it will crash and burn. There's no way for Libby to know for sure. But in this moment, it feels so good, so very good, to be understood, to talk to someone who has lived through this difficult thing she's been grappling with on her own for so long.

Their waiter appears beside their table, holding out a leather billfold. "Would you care to see a dessert menu?"

Libby looks at Peter across the table. She isn't ready for the night to end. She hopes he's feeling it too, this connection that seems to be growing between them.

"Life is too short to skip dessert," Peter says. He tosses Libby a wink as he takes the menu from the waiter's hand.

LIBBY FEELS LIKE SHE'S FLOATING as she drives home. It was a wonderful evening. She and Peter stayed at the restaurant talking, sipping wine, sampling decadent desserts, lost for hours in their own little world until they noticed the staff mopping the floors, the hostess yawning at her stand waiting to close up for the night.

Libby can't remember the last time she smiled so much, the last time she had so much to say. She found that Peter was easy to talk to. Libby loved the way he really seemed to listen to her, never once reaching for his phone, never glancing down at his watch. She'd forgotten what it was like to have someone take an interest in her.

She takes the Sterling Valley exit off the highway and she's back on more familiar roads. She hopes she didn't talk Peter's ear off tonight, but she doesn't think he minded. He'd asked her a lot of questions and even suggested a second date at the end of the evening. Libby smiles again just thinking about it.

"Listen," he said as he walked her back to her car, opened the door for her. "I know this is terrible form, and I'm supposed to do that whole thing where I don't call you for four days. Or is it three?"

"Pretty sure it's four."

"Right, four, then. But would you mind terribly if we skipped all that? I like you, Libby. And I'm not interested in playing games at this stage in my life. So if it's all the same to you, I think I'll just tell you right now: I'd like to see you again."

"I'd like to see you again too, Peter." She smiled up at him, her eyes sparkling.

He tucked one of her blond curls behind her ear, his touch as gentle as a brush of feathered wings. "Then it's a date. Just tell me when."

Libby rolls to a stop at an intersection, the red light suspended above the street glowing bright in the dark night. It takes her a moment to register where she is. If she makes a right at this intersection, she'll be headed back home, to Hawthorne Lane, but if she makes a left, the road will take her to Bill's town house.

Libby realizes with a start that this is the first time all night that she's thought of Bill. Of Heather. Tonight, with Peter, was the first time in the past year that her mind hasn't been consumed with regrets over mistakes she'd made in her marriage, with worries about the future. Tonight, she wasn't Bill's soon-to-be-ex-wife, she wasn't Lucas's mom, she was just . . . Libby. And that was enough.

Libby doesn't know whether things will work out with Peter in the long run—after all, this was only their first date—but she knows now that either way, she'll be okay.

As the light turns green, she looks in both directions down the empty stretches of pavement, at the crossroads of her life.

She flicks on her right-turn signal. It's time for her to move on.

32

HANNAH
Hawthorne Lane

Hannah's fingers twitch over the keyboard of her laptop. She tells herself there's no point in checking her email again, that there will be nothing new, that it's a dead end, that it always has been. But still, she feels drawn to it, as if it's a compulsion she can no longer resist, the way one might pick at an old scab.

"Good morning, gorgeous."

The sound of Mark's voice just over her shoulder makes Hannah jump in her seat. She slams the top of her laptop shut as he nears the back of the couch; his strong hands reach over it to massage her shoulders.

"You're up awfully early," he says before leaning down to tenderly kiss Hannah's neck.

She forces a smile as she looks up at her husband, into his kind, guileless eyes. "Just wanted to get a head start on some of the event programming for the library next month." The lie is thick and filmy on her tongue.

"I love how much you love your job," he says, trailing his fingers along Hannah's collarbone. "But if you're open to a distraction..."

Mark's hand travels lower, dips under the neckline of her shirt, fingers the lace at the edge of her bra. She feels a swell of want as he cups her breast, his thumb moving methodically over the mound of her nipple, his breath warm in her ear.

"Come back to bed," he says, his voice a low growl. "I can be a little late getting to the office today..."

"I..." Hannah wants to. There is nothing she wants more than to follow Mark back to their bedroom. She wants to be the kind of newlywed bride who makes love to her husband on a sunny morning. But she isn't. She can't be. Not with all the lies that have built up between them, the threat to their marriage that lurks around every corner. How can she let herself go? How can she be in the moment with Mark while knowing that she could lose him at any second? "I should probably finish up here."

Mark sighs. He walks around the side of the couch and positions himself next to Hannah. Gently, he lifts the laptop from her thighs, sets it on the coffee table in front of them, and takes her hands in his.

"Talk to me," he says, his fingers massaging the inside of her wrist.

"About what?" The words spring too lightly from her lips.

"Is it me? Have I done something to upset you?"

"Mark, no, of course not. Why would you think that?"

Mark lets go of her hands, pulls his own back into his lap. "I'm at a loss here, Hannah, I really am. I feel like . . . you've changed since we moved here. You've been so distant. Secretive. At first I chalked it up to the move. I know coming here, to Hawthorne Lane, was a big adjustment for you. But it's been almost three months now, and it feels as though this space between us is only getting bigger. Was this move a mistake? Are you happy here?"

"I am," she responds without hesitation. "I love my job, I've made friends, I *am* happy here."

"So, then, what is it? What's changed between us?"

Mark's eyes search Hannah's face, and she can see the hurt in them. The confusion. It's enough to make her feel as if her heart is being torn out of her chest. She wants to tell him the truth. She wants to assure him that *she* is the problem, not him. But she knows that she can't. She thinks of the notes, the threat that is circling her like a shark in open water. Hannah doesn't know how it's possible, but someone, somewhere, knows about her past, about the worst thing she's ever done, and they're going to use it against her. She can't let Mark be dragged down with her. Hannah hates that her lies are hurting him, but she knows that the truth would do more than hurt him—it would destroy him. "Nothing has—"

"Please don't," Mark cuts in. "Please don't pretend you don't see it. I'm losing you, Hannah. Piece by piece, day by day, I'm losing you. And you won't even tell me why. It feels like torture, just sitting here watching it happen without knowing how to fix it."

"I'm right here, I promise you. I haven't gone anywhere."

"Maybe physically you're here, but . . . I can see it when it happens. When you drift off to somewhere I can't reach you. I thought we were closer than this. I thought . . . God, I thought we were going to start trying for a baby. But now you won't even let me near you."

Hannah winces at the cold jab of truth in his words. They *were* supposed to be starting a family. It's what they'd both wanted. But things have changed for Hannah and she can't tell Mark why. She can't explain how terrified she is to bring a child into their lives when her past is hanging over her head like a swinging blade. She can't explain how much she wants this, how every time she walks past an empty bedroom in their house, she imagines the nursery it could someday be and how having this dream, this baby, ripped from her arms feels like her punishment for all the mistakes she's made. She can't tell her husband that every time he reaches for her in the dark, her mind is somewhere else. How when she closes her eyes, she feels not his hands on her but her own hands on skin slicked with warm blood, her fingers fumbling for a pulse she already knows she won't find. She can't tell Mark any of it. Not without telling him all of it.

"I'm sorry," she says. Because it's all she can say. And she *is* sorry. Desperately sorry that she dragged him down into the dark well of her past. She'd thought she could outrun it, that marrying Mark was her chance at a fresh start. But she should've known that it would catch up with her eventually and that when it did, it would drown them both.

Mark watches her as if waiting, hoping, for more, but it doesn't come. He nods, and there's a new heaviness to it, his gaze drifting away from Hannah as he stands. "I'm going to take a shower," he says. "When you're ready to let me in, you know where to find me."

Hannah leans back into the couch, the sound of her husband walking away from her causing tears to prickle at the backs of her eyes. She's done this to them. To him. She hates herself for it.

Outside the window, morning sun shines on another day on Hawthorne Lane. Birds twitter in the trees, which are resplendent in their autumnal palette—splashes of fiery reds, vivid oranges, golden yellows. Porches have been festooned with hand-carved pumpkins and bumpy, curling gourds, and crisp brown leaves dot the paved sidewalks. The bucolic scene clashes so harshly with the gray gloom that hovers over Hannah's living room that she stands up and goes to pull the curtains closed, ready to shut herself away from it. But as her fingers curl around the fabric, she sees something that gives her pause.

Georgina. She jogs lightly down her front steps in sneakers and black Lycra pants with a matching quarter-zip top, and her long red hair has been pulled back into a shiny ponytail that swishes behind her as she moves. Oversize sunglasses hide her eyes, but from what Hannah can see, her face looks as flawless as ever, no trace of the swelling Hannah had noticed days earlier.

Hannah feels her muscles coiling beneath her skin, anger clouding her vision. Georgina reminds her so much of her own mother. The way she'd dab at her face with foundation and concealers, wincing as the blending brushes dusted over her broken skin. The way she'd avoid her friends, their neighbors, blaming chronic migraines for her absences. Hannah had felt so powerless then. Much the way she feels now, her marriage on the verge of implosion with no means to stop it. But Georgina. Georgina she can do something about. It might be too late for Hannah to divert the course of her own life, but maybe it's not too late for her to help Georgina.

Hannah quickly pulls on a pair of sneakers, shrugs a jacket over her T-shirt, and runs outside just in time to fall in step with Georgina as she passes the driveway.

"Good morning," Hannah says.

Georgina slows, jogs in place. "Good morning! I was just heading out for a run."

"Mind if I join you?"

"Er . . ." Georgina looks uncertain. Hannah can see an internal battle playing out across her face, but in the end, politeness wins, as Hannah hoped it would. "Of course. I didn't realize you were a runner."

Hannah looks down at her ensemble. Bright white sneakers, a bulky jacket. "I'm not, usually. But I'm trying to get into it."

"All right, well, I'm just headed up to the jogging path if you'd like to come along." She nods toward the entrance to the woods that surrounds their cul-de-sac.

"Great!" Hannah chirps, though she's not certain she'll be able to keep up with Georgina. Just looking at her, at the lean, toned muscles of her body, her expensive athletic wear, Hannah can tell that she's outmatched.

Georgina sets off, her strides long and graceful, and Hannah clumsily trots along at her side like a puppy.

"Do you . . . run . . . often?" Hannah asks as they approach the entrance to the jogging path. She's embarrassingly out of breath already.

"I try to. Whenever I find the time." Georgina's words effortlessly float from her lips, as weightless as clouds. Hannah makes a resolution to start doing this sort of thing more often.

They turn off the sidewalk and onto the paved path through the woods. Hannah has walked by this place so many times, but she asks herself now why she never made the time to explore it. She feels like she's entered a different world. In the woods, the autumn trees form a kaleidoscopic canopy, a collage of vibrant colors and rich textures that arch over their heads. The air feels fuller here, saturated with the scent of morning dew and fresh soil. There's something almost sacred about it, the way that the spongy ground, the soft bark of the trees, has created a lush silence around them. If she didn't know better, she would think they were a million miles away from their neat suburban town. Hannah jogs beside Georgina for a while, savoring the solitude of this place, the fresh air filling and expanding her lungs, and suddenly she finds that her breathing is not as labored, her legs not as tired. As if just being here in these woods has transformed her into someone new.

"I'm sorry, you know," Hannah starts, her voice small against the vastness of the forest around them. "About the other day. I shouldn't have approached you at your house like that."

"It's all right," Georgina tells her. "It's already forgotten."

"It's just..." Hannah pushes herself forward, striving to keep up with Georgina. "I know what you're going through. And I know how lonely it can feel and—"

"I appreciate the concern," Georgina says. "But, really, there's nothing to worry about."

"My mom used to say the same thing." The words ring out among the quiet trees. "Her name was Julie." There's something freeing in saying it aloud, in releasing her memory here in the wilderness.

Georgina's pace slows and Hannah hopes that means that she has her attention, that she's willing to listen. "My father. He was like Colin. Well, in a lot of ways he wasn't. He was broke, he drank too much and worked too little, but he was like him in other ways. He was controlling, always putting down my mother. And he'd... hurt her. She thought I didn't know, thought that she was hiding it from me, but she wasn't."

Georgina stops, turns to face Hannah. "I'm so sorry you went through all that. Truly, I am. It sounds like it was terrible. But my marriage, it's nothing like that."

Hannah's heart sinks. For a moment there she'd thought she was getting through to Georgina, but it seems that she's still beyond reach.

"And even if it was," Georgina continues, her voice uncertain as she resumes a slow jog, "even if you were right about Colin, there's nothing you or anyone else could do to stop it."

"Maybe I can't," Hannah says, following behind Georgina as they round the next bend, turning out of the woods and back onto Hawthorne Lane, "but you don't have to go through it alone. There are places you can go, you—"

"Please," Georgina begs. "Just let this go."

"I can't," Hannah says. "If you won't get help for yourself, do it for your daughter."

"Christina doesn't need help. Colin would never hurt her."

Hannah shakes her head. "You might not see it now, but living with a man like that, it does things to a kid. You might think you're shielding her from it, just like my mother thought, but Christina knows, Georgina, I promise you she does, and when she gets older it's—"

"Hannah."

The tremor in her tone stops Hannah in her tracks. She follows the older woman's gaze to her front door, where Colin leans against the frame, one hand raised in greeting, a plastic smile pinned to his lips.

"Please. I'm begging you. Just stay away from me and my family."

33
CHRISTINA
Hawthorne Lane

Christina Pembrook bends to pick up a fallen leaf from the walking trail. It's a maple, once red but now browned with age to the color of toasted cinnamon. She adds it to the bundle in her hand that she's already collected. It's an old habit, picking up leaves as she walks. It's something she used to do when she was little, when she'd walk this trail with her mom. Her mom was always good with stuff like that, making things fun for her and Sebastian. They weren't just out for a walk—they were on a scavenger hunt, gathering leaves in every color they could find, willowy stems clutched in small palms like discovered treasures.

Lucas looks over at the growing collection in Christina's hand, but he doesn't comment on it. He probably thinks she's such a weirdo, picking up leaves like a little kid. Christina should just drop them.

But then he leans down and grabs a leaf of his own, this one canary yellow. He inspects it for a moment, then hands it to her. "You don't have one like this yet."

She blushes. "Thanks."

"I'm glad you were able to meet me today," he says, his hazel eyes tinted a more mesmerizing shade of green than any of the foliage around them.

"Me too."

"It's strange, hanging out with you in broad daylight. I was beginning to think you were a vampire or something."

Christina laughs. "No. No fangs. I just have strict parents and it's easier to sneak out at night." Well, it *was* easier, until one of the new neighbors saw her creeping across the front lawn one night and texted her mom. That sort of put an end to all the cloak-and-dagger meetups.

"Well, I like the daytime version of you."

He sweeps a lock of her blond hair off her cheek and gently tucks it behind her ear. Christina feels a warm flush travel up her neck, ending where his fingers had grazed her skin.

She and Lucas have known each other for most of their lives, but only recently has she started to get the sense that he really sees her, as maybe more than just the girl who lives across the street. She kind of still can't believe it. She's not exactly at the top of the social pyramid at school, which never really bothered her before, but Lucas is right up near the peak. Christina can certainly see why. He's a star athlete, an honor student, and he looks like . . . *that*. She risks a glance up at him now, at the swoop of his dark hair, the square set of his jaw, the muscular slope of his shoulders. Somehow, *that* boy has chosen her. She's pretty sure this is what it feels like to win the lottery.

Christina hasn't told anyone about Lucas yet, about this growing thing that's sprouted up between them. Her best friend, Amy, would absolutely *die* over the news that she's seeing Lucas Corbin. But her parents would be apoplectic if they found out that she's been sneaking around with her maybe sort-of boyfriend. Besides, she likes having this for herself, this amazing, bubbly secret that makes her feel lighter than air. She isn't ready to share it with anyone but Lucas yet.

Lucas takes her hand, weaving his fingers through hers, and leads her off the paved path and onto a narrow dirt trail carved by the footprints of teenagers before them. She knows where they're headed: to the clearing where kids hang out sometimes, hidden away from parents and teachers and every other adult who wants to tell them what to do. She and Lucas have found the occasional beer bottle here, cigarette butts left behind by other people, but over the past weeks, Christina has come to think of the clearing as *their* spot, hers and Lucas's. She likes to imagine it that way, as if it exists only for them.

The trail narrows, and Lucas steps in front of Christina. He ducks under a low-hanging branch and holds back the foliage for her as she passes beneath it.

It's so different, being here in the middle of the afternoon. At night, lit only by silver moonlight, the forest is all monochrome shadows and rustling branches like hollow bones knocking together in the wind. But now this place feels softer, more alive. Chipmunks scurry up tree trunks, their cheeks stuffed with plump acorns, and the ground, padded with a bed of fallen leaves, is spongy beneath the soles of their sneakers. Somewhere in the distance, a pair of cardinals whistle their melodic tune, and a gentle breeze, heavy with the fresh scent of sap, winds lazily between the trees.

"Here we are," Lucas says as he leads Christina into the clearing.

There isn't much to the place. A fallen log that serves as seating, a circular patch of grass, and a small firepit that was both built and extinguished long ago. But there's still something magical about it. Or maybe the magic is in who she's with.

Lucas sits on the log, stretching his long legs out in front of him, angling his face up to the sun as if soaking up the final rays before winter sets in. Christina wonders what they'll do then, if they'll still be able to come to this place when the trails are frozen over, buried under a blanket of snow. And then she wonders what will happen after that, if, when the leaves turn again next fall, she'll still be here to see it.

Christina hasn't told Lucas about her plan to apply for the exchange program in California next year. Not that she thinks he'll try to talk her out of it—this thing between them isn't nearly that serious yet, and she can totally imagine Lucas being supportive of her dream—but because she's afraid of how much it will hurt when he doesn't. Not that it matters. Christina knows she'll never be able to convince her mom to let her go, even if she does manage to get accepted.

Lucas nudges her with his elbow. "What are you thinking about?"

"My mom."

Lucas laughs and it's as wild and free as the forest around them. "I take a girl out on a romantic walk through the woods and she's sitting here thinking about her mom."

Christina smiles, swatting him playfully on the arm. "Wasn't what you had in mind?"

"Not exactly," he replies. "But I think I can change that."

He leans toward her, his eyes slowly closing, and then his lips are on hers. Christina relishes the softness of them, the gentle intention of his hand as it reaches out to hold hers, the moment as sweet as cotton candy on a summer night. This is how it always is between them: innocent, reverential. Lucas is the first boy she's ever kissed, and though she's never admitted that to him, she suspects he knows it.

Christina is grateful that Lucas never complains when she pulls away from him, that he seems to understand and accept her unspoken boundaries. She wonders if it was the same with the other girls, the ones who came before her. Somehow she doubts the kinds of girls Lucas Corbin usually dates would cut him off at a kiss, and she hopes he's not quietly growing bored of her. Hopes that one day soon he won't be looking for someone willing to give him more than a chaste kiss on a fallen log.

The kiss grows more urgent, their tongues probing and exploring, as if they're starving for each other. Christina feels a flutter of warmth low in her belly, her skin tingling with the aftershock of it, and she realizes that she wants more of him. So much more of him. She wants to know what his hands would feel like on her skin, what his body would feel like pressed against hers. Lucas must be feeling it too, losing himself in the heat of the moment, because his hand travels to the hem of her shirt; the tips of his fingers slip beneath it to graze the soft flesh of her stomach. A shudder rolls through her, and she wills his hand higher, feels like she will come undone if he doesn't touch her.

But no. She can't. She pulls away from him so abruptly that she nearly falls off the log, her lips plump and swollen from his kiss. "I . . . I'm sorry."

"That's okay," he replies, wiping his lower lip with the pad of his thumb. "You don't have to apologize." He stretches out again, a picture of relaxed composure.

But Christina thinks again of the other girls, the ones who would have given him exactly what she knows he wants. "It's just... my parents. Like, they have all these rules. About boys and stuff, and I think they got into my head about it, and, see, they have this thing about me not being allowed to date—" She realizes her mistake, her cheeks burning a crimson red. "Not that we're *dating*, necessarily. I didn't mean to assume we were, like, officially together or anything."

"Are we not?" Lucas smiles, and the heat it stirs in Christina's belly is enough to melt the polar ice caps.

"I... I guess I wasn't sure." She adjusts her glasses, straightening them on her nose.

"Let me clear it up for you, then," Lucas says, his smoky green eyes meeting hers. "I want to be with you. And you don't need to explain yourself to me. If you're not ready to go further, then you're not ready." He shrugs. "You're worth the wait."

She feels like she could cry, but she doesn't know why. He's saying all the right things, but she still feels like she's messing this up.

"Besides," Lucas adds, sparing her from having to find the words to respond, "I think it's cool that you're so close with your parents."

Christina looks at the ground, tracing circles in the dirt with the toe of her sneaker. "I don't know that I'd describe us as close, exactly..." She doesn't know how to explain her relationship with her parents to Lucas, how to tell him that the idyllic version of her family that he sees, that everyone sees, feels like a performance to her. How can she put into words the cold detachment she's always felt for her father, the way she can't ignore his obvious preference for her brother? Or the way she loves her mother but doesn't feel like she knows her, the woman she is under the flawless facade she wears like armor? "It's complicated."

There's a beat of silence before she continues, eager to push the spotlight off her. "What about you, though? You and your mom always seemed super close."

"We are. Were." Lucas grows pensive, his eyes scanning the trees as he seems to search for an explanation among the branches. "I guess it's complicated for us too lately. Ever since she and my dad split up, I've been kind of a dick to her."

"Why?" Christina appreciates his honesty, recognizes that it's a rare quality in a teenage boy, the ability to admit to his own shortcomings.

"I don't know. I don't blame her for their divorce or anything. Honestly, my dad is the one who deserves the blame. He just, like, walked out one day and decided he didn't want to have any responsibilities anymore. I looked up to him before that, you know? And then suddenly I couldn't anymore. I couldn't respect him. What kind of man does that? And I was just so mad about it. Like, really pissed off all the time. And my mom was there, and, well, he wasn't. She's always there. So I kind of took it out on her. Like, I was afraid that if I took it out on *him,* he'd just walk out of my life entirely. But my mom, she's not like that. She's solid."

"I'm sure you guys will work through this." Christina squeezes his hand. She loves that she gets to have this version of him. That the tough jock he is at school allows himself to be emotional, introspective when he's with her.

"Yeah. We will."

She leans toward him, this beautiful, vulnerable boy, and kisses him again. He seems surprised at first, his lips frozen against hers. But she feels him softening, opening to her as she parts them with her tongue.

She takes his hand, slides it under the hem of her shirt so his fingers are splayed against her bare stomach.

"Are you sure?" he breathes into her mouth. "We can just keep kissing..."

"I'm sure."

"What the fuck is this?"

The sound of someone in the clearing shatters the moment as if it were glass.

Lucas whips his hand from beneath Christina's shirt and both of them jump apart as if they were repelling magnets pushed too close.

"Are you fucking kidding me right now?" Sebastian stalks across the clearing, heading directly for Lucas.

Christina stands up and puts herself in Sebastian's path so she's positioned between the two boys, but it's as if her brother doesn't even see her. His eyes, as sharp and murderous as daggers, are trained on Lucas.

"Whoa, chill out," Lucas says, holding up his palm in a placating manner.

And it is the exact wrong thing to say. Christina sees Sebastian's nostrils flare, the muscles in his jaw clench.

"I will not *chill out*," he spits, his voice a mocking whine. "What do you think you're doing with my sister?"

"It's none of your business, Sebastian," Christina says, her hands pressed flat on her brother's chest. Her heart starts to hammer against her ribs as she stands here with these two angry boys towering over her, but she doesn't move.

"Like hell it's not," Sebastian retorts, his eyes never leaving Lucas's. He lifts a hand and shoves Lucas hard in the chest. In doing so, he knocks Christina off balance, and she stumbles.

If Sebastian notices what he's done, he has no reaction to it. But Christina can see the way it ignites something in Lucas, something dangerous and fierce, an untapped rage in him that she didn't know existed.

"Watch it," Lucas growls, stepping around Christina and shoving Sebastian so forcefully that it knocks him back a step.

Sebastian wastes no time. It's as if Christina is watching it all unfurl in slow motion: the way her brother pulls back his fist and sends it in an arc that connects with Lucas's face, the blood that flies from Lucas's split lower lip. The way Lucas touches his face as if in disbelief, wipes the blood away with his sleeve. How he makes a fist of his own, but Sebastian's knuckles slam into his ribs before he has a chance to throw a punch.

"Stop!" Christina screams, the world suddenly moving at full speed again. "Sebastian, stop!" She throws herself in front of Lucas, both palms in the air, pleading with her brother.

"Stay the fuck away from my sister," Sebastian growls at Lucas, his upper lip curling in distaste. He spits on the blood-spattered ground at Lucas's feet, then grabs Christina by the arm, pulling her toward the path home.

"Christina." Lucas reaches out for her, but she shakes her head.

"Don't," she says, her voice barely above a whisper. Then she allows herself to be led away from him.

34

MAGGIE
Benton Avenue

"Let's go."

Maggie startles, the knife she was holding clattering to the floor. "Go where? I'm just getting started on dinner," she says with some effort. Her jaw is still tender from the last time she'd questioned Dean. She prods one of her molars with her tongue. She's pretty sure it's loose.

"You can do that when we get back."

Maggie wants to ask again where it is that she's going, but she can tell that she won't be getting an answer from Dean. And so instead, she picks the knife up off the floor and carries it to the sink. She grips the handle for a moment, feeling the heft of it in her hand.

I could kill him, she thinks. She imagines the expression on his face if she were to plunge the silver blade into his neck. The mix of surprise, horror, defeat that would play across his features. She slides her thumb over the smooth wooden handle.

"What's taking so long?" Dean barks.

Maggie drops the knife into the sink where it lands with a clang. She doesn't have it in her. She isn't a killer.

"I'm coming," she says.

Maggie follows Dean out to the driveway, feeling more trapped than she ever has before. She wonders what Sam would say if he were here right now. She's been thinking about Sam a lot lately. She could call him. She knows he'd help her, even after she'd been so awful to him. But it wouldn't be right. She can't ask Sam to ride in like a white knight and rescue her from her own life, not after the way she'd treated him, casting him off like his friendship meant nothing to her. Besides, what if Sam got hurt because of her? What if he were to show up here and Dean did something terrible? She imagines that knife again, but this time it's in Dean's hand. She watches the scene play out in her mind: Dean stabbing the knife into Sam's chest, the blade sliding between his ribs, Sam clutching at the hilt, thick, black-red blood dripping between his fingers. She imagines the way his beautiful blue eyes would look as he took his last breath, the life draining away from them, and the way she's certain he'd still have come for her even if he knew what it would cost him. No, Maggie can't take that risk. Not with Sam. She made her bed with Dean, and now she has to lie in it.

Dean climbs into the driver's seat of his old Camaro. He doesn't drive it often, in part because he prefers his bike and in part because it's unreliable. Dean bought it off the owner of the chop shop down the street. It needs a lot of work, work Dean knows how to do himself, but the repairs require parts, and those require money, something that's always been in short supply and is getting even shorter since Maggie hasn't been able to go to work nannying for the Sullivans this week. Not in the state she's in. Her back has been hurting her too much to get on the floor and play with the children, and she knows her appearance would raise questions she isn't ready to answer. She had to pretend to be sick with the flu.

Maggie gets into the car and buckles her seat belt while Dean turns the key in the ignition. The Camaro starts on the first try, the car roaring to life. He backs down the driveway and the tires kick up gravel and a cloud of dirt that balloons out around them.

As he starts down Benton Avenue, one arm languidly draped over the steering wheel, Maggie notices him looking at her from the corner of his eye.

"We're going to scope those big fancy houses across town," he tells her, offering the explanation like a gift. But Maggie knows it's a Trojan horse.

She says nothing, keeps her eyes on the road in front of her.

"The ones that look like kids live in 'em, those are the ones we hit. Most likely to be empty on Halloween."

Maggie stares listlessly out her window, watches as they leave their usual stretch of town, passing the run-down gas stations, the barbershops, and the check-cashing places.

"You're going to be the one to ring the doorbells. Just in case someone answers. You're less . . ." He looks at her again, his eyes roving over her body. Maggie wills herself not to move. "Threatening."

"Of course," he continues, talking more to himself than Maggie now, "we're going to skip the houses with those fuckin' doorbell cameras. Although those are probably the ones that have the good shit in them. Are you listening?"

Maggie nods, pretends to be interested in the scenery outside her window. They're passing a heavily wooded area now, and the trees look like a green-brown blur as they speed by.

"I don't think you are," Dean says. "You're not listening to a damn word I say."

"I am," Maggie insists.

"We're in this together, Maggie. Me and you. Whether you like it or not. And I'm sure I don't need to remind you that we wouldn't have to be doing any of this if it weren't for you."

Maggie wonders, not for the first time, how much of Dean's insistence on robbing the houses of their wealthy neighbors is to pay off their debt to Mike and how much is because he enjoys the idea of it, the satisfaction it would bring him to take from those who have always had more than he has.

Dean rolls up to a red light, bringing the car to a stop. He pulls a small plastic bag from the pocket of his leather coat. Maggie pretends she can't see him in her peripheral vision as he shakes a tiny mound of white powder onto the side of his hand and inhales it up his nose in one quick breath.

He exhales loudly as the drug courses through his veins, the high taking hold of him.

Maggie's hands start to shake in her lap. "Do you want me to drive?" she asks.

Dean works his jaw, his teeth grinding together, and it makes Maggie's skin crawl.

"You know, just so that you can get a better look at the houses," Maggie says, forcing her face into a watery smile.

"Is there something wrong with the way I drive?"

Maggie feels the car accelerating, the tires of the Camaro spinning faster over the asphalt. She clasps her hands together, her fingers interlaced so tightly that her knuckles blanch. Dean does this sometimes—drives too fast, takes turns too sharply—because he knows it frightens her.

Maggie swallows hard, her throat still sore from where Dean had grabbed it. "No," she says. "Sorry." She hates the timidity she hears in her voice.

She wasn't always this way, this meek little mouse of a person. She tries to remember who she was before. She knows she was stronger, more capable, but the memory feels so far away to her now. Dean has broken her down so completely that she hardly remembers that version of herself. *It's sad,* she thinks. She feels it like a loss. The death of the person she should have been.

"What's the matter, Maggie?" Dean asks, a taunting lilt to his voice. "Am I scaring you?" He pushes his boot down harder on the accelerator, and the Camaro jolts forward, barreling even faster down the empty stretch of road.

"N-no," she stammers, but Dean laughs.

"Oh, good. Let's go a little faster, then."

The Camaro's engine roars, the hood shaking as the pistons fire rapidly beneath it.

"Do you want me to slow down?" Dean asks.

Maggie doesn't respond. She knows it doesn't matter what she says. There is no right answer.

"I asked you a question, Maggie."

The car begins to rattle, a metallic jangling, as Dean pushes it past its limits. Maggie squeezes her eyes shut, her stomach quaking.

"Look at me, Maggie."

She doesn't; she can't. She's so frightened that she can't bring herself to open her eyes.

"I said look at me." Dean is angry now, the words leaving his lips like thrown jabs.

Maggie forces her eyes open, her chin trembling as she turns to face him.

Dean is watching her intently, his head fully turned toward Maggie in the passenger seat. He's not looking at the road.

"Please stop," Maggie manages, her voice a strangled squeak.

"What did you say?" Dean smiles, a Cheshire cat grin. "I didn't quite hear you." He's still not looking at the road, and Maggie knows it's intentional. She knows he's doing this to scare her.

"Stop!" she shouts. "That's enough, Dean!"

The edges of his smile creak upward. "Didn't think you had any of that left in you." He pushes down even harder on the accelerator and the red dial of the speedometer quivers. Maggie can feel the back tires of the Camaro fishtailing across the pavement.

She looks out the windshield and her eyes go wide, the air vanishing from her lungs as she sees what's ahead of them. "Dean!"

He looks now too, and he slams on the brakes. It's the first time Maggie has ever seen him truly afraid.

35

GEORGINA
Hawthorne Lane

"What were you thinking?" Georgina shouts. She rarely loses her composure, but after the call she just got from Libby Corbin, she can't help it.

Sebastian huffs. "Of course Lucas would go crying to his mommy."

"That's hardly the point, Sebastian!" Georgina throws her hands up in frustration. Behind her, the last rays of daylight stream in through the picture window of her kitchen, golden and bold. "You can't just go around hitting people!"

"When he's feeling up my sister, I sure as hell can." Sebastian opens the refrigerator, pulls out a bottle of water.

His casual reaction to the whole ordeal has Georgina feeling irate. According to Libby's frantic phone call, Lucas came home with a bloodied face. He didn't want to tell his mother what had happened at first, but he eventually relented and informed her that Sebastian had punched him. *Punched him!* Georgina was equal parts mortified and horrified, issuing a slew of apologies to an incensed Libby. But Sebastian? He doesn't seem the least bit fazed. He hurt someone, really hurt him, and as far as Georgina can tell, he doesn't seem to care one bit.

"No!" she tells him. "No, you cannot! This isn't how you deal with things, it's just not . . . it's not acceptable!"

"Well, I'm sorry if my behavior was not 'acceptable' to you"—he gestures quotation marks in the air—"but it's already done, so I guess that's that." He chugs a long sip of water, his Adam's apple bobbing in his throat as he tilts his head back.

"That is not that! You're going to go upstairs and apologize to your sister, who is extremely upset over this entire episode, and then you're going to apologize to Lucas."

Sebastian sets his water down with such force that some of the liquid jumps from the bottle and splashes onto the counter. "Like hell I am." His eyes narrow to slits as he glowers at his mother.

Who is this man? she wonders. *What happened to the boy I raised?* And then the guilt washes over her again. Guilt that she wasn't a good enough mother, that despite her best intentions, she'd failed him somehow. She *must* have, because here he is, fully formed and frightening. This, this anger, this rage inside him, surely it's her fault. Perhaps it grew in the empty space between them, the gap she couldn't close between mother and son. With Christina, it had felt so natural, so easy. The first time she'd held her daughter in her arms, she looked down into her big, round eyes and she knew that she belonged to her. But Sebastian . . . he'd always belonged to Colin. Perhaps it was the depression that consumed Georgina after his birth. Maybe he could sense that ugliness in her; maybe he'd felt it like a rejection that left him floundering for someone, anyone, to attach to. A drowning sailor desperately clinging to the only life ring in sight. Or maybe Colin had taken him, the son he'd always wanted, and slowly and methodically turned him away from the light of his mother's love. Georgina can't be sure how it happened; she knows only that she'd let him down, that one way or another, she'd lost him.

"You are going to apologize," Georgina insists. "You are." Because that's what kind people do. They don't just hurt someone and feel entitled to walk away without consequence. How could her son not know that? It can't be too late to set him on the right path now. It just can't. She can still be the parent he needs; she can still set this right.

"Enough!" Sebastian shouts, the deep timbre of his voice reverberating off the walls. "Leave it the fuck alone already!"

Georgina is stunned, her feet frozen to the floor. "Sebastian Pembrook! You absolutely cannot speak to me that way."

Sebastian steps toward her and she sees a familiar glint in his eyes, an icy reflection of his father. "I said leave it alone!" he shouts, both of his hands rising to meet Georgina's shoulders.

Sebastian shoves her, and Georgina feels her back collide with the hard stone of the counter before she falls to the floor. She scrabbles along the cool tiles, trying to pull herself to a sitting position, the small of her back already aching.

Sebastian takes a step toward her, and for a moment she thinks he's going to reach down and help her, or maybe fall to his knees and cry tears of remorse for what he's just done to his own mother. But he doesn't. Instead, he stands over her, scowling down at her on the floor, disgust twisting his handsome face, as if she were something vile and loathsome.

"Are we finished talking now?" he says with a sneer. Then he turns and walks away.

Georgina hears the back door slam before she finds the will to get up. She does so gingerly, assessing the damage to her body. She's not injured, not really, though she knows she'll never be the same again nonetheless. Not after she's seen what her own son is capable of. Georgina knows now that she's let things go too far for too long. She's allowed Sebastian to become the very thing she spent his entire life trying to protect him from: his father.

GEORGINA KNOCKS ON CHRISTINA'S BEDROOM door, her knuckles softly tapping the wood. "Honey, it's me. Can I come in?"

"Okay." Christina sighs dejectedly.

Georgina pushes open the door and steps into the room. She finds her daughter sitting on her bed, her knees tucked up against her chest, tears in her eyes. She looks so young to Georgina in this moment. Like a little girl. Although Georgina knows she's not. She's growing up so quickly. Christina is in that strange in-between time, suspended between being a girl and a woman, where she's not fully either and yet the world expects both of her.

"Do you want to tell me what happened today?"

Christina props her head on her knees, her arms around her shins. "Not really."

Georgina sits on the bed beside her and smooths her daughter's golden-blond hair. "Libby already told me some of it."

Christina's bottom lip starts to quiver. "Is Lucas okay?"

Georgina nods.

"It was awful, Mom. So awful. I was with Lucas in the clearing." Her cheeks pink.

"Go on," Georgina encourages her, glossing over this small confession.

"We were sort of... well, we were kissing. And Sebastian showed up, and he hit Lucas. And oh my God, he was bleeding and stuff, and it got all over his shirt, and then I tried to stop Sebastian, but he just wouldn't stop, and he hit him again . . ." She starts to cry, fat tears sliding over the round crests of her cheeks. "He didn't have to do that, Mom. It wasn't like Lucas was taking advantage of me or anything. I *wanted* to be there with him. We're sort of... together? Or at least we were. He'll probably never want to see me again now. And we were just kissing. That's all, I swear." She sobs, burying her face in her knees.

"Christina," Georgina says, her voice gentle and coaxing. "I need to explain something to you. Something very important."

Christina slowly picks up her head, her watery eyes turning to her mother.

"Sebastian had no right to do what he did today," Georgina continues. "It wasn't his place. And it's not mine or your father's either. We have rules about boys and dating because you're still young, and we don't want you to make mistakes that you'll regret when you're older. I want you to understand what it means to love and feel loved and how special it is to be with someone who cares about you the way he should."

"Lucas does."

"I'm glad for that. I really am. But what I'm trying to say is that you are your own person and you get to make your own choices. Your value as a woman doesn't lie in what you choose to do or not do with a boy."

Christina's face turns various shades of red, but Georgina knows that she needs to finish. She needs her daughter to hear this. *Really* hear it. Her daughter can—will—be so much more than she is.

"As your parent, I always want to you guide you and protect you whenever I can, but I haven't always gone about it the right way. In fact, I've made so many mistakes that I wish I could take back. But despite all of that, when I look at you, I see someone stronger, braver than I've ever been. You're going to go so far in life. I just know it."

"Mom?" Christina says. She pauses, her lips parted as if she wants to say more, but she closes them again.

"If there's ever anything you want to talk about, anything at all, I'm here." Georgina takes Christina's hand in hers, gives it a reassuring squeeze. "I'll always be here."

36
AUDREY
Hawthorne Lane

Audrey's sneakers hit the deck of her treadmill in a steady pattern. She turns up the music streaming through the speakers of her home gym. It was part of the recent renovations she and Seth made to the house, a state-of-the-art gym in their finished basement. She's been more grateful for it than ever these past few days, since Colin cornered her in the alley next to her office building.

Audrey hates to admit it, even to herself, but ever since that incident, she's been somewhat afraid to leave her house. She's avoided their local grocery store, driven her car into the office (despite the exorbitant cost of New York City parking), and she's skipped her sessions with her personal trainer. None of it was worth running into Colin again.

Audrey picks up her pace, her feet thudding against the spinning band of the treadmill below her. She hates Colin. Hates that he's made her a prisoner in her own home, too frightened to so much as collect the mail from her mailbox. Audrey has never been the type of person to shy away from . . . well, anything. But with one swift movement, Colin has managed to reduce her to a shaking, quivering wisp of a woman. She clenches her teeth, running harder as she thinks about it, the way she'd cowered and caved to him. The heart rate on her fitness watch ticks higher as she remembers the feel of his hands gripping her arm, her throat. The way she'd been so meek and pliant—"Yes, Colin"; "No, Colin"—the way he'd smiled, his voice in her ear like a purr: "Good girl."

Audrey refuses to be that person ever again. She's stronger than that, stronger than he thinks she is. And next time he comes for her, she's going to be ready. She's not going down without a fight.

That's the part that's stuck in her mind, that's haunted her in the early-morning hours while she lies awake listening to Seth snoring in bed beside her. Why hadn't she fought? Why hadn't she kicked and screamed and clawed at him? Why had she crumbled into dust, letting him trail his fingers over her body even though they'd felt like razor blades against her skin?

She senses movement in the fitness mirror mounted on the far wall of the gym. Seth is back from picking up their dinner. She dials down the pace of the treadmill, slows herself to a stop, and clicks the remote to cut off the music, which she now realizes was blasting over the whir of the treadmill. Audrey takes a sip from her water bottle and whisks the sweat from her brow with the small towel she keeps looped around the bar of the treadmill.

"That was fast," she says, sweat dampening the black Lycra sports bra she wears as a top. Her body feels good after her run, fit and strong. This was exactly what she'd needed.

Seth offers no response, and Audrey turns to face him. But it isn't Seth hovering in the doorway like a specter. It's Colin.

Audrey gasps, and Colin casually steps into the room and shuts the door behind him. Suddenly it feels like her air supply has been cut off. Audrey panics, scanning the walls, the few shoebox-size windows near the ceiling, the firm surface of the thick metal door. Seth had insisted on that door. He wanted to soundproof the gym, isolate it from the rest of the house so he could write in peace while Audrey worked out. There's no escape, she realizes now. She's trapped down here. With him. Her breathing quickens.

"What are you doing here?" she demands, forcing herself to remain calm, not to let him sense her fear.

"Just thought I'd drop by for a little chat."

"You can't just show up at my house! Seth is home," she lies. "He'll be down here any second, so you should just—"

"Audrey, I know Seth isn't home. His car isn't in the driveway."

"That doesn't mean he's not home. Maybe his car is in the shop. Did you think of that?"

"No," he responds, infuriatingly calmly. "Is it?" Audrey hates the amusement that dances in his eyes as he challenges her obvious lie.

"Y-yes," she stammers.

"Well, in that case..." Colin cracks open the basement door and yells up the stairs, "Seth, would you come down here a moment? I think Audrey would like your assistance with something." He cups his hand to his ear theatrically, leaning toward the stairs. "Nope. Nothing. Guess he must have left." Colin slams the basement door shut once again and stands in front of it, sealing off Audrey's only hope of escape.

"Now that that's settled," he continues, "I think it's time we had a little talk."

Audrey doesn't respond. She can't find the words.

"You remember our last chat, don't you?"

She nods.

"Well, it would appear that you've forgotten the message. I think I was clear with you, was I not? When I call, you are expected to answer. And yet I've called you several times, and it seems that my phone number remains blocked. That's not very nice, Audrey. Not to mention inconvenient. It's left me with no choice but to come here and talk to you in person."

"What do you want, Colin?"

"I think you know what I want."

Colin's eyes slide over the curves of her body, and it leaves Audrey feeling exposed. She wraps her arms around her bare midsection.

"Oh, no point in getting shy with me now." Colin laughs.

The easy, bubbling sound of it sparks a fury in Audrey. "You have to leave. What happened between us was a mistake. A mistake I won't be making again. It's over, Colin. You need to understand that. I'm married."

Colin's eyes harden to stone; a muscle in his jaw twitches. "Now you care that you're married? It never seemed to bother you before when you were taking your clothes off for me like the whore you are."

The words hit Audrey like a slap across her face.

Colin steps toward her, closing the gap between them. He runs his hands along her Lycra-clad hips. "Why can't you just play nice?"

Audrey pushes away from him, her long dark ponytail swishing over her shoulders as she vehemently shakes her head. "Don't touch me."

"Wouldn't it be a shame," Colin says, feigning thought as he taps a finger against his chin, "if Seth were to find out about the 'mistake' you made with me?"

The sound of her husband's name in Colin's mouth is the final straw for Audrey. It's gasoline on the spark of rage he's been stoking inside her, and it sets off an explosion.

"Don't you dare talk about my husband to me. You're not even worthy of speaking his name. And if you ever show up here again, if you ever put your filthy hands anywhere near me, I'll tell Georgina everything. I swear to you, I'll do it. You seem to forget that you have something to lose here too, Colin."

Colin smirks, and it takes all of Audrey's self-control not to reach out and smack the smugness off his face. "I've always found that fiery side of you so sexy. But there's something you're mistaken about." The smirk is gone, and Audrey never thought she'd be so sorry to see it go. The stony severity left in its wake is far more frightening. "You do not call the shots here. And I have nothing to lose. You're going to tell Georgina about us? Go right ahead. But I warn you, you're going to be disappointed by her reaction. She already knows. Maybe not that it's you that I'm fucking this time, but she knows that our marriage is not a . . . traditional one. That I come and go as I please."

Audrey's eyes grow round, her mouth agape.

"You look surprised," Colin comments. "Poor Audrey—did you think you were the only one? That you were special?"

Audrey doesn't reply as she watches the only card she was holding slip between her fingers.

Colin steps so close to her that their chests are nearly touching, and then he reaches out, brushing his fingers over her ponytail. "So beautiful," he breathes.

Audrey's own breath is caught in her throat as she waits for him to do whatever he's going to do next.

"But I'll tell you this," Colin says, glowering at Audrey, his words like cut glass, "if you threaten me again, it will be the last thing you ever do."

He turns away then, and Audrey feels like she can finally exhale. She watches him walk away from her, those long confident strides, but when he reaches the door, he stops, turns to her once more.

"And, Audrey? You really should be more careful about remembering to lock your doors. *Anyone* could have just walked right in."

37

GEORGINA
Hawthorne Lane

"There you are," Georgina exclaims with a breathy sigh of relief. Rarely is she ever happy to see her husband darkening their doorway, but today she needs his help.

"And hello to you too, my darling wife." He glares at her, eyes narrowed. She's already made a misstep and she can't afford many, not if she's going to get him on her side about Sebastian. Colin has always had blinders on when it comes to his golden son's shortcomings, but surely his willful ignorance can't extend to physical violence.

"I'm sorry," she says. "Of course. Hello, Colin." She goes to him and rises on her toes to kiss his cheek, the way he likes to be greeted.

He takes off his suit jacket, tossing it over the banister. It will remain there until Georgina picks it up and brings it to be dry-cleaned for him. She knows this without his having to tell her. He drops his briefcase and takes off his shoes. They too will remain where he's dropped them until Georgina tidies them away.

"It's been a long day," he says, "and now I have to come home to you nagging me the moment I walk through the door?" He scowls at her.

"You're right," she concedes. "That was thoughtless of me."

"You have no idea what it's like. The kind of pressure I'm under at work." Colin rubs his temples.

Georgina knows how the evening is supposed to go: She's expected to serve her husband a quiet dinner, being careful not to disturb him, and he'll follow that with a nightcap and perhaps a sleeping pill that will allow him to drift off to a blissful, dreamless sleep while she lies awake fretting about their son. But she can't let that happen, not tonight.

"Do you want to talk about it?" she asks.

"With *you*?" Condescension pours out between his words. "You wouldn't understand the first thing about it."

"Sorry," Georgina says again. She reminds herself that she needs Colin's help with Sebastian, so she can't let herself be baited into the argument he's clearly spoiling for. "I only wanted to help."

"Well, you can help by cleaning this stuff up." He gestures to his belongings that he's strewn about the open foyer. "You know I hate to come home to a mess."

"Yes, sure." Georgina picks up Colin's shoes, folds his jacket neatly over her arm. She thinks she catches a faint whiff of a woman's perfume but she ignores it.

Colin turns and starts up the stairs.

Georgina follows a few steps behind him, cautiously, tentatively. Something has Colin in a particularly bad mood tonight. Normally she leaves him be when he's like this and waits until the tides shift, until the right moment presents itself for her to ask something of him. But tonight, it simply can't wait.

She thinks again of Sebastian, of the scene Christina described. How he'd hit Lucas, leaving his face a bloody mess. Of how, when she'd confronted their callous, remorseless son, he'd shoved his own mother without an ounce of shame or hesitation. She and Colin have let Sebastian become this thing, this monster, and now she owes it to him to set things right, to do better for him. She can't let it go on a moment longer. No matter what it might cost her.

"Colin?" Georgina steps into the bedroom to find him unbuttoning his dress shirt, his belt already unbuckled. Seeing him this way unleashes visions of the other night as if they'd been pushing on a barricade in her mind and just broke through: Georgina bent over the bed, Colin taking her from behind, her tears soaking into the mattress. She can't—won't—go through that again. In this moment Georgina feels as if she'd rather die than let him degrade her in that way ever again. Perhaps she should give him a few minutes, wait for him to come downstairs, maybe have a drink ready for him. That should help take the edge off the difficult conversation they're about to have.

But it's too late. She's already spoken, and Colin is watching her expectantly, a look of mild annoyance on his face.

"What? What do you want?"

"I...uh..."

"Come on, Georgina. Out with it already. As I said, it's been a long day and I'm not in the mood for your dramatics tonight."

Georgina swallows hard. Colin isn't going to like this, but it's now or never. She reminds herself that she's doing this for her son. "There was an incident with Sebastian today."

"What kind of incident?" Colin's voice is a cocktail of irritation and impatience.

"He got into a fight. With Lucas Corbin."

"Corbin? Is that the kid down the block?"

"Yes."

"Is Sebastian hurt?"

"No, but Lucas is."

"So what's the problem?"

"The problem," Georgina explains, irritation rising in her own voice now, "is that our son hurt someone and he doesn't seem to care."

"He's a boy, Georgina. This is what they do."

"I don't think it is, Colin. I don't think this is normal kid stuff. Sebastian, he's... so angry. All the time."

Colin rolls his eyes, pulls a T-shirt over his head. "That's a tad dramatic. The boy is perfectly fine."

"He's not. I'm telling you. He... he pushed me today."

"Pushed you?"

"I was trying to talk to him about what happened with Lucas and he turned on me. It was like he just snapped."

Colin looks Georgina over, his eyes scanning her from head to toe. "Well, I'll have a chat with him if you want, but you seem fine to me."

"That's not the point!" Georgina is shouting now, unable to hold back her anger, her incredulousness that Colin isn't seeing the same warning signs that she is.

"Watch your tone, Georgina." The words curl from Colin's lips in an angry growl.

But she can't rein it in anymore, her anger, her disappointment, her driving need to help the son she's so bitterly failed. "I'm his mother, Colin, and he put his hands on me! I was frightened of my own son today. We're destroying him, don't you see that?"

"I don't have the faintest clue what you're raving about. Now this is *my* fault?"

Hannah's words float to the surface, bubbling up from somewhere in the back of Georgina's mind: *Living with a man like that, it does things to a kid.* Georgina thought she'd spared them from knowing what their father was like behind closed doors. She thought that this was her own private hell, but now she sees the truth. The evil in him has infested her home—it's leaked under locked doors, traveled through the walls. Her children were never safe from it; they were raised on it. Steeped in it. And it changed them, harmed them in ways she wasn't ready to see. Until now.

"Yes, Colin. It is your fault. Your anger, your violence—"

Colin steps toward her, his jaw clenched. "I've never laid a hand on those children." The words are pushed out from behind his teeth.

"You didn't have to. You damaged them just the same."

"This is your friend, isn't it?" Colin's eyes narrow in anger. "That nosy bitch that moved in across the street. She's putting all this shit in that stupid fucking head of yours." He taps her on the temple. "I don't trust her. This whole friendly-neighbor act. Everyone has something they're hiding, Georgina. Some are just better at it than others."

Colin unclasps the silver watch on his wrist. "I saw you with her again, you know. Even after I told you to stop talking to that woman."

"No." Georgina shakes her head. "No! I see what you're doing. You're trying to manipulate me, to change the subject. You don't get to twist this around and make it about some perceived infraction of mine to take the focus off you and what you've done to this family. I—"

The back of Colin's hand collides with Georgina's cheek before she can finish getting the words out. Her mouth fills with something warm, a metallic taste twisting on her tongue. She swallows it down. "Does that make you feel like a strong man, Colin? Does it?"

This time his closed fist lands a blow to her stomach, knocking the air from her lungs.

Georgina doubles over, gasping for breath. She knows she should stop, that she's outmatched. But there's more she needs to say. More he needs to hear. She's feeling emboldened by the pain, the anger she feels toward him, toward herself, for the way they've failed their children. It's as if she's taking his blows and harnessing their power for herself. It's been a long time since she stood up to Colin, and now that she's started, she can't seem to stop. The words come in a wheeze, but she pushes them out. "Is this the kind of man you want your son to be? Because it's what you're turning him into."

Colin grabs her by the throat, his fingers digging into the pale, delicate flesh. "Shut the fuck up."

Georgina can't speak, she can barely breathe, but she shakes her head: *No.*

Colin squeezes tighter, so tight that the edges of Georgina's vision start to blur and stars burst before her eyes. She panics now, scrabbling at his hand, kicking, scratching, fighting for her life—but Colin is so much stronger than she is. He stands back, his wife pinned against the wall, watching her thrash like a fish on a hook. Georgina looks into his eyes, silently pleading with him to let her go, but the only thing she finds there is a void of cold detachment. He is no longer human. Maybe he never was.

Georgina can feel the moment that her body gives up. Her brain is telling her to fight, but she has nothing left to give. Her muscles slacken and her breathing slows. She is going to die.

Her last thought is of her children. How much she loves them, how sorry she is to be leaving them behind with *him.* How, if she could go back, she'd do things differently. For them, for her. But it's too late now. Her time is up. Georgina's world goes black, and she begins to slip away, as quiet and unobtrusive in death as she was in life.

Colin lets go of her neck, and Georgina's limp body falls to the floor. It takes her a moment to realize that she can breathe again, but when she does, she sucks in greedy gulps of air that feel like knives swallowed down her ravaged throat.

Her husband stands over her, casting a long dark shadow over her crumpled and broken body. And Georgina knows, with piercing certainty now, that it's only a matter of time until he kills her.

38
HANNAH
Hawthorne Lane

Hannah curls her knees up to her chest, wraps her blanket tighter around her shoulders. The porch swing creaks as it slowly rocks beneath her weight. Hawthorne Lane looks so different at night. The lush green lawns and vibrant fall foliage are hushed now, blanketed in silver moonlight. The usual sounds of whirring lawn mowers and laughing children are replaced with the distant hoot of a great horned owl, a chorus of chirping crickets. Hannah looks out over the darkened forest, the bristles of treetops that reach toward the glowing moon, and the dark copse of trees below them, so thick and deep that they blur into an endless black mass. Hannah wonders what kind of creatures come out at night when the curved paths belong only to them. When the mothers pushing strollers have safely tucked their children in for the night and the joggers have had their fill of nature and returned to the tidy confines of their big houses.

There's a light out, she notices. One of the streetlamps meant to lull the residents of Hawthorne Lane into a false sense of security, a pretextual barrier between them and whatever lurks in the anonymity of those woods after dark.

Hannah should be asleep like everyone else in the darkened houses on her cul-de-sac, like Mark, who is upstairs in their bed, unaware that Hannah's side is growing cold yet again as she wanders their property. She's been so restless lately, her conversation with Mark hanging heavily on her mind. He was right to say what he did.

Hannah *has* changed. Those anonymous notes have eaten away at her, turned her into the kind of person who is too afraid to be happy, who is so frightened of the future that she is destroying her present. She can feel it, the distance between herself and Mark, like a black hole that's opened in the center of her, sucking up everything good and right that they'd built together.

She sits up straighter, pulls her laptop onto her lap. She brought it out here with her earlier. It's become an addiction now, checking her secret email account, as habitual as brushing her teeth, driving to work. She lifts the top; the screen slowly wakes, and she navigates to her email account. The one that shouldn't exist, the one she was supposed to get rid of three years ago. The one she isn't sure why she kept but knew she had to. Just in case she ever had to go back there.

Hannah blinks at the screen. She shouldn't be surprised—she's been waiting for this moment for some time now—but yet she is. The inbox that has been empty for so long has one new message waiting for her. Hannah clicks to open it with a shaking hand. It takes a moment for the image to load, another for Hannah to process what she's seeing. It's the photo Audrey had taken at brunch weeks ago, an image of raised glasses clinking over a table strewn with menus and artfully arranged breakfast pastries, and there, in the edge of the frame, is Hannah. She zooms in closer, sees that it's a screen grab from Audrey's Instagram account with a caption reading *Brunch with the ladies in our favorite spot!*

Below the image is a single line of text:

I found you, Maggie.

39
HANNAH
Hawthorne Lane

Hannah can't breathe. She can't move. She can't think. She no longer hears the owls, the melodic song of the crickets. All she hears now is the roar of blood rushing in her ears. The world around her has melted away, ceased to exist outside of those four words: *I found you, Maggie.*

A scream pierces through the still night air and Hannah jumps up, her laptop falling onto the concrete at her feet with a clatter. They're coming for her. She doesn't know who sent that email, but whoever it is has found her. Has found *Mark*. Panic overtakes her, icy-cold fear flooding through her veins.

"Sorry," a voice calls from the sidewalk, breaking through Hannah's pulsing fear.

Hannah turns with a jolt to see the young woman who works as a nanny for the family down the block. She's pushing a stroller around the rounded bend of the cul-de-sac, a thrashing baby kicking at the blankets inside. "Couldn't get this little one to sleep. I thought a walk might help, but we didn't mean to disturb you."

Hannah tries to force a smile but her teeth rattle in her skull and her entire body quakes, a jumble of frazzled nerves.

"Are you okay, ma'am?" the young woman asks, the stroller coming to a stop in front of Hannah's driveway.

"Y-yes," she stammers, forcing out the familiar lie. She's not okay. She may never be okay again. That email has changed everything.

"All right, then . . ." The woman eyes her skeptically as she takes hold of the stroller's push bar and edges it forward. "Have a good night."

Hannah watches her disappear down the block, back into the darkness, and those four little words round on her again in the silence. They spin and swirl in her mind, repeated over and over until the sounds lose all meaning, until they become an echo in her head, a broken record she can't turn off: *I found you, Maggie; I found you, Maggie; I found you, Maggie.*

Hannah hasn't heard that name in over three years. Not since the night of the accident. It all comes rushing back to her, so clearly that the memory is like a film projected in her mind.

She remembers the way Dean's heavy black boots looked as he pushed down on the accelerator, how the red dial of the speedometer quivered as they barreled forward, Dean's eyes on her and not the road. She remembers the feel of the Camaro's back tires fishtailing across the pavement, and she remembers the moment she looked out the windshield and saw the guardrail ahead of them.

She saw it before Dean did, and by the time he processed what was happening, it was too late. He jammed on the brakes, the tires squealing, the smell of smoke and burning rubber filling the car.

Maggie didn't know what to do. They were going to crash; they were going to die. She grabbed the steering wheel with both hands and pulled on it as hard as she could.

"What the fuck are you doing?" Dean shouted, panic flooding his voice.

Maggie wasn't certain, she just knew that she had to do something, that she couldn't sit by and wait to die, forever trapped in that car with him.

The Camaro spun out of control, careening wildly across the pavement. They missed the guardrail but veered off the opposite side of the road. Maggie felt the asphalt give way to dirt and gravel, the last thing she remembers before they slammed into a tree and her world went dark.

When Maggie woke, she was lying against a deployed airbag, her ribs aching, her nose gushing thick red blood. It trailed into her mouth, a viscous river. She tentatively lifted one arm and then the other, rolled each ankle. Though her entire body felt like it was on pins and needles, she was surprised to find that she was relatively uninjured. Maggie sat up; the world spun around her, and her skull throbbed. She lifted a hand to her forehead. More blood poured from an open gash. But she was alive. She'd survived somehow. And then she looked at Dean.

He was collapsed over the steering wheel, his jaw slack, his arms limp at his sides. Dean's airbag hadn't inflated, even though, Maggie saw, it was his side of the car that had collided with the tree; his window was shattered, the driver's-side door dented in. Maggie was certain Dean had never checked the airbags. Never took the time to make sure the car was safe to drive.

But that didn't matter anymore. Because Maggie had killed him. When she'd grabbed that steering wheel and caused Dean to lose control of the car, she'd killed him. *It wasn't my fault. It was an accident.* That's what she told herself, but somewhere in the back of her mind, a small voice reminded her that this was exactly what she'd wanted, what she'd wished for when she'd held that knife in her hand only hours before.

Maggie unbuckled her seat belt, pushed her shoulder, which screamed in pain, against the passenger door, and nudged it open.

"Mags."

She heard it, her name nothing more than a exhalation, but it stopped her in her tracks as she was stepping out of the car. To freedom, to a world without Dean.

She looked back into the car as one of Dean's eyes slowly fluttered open. "Help," he breathed, blood bubbling from between his lips.

Maggie watched him, his feeble, wheezing breaths, the fear in the one eye he had managed to open. But she made no move to help him. It was like she was frozen while the world still spun around her. Maggie knew she should be feeling something in that moment—grief, guilt, regret—as she stood there, watching her husband's breaths slow to nothing, his chest no longer rising and falling. But she felt nothing. Nothing at all.

It wasn't until Dean's eyes drifted closed and his pallor became a ghostly white that Maggie came back into her body. She had no idea how long she'd been standing there watching him die, but her hands had grown numb with the cold by the time she forced herself to climb back into the car. Maybe the crash had been an accident, but this, this was intentional. She'd chosen to let Dean die. What had she done?

Maggie reached for Dean with an unsteady hand, the muscles of her arm protesting in burning pain as she held two fingers to his throat. She felt his blood, viscous and sticky between her fingers as she searched for the pulse she already knew she wouldn't find. Dean was gone. She was a murderer.

I found you, Maggie. The words cut through the memory. Someone knows what she did on the empty stretch of road that night. Though Hannah can't fathom how. She was so certain that they were alone, that no one was there to witness the most terrible thing she'd ever done. *And yet . . .* She thinks of Mike, of his leering, oil-slick eyes, his promise that he'd make her pay her debt one way or another. Has he somehow figured out that she survived the accident and he's looking for what he's owed? Or is he after something else—retribution for his friend's death?

Mike would have her old email address, Hannah supposes. This is why she'd kept it active all this time, one final tether to her previous life that she'd never cut. When her past came for her, she wanted to see it coming. But now that it is, she doesn't know how to stop it. It's barreling toward her like a freight train and she's standing, frozen, on the tracks. *I found you, Maggie.*

HALLOWEEN NIGHT

Transcript of interview with Beth Patterson
October 31, 2024

Detective Olsen: Thank you for coming down to the station, Ms. Patterson.

Ms. Patterson: Sure, of course, anything to help. And please, just call me Beth.

Detective Olsen: All right, then. Beth. You told the officers at the front desk that you had information pertaining to our current investigation into an incident that occurred earlier this evening on Hawthorne Lane?

Ms. Patterson: I do, yes. I heard this is being considered a homicide. Is that true?

Detective Olsen: At this time, we're still exploring all possible avenues.

Ms. Patterson: So you really have no idea what happened, do you?

Detective Olsen: As I said, ma'am, we're still exploring all avenues. Now, what was it that you wanted to report?

Ms. Patterson: I don't know if you've heard about this yet, and, mind you, I hate gossip, but as it's part of your investigation, I thought it best that I mention it . . . there was an argument at the fall festival. Earlier in the evening. Before, you know . . . everything.

Detective Olsen: An argument?

Ms. Patterson: I guess I'd go so far as to call it a fight. I saw at least one person try to throw a punch. It was really quite shameful, a group of adults behaving like that in front of all the young children just trying to go trick-or-treating.

Detective Olsen: Can you tell me who was involved in this altercation?

Ms. Patterson: I certainly can. I'm the head of the PTA. I know pretty much everyone in this town. It was most of the people who live up on Hawthorne Lane: Libby and Bill Corbin, Audrey and Seth Warrington, Georgina and Colin Pembrook, and there were some others there as well. The new neighbors, I think. I don't know their names yet. There was a pretty large crowd gathered by then. It was hard to tell who was actually involved.

Detective Olsen: Thank you. Ms. Patterson, do you recall anything else that occurred during this altercation?

Ms. Patterson: All I know for sure is that when the fight broke out, someone yelled, "I'm going to fucking kill you"—excuse my language—and then I got as far away from those crazy people as possible.

SIX HOURS EARLIER

40
AUDREY
Hawthorne Lane

Audrey looks at her reflection in the full-length mirror that hangs on her bedroom wall, fastening the backs of her diamond stud earrings. It's been only two days since Colin waltzed into their basement with his threats and his swaggering bravado, but Audrey feels like she's become a different person since then. Her hair, which she usually pampers with regular trips to the salon, is dull and lanky, and there are purple circles under her eyes that look like two pressed bruises.

"Are you sure you want to go to this thing?" she asks Seth, who lies on the bed behind her, scrolling through his phone.

"Audrey, the fall festival is going on right outside our house. Of course we have to go. How would we look if we were the only house on the block not handing out candy?"

"Does it matter how we look?" She watches Seth in the mirror as he puts down his phone, looks quizzically at the back of her head.

"Who are you and what have you done with my wife?"

Audrey knows he meant the question in jest, but the truth is that she doesn't know who she is anymore. She once prided herself on her confidence, her self-assurance. But now? Now she's the type of pathetic, insecure woman who carries on an affair with the man next door just because she was feeling a bit neglected. The type of woman who's gotten herself in so deep with a dangerous man that she's afraid all the time, even in her own home. She can't sleep; she can't eat. The guilt, the regret, the fear . . . it's all chipping away at her. And she hardly recognizes the shell of the woman it's left behind.

"I'm just saying..." Audrey continues. "We could skip it if you wanted to."

"Do *you* want to skip it?" Seth's eyes narrow as he watches his wife appraisingly. Audrey should've known he'd see right through her. "Is there a reason you don't want to go, Audrey?"

There *is* a reason. And his name is Colin Pembrook. He's undoubtedly going to be there, with his smug face and his piercing blue eyes, standing next to his perfect wife, handing out candy apples to children as if he's not some kind of monster in disguise.

Audrey looks at herself in the mirror one last time before turning to face her husband. She knows what she has to do. She's known for some time now. But that doesn't make it any easier.

Telling Seth the truth is the only way for Audrey to free herself from the hold Colin has on her. If she tells Seth everything, Colin will no longer be able to dangle the threat over her head. It's only a matter of time until he makes good on it anyway. Audrey knows that. He's just a cat toying with its prey before it goes in for the kill.

Audrey had wanted to spare Seth the pain of learning the details of her affair. Of finding out that it was with Colin, of all people. He might have his suspicions about Audrey's infidelity, but she knows that everything will change the moment he finds out the truth. There will be no more pretending, no more hiding from it after that, and it's only going to bring him more pain. These past months haven't been easy on Seth. Coping with the loss of his career has nearly broken him, and the last thing Audrey wants to do is shatter him beyond repair. But now that it seems inevitable that he will find out, isn't it better, kinder, for it to come from her lips, from a place of love and remorse rather than revenge?

"Seth," she says, swallowing back the bile that rises in her throat. "We need to talk."

She walks toward him, perches on the edge of the bed. She tries to take his hand but he pulls it away.

"Just tell me." His words are steely, as though he's already armoring himself against what he knows is coming.

Audrey lets out a sigh, her head hung low in shame. "I had an affair." Speaking the words aloud feels like releasing shackles from her wrists. But she knows she has no right to feel relief in relinquishing this burden as she shoves the weight of it onto her husband.

"I'm so sorry," she tells him. "More than I can ever put into words. It was a mistake, and it's over now."

"Why?" Seth asks, the single question ringing out into the silence of their bedroom. "Why? Have I not given you everything? The life you always said you wanted?" His arms spread wide, gesturing to the beautiful home they share.

"You did. You do. It wasn't about that, Seth. It wasn't about the things, the cars, the house. It was about how I felt. How lonely I was. You were gone all the time, and—"

Seth holds up a stony palm. "Don't you dare blame this on me."

"I'm not. I promise you I'm not. But you asked why I did it, why I made the choices that I did, and I'm trying to tell you how I felt. It isn't an excuse, it isn't a justification for what I did, but it's the truth. I felt like I'd lost you. That you'd moved on from me, from us. God, there were times when I felt like you didn't even see me anymore. Like if one day I were to quietly disappear, you wouldn't even notice."

Seth is silent, waiting for her to continue, but Audrey can see the anger simmering to a boil behind his eyes.

"I ended it because I wanted to work on us, on our marriage. I couldn't stand the thought of losing you." Even as she speaks the words she knows she's supposed to say, she isn't sure how much of it is true. Audrey has been lying for so long, to Seth, to herself, that somewhere along the way, the truth has become a slippery, evasive thing, a minnow darting between her fingers that she can't quite grasp. Had she ended the affair, scrambled to save her marriage, out of love for Seth or because she was simply too afraid to disrupt the comfortable complacency of their lives?

"I just . . . I hope you can find it in your heart to forgive me," she adds. "I know it won't be today or even tomorrow, but I want the chance to earn your trust back. I hope that, in time, we can—"

Seth shakes his head. His next words are glacially cold: "No. You're not finished yet. I need to hear all of it. From the beginning." He reaches into his bedside drawer, takes out two white pills, crushes them between his teeth, and swallows them down.

Audrey winces. She'd been hoping to leave out the sordid details, but if this is what Seth needs from her, she owes him that much.

And so Audrey lets go of her pride and she tells Seth everything. About how she'd met Colin at the martini bar where they'd drunkenly shared their first kiss and about how that kiss led to an affair that lasted six months. She tells her husband that she'd ended things with Colin when she'd come to her senses, realized that she wasn't willing to destroy their marriage for a man who meant nothing to her, and that he'd been reluctant to let her go.

The more she talks, the more easily the words flow, like a river breaking through a dam.

She tells him how Colin flooded her phone with calls and texts. How she blocked his number, so he'd shown up at her office, dragged her into an alley, and forced himself on her. And how, when she still wouldn't go back to him, he'd strolled into their home as if he had every right to be there and cornered Audrey in the basement, threatening her and terrifying her beyond belief.

When Audrey is finished, when she feels wrung out, like she sliced open her veins and bled herself dry of every last drop of the truth for him, she looks at her husband, nervously awaiting his reaction. She'd expected him to be furious, to scream and shout. She'd expected broken glass and smashed picture frames. She'd expected him to demand that she pack her things and leave. But Seth remains terrifyingly silent.

Audrey watches him, the emotions trotting across his face like actors on a stage: sadness giving way to disappointment, disappointment becoming hurt, and, finally, hurt turning into burning anger. But still he says nothing.

"Seth?" she says after several moments, her voice tentative and unsure. "I can't imagine how you must be feeling right now, but please, talk to me. Just say something. Anything."

His face hardens into an iron mask, and when he finally speaks, his words are scalpel-sharp, as if all of the anger he's been holding inside for the past two months over the loss of his career, over the affair he's long suspected, is concentrated into six words:

"I'm going to fucking kill him."

41
GEORGINA
Hawthorne Lane

"Thank you!"

The little girl's face lights up in delight as Georgina hands her one of the homemade cookies she baked for the fall festival. They're orange cardamom with a hint of vanilla in the shape of pumpkins, and they're decorated with a shiny layer of royal icing. She'd spent hours piping those little curling vines, packing individual cookies into cellophane treat bags, but it was a labor of love. In her kitchen, Georgina feels confident and capable. There, she can gather her ingredients and make something that brings people joy. Colin tends to leave her to her own devices while she's cooking—he has very little interest in what she does in the kitchen—so she can take her time. She can pipe and frost and decorate to her heart's content, until she's created a thing of beautiful perfection.

She looks out over the crowded cul-de-sac. The fall festival is starting to get busy now. Families peruse the vendor stalls, children in costumes—astronauts and ballerinas, dinosaurs and butterflies—run happily through the streets, collecting treats, their eyes bright and shining with excitement. Across the street, Hannah lifts a hand in greeting, and Georgina returns the gesture with a subtle wave before adjusting the collar of her turtleneck sweater. She has the distinct impression that the other woman knows exactly what she's hiding beneath it, the purple bruises that snake around her neck in the shape of Colin's fingers. Georgina finds it almost unnerving how well Hannah can see through her when no one else ever has. She remembers Hannah's story about her mother. Maybe that's how she does it, but . . . why? Why does she care so much about helping Georgina? And can't she see that it's a lost cause? That with a man like Colin, there is no winning, no way Georgina walks out of this unscathed. And then she remembers what Colin said about Hannah: *Everyone has something they're hiding. Some are just better at it than others.* Georgina wonders whether there was some truth to his words. She can't help but feel like there's more to Hannah's story.

"Where's Dad?" Sebastian asks, pulling Georgina from her thoughts as he drops a cookie into another child's bucket. He doesn't take care with it like she does, just lets it land in the orange plastic pumpkin with a *plonk*. The delicate cookie will be broken now, the icing cracked. She wonders if she should offer the little boy another one—she doesn't want him to be disappointed—but he dashes away to the next house, his treat bucket swinging wildly at his side.

"In the garage," Georgina replies. "He was going to get an extra table out of storage." She turns and looks over her shoulder, sees Colin standing in the garage holding a drink in one hand, a Maglite flashlight in the other. One of those heavy, expensive ones he'd insisted they needed for some reason that still evades Georgina. He shines it into the upper rafters.

When she turns back around, Sebastian's attention is already elsewhere. His eyes are trained forward, a muscle in his jaw working. "Does this guy never fucking learn?"

"Language. There are children here," Georgina chides him, following his line of sight to Christina and Lucas, who are standing on the opposite side of the cul-de-sac sharing a pink cloud of cotton candy.

She sees how Christina looks up at Lucas, her body angled toward his. There's something so sweet about it, the way he takes her hand in his, weaving his fingers between hers as he gives her the sugary treat. Georgina knows that she's witnessing her daughter's first love. And that there's magic in that. As Christina gets older, there will be other boys, other, bigger loves, but there will never be another one like this one. She's going to remember this boy for the rest of her life.

"Couldn't find it," Colin says as he approaches the table. He sets the flashlight next to the basket of pumpkin cookies and takes a large sip of the amber contents of his glass. Living with Colin has made Georgina extremely adept at predicting his moods. She can sense them like the changing tides, knows when it's best to appease him and when she should avoid him altogether. But there's something off about him today, something she can't quite read. He seems to be on edge as he looks over the crowd gathered for the festival. It's like he's waiting for someone. She wonders who that might be and why he's draining his glass so quickly while he waits.

"What's going on?" he asks.

"That," Sebastian responds, nodding toward Lucas and Christina. Christina is laughing at something Lucas said, her head tipped back, her blond hair tumbling behind her like a waterfall.

Georgina can feel Colin tense beside her, the muscles in his body coiling.

"I thought I was clear about the rules," he says, his voice a snarl. Georgina can smell the liquor, sour on his breath. She hates when Colin drinks. It makes him too unpredictable.

"I'll go talk to her," Georgina quickly offers, and sets off across the street. Maybe she can run interference before Colin humiliates their daughter by dragging her home in front of all their neighbors.

But Sebastian darts ahead of her and reaches Lucas and Christina before Georgina can. He pushes Lucas from behind, sending him tumbling to the pavement.

"What are you doing?" Christina screeches as she reaches for Lucas, her glasses clattering to the ground, the lenses cracking on the asphalt.

But Lucas is quick to jump to his feet, and he shoves Sebastian hard in the chest. "Keep your hands off me," he growls.

"I thought you would have learned your lesson by now," Sebastian retorts, his eyes narrowing on the other boy. "Don't want to have to send you crying to Mommy again."

Lucas's hand curls into a fist. "Try it."

Georgina grabs Sebastian's arm. "Sebastian, don't!" she yells just as Lucas's fist collides with the side of Sebastian's jaw.

Sebastian flings his mother off his arm as easily as if she were a rag doll. She watches in horror from the ground as her son swells with rage, his chest puffed out, a trickle of blood trailing over his lower lip. He clenches his hands into fists, and Georgina scuttles away from him.

"Sebastian! Don't!" she cries again. She is terrified to find out how far her son is willing to go. She has the awful feeling that if he lets fly that anger inside him, he won't be able to rein it in again.

And then suddenly Colin is there, standing between the two boys. For a moment Georgina is relieved, thinking he's come to end the fight, but instead he grabs Lucas by the collar of his shirt, twists it in his fist, and lifts him off the ground.

Lucas clutches at his neck, kicking and thrashing, as Sebastian steps up next to his father. Seeing them like that, side by side, mirror images of each other, brings on a bout of nausea in Georgina.

Christina starts to cry, fat tears rolling down her face as she pleads with Colin to let the boy go. "Daddy, please!" she cries. "Please!"

But Colin is unfazed by his daughter's distress. "Shut up," he barks. "I'll deal with *you* later."

Christina startles. She doesn't understand it yet, but Georgina does. She knows that look in Colin's eyes, that singular focus—Christina's father, the man she has always known him to be, is gone. Georgina tried so hard to keep this version of Colin from her children. She'd sacrificed so much of herself to spare Christina from seeing the kind of violence that's playing out before her eyes, and Georgina understands now that there's nothing more she can do. She can't protect her child from the world. Maybe she never should have tried.

A crowd has started to gather, and Georgina scrambles to her feet and shields her crying daughter. "Colin!" she shouts. She grabs her husband's arm, digging her nails into his skin and shaking him as if she's trying to wake him from a trance. "Stop!" she commands. "Get your hands off that boy! You're out of line, Colin!"

Colin drops Lucas's collar, and Georgina hears the sharp intake of air filling Lucas's lungs as his feet land back on the pavement. But Colin isn't looking at him; his eyes are locked on Georgina, cold, hard, and unforgiving.

Georgina can feel the stares of the crowd, the eyes boring into her back, but she looks only at Colin, her chin held high, righteous and defiant. She knows there will be a price to pay for what she just did, but it doesn't matter. She did what she had to do. Let him take his anger out on her, as long as he spares her children.

42
LIBBY
Hawthorne Lane

Libby has finally reached the front of the line for mulled wine. Maybe it's her imagination, but it feels like the whole town has crowded onto Hawthorne Lane for the fall festival this year. Georgina really has done a fabulous job of it, she can't deny that. The streetlights are wrapped with fall garlands, and a hand-painted banner stretches across the length of road leading into the rounded cul-de-sac. Each house has taken care to decorate its porch with fat, round pumpkins and stalks of multicolored corn. The smell of buttery popcorn and melting sugar wafts from the vendor stands, and families slowly walk through the closed-off street pulling red wagons full of costumed children with sticky hands and smiling faces.

"One cup, please," Libby tells the woman working the wine stand as she fishes for her wallet in her purse.

"Make that two," a familiar voice calls over her shoulder.

"Just the one," Libby tells the woman, handing over the cash before turning to address her soon-to-be-ex-husband. "Hello, Bill."

"Hey, Libs." He loops his thumbs into his pockets, rocks back on his heels, and offers her a disarming smile. "How've you been?"

"Just peachy," she deadpans. "What do you want, Bill?"

A few weeks ago, Libby would have been elated to see him standing here outside the house they once shared. She would have taken this as a sign that there could still be something between them. But now all she feels is mild curiosity about what brought him to her doorstep and a twinge of annoyance that he hadn't bothered to tell her he was coming. *Typical,* Libby thinks. Of course he'd assume that she'd be eager and available to see him whenever he felt like waltzing back into her life. Not that she can really blame him for that. Libby has always molded her life around Bill and his needs. But he doesn't see that something's changed in her. That she's doing her best to move on from him, that she's actually invited Peter here today. Libby looks out over the crowd. He hasn't arrived yet, but he should be along any minute now.

"Nothing," Bill says.

"Then why the hell are you here?"

"Lucas asked me to come," Bill replies. "He was supposed to spend the night at my place, but he insisted he wanted to stay for the festival. I suppose there's a reason for that?" He raises one eyebrow, breaks into an off-kilter grin.

"Her name is Christina." Libby assumed Bill already knew about Lucas's new girlfriend. She's all he can talk about at home with Libby. Libby can't deny the small thrill of satisfaction she feels that their son has confided in her and not his father, but she quickly pushes it away. She'd thought for sure that Lucas would have mentioned his new relationship to Bill, especially after the altercation between him and Sebastian. God, Libby had been furious when Lucas came home with his face a bloody mess. Maybe she should have called Bill then, told him what happened herself, but she assumed Lucas would tell him. And besides, she'd handled the situation. She immediately called Georgina, who assured her that she would straighten out her vicious thug of a son. Libby could tell something was off about that boy even when the kids were small. She couldn't put her finger on it, but there was always a coldness about him that made her wary.

"Ah, a girl." Bill sighs theatrically. "I should have known. It's always a girl."

"Something the two of you have in common these days."

"Funny," Bill remarks.

"It wasn't meant to be. Where is Heather today anyway?"

"She had a ... doctor's appointment. And I, uh, I thought maybe we should talk anyway. Just the two of us. About something kind of important."

A sinking feeling opens in the pit of Libby's stomach. It's almost as if she knows what Bill is going to say before he utters the words that will change everything.

"Heather is . . . pregnant."

"No, she—she can't be." Libby feels as though the ground has opened beneath her feet, leaving her in free fall. Heather. Pregnant. This explains why Bill moved her into the town house so quickly, but understanding does little to ease the pain of the wound to Libby's heart.

Bill is going to have another baby. The second child they'd once both longed for. In a flash Libby sees the pile of negative pregnancy tests accumulated in the trash can, the slow shake of the doctor's head, the silent sonograms that would never show the flutter of a heartbeat. But now Bill is going to have another chance . . . with someone else.

"I'm sorry, Lib. I know this can't be easy." He takes her hand, but Libby yanks it away as though she's been scalded.

"Of course it's not *easy*."

Her mind goes back to the early days of Lucas's life, to the way he'd felt, warm and steady, in her arms as she'd rock him to sleep, the hazy golden sunlight that poured into his nursery as he'd taken his first steps. She remembers the day Bill taught him to ride a bicycle, all gapped teeth and scraped knees; she remembers the first days of school, the birthdays where they'd all crowded around a frosted cake together, watching Lucas scrunch his eyes closed and make a wish before blowing out the candles. An entire lifetime of memories. Moments that exist for Libby only in the past; fragile, fading things that she can pull out, look back on fondly, and reshelve like dusty photo albums. But Bill, he's going to get to live it all again. Only this time, he'll be experiencing that joy with someone else.

"Obviously this is going to complicate things," Bill continues, "and of course we're going to have to finalize the divorce now, but—"

He's still speaking, but all Libby can hear is the ringing in her ears. She feels her sadness giving way to molten anger. It roils and churns inside her, sloshing in her gut like lava. Complicate things? Is that all she is to him now, a complication to be dealt with before he can start his new family? Libby pictures the three of them nine months from now: Heather dewy and glowing in a hospital bed, a new baby bundled in Bill's arms, tears of joy filling his eyes. And then she imagines her own life: Lucas leaving for college, his bedroom boxed up, the posters pulled from the walls, leaving only a faint outline of the boy who used to live there, and Libby all alone in the big empty house that once held her family.

How much more is she meant to take? When Bill said he needed time away from their marriage, she lay down like a doormat and let him walk away; when she found out he was dating again, she was hurt but she did her best to move on too, and now, just as she was finally coming to terms with the end of their marriage, just as she was starting to find her own glimmer of happiness, there's going to be a baby. It's almost more than Libby can bear.

She clenches her fists at her sides, concentrating on the pain of her nails digging into the flesh of her palms, willing herself to contain the bubbling rage that threatens to boil over. "How can you be so—"

"Wait," Bill interjects. "I think something is happening." He points over her shoulder toward the center of the cul-de-sac.

Libby turns, sees the crowd that has gathered in the middle of the street, hears the din of raised, angry voices churning like a gathering storm. Her first instinct is to look for Lucas. She's a mother. No matter how old her son gets, when she sees trouble, her first thought will always be to seek him out, keep him safe. "I don't see Lucas." The words come out panicked and clipped.

"I'm sure he's fine, but let's go find him." Bill starts toward the throng of people, and Libby hurries behind him. He pushes his way through the crowd, aiming for the center of the circle. "Excuse me. Sorry."

Libby is jostled by the onlookers, who all seem to be focused on something going on in the center of the cul-de-sac, but she can't see what it is through the mass of people. She tries to stay close to Bill as he parts the crowd, but somehow they get separated. Someone elbows her drink, sending the cup flying and mulled wine spilling down the front of her shirt. She can't be bothered to care right now. Her only thought is of finding her son. She doesn't know what it is, a mother's intuition maybe, but the longer she goes without setting eyes on Lucas, the more certain she is that something has happened to him.

Finally, she reaches the middle of the crowd and time seems to stand still as Libby surveys the scene before her. Colin towers over Lucas, who's staring up at him with a look of terror frozen on his face. Lucas's shirt collar is stretched and twisted, and a vein on Colin's forehead bulges as he bears down on Libby's son, fists clenched. Behind him, Georgina is pushing Sebastian and Christina through the crowd, away from the scene.

"Stop!" Libby shrieks, and in a flash, time is set in motion once again.

Libby rushes to her son and positions herself between him and Colin. "Leave him alone!"

Colin whips around so that he's facing Libby, his shoulders squared, a roaring fire burning behind his eyes. Libby has never seen her neighbor like this before. She's always known him to be so pleasant, charismatic. Mixing up mojitos at neighborhood barbecues, offering a smile and a wave as he collects his mail, asking after Lucas if they happened to cross paths. All in all, Colin Pembrook seemed like the perfect neighbor. But now, as he glowers at her, the heat in his gaze so strong that Libby can almost feel the burn of it on her skin, the illusion shatters around her. It was all a facade, a cheap plastic disguise.

"You better not have harmed a hair on his head," she growls, her eyes locking on Colin's, refusing to allow him to intimidate her.

"Or what?" He scoffs.

The sound of it, the casual flippancy, enrages Libby. She's tired of being underestimated, disregarded, and ignored. She's tired of being Libby, the woman who is expected to take it all on the chin, to be okay, to retain her composure no matter what life throws at her. She's tired of everyone, including herself, glossing over her feelings. She's held back so much for so long—the separation, Bill dating, and now Heather's pregnancy—that she feels like a bomb on the verge of detonation. And this, Colin threatening her son, this is the very last spark that sets her off.

"Or it'll be the last thing you ever do." Libby levels the words at Colin, savoring the bite of them on her tongue.

Colin smiles pityingly, and Libby feels the flames of her rage climb so high that she's engulfed by them. Lucas is everything to her, the only thing in her life that really matters. She charges at Colin, shoves him hard with both hands, channeling a primal strength she didn't know she possessed. She doesn't recognize herself in this moment; it's as if she passed through the fire of her own anger and emerged, reborn, as someone new. Someone strong and capable, someone who won't be pushed around.

Colin stumbles on his feet, a look of surprise passing across his face before his hand shoots out, trying to grasp Libby's throat. She leaps backward as his hand swipes through the air, so close that Libby can feel the heat of his skin on hers.

"Get away from my wife." Bill shoves his way through the throng of people and then charges at Colin, nearly knocking him to the ground. "And what did you do to my son?"

Libby has never seen this side of Bill before. There's something wild and animalistic in the way he stands, the muscles in his shoulders tense, his teeth bared.

"That boy," Colin spits, "needs to stay the hell away from my daughter."

Bill shakes with anger. "If you touch either of them again, I swear I'll—"

But before he can finish the threat, Seth Warrington breaks through the crowd, his features twisted with hatred as he sets his sights on Colin.

"You!" he shouts. He lunges for him and swiftly tackles him to the ground. Colin's eyes grow wide, his mouth a rounded O of surprise as he lands on the asphalt. "I'm going to fucking kill you!" Seth exclaims.

Libby watches in horrified astonishment as the two men grapple on the pavement. What the hell is going on? Why did Seth, of all people, decide to intervene?

Bill seizes Colin by the shoulders and tosses him off Seth, sending him rolling onto his side.

Libby feels her heart pounding in her chest as Colin scrambles to his feet, and the three men stare each other down, breathing heavily, the anger radiating off them thick and palpable.

Lucas tries to dart around his mother and into the fray, but she grabs him by the arm and holds him back. "You're staying out of it."

Tension crackles through the air as Colin looks from Bill to Seth. The crowd has gone silent, and even the cool October breeze holds its breath as if it too is waiting to see what will happen next.

And then, to Libby's surprise, Colin takes a step back, surely realizing he's outnumbered. "Just keep your son away from my daughter." The words are venom dripped from his lips.

Bill glowers at him. "If you ever come near my family again, you won't live to regret it." He speaks clearly and evenly, as though this isn't a threat but a promise. "I swear to you, Colin. I'll fucking kill you."

Bill turns then, folds Lucas and Libby under his arms, and leads them through the gathered crowd.

"ARE YOU SURE YOU'RE ALL RIGHT?" Libby asks Lucas for the third time as they make the short walk to their house.

"I'm fine, Mom. I told you." But his voice comes out as jagged as broken glass.

"How about you and I go for a walk together?" Bill suggests, herding Lucas toward the opposite sidewalk. "Give you a minute to cool off."

"Yeah," Lucas responds, nodding. "Yeah, okay."

Libby isn't keen on letting Lucas out of her sight at the moment, but he'll be with Bill, and she knows Bill won't let anything happen to their son.

"Be careful!" she calls after them nonetheless as she watches them go off together. "I'll see you at home!"

Libby feels herself deflate as soon as they turn off the street, away from the crowded festival, and walk toward the path through the woods. *They'll be back soon,* she reminds herself. *Lucas is okay.* She repeats it like a promise in her head. *Lucas is okay.*

But what if he hadn't been? What if she and Bill hadn't gotten there in time? The thought makes her shudder with a cold chill. *I would have killed Colin tonight.* The thought comes to her clear and final. If he'd hurt her son, Libby would have murdered Colin in cold blood, and she would have done it without an ounce of remorse. The idea is both frightening and liberating, like peering into the dark, unexplored depths of her own rage. Libby never knew she was capable of such things, but she's certain now that she is. She would do anything to protect her son.

Libby forces herself to take deep breaths as she walks the rest of the way home, climbs the steps to her front porch. *We* did *get there,* she reminds herself, *and Lucas is okay.*

"Is this a bad time?"

The sound of a man's voice on her porch startles her, and her hand rises to her chest in alarm.

Peter stands up from the rocking chair where he's been waiting for her. "Did I scare you? I'm so sorry!"

"No, it's..." Libby exhales. In all the commotion she'd forgotten about Peter entirely. "It wasn't your fault. There was an incident with Lucas, and he's fine now, but—you know what?" She stops herself, leans in to kiss him deeply. As she does, she feels the anger, the tension begin to drain away. It takes everything not to collapse in his arms as he wraps them around her, safe and secure. "I don't want to talk about it right now. I'm just glad you're here."

A smile breaks across Peter's face as they part. "With a greeting like that, I am too."

"Libby?" a small voice calls. Libby peers around Peter's shoulder to find Hannah slowly ascending the steps to her porch. "I saw some of what happened just now, and I wanted to make sure everyone is okay."

"Oh, we'll be fine. I appreciate you checking in, though. Peter," she says, "this is my friend and neighbor Hannah. Hannah, this is Peter."

She watches as Peter turns to face Hannah, smiling brightly as he extends his hand to her, but Hannah doesn't return the gesture. In fact, she looks from Libby to Peter and back with the strangest expression on her face. Libby realizes the state that she's in—wine splashed down her shirt, her hair a wild mess of curls. She must look absolutely deranged.

"If you'd both excuse me for just a moment, I should probably change out of these clothes. I'll be right back." She opens the door and dashes inside, leaving Peter and Hannah alone together.

43

HANNAH
Hawthorne Lane

"Dean? What—what are you doing here? H-how—" Hannah stammers.

"It's nice to see you too, *Hannah*."

Bile rises in Hannah's throat at the sound of her new name on his lips. Dean looks different these days—less lean than she remembers him, with his hair combed neatly to the side and glasses perched on his nose. He's dressed differently too, in khaki slacks and a button-down shirt, no hint of the leather jacket and boots that she sees so vividly in her mind whenever she thinks of him. Though when she does think of him, it's usually of the last time she saw him: one eye swollen shut, the pink-tinged spittle that foamed between his lips as he used his last breaths to plead with her for help that would never come.

How is this possible? How could Dean have survived the accident? All this time she thought he was dead, that she'd killed him. Hannah feels herself going back there, falling into the memory. She'd limped away from the Camaro, from the smell of burning rubber and leaking gasoline, her body aching with pain, her mind capable of forming only one thought: *Run.* She'd tried, forcing one foot in front of the other, faster and faster, feeling her feet colliding with the asphalt of the desolate road, the sensation reverberating painfully through her shins. But she ran. As best she could, she ran. And as she did, the fog began to lift; her thoughts began to clear. The numbness that had taken her over earlier, allowed her to do the thing she knew she needed to do, subsided and reality broke over her like a cresting wave. She had left Dean to die. She hadn't called for help; she hadn't tried to save him, to pull him from the wreckage. Because she'd *wanted* him to die. It was the only way she'd ever be free.

But she hadn't killed him. Because now he's here, standing on Libby's porch, calling himself Peter.

"What do you say we go for a little walk?" He loops his arm though Hannah's, pinning her to his side as he leads her away from Libby's house.

"How did you find me?" Hannah asks as they walk, her voice quaking. She feels like a prisoner being led down death row.

"Did you know that when you marry one of those high-society types, there's usually an announcement in the newspapers about it?" He speaks so casually, as if they're just out for an evening stroll. "There was a photo of you and everything, right under your new name, Hannah Wilson."

Hannah thinks of Mark's mother. How appalled she'd been by their insistence on a small wedding. She must have taken it upon herself to run the marriage announcement.

"I'd been looking for you for a long time, Maggie. Ever since you tried to kill me three years ago. Truth be told, I'm not a patient man, but when I want something badly enough, I'm willing to do what it takes. I knew it was only a matter of time until you scurried out of whatever hole you were hiding in. Rats always do, eventually. I paid for a subscription to a service to alert me if a photo of you ever surfaced online. It took a few years, but then there you were. And I had the name of your new husband too. That was an unexpected windfall that made it pretty easy to track down his address in Manhattan. Of course, you'd already moved, but I had no way of knowing that then. I sent a few letters. I hope you got them."

"Why didn't you tell me it was you in the letters? Why didn't you tell me you were alive?"

"It was a lot more fun this way, don't you think? I wanted you good and scared, thinking about everything you'd done, before I showed up. I wanted that moment—I wanted to see the look on your face when you realized I'd come back from the dead. I do love a good surprise. Take, for instance, finding a second photo of you online, only months after the first. It's funny how life works sometimes. It took me almost three years to find you the first time, and then, surprise! There you were again in a photo posted on a public Instagram page by someone named Audrey. Out to a fancy brunch like you're some sort of socialite now."

Dean yanks Hannah's arm, pulling her off the road and onto the path through the woods.

"I will say," he continues, "I never took you for the type." His eyes trail over the contours of Hannah's body before landing on the diamond engagement ring that sits on her left hand. She tries to pull away from him, but he holds her tight, a look of disgust souring his face as he stares at the stone.

She's become the very thing he hates most in the world, the type of person he's always been obsessively jealous of. Dean might not have known Hawthorne Lane existed before he found her—they'd lived in another town, far from here, but one that had its own version of Hawthorne Lane. The type of place where the streets are lined with big houses, expensive SUVs parked in every driveway. Where the men dress in suits each morning and the women casually wear diamonds worth more than Dean could make in a year. He hates her, Hannah knows. Not just for what she did to him but for who she's become without him.

"I befriended your neighbor, the one tagged in the photo, to get closer to you," Dean continues. "Libby. Found her on a dating website. Honestly, I wish I had thought of that back in the day. It's a great angle. And you gave me the idea, you know. New name, new me! Anyway, Libby practically welcomed me into her life with open arms. If she had been my mark, it would have been all too easy. But Libby was just a means to an end. You were the one I wanted, Maggie. And thanks to Libby's endless droning, I learned quite a bit about your new life. Like your address here on Hawthorne Lane. And the kinds of people you associate with now, about the comings and goings of the neighborhood. I needed to know what I was walking into." He glowers at her. "Seems to me you did pretty well for yourself. But while you were off convincing some rich moron to marry you, *I* was going through hell."

Hannah bites her tongue at the mention of Mark. She wants to defend him, tell Dean that he doesn't know the first thing about him, but she knows it will only make him angrier.

"I got lucky that night," Dean says, leading Hannah farther into the darkened woods, farther away from the festival and anyone who might be able to help her. "A car came down the road, saw the wreck. They called for an ambulance. The doctors at the hospital told me I was lucky to be alive, that I'd barely had a pulse. If I'd gotten there only a few minutes later, I wouldn't have survived. But I *did* survive. No thanks to you."

Hannah thinks back to that moment, her shaking hand searching for Dean's fading pulse beneath the congealing blood. She must have missed it; she must have made a mistake.

"Not that it was easy, mind you," Dean continues. "There were so many surgeries, months of rehab. I couldn't even stand up to take a piss by myself. Not that you cared."

He stops then, grasps Hannah tightly by the upper arm and forces her to look at him. "When they cut me loose, I went home and found the house ransacked. The guys Mike worked for, it turns out they weren't willing to wait for me while I got back on my feet. They took my bike, took everything that wasn't nailed down, to settle *our* debt. And then Mike cut me loose too. After all the years we'd known each other, he said I'd become too much of a liability. That he never wanted to see my face again. So there I was, barely able to walk, with no one to take care of me and nothing left to my name. And do you know whose fault that was, Maggie?" He glares at her, his eyes shining like onyx in the light of the full moon as he leans in closer. "Yours."

44

HANNAH
Hawthorne Lane

Hannah twists her body, pulling her arm from Dean's grasp. She briefly catches the look of surprise that flashes across his face as she turns and begins to run. She doesn't know where she's going, but she knows she can't slow down even as she leaves the safety of the paved path, crashing through thickets of knotty branches and creeping vines that grab and claw at her as she passes.

It's just like the last time she left him behind, only that time, she knew he couldn't follow her. Maggie ran then too. Ran until her legs gave out. She hadn't realized where she was heading until she came to rest under a streetlight, doubling over to catch her breath, coughing and sputtering, blood still flowing from her nose and lips. She looked up then and saw where she'd ended up. Without realizing it, she'd run to the one person she'd always known she could come back to: Sam.

Maggie knocked on his door, the effort of lifting her arm almost more than she could manage. When Sam opened it, he took one look at her and caught her in his arms just as she collapsed.

When Maggie came to, she was lying on Sam's couch, an ice pack on her swollen wrist, a wet rag on her forehead. She blinked, and his face slowly came into focus over her, his eyes brimming with worry.

"Thank God," he breathed. "What happened? Was it Dean? Did he do this to you?"

And Maggie slowly but surely told Sam everything. She started from the beginning. She told him that when she aged out of foster care at eighteen, she didn't know how she was going to survive. She was all alone in the world, without her mother, without Sam, who was away at college by then. She struggled every day just to make ends meet, just to keep her head above water. She was so scared, always worried about her next meal, the next bill she'd have to pay. And then there was Dean. When he waltzed into the diner that first night, he seemed like a dream come true. Here was someone who could love her, someone who wanted to build a life with her. And suddenly she didn't feel so alone anymore. Suddenly, and for the first time since cancer took her mother from her, Maggie was truly happy.

Until the abuse started. Maggie couldn't look Sam in the eye as she told him about that part. She explained how it had started so small—an insult from Dean when he was having a bad day, a shove that could have been an accident. But it escalated as the months and years passed. Escalated to the point where Maggie feared for her life.

She told Sam about the money Dean owed, about the drugs and the gambling and the jam jar. She told him about Dean's plan for Halloween and the accident she'd caused, and finally, she told him about how Dean had died in a ditch that night because she'd chosen to let him.

"You're safe now, Maggie." It was all Sam said as he took her hand in his. "No one is ever going to hurt you again. I just wish you had told me what was going on sooner. I would have helped you."

"I knew you didn't want to speak to me. Not after the way I'd treated you. And I understood, I really did. It wouldn't have been fair to call and dump all this on you when—"

"What do you mean, I didn't want to speak to you?"

"I called you. The day after we had that argument. I wanted to apologize, but you never called me back."

"Maggie, I did. So many times. I called, I texted . . . when you didn't answer, I thought that *you* were the one who didn't want to speak to *me*."

"Dean." Realization dawned on Maggie then. "He must have blocked your number in my phone. I never got any of your messages."

Sam scowled. "Is it too soon to say I'm glad he's gone?"

Maggie dropped her head into her hands. "I just don't know what I'm supposed to do now."

"We'll call the police," Sam said, sturdy and assured. "We'll tell them what happened. Dean was on drugs, he was being reckless, the accident was his fault, not yours."

Maggie shook her head. "But I left the scene of an accident. I left him there to die."

"They'll understand. When you tell them what you told me, they'll understand why you were scared, why you ran."

"I didn't just run," she insisted. "I stood there and watched him die. I *wanted* him to die, Sam."

"No one else has to know about that."

"The police aren't the only ones I have to worry about, though," Maggie reminded him. "Dean got us involved with some pretty bad people. Even if the police don't come after me, those guys are going to."

"I won't let anyone touch you," Sam said, holding her hand even tighter. "No one will find you here."

"And what if they do?" Maggie struggled to sit up. "What if they do and something happens to you because of it?"

"I don't care what happens to me."

"But I do. I couldn't live with myself."

"What do *you* want to do, Maggie?"

Maggie was quiet for a moment. It had been so long since someone had asked her that, since someone had cared what she wanted. "I think it would be best if I . . . if I disappeared."

"You can't, you—"

"I can, Sam. I've done it before. With my mom, after we escaped from my father. He . . . he was like Dean. But she was braver than I was. She got us out of there, and we disappeared. We spent the rest of the time we had together hiding from him. Using fake names, moving from place to place whenever Mom thought there was a chance he might find us."

Maggie thought back to those years, the back seat of her mother's Buick stuffed with their belongings, bags they never fully unpacked, shuttling between sketchy motels and cheap rental apartments. There were some stretches of time, like when she'd lived next door to Sam, that they thought they were safe enough to settle down, to call someplace home. But inevitably, Maggie's father would track them down again and they'd have to move without so much as a goodbye. Sam was the only person she'd kept in touch with through each move, the one thing she couldn't give up. Until Dean forced them apart.

"Is that why you left so suddenly? Back then, I mean?"

"Yes. It was." *Come on, baby, it's time to go. He found us.*

"I . . . I had no idea." He paused then, as if absorbing this new reality. "What was your name? Before you were Maggie."

"Melody." The name felt strange and misshapen in her mouth, withered with disuse. It had been so long since she'd spoken it aloud.

"Melody," Sam repeated, rolling the name on his tongue. "I can't believe this. All this time, and I never knew."

"Because you couldn't. Because it didn't matter. I wasn't that person anymore. I haven't been for a very long time. It's part of the reason I can't call the police now, I can't have them digging into my past. I'm pretty sure what my mom and I did wasn't exactly legal. But now I need to do it again. I need to become someone new. My mom taught me how, but I'm going to need your help."

Sam looked at her, tears gathering in his eyes. They both knew this was goodbye, but they also knew that he'd help her anyway.

Sam reached out to some of his less-than-savory contacts, people with the resources to repay the favor they owed him when he was arrested for stealing a car they had taken. They'd gotten Maggie a new ID, a new name. She didn't ask where they'd gotten it, and she didn't want to know.

On their last day together, Maggie stood in Sam's doorway, a duffel bag full of new clothes strapped over her shoulder, a fake driver's license—her photo above her new name—in her pocket.

"I don't know how I'm ever going to repay you for all of this," she said, adjusting the nylon strap on her shoulder. "You're giving me a chance at a fresh start."

"You don't need to," Sam replied. "This is what friends are for."

"Committing identity fraud? Evading the police?" Maggie joked, tears already forming in the corners of her eyes over the goodbye she knew was coming.

"Okay, maybe this is a little beyond the call of duty, but I still have one last thing to give you." He held out a slim manila folder, offering it to Maggie. "I know you promised your mother that you'd never go digging into the past..."

Maggie remembers the words her mother had made her repeat like a solemn vow—*Never look back*—as she took the file from Sam's hand.

"But I did some research. If you ever want answers, the closure you deserve after everything you've been through, it's all in there."

Maggie rose onto her toes and kissed her best friend on the cheek, her lips lingering against the rough stubble a beat too long. "Thank you, Sam. For everything."

As his front door closed on a tearful goodbye, Maggie knew that if this was going to work, she'd have to close the door on her past for the very last time. And so, after so many years of running, Maggie broke the vow she'd made to her mother and opened the folder Sam had given her.

She read the documents Sam had acquired, learned about how her father had died, alone in the house he'd once shared with Maggie and her mother, two years prior. Maggie wasn't sure what she was supposed to feel in that moment—relief, sadness—but what she did feel was hope. Hope that she could really do this. Her mother's plan had worked; they'd outrun the demons of their past—they'd won. And now she could do it again; she could have a second chance after Dean and all the darkness he'd brought into her life. Maggie closed the folder, placed it neatly in Sam's mailbox. What was in that file was part of someone else's story. She was Hannah now.

45
CHRISTINA
Hawthorne Lane

> Where are you?

Christina stares down at her phone screen, glowing white in the darkness of the woods. It's a brisk October night, the kind that smells faintly of burning wood and decaying leaves, where the air is just cold enough to remind you that winter is lingering somewhere on the ever-nearing horizon. She's well beyond the streetlights now, and the sounds of the festival fade to a murmur as she ventures farther down the paved path.

> Took a walk with my dad. Almost home now.

Christina squints down at the phone, struggling to read the message without her glasses, and then sighs with relief that Lucas actually answered her. She wasn't sure if he would. Not after what her dad and Sebastian had pulled today. That was bad. Like, really bad. Christina was completely humiliated in front of basically the entire town, and she wouldn't blame Lucas if he never wanted to see her again. She can still picture her father's fist gripping Lucas's shirt, the fear in Lucas's eyes as he fought to breathe. She'd never seen her father like that before. It was like someone she didn't recognize had slid into the driver's seat and taken control of him. The father she knows would never have shown his true colors in public. He's usually far more careful about keeping up appearances, making sure that his rage is contained behind closed doors. No, Christina was not surprised by her father's capacity for violence, only that he'd forgotten to hide it.

She thinks of her mother. Of the storm they all know is coming. Christina isn't stupid. She's seen the bruises over the years, heard about her mother's "accidents." She's listened to the shouting through the walls, her mother's whimpered cries. When Christina was small, she'd cry too. She'd bury her head under her pillow, waiting for it to be over, tears soaking her sheets.

But the next morning, her mother would pretend everything was fine. Christina would find her in their spotless kitchen mixing up waffle batter or slicing fresh strawberries, always with a smile on her face. It was all picture-perfect, just as her mother wanted it to be. And so Christina would pretend too.

After a while, all they did was pretend. They pretended that Mom was okay, that Christina didn't know the truth, and that her father wasn't a monster. Reality, at least inside their house, became this strange, plastic thing for Christina. Warped and stretched until it became unrecognizable. At some point along the way, she could no longer tell what was real and what was pretend. Which of her mother's smiles were genuine and which were put on. It made it impossible to truly know her.

She looks down at her phone again, types out another message:

> I'm so sorry about what happened. Can we meet at our spot? Talk?

Lucas's response follows quickly:

> I'll try. Dunno if my parents are gonna be cool with me going out tho.

> I'm heading there now. Please try to come.

She slides her phone into the pocket of her jeans as she turns off the paved pathway and onto the dirt trail that leads to the clearing. She switches on her dad's Maglite, and a cone of warm light illuminates the path ahead. She doubts her father would be too happy to know she'd taken it without asking, but he'd be even less happy to know that she was using it to walk through the woods at night with the hope of meeting up with Lucas. There would certainly be consequences for that.

Christina's father has never hurt her—at least, not in the physical sense—but then again, she'd never given him a reason to before. For the most part, she was an easy kid. Never gave her parents any trouble. Because she knew what would happen if she did.

Once, when she was five, the ice cream truck had driven down Hawthorne Lane. It was a scorching summer day, and Christina had wanted an ice cream more than anything in the world. She imagined the swirl of vanilla on top of a pointed cone, the bright rainbow sprinkles. She could practically taste the cold treat melting on her tongue. She'd begged her parents to get her one, but her father said no. They hadn't eaten dinner yet, and he didn't want her spoiling her appetite. She looked longingly out the window at the colorful truck, listened to the tinny, tinkling music. "Please, Daddy," she begged.

"The answer is no."

"But Mommy lets us have it!"

"I said no!" Her father's response was swift and unmoving.

"You're the meanest!" she'd cried.

Later that night, as Christina lay in bed, she overheard her parents arguing.

"She's just a little girl," her mother said. Her voice, usually so warm and loving, sounded strange, different. Christina sat up, listening closer.

"You've spoiled her. Turned her into a little brat. Talking back to her own father like that."

"Colin, she's a child. She just wanted an ice cream, she didn't mean—"

Christina heard the slap, the sharp intake of her mother's breath. She squeezed her eyes shut. *It's my fault. I've been a bad girl and what's happening to Mommy is all my fault.* She promised herself that she was going to be better. She was going to be *perfect*.

The flashlight in Christina's hand flickers, momentarily throwing the trail into darkness. Christina doesn't like being here alone at night. The trees with their knotted eyes and gnarled limbs seem to stare down at her, and every rustle in the brush is a potential threat creeping ever closer. She gives the metal flashlight a shake, hoping the batteries aren't going.

If her mother were here, she'd probably have backup batteries in her purse for just such an emergency. Christina sighs. She hopes her mom is okay. Maybe she shouldn't have left her at home with her father. They were arguing when Christina left—it was the only reason she was able to sneak out—and she knows this is going to be a bad one. She saw how angry her father was earlier, heard her mother stand up to him in front of everyone. She'd been so proud of her in that moment.

When she was a child, Christina loved her mother in a clear, singular way. It was simple: Georgina was her mother, and she loved her. But now that Christina is older, her feelings toward her mother have become so much more complicated. She knows how much her mother loves her, has sacrificed for her. She's seen her bear the brunt of her father's anger all of her life, but why? Why does she let him treat her that way? Couldn't she tell that Christina knew the truth, that it was destroying her to have to watch it? Why didn't she get them out of there, away from him? It's as if all the things she feels for her mother—love, resentment, disappointment, gratitude, pity—have formed into individual strands, and they've become so knotted, so tightly wound, that she can no longer feel one without the others.

All she knows for sure is that she doesn't want to end up like her mother. Growing up, she almost thought it was normal. That love and fear went hand in hand. It was the only example she had of what love was supposed to look like. But it's not like that with Lucas. He makes her feel safe. She hopes he can forgive her.

The flashlight flickers again and the light gently dims until none remains. "No," Christina mutters, rattling the batteries. "Not now."

But the light won't turn back on. *Useless,* she thinks. The thing weighs a ton and she carried it all the way out here for nothing. She looks over the trail ahead of her, squinting her eyes as they adjust to the dark. She's almost at the clearing. Or at least, she *thinks* she is. It's hard to tell without her glasses. And she's never taken this trail at night before, not without Lucas leading the way. She probably should have been paying attention to the directions instead of watching the back of his head, memorizing the constellations of freckles on his neck.

I'm not lost, she tells herself. *I can't be lost.* The tree beside her, the one with the creeping vines, definitely looks familiar. But then again, they kind of *all* look familiar. Christina turns back, retracing her steps. If she could just find her way back to the paved path . . .

A rustling in the trees gives her pause. She stops. Listens. Christina knows that she and Lucas aren't the only ones who walk in these woods at night. She remembers the empty cans, the stubbed-out cigarettes they'd found around the clearing. But still, the idea of someone else being out here with her, the sound of heavy feet crunching through the bed of leaves on the forest floor, causes the skin on her arms to prickle.

"Lucas?" she calls, giving the flashlight one more useless shake. "Lucas, is that you?"

Maybe he'd come to meet her. Maybe they'd be laughing over this a few minutes from now. About how she'd been so spooked, lost in the woods on Halloween like something out of a scary movie.

But Lucas doesn't answer, and the source of the sound seems to be drawing closer. Christina's pace quickens. She hopes it isn't a raccoon. They're pretty cute and all, with their little masks and bushy tails, but she'd prefer not to meet one face-to-face in the wild.

She breaks into a jog, ducking under low-hanging branches and hopping over fallen logs. She hears the sound of her own heavy breathing, the snapping of twigs beneath the soles of her sneakers, and that rustling growing increasingly louder. There's definitely someone else out here with her. She's certain of it now. A raccoon wouldn't be following her.

Her heart pounds in her chest. There's someone behind her. She can feel it, sense the eyes on her back. But she's too frightened to turn around to see who it might be. She thinks she can hear breathing now, the person gaining on her as she forges through the undergrowth. Up ahead she sees a break in the trees—the jogging path, the smooth asphalt like a silver lake in the light of the full moon. She just needs to get there...

Christina breaks into a run, a full-on sprint, her arms pumping at her sides. She ignores the branches that scrape her face, the detritus that tangles in her shoelaces.

Finally she reaches it, the relief of hard pavement beneath her feet. She knows where she is now. She knows she can make it out of here.

And then someone grabs her.

A PAIR OF STRONG ARMS wrap around Christina's chest so forcefully that it knocks the wind from her lungs.

"Help!" she yelps, her voice a breathless rasp.

"Don't," a man's voice growls in her ear. "Make another sound and I'll kill you."

A frightened whimper escapes Christina's lips.

"I've been looking for you for a long time, Maggie, and you're not going to get away from me again."

Who is Maggie? Christina wonders. She wants to tell the man that he's wrong, that she's not who he thinks she is, but she's too scared to say a single word.

"Now you're going to do exactly what I tell you, do you hear me?" the man says.

Christina's body goes rigid with fear.

"I'm going to let go of you now, and you're going to be a good girl. Understood?"

Christina doesn't respond; she can't. All she can focus on is the feeling of his hands on her body, the sour smell of her own panicked sweat.

"I asked you a question," he barks, his grip tightening around her ribs. "Is that understood?"

She manages a tight nod, her teeth chattering.

"Good," he says, his hold on her slowly loosening.

Christina wonders if this is how her mother feels, if sometimes she can't force her body to move even when she knows what's coming.

But she's not her mother.

The man's hand clasps onto Christina's shoulder as he spins her around to face him. And when he does, she's ready. She's holding the Maglite in both hands, gripping it like a baseball bat, and she swings it directly at his head.

The heavy metal flashlight collides forcefully with his temple, the impact echoing through Christina's forearms.

She watches as he stumbles back, his hand rising to his head, his mouth agape, his eyes wide in surprise. He looks dizzy, like a boxer staggering toward the ropes, and then he begins to fall.

Christina squeezes her eyes shut in horror as the man collapses to the ground.

"Oh my God," she cries.

"Christina?"

Her head snaps up; she looks wildly around the darkened woods.

"Christina, honey, it's me. Hannah."

Hannah emerges from between the trees, and she takes in the scene before her: Christina's chest rising and falling with her rapid breaths, the bloody flashlight dangling limply from the end of her arm, the man sprawled at her feet.

"It's okay, Christina," she says, her voice steady and calm. "Everything is going to be okay."

Hannah goes to the man, bends over him, and reaches out her hand so that it hovers just above his lips.

"Is he . . . dead?" Christina whimpers, her fingertips trembling at her own lips.

"No. He's not." Hannah shakes her head as she stands. "But we need to get you out of here. Now."

46

GEORGINA
Hawthorne Lane

Knock, knock, knock.

Georgina slowly sits up on the bed in the guest room, pressing her palm to her forehead to quell the dizziness that washes over her.

Knock, knock, knock.

She slides her hand over the contours of her face, assessing the damage. Swelling under her left eye, dried blood crusted under her nose, tenderness in her jaw. Her scalp aches from where Colin grabbed her by the hair and dragged her up to their bedroom after the incident with Lucas, and she's fairly certain that her right wrist is sprained; it pulses with pain as she props herself up.

She doesn't care who's at her door—a trick-or-treater, a vendor looking to be paid—whoever it is can go away. She's not opening that door for anyone. Christina is safe in her bedroom, and Sebastian is spending the night at a friend's house. He stalked off after she dragged him away from the fight. Her children are accounted for and Georgina can't bring herself to care about anyone else. That there's still a festival going on outside—children laughing, families sharing popcorn from paper sleeves—feels like a personal affront. A mockery.

"Georgina," a muffled voice calls through the front door. "It's Hannah. I have Christina with me. It's an emergency."

Christina? She must have snuck out of the house while Georgina and Colin were arguing.

Georgina has already started to block it from her memory. She remembers it only in scattered fragments now: Colin's fist colliding with her cheekbone, the toe of his shoe meeting her ribs as she lay crumpled on the ground, strands of her long red hair clutched between his fingers. This had been bad, even for him. Georgina knew it was partly because she'd stood up to him, embarrassed him in front of their friends and neighbors, and partly because he'd had something to prove to himself. Being forced to back down from Bill Corbin and Seth Warrington must have been a devastating blow to Colin's ego, but with his wife, in his home, he was still powerful. It was like he was a man possessed. His blows landed wildly—he was unrestrained, unable to stop himself, even though it meant that Georgina wouldn't be able to show her face in public for weeks. And when it was over, his knuckles swollen, sweat soaking through his shirt, he'd gone to sleep. It was as if, in exorcising the demon that possessed him, there was nothing left of him at all.

Georgina knows that tomorrow Colin won't remember most of this. The details will feel fuzzy in his head; he'll look at her and be surprised at the extent of the damage he caused. And it feels so profoundly unfair. He should be forced to face what he's done, her bruises a penance, the memories lashes on his back.

Georgina climbs out of bed and tiptoes down the stairs as quietly as she can, though her side aches with the effort. She wonders if her rib is broken, but she can't make a sound—she doesn't want to risk waking Colin—so she clutches her side and keeps moving forward.

When she reaches the front door, she pauses for a moment with her hand wrapped around the knob. As soon as she opens it, Hannah and Christina are going to see what Colin has done to her. There will be no excuses this time, no stories of walking into doors or falling down the stairs. This time, there will be only the cold, ugly truth of it. She's ready.

Georgina pulls open the door to find Hannah on her doorstep, Christina standing beside her, swaying slightly on her feet. Her hair is mussed, dirt and twigs tangled in the blond locks, and Colin's flashlight dangles from a lanyard looped around her wrist.

"Christina?" Georgina rushes to her; her hands grip her shoulders as she looks over her daughter, assessing her for injuries. "Are you okay?" Christina stares at her blankly, and a sinking feeling opens in the pit of Georgina's stomach. "What happened?"

"There was an incident," Hannah starts. "I found her in the woods."

"A man attacked me," Christina says, her voice reedy and thin. "I hit him with this." She lifts her wrist and now Georgina sees the blood slicking the end of the metal flashlight. She feels as though she might be sick.

Georgina pinches the lanyard between two fingers, gently lifts it from her daughter's wrist. "Is he . . ."

"He's alive," Hannah cuts in. "But I think . . . I think you and I should talk."

Georgina looks back over her shoulder into the house where Colin is still asleep. Her daughter is not safe here.

"Christina, honey, go to Libby Corbin's house. Tell them only that there's been a family emergency and that I'd like you to stay there for the time being. You'll be safe with them, I promise, okay? I'm going to get your father. He'll handle this."

HALLOWEEN NIGHT

Transcript of interview with Georgina Pembrook
October 31, 2024

Detective Olsen: So you were woken by the sound of your daughter coming home, is that correct?

Ms. Pembrook: It is. Christina was quite shaken, and her hair and clothes were a mess. She told me that she'd been attacked by a strange man in the woods, that he'd grabbed her and tried to drag her off the path, but she managed to break free. I sent her to go stay with our neighbors the Corbins, and then I immediately woke my husband to tell him what had happened.

Detective Olsen: And how did he take the news that his daughter had been attacked?

Ms. Pembrook: Not well. He was incensed, furious. I begged him to call the police, but he insisted on going to find the man himself. My husband, he's . . . he can be impulsive, violent. I'm certain you've noticed the marks on my face, Detective. That should give you some idea of what he's capable of. But when I told him about what happened to Christina—well, he was angrier than I've ever seen him. He was completely out of control.

THREE HOURS EARLIER

47

GEORGINA
Hawthorne Lane

Georgina watches Christina cross the street, weaving around the families who have set up their chairs in the cul-de-sac in anticipation of the fireworks, and step into the warm light of Libby's front porch.

"You said we should talk," Georgina says to Hannah, her eyes still lingering on her daughter as Bill Corbin opens the front door, welcomes Christina into the safety of their home. "So tell me."

And Hannah does.

GEORGINA'S MIND IS REELING BY the time Hannah is finished. Her story, though so different than Georgina's own, is, at its core, hauntingly familiar. But Hannah had done what Georgina wasn't strong enough to do—she'd escaped. She'd started over, built a life for herself under a new name. For a moment, Georgina lets herself imagine what it would be like to be brave enough to do that, to start over, her and her children, far away from Colin. Someplace he could never reach them. She imagines herself in a little house in California. It's nothing like the cold, sterile mansion on Hawthorne Lane. In California, there's a tiny balcony where she can smell the ocean air as she sips her morning coffee, where sand is somehow always scattered on the floor and flip-flops are piled by the door. She pictures her family of three sharing a greasy takeout pizza and watching the sunset on the beach. It feels so tantalizingly real that Georgina can almost touch it.

And then the illusion shatters at her fingertips. Colin would come for them. He would find her and drag her back to hell, just as Dean has come for Hannah, clawing his way back from the dead to do it.

"I think Dean mistook Christina for me," Hannah explains. "I was the one he was after."

Georgina studies the younger woman, her slight build, her golden-blond hair so much like her daughter's. She can see how it might have happened, the confusion in the dark.

"We'll call the police," Hannah says. "What Christina did was self-defense. I just thought you deserved to know the truth. I brought this to your doorstep, and I'm so sorry, Georgina. Truly I am."

"But if we call the police..."

"They might find out that I've been living under a fake name. And Mark will too. I probably committed some sort of identity fraud; I almost killed a man, and I left the scene of an accident. I know all that. But it doesn't matter. It doesn't matter what happens to me. This is all my fault."

"I want to see him," Georgina says, her words slow and measured. Georgina thinks of Hannah, of the second chance she'd fought so hard for being ripped out of her hands. The one Georgina would kill to have for herself. She thinks of her daughter, so young and innocent, being assaulted in the dark, that man's hands on her body. How scared she must have been, but how brave she was to have saved herself. And then she imagines the sirens, the handcuffs, her baby being pushed into the back of a police car and interrogated about something that wasn't her fault. Something that the two women standing here now could have protected her from if they'd made different choices.

"Are you sure?" Hannah asks. "He wasn't looking good when we left him. I think he hit his head on something when he fell. I didn't want to tell Christina that, but there was a lot of blood. I'm ... I'm not sure he's going to make it."

"I want to see him for myself before we make any decisions."

Georgina walks over to her garage, lifts the door. She leaves the bloodied flashlight on Colin's workbench, shrugs on a jacket two sizes too large for her, and closes the door once again.

She looks back at the house where her husband is sound asleep one last time. She told Christina she'd have her father handle this situation, but there are some things only a mother can do. "Let's go," she says.

48

LIBBY
Hawthorne Lane

Libby hands Christina a blanket. "Are you sure you're all right?" she asks.

"Yes, Mrs. Corbin. Thank you again."

Libby wants to ask what put that haunted look in the young girl's eyes, why she appeared so suddenly on her doorstep. But she doesn't. She can sense that this isn't the time, so she gently closes the door to the guest room.

The poor girl is obviously badly shaken, but she hadn't offered much of an explanation about what happened, saying only that it was a "family emergency." Libby wonders if it has anything to do with Colin and what he'd done to Lucas earlier in the day. Libby is still feeling pretty shaken by that herself, and she's not a teenage girl.

It's certainly been a strange night. First Peter disappears into thin air in the few minutes it took Libby to change her clothes, without so much as a text explaining his sudden departure, and then a little while later, Christina shows up out of the blue looking like she'd been through hell. Libby had meant to check in with Peter, make sure everything was okay, but she got distracted by Christina's arrival. She pulls out her phone now, but there's nothing new from him.

This isn't like him, she thinks as she stares at the blank screen. She's always known Peter to be rather communicative. She hopes there hasn't been some kind of emergency with him too. Libby isn't sure how many more fires she can put out today.

"Mom?" Lucas asks, tentatively poking his head into the hallway. "Is Christina okay?"

Libby wants to lie to him, tell him that there's nothing to worry about, but she finds that she can't. Her son is not a child anymore, and not every story has a happy ending. "I'm sure she will be. All we can do is be here for her right now. Just keep an eye on her, okay? Let me know if she needs anything."

Lucas nods. "Yeah. I will."

Libby looks at her son, nearly a man now, as he stands protectively outside the guest room, and she's overcome with emotion.

"I love you," she says.

Lucas grins, and for a moment he's her little boy again. "I love you too."

"I know this past year has been hard on both of us, but you're a good kid, Lucas. I'm proud of you, of the man you've become. I hope you know that."

"I know." He looks down at the ground. "And, Mom? I'm proud of you too. Thanks for, you know, being here."

Tears gather in the corners of Libby's eyes. "Always," she says, as she turns and heads back downstairs.

"All good?" Bill asks as she walks into the kitchen.

The sight of him there, drinking coffee from her favorite mug, Jasper sprawled at his feet, is comfortingly familiar and yet so out of place, as if he's always been a visitor just passing through. The anger Libby felt at him earlier, her searing jealousy over Heather's pregnancy, had drained out of her after her confrontation with Colin, Bill jumping in to protect her. All that's left is a sort of nostalgic emptiness, a hollow resignation that echoes with the promise of what they could have been.

"Yeah," Libby replies. "Christina wanted to get some rest."

"Did she tell you any more about what happened?"

"No." Libby pulls out a stool from under the counter and perches on it. "She didn't."

Bill leans against the counter, the mug cradled in both hands.

For a moment they're both silent, existing in the rare peace that's settled between them.

"I didn't mean for things to be this way between us." Bill's words come to her softly, and, for the first time in nearly a year, Libby gets the sense he's letting his guard down, that, finally, he's not pushing her away. "You were right about what you said. I should have tried harder to work through things, to fix us, instead of walking away. I should have told you how I was feeling sooner. I just . . . I didn't know how. Not until it felt like it was too late to fix it."

"And I should have realized how unhappy you were," Libby concedes. "I think maybe I did know, on some level. I just didn't want to face it." It's an admission, Libby realizes, that has been a long time coming. A truth she hadn't, until now, wanted to admit even to herself.

They haven't made things easy on each other, she and Bill. When Bill ended their marriage, it felt like a sudden blow to Libby. A hasty decision, cavalierly made. She'd been blindsided by it and so she'd lashed out, blaming Bill for everything that had gone wrong in their lives. She'd wielded her pain like a sword to cut him down with, and the more she swung at him, the farther he backed away from her.

But it hadn't been sudden to Bill, had it? His leaving was something he'd been building toward, slowly preparing himself for, so by the time he'd ended things, he'd already put up walls around himself, so thick that they'd felt impenetrable to Libby. They'd both made so many mistakes. If only he'd talked to her sooner. If only she'd been easier to talk to . . .

"I still can't believe I'm going to be a father again," he says, shaking his head slowly. "At my age! This wasn't exactly the plan . . ."

"I know. Or at least, I suspected."

"I never meant to hurt you or Lucas."

"I know that too." Libby looks down at the counter, tracing circles with her finger. "But life doesn't always go according to plan." A fact Libby has only recently come to accept.

She lifts her head, watches the familiar scene before her, Bill rinsing his mug in her sink, and she sees, for the first time, how much he's changed. He's no longer the boy she'd met at nineteen. Libby feels like she's lived one thousand lives since then. She's changed—through motherhood, through the career she built for herself—she's grown and evolved and become someone new. And she understands now that Bill changed too. How had she not realized it sooner? Although they'd navigated the currents of life together, the tides shaped them in different ways. Formed them into people who no longer fit together. All this time she's been clinging to a version of Bill that no longer exists. Perhaps it's time now to let him go.

"You're going to be a great dad," she tells him. It's a peace offering, an olive branch extended, but she finds that she means it too. In a flash, she pictures Bill pushing a little girl on a swing, teaching another little boy with his distinctive smile how to catch a ball. "You always have been."

"I can't tell you how much it means to me to hear you say that." Bill turns to face Libby, drying his mug with a tea towel, and their eyes meet.

They're going to be okay. Things will never be the same between them, but they'll be okay. *Libby* will be okay.

Bill places the mug back in the cabinet. "I'm going to head home. But you call me if you guys need anything. Anything at all, okay? I can be back here in fifteen minutes if you need me."

"We're fine. Thanks, Bill. I'll walk you out."

Libby follows Bill to the door and watches him walk down her front steps. He stops as he reaches the driveway and turns back to look at her one last time, his hand raised in parting.

Goodbye, Bill, she thinks as he disappears into the crowd.

LIBBY WATCHES THE FESTIVITIES PLAYING out outside her window, the children running, the parents following behind them carrying half-eaten candy apples and plastic buckets filled with candy. It's been a very long, emotionally draining day and she's exhausted.

She's about to turn away to check on Lucas and Christina when she sees something unexpected: Hannah and Georgina rushing down the sidewalk, their heads ducked low, Georgina bundled in an oversize hunting coat that Libby would have thought she wouldn't be caught dead in.

"Hey!" Libby calls, but they don't seem to hear her.

Libby quickly pulls on a pair of sneakers and yanks a jacket off the rack by her door.

By the time she steps outside, Hannah and Georgina are halfway down the block. And Libby, curious, sets off after them. Where could they be going in such a hurry? What kind of emergency necessitated Georgina sending Christina to Libby's house?

"Hey!" Libby yells again as she draws nearer, jogging to close the gap between herself and the other women, but again she's met with no response from her neighbors.

"Georgina!" she finally shouts. They've almost reached the woods, and Georgina turns and stops in her tracks, stiff-backed and rigid, under the broken streetlight. Libby wonders how long that light has been out and why she never noticed it before. "Georgina, what the hell is going on?" It comes out sharper than Libby intended, but she can't help feeling irritated with the other woman. Georgina's son and her husband had *assaulted* Lucas, and then she sent Christina over to Libby's house without a word of explanation, and now here she is wandering through the fall festival, apparently without a care in the world. Did Georgina not feel that she owed Libby some answers?

"Libby, I..." Georgina starts, but the words trail off, carried away on the October wind. "Is Christina okay?"

Libby feels herself becoming exasperated. "She's fine, but I'd like to know what this is all about. I think after what happened today, you owe me an explanation at least!"

"Georgina," Hannah says, her voice gentle and coaxing, her hand touching Georgina's wrist. "I think we need to tell her. She deserves to know. She's mixed up in this too."

"Mixed up in what?" Libby throws her hands up in frustration.

Georgina's eyes slide toward old Ms. Woodrow's house, where a television flickers through the living-room window. As she turns, her face is lit by a shaft of moonlight, and Libby gasps.

"Georgina, what happened to you?"

"Nothing," Georgina replies. "It doesn't matter now."

A shiver of understanding trickles down Libby's spine. "Was that...Colin? Did he do that to you?" In a flash, Libby can picture it: Colin towering over his wife, the same way he'd done with Lucas, his hand reaching for her neck the way it had for Libby's.

Georgina nods, her eyes unable to meet Libby's as she adjusts her enviable red hair so that it conceals half her face as though by instinct. And Libby knows in her gut that this wasn't the first time.

"Libby, there's something you need to hear," Hannah says. "It's about Peter."

"Wait—Peter?" The change in direction is disorienting. "What does Peter have to do with anything?"

"Hey!" A familiar voice calls. Audrey. She marches up to them, her hands shoved in the pockets of her coat. "Have any of you seen Seth? I've been out here looking for him for ages. He stormed off after the whole ordeal with Colin and—" She stops, her eyes passing over the group. Realization dawns on her face as she takes in the somber looks all around her. "Wait, did something happen?"

"That's what I'd like to know," Libby replies, her gaze landing on Hannah. "Will someone please tell me what exactly is going on?"

WHEN HANNAH FINISHES TELLING HER story, evidently for the second time that night, Libby feels like she's going to be sick.

"So, Peter . . ." she says, trying to wrap her mind around what she's just heard. "All this time he's really been Dean?"

Hannah nods.

"Your abusive ex-husband, whom you thought you'd killed, tracked you down to Sterling Valley and was using me as a way to get to you?"

Hannah winces. "I'm sorry, Libby. I really am. But the man you thought you met . . . he's not real. Dean is a con man. This is what he does. He shows you what he thinks you want to see. He uses people, hurts them, then throws them away when they no longer serve a purpose for him."

Now Libby is sure she's going to be sick. "And so, tonight, I invited him here . . . and now Christina . . . Oh God." Bile rises in her throat.

"We're going back there," Georgina says. "To where it happened."

"I'm coming," Libby replies resolutely. She needs to see Peter, or Dean, or whoever he is, for herself. This man that saw her broken heart and used it to his advantage. She deserves that closure.

"Me too," Audrey adds.

Hannah nods solemnly. "Okay," she says. "But we'd better hurry."

She leads them all into the woods just as the first of the fireworks explode over Hawthorne Lane.

49
GEORGINA
Hawthorne Lane

The forest is unnaturally quiet; even the crickets have stopped chirping. Georgina, Hannah, Audrey, and Libby stare down at Dean's dead body lying on the pavement of the jogging path. There's a halo of red-black blood framing his head, and his complexion is pale and waxy under the light of the full moon. His eyes, clouded and lifeless, stare unmoving into the inky sky above their heads, and his jaw hangs slack, his lips parted in a silent gasp.

"He's really dead." Hannah is the first to speak, and when she does, she sounds almost skeptical, as if part of her still expects him to jump up and grab her.

Georgina squats down next to the body. She can't think of it as a person. If she starts to think of the body as a person, she'll have to think about the fact that her daughter killed him, and she's not ready to grapple with that just yet. "It looks like he hit the back of his head on that," she says, pointing to a large, jagged rock beside the body, the edge of which is smeared red with blood.

"He fell backward when Christina hit him with the flashlight," Hannah explains, nodding. "He must have hit the rock on the way down."

How is Georgina going to tell her daughter this? How will she ever be the same? As much as Dean might have deserved exactly what he got, Christina took a life, and under any circumstances, that has to be a heavy burden to bear. *God, she's only a child.* Georgina chokes back a sob.

"Now what happens?" Libby says. When Georgina turns to look at her, she's staring down at the body of the man she knew as Peter, her fingers trembling at her lips.

"We call the police," Hannah says. "And whatever happens to me happens. Christina will be okay, though. It was self-defense. Surely the police will understand that."

Georgina huffs. She's supposed to put her daughter's future in someone else's hands? To unquestioningly trust that the police are going to do the right thing? In Georgina's experience, the people who were meant to protect her—her parents, her husband—were the ones who ended up hurting her the most. But now Hannah expects her to believe that the police, a judge, a jury, will keep her daughter safe? No, it's a risk she's not willing to take. Georgina is going to have to look after Christina herself.

Georgina feels the anger rising in her like a tide. She imagines her daughter on a witness stand, reliving the worst moments of her life, cutting herself open, bleeding for a jury, begging to be believed, bargaining for her freedom. And what if they don't believe her? What if they look at her and decide that she'd gone too far in protecting herself? What if they hold her accountable for saving her own life; what if, once again, an abuser wins? Georgina won't let that happen.

And then there's Hannah to consider. What happens to her in all this? Does she deserve to lose the life she made for herself here, and potentially her freedom, because of Dean? She already escaped him once, and it feels deeply unfair that it was all for nothing, that he'll still drag her down with him in the end. *But what if . . . what if . . .*

"There's another way," Georgina says, the wisp of an idea forming, taking shape in her mind, becoming something solid and sure.

A crow calls out from somewhere among the shadowy tree branches, and Georgina imagines its curved beak, its sharp black eyes shining like polished stones, watching her in the dark, waiting for her to make a decision. She hears it take flight, feathery wings beating against the velvet night sky, and she nods. "Colin did this. Colin killed this man."

"What?" Libby exclaims. "But . . . how?"

"I have an idea. But we're going to have to do this together."

Together they can do what Georgina could never do alone.

She's done the research. She knows the statistics; she's read them so many times that they're burned into her memory. She knows that children who grow up surrounded by domestic violence experience significant psychological trauma that makes them more likely to commit suicide or acts of violence toward others, and that they're three times more likely to be involved in domestic abuse in adulthood, repeating the cycle and becoming victims or abusers themselves. She looks at Hannah, thinks of the violence she endured at the hands of her father, how she escaped only to find herself married to another monster in a prettier disguise. How easily that could be her own daughter... how easily her son could become the monster. *No more,* Georgina decides. *It ends now.*

Georgina looks at her neighbors, her friends, their eyes wide with fear. No one speaks. They don't agree, but they don't object either.

She wonders what they must think of her, that she's stayed with Colin for as long as she has. That it's taken her all these years to break through the shame that kept her isolated from those closest to her. But Georgina isn't alone anymore. "It's the best solution. For all of us."

She looks at Hannah, who deserves to keep her secret, her second chance, and Libby, who just hours ago was willing to do whatever it took to protect her son from Colin. And then her eyes meet Audrey's.

50
AUDREY
Hawthorne Lane

"I'm in." The others look at Audrey in wide-eyed disbelief. "What? Colin deserves it," she says, folding her arms over her chest. "You might not want to admit it, but we all know it's true. Georgina is right. This is the best solution. For *all* of us."

Libby looks like she might puke, and Hannah stares, eyes unfocused, into the thick darkness of the woods around them, but Georgina is harder to read, a mixture of both relief and confusion playing across her face.

Audrey opens her mouth to explain, but then closes it again. She grabs the collar of her sweater, pulls it down, slides it off her shoulder. She lets the deep purple bruises in the shape of Colin's fingers, stark against her moonlit skin, say everything she can't put into words.

She sees the moment that recognition, understanding, slots into place for Georgina.

"I'm sorry," Audrey says. And she means it. More than Georgina will ever know. "For everything. I should never have gotten involved with Colin." She turns to Hannah. "And I never should have posted that photo. If it weren't for me . . ." A wave of guilt overtakes her. If she hadn't been having an affair with Colin, if she hadn't allowed herself to be goaded into his twisted mind games, Dean wouldn't have found his way to Hawthorne Lane, and none of this would have happened.

But Georgina lifts a palm, stopping her. "It doesn't matter now. What we need is a plan."

Audrey watches in awed amazement as Georgina takes control, orchestrating a plot to frame her husband for murder the same way she might organize a dinner party. She lays out each of their parts as if they're actors in a play.

"Hannah," Georgina says, "you were never here, understood? You never met Peter, you've never seen this man"—she gestures at the body lying at their feet—"and you've never been anyone but Hannah Wilson. We need to leave you out of the story entirely if we're going to keep the police from looking into you."

Hannah swallows, her lower lip quivering. And then she nods. "Thank you."

"And Libby..." Georgina turns to the other woman. "The police will surely find the messages between you and Peter, so they're going to be able to connect him back to you. If you tell them that you last saw him with Hannah, that will bring up questions we don't want her to have to answer. So we need another story—one that doesn't involve Hannah—to explain why he was out here in the woods tonight and why he might have attacked Christina."

Libby is quiet. And for a moment Audrey isn't sure which direction she's going to go. She can tell that Georgina feels the same way, unease etched in the lines around her mouth. But after a moment that feels like an eternity, Libby finally speaks:

"I . . . I think I can do that."

"As for me," Georgina continues, breathless with relief, "I'll make sure all the evidence points to Colin. Christina will never have to know the truth about what happened here tonight. I'll talk to her before we go to the police, but as far as she knows, Dean was alive when she left the woods. Let her think her father did this. She's only a child. Even if the police do believe she acted in self-defense, this isn't something she should have to carry for the rest of her life. Let Colin shoulder that weight for her. It's the very least he can do."

"Do you think," Hannah says hesitantly, "do you think this actually will work?"

"What if it's not enough?" Libby adds, her face a pale oval in the moonlight. "I mean, it's not like we can say we saw Colin out here. What if he talks his way out of this and we've only made things worse?"

"I can help with that," Audrey says. "Leave it to me." She wants to do this; she has to. Not just because of the guilt she feels for her part in bringing them all here, and not just to protect herself from Colin, but for all of them. She's doing this for Hannah, who doesn't deserve to have her life torn apart for a man like Dean; for Libby, who deserved better than what Peter did to her and whose son will not be safe as long as Colin walks free; for Christina, who is just a child, the only innocent in all this; and for Georgina and every other woman like her who has ever been hurt by a man like Colin. It's time that they take their power back. It's time that they come together to make things right.

The four women look at one another, their eyes meeting in the dark, and it's as if they're seeing each other, *really* seeing each other, all the little ways in which their separate lives have become irrevocably intertwined, for the very first time. And slowly but surely, each one nods. They're in this together now, and there's no turning back.

51

DETECTIVE OLSEN
NOVEMBER 1

Detective Frank Olsen props his elbows on the table and massages his forehead. He can't remember the last time he was this tired. It's been one hell of a night, interviewing one witness after another. Maybe he's getting too old for this. He remembers back in his early days on the force when an all-nighter was nothing, a stiff cup of coffee and he was good to go. But now? Now he feels the exhaustion in his bones. Maybe Mary was right when she said it was time for him to start thinking about retirement, spending more time with their grandkids, buying a little house in one of the Carolinas. But whenever he begins to consider it, a case like this falls into his lap. Something that gets his wheels turning, really makes him think.

He worries that if he retires, he'll end up driving both of them up a wall. What would he do with himself? Detective Olsen has never been the type to sit still—he can't picture himself on a fishing boat, staring out at the glassy water, his mind as empty as his hook, or doing crossword puzzles in a rocking chair for hours on end. What else are old retired guys meant to do? Hell if he knows. He just knows that he's not ready to give this up yet, not when there are still cases like this one in the cards for him. The majority of the time, being a detective in Sterling Valley isn't the most riveting job. Most of the cases he catches are about a cleaning person who allegedly stole a family heirloom, and there was that one string of break-ins last summer that turned out to be a bunch of kids with nothing better to do. But this case is looking more and more like a real homicide, something he can sink his teeth into, and he feels like he's shaking the dust off, finally doing some real police work for a change.

See, Mary? I've still got it.

Detective Olsen spreads the latest witness statements out on the conference-room table. There are four of them, one for each of the witnesses who are still holed up in the interrogation rooms while his team conducts a search of the Pembrook house. Detective Olsen shuffles the pages, ordering and reordering them into a sequence that makes sense. With the papers laid out like this, a story is emerging. He reads the relevant portions again:

Libby Corbin
I'd invited a man I met online, Peter, to the fall festival tonight, but when he arrived, things didn't go as I'd anticipated. He was behaving rather aggressively, making unwanted advances toward me, and when I refused him, he became quite angry. He said something to the effect that he hadn't come all this way to leave without getting laid. He stormed off after that in the direction of the woods. I'm making this report because I'm concerned that he might have been mixed up in whatever happened out there tonight.

Detective Olsen had shown her a photo of the deceased, and she'd identified him as the man she'd known as Peter. Evidently, he'd given her a fake name in their exchanges, as the driver's license they'd found in his pocket listed his name as Dean Tucker. Detective Olsen had done some digging into Dean Tucker. As it turns out, this last run-in with the law was far from his first. He'd found arrests for shoplifting, assault, and more than a few complaints from ex-girlfriends accusing Dean of roughing them up. It looks like Ms. Corbin had been rather fortunate, in the grand scheme of things.

He looks at the next statement in front of him:

Christina Pembrook
I was on the walking path through the woods when some man just grabbed me out of nowhere. I yelled and screamed but he wouldn't let me go. I was kicking and fighting, and I think I must have kicked him in his genitals, as he let out a yelp and I was able to break free. I ran home and told my mother what had happened. She sent me to stay with Mrs. Corbin and said that my father would handle things from there. I'm not sure what happened after that. My mom came and woke me in the middle of the night to tell me that I needed to come down here and tell you what happened to me in the woods.

Detective Olsen pauses, considers this one again. On the face of it, the girl would have no reason to lie about being attacked by Mr. Tucker, and given the man's rap sheet, it wouldn't take a stretch of the imagination to believe it. But there's something about the wording, something about the strange, detached way the girl recounted the story in the interview, that makes Olsen feel uncertain. He remembers the way she seemed to look over his shoulder as she spoke, her eyes drifting upward as if she were trying to remember her lines rather than the event itself. He gets the impression that there's something missing here, something the girl intentionally left out; he's just not certain what it is. He moves on to the next statement: Georgina Pembrook's.

After I told Colin what happened to Christina, he was furious. I followed him out to the garage, where he put on his coat and took a flashlight from his workbench. I begged him to call the police, to leave this up to them to resolve, but there was no reasoning with him. He was determined to go into the woods on his own and find the man who attacked our daughter.

He'll come back to this one later. He jumps to the final statement, reads the relevant section again, the narrative unfurling more clearly now.

Audrey Warrington
I was at the fall festival when I saw Colin Pembrook walk out of the woods, heading in the direction of his house. He seemed to be in a rush, but I followed him. I'd wanted to talk to him about something important. I'm not proud of this, but Colin and I had an affair. He tried to blackmail me into continuing our arrangement, but I'd told my husband, Seth, the truth earlier that night. You can ask Seth yourself if you'd like. He will tell you the same thing. I wanted to tell Colin that it was over, that my husband knew about us and he had nothing left to hold over me, but when I caught up with him, I could see that there was blood on the sleeve of his jacket. He was holding a flashlight that had blood on it as well. I asked what happened and he told me to mind my own fucking business. In the time I've known Colin, he's been a violent and vengeful person. I'm concerned he had something to do with the person that died in the woods tonight.

Detective Olsen flips back to Georgina Pembrook's statement, where the story reaches its conclusion:

I hid in our guest room while my husband was out looking for the man who'd hurt Christina. I don't know how long he was gone. I must have fallen asleep, because when I woke up, it was pitch-black outside. I went to our bedroom to check if he was home, and I found him in our bed with blood on his clothes. That's why I came to you. I don't know exactly what my husband did, but I know what he's capable of. He would kill me if he knew I was here, but I had to say something. I couldn't live with myself if I didn't.

Detective Olsen had watched her carefully as she recounted her story. He'd have to have been asleep at the wheel to miss the signs of abuse on her: the swelling around her eye that was blossoming into quite a shiner, the wavering note of fear in her voice as she spoke about her husband, the way she seemed to flinch whenever Detective Olsen so much as cleared his throat. There was no question that this woman was afraid of her husband, that it had taken a lot for her to come forward and speak out against him, but she was whip-smart too. Probably, Olsen suspected, smarter than most people gave her credit for. Olsen wanted to believe her, he really and truly did, but he wasn't entirely sure that he could. Just as with the daughter's statement, something felt off about the whole thing. He just couldn't put his finger on what it was.

And then there's the anonymous call to consider. The tip he'd received earlier about looking into a strange man who had been casing the houses on Hawthorne Lane. He rewinds the recorded call and listens to it again now:

There was this man wandering around the block. And he just, I don't know, something felt off about him.

The voice sounds faintly familiar. Almost like Libby Corbin's, but he can't be sure. Whoever had made the call had done her best to disguise her voice.

But why would she have made that call? Was it possible that she was trying to shape his perspective on Dean Tucker, get him to see Dean as a criminal prowling the neighborhood with nefarious intent, and to direct his attention away from whatever is hiding underneath these statements, the ones that are painting a tantalizing picture of one dangerous man killing another?

Detective Olsen may never know for certain. But what he does know is that the women's statements were enough to warrant a search of the Pembrooks' residence, something he'd dispatched his team to do while he finished interviewing the witnesses.

His cell phone buzzes now, rattling on the metal table beside him. It's the call he's been waiting for. "You find anything?" Olsen barks.

"Sure did," his partner, Ruth Sutherland, responds. Sutherland is a good kid with the makings of a great cop. "The guy was asleep when we got here. Caught him red-handed. Literally. His knuckles are all swollen, and there was blood all over his hands. And we found his jacket and flashlight in the garage, both with blood on them too.

Forensics is lifting the bloody prints on the flashlight now, but given the blood on his hands, I think it's safe to assume they'll be a match."

"Why wouldn't he have washed up?" Colin Pembrook is a lawyer, and a good one from what Olsen can gather. Why would he let himself be caught so easily? "It doesn't make sense to me. This guy goes out and kills someone and then just goes to sleep without even washing the blood off his hands?"

"No idea, old-timer." Olsen pretends to hate it when the kid calls him that. But he smiles on the other end of the line despite himself.

"Maybe he wasn't thinking straight," Sutherland continues. "Or maybe he passed out before he had a chance. We found some sleeping pills on his nightstand. Who the hell knows. But there's an ADA on the scene now. She's telling me that with the statements we have and the evidence in the house, we have enough to make an arrest. Do you want to come down here and do the honors?"

"This one is yours, kid." Olsen doesn't have to see Sutherland to know that she's smiling as she ends the call.

He should be happy. Wrapping up a case like this in record time, evidence served up on a silver platter. But something is still nagging at him. Maybe how easy it all was, the way it'll all be tied up with a neat little bow as they hand the case off to the district attorney's office. Justice served. It's possible it's all in his head, but the truth, Olsen knows from experience, is often far messier than meets the eye. He thinks again of Georgina Pembrook, of the bruises on her face, and for the first time in his long career, he wonders if justice and the truth must always be one and the same.

He's starting to be able to picture it now, that little house in North Carolina, his wife in a rocking chair by his side, his grandkids running through the grassy yard. Maybe, just maybe, this is an ending he can live with.

52

GEORGINA
Hawthorne Lane

Georgina's hands shake nervously in her lap, and she clasps them together, willing herself still. She's been at the police station for ages. Or at least she thinks she has. Time seems to follow a different set of rules here; minutes languish into hours. Surely it can't be much longer... can it? Georgina doesn't have the faintest clue how long it takes to conduct a search of a crime scene (her house, a *crime scene*!), but she's certain they'll find what they're looking for. She hadn't exactly made it difficult.

That is, of course, unless Colin has already woken up and destroyed all the evidence she'd carefully laid out like breadcrumbs before the police arrived. The idea makes her dizzy. If he figures out what she's done... Georgina shakes off the thought. *No. That won't happen.* She's almost certain that Colin took one of his sleeping pills last night. She'd seen the familiar orange bottle on his nightstand when she crept in with his jacket, stained red with Dean's blood, and the Maglite that had been used to kill him. It would explain why Colin fell asleep so quickly after their altercation and why he stayed asleep as Georgina used the discarded T-shirt he'd been wearing earlier that day to wipe away Christina's fingerprints on the handle of the flashlight, then gently touched Colin's fingers into the thick, congealing blood. He didn't even wake as he turned over in his sleep, smearing streaks of blood on their starched white sheets. It would explain why he hadn't heard her sneak into the garage to drop the bloodied jacket and the offending flashlight onto the concrete floor, and it would explain why he'd still been asleep when she got in the car and headed out before dawn to file her police report, an attempt to drive the final nail into his coffin.

What could possibly be taking so long? Georgina looks up at the one-way mirror, startled again by her own reflection, the swelling at her cheekbone blooming into a mottled tangle of bruises, her hair unbrushed and wild. She runs her fingers through the knotted locks. She's going to cut it, she decides. As soon as it's appropriate, given the circumstances. She imagines walking out of the salon, how light and free she'll feel, the autumn breeze on her neck. Then she remembers herself, remembers that the mirror isn't actually just a mirror but a window. She wonders if Detective Olsen is watching her on the other side of the glass, studying her movements the way they always do on television. Georgina drops her hand and straightens her posture, sitting taller in her chair, just in case.

She'd found it hard to get a read on Detective Olsen during her interview. He'd listened intently as she spoke, jotted down notes here and there, but mostly he'd watched her with the sort of analytical detachment one might expect of a therapist. It made Georgina feel uneasy. Was it possible that Detective Olsen could see right through her? Had he somehow pieced together what she'd done?

The plan wasn't perfect. Far from it. Everyone involved—Georgina, Libby, Audrey, and even Christina—had a motive to lie, obvious reasons for wanting Colin to take the fall for what happened to Dean. But there was nothing that could be done about that. Audrey couldn't hide the evidence of her affair with Colin any more than Georgina could hide the abuse she'd suffered at his hands, and there had been dozens of witnesses who saw Colin assaulting Libby's son. For that reason, they'd had to stick as close to the truth as possible in giving their statements, bending it only where they needed to in order to make the pieces of the new narrative fit. She just has to hope that it's enough.

It had been difficult to convince Christina to go along with the story Georgina crafted at first. She was hysterical when Georgina collected her from Libby's house on her way to the police station, when she'd had to tell her that her father had gone out looking for the man who'd attacked her and Georgina feared he'd taken matters into his own hands. It took a rather long time to get Christina to understand that she needed to leave the part about the flashlight out of her statement to the police—it would only complicate things and she couldn't throw away her future over something her father had done; that wasn't what any of them wanted for her.

The sound of a door slamming in the distance pulls Georgina's attention. *Is Detective Olsen finally coming back with news?* She stands, her metal chair scraping along the linoleum floor as it's pushed back from the table, and walks to the closed interview room door. She wonders if she's allowed to open it. She came here voluntarily; she should be able to come and go as she pleases, shouldn't she? And yet she hesitates, her hand on the knob, until she hears Colin's venomous, muffled voice seeping through the door.

He's angry, Georgina can tell, screaming that there's been a mistake.

She cracks open the door to the interview room, peers cautiously into the hallway of the police station. She can hear Colin yelling more loudly now, bellowing with indignation.

"I don't need a lawyer, I *am* a fucking lawyer, and I'm telling you that I have no idea what you're talking about! I didn't do anything!"

"Please calm down, sir," a male officer says gruffly as he helps escort Colin through the station, his hands pinned behind his back with a pair of silver cuffs.

Colin tries to pull free, but the pair of officers flanking his sides tighten their grips on his arms. "You're making a big mistake," Colin spits. "I'll sue this whole fucking department. You'll see!"

"I'm sure you will, sir," the same officer replies drolly.

Colin looks around, his cold blue eyes wild with alarm, and then he sees her. His eyes meet Georgina's and he tries to dart toward her. "I was home all night last night, asleep in bed! Just ask my wife, she'll tell you!"

"We already have," Detective Olsen says, stepping out of one of the other interview rooms so that he's face-to-face with Colin. "And it turns out she had a lot to say."

At first Colin seems confused; his lips move but no sound comes out of his mouth. And then realization dawns on him—Georgina can see it like the sun cresting over the horizon. She watches the transformation she's seen so many times before, Colin's loosely held pretense of humanity slipping away from him, giving way to a primal rage.

"You!" he shouts. "You fucking bitch! What have you done?"

Georgina pushes the door to the interview room fully open now and stands tall, her head held defiantly high. "All I did was tell the truth. Something I should have done a long time ago."

"I'll kill you!" Colin spits, struggling against the officers keeping him at bay. He reminds Georgina of a rabid dog yanking uselessly at the end of its chain. "I'll fucking kill you!"

"I think we've heard enough," Detective Olsen remarks coolly. He nods to the uniformed officers, who shove Colin, still spitting and raving, forward. "Are you all right, ma'am?" Olsen asks, turning his attention to Georgina.

Georgina's eyes track her husband as he's dragged through the police station. "I will be."

Sterling Valley Community Board

Forum: Neighborhood Happenings
05/27/25

Poster: Harper Jensen
Has anyone else been following the Colin Pembrook case? This is insane!

> Reply: Lauren Arca
> I have. Honestly, I hope they throw the book at him!
>
> Reply: Jeff Scarlotta
> I don't know. If it was MY daughter that was attacked, I would've done the same damn thing. I hope the judge takes that into consideration.
>
> Reply: Jessica Seldin
> Still, you can't just go around hunting people down and killing them. The man had a propensity for violence. Just look at what he did to Georgina! Even Audrey Warrington (who he was having an affair with?!) testified that he was a violent creep. I hope the judge takes THAT into account.
>
> Reply: Lisa Marie
> Did he really "hunt him down" though? I mean,

if I was planning to go kill someone, I'd probably arm myself with a little more than a flashlight.

Reply: Harold Knut
Former lawyer here, and that right there will be the difference between getting the murder conviction the prosecutor wants and a lesser conviction for manslaughter. What was his intention when he went into those woods, when he swung that flashlight? Did he intend to kill the man? Was he just trying to injure him? And is there enough evidence to prove either theory beyond a reasonable doubt? I suppose we'll all have to wait and see what the jury believes.

Reply: Beth Patterson
All I can say is that I never would have suspected this of Colin. It really makes you wonder how well you know your neighbors . . .

53
HALLOWEEN NIGHT
One Year Later

The doorbell at 5 Hawthorne Lane rings, and Hannah lifts her head off Mark's shoulder. "Is it your turn or mine?"

"Definitely yours," he replies, grabbing another handful of buttery popcorn from the bowl nestled between them. "But I'll pause the movie for you."

"All right," Hannah says with an exaggerated sigh, tossing the warm blanket off her lap. "But don't finish all the popcorn."

"I make absolutely no promises to that effect!" Mark calls after her as she makes her way to the front door.

Hannah smiles to herself. A year ago she couldn't have imagined them here. Happy, together, with no secrets left between them. It hadn't been easy for Hannah to tell Mark the truth about her past, but in the end she felt she had to do it. Once Dean and all the danger he brought with him was gone for good, Hannah knew she couldn't live the rest of her life wondering whether she was as bad as Dean had been, if she'd conned Mark into loving a false version of her. He deserved to know who he'd married, and, well, if he didn't want to be with her anymore, maybe that was exactly what she deserved.

She'll never forget how worried he looked when she sat him down on their living-room couch, took his hands in hers, and told him that they needed to talk.

It was hard to find the words, but she knew she had to say them. She had to do this for Mark. "I . . . I haven't exactly been honest with you. About a lot of things. I'm not . . . I'm not who you think I am."

Mark had looked confused at first as she explained that her name wasn't really Hannah. That before that, there had been Maggie, and Melody before her. She watched his confusion turn to hurt as she told him she'd been married before and then to revulsion as she detailed the abuse she'd suffered at her husband's hands.

Mark was quiet as she told her story, absorbing her truth, her pain, as if by holding it in his own heart, he could somehow take the weight of it from her.

Hannah told him about the drugs and the debt and the jam jar. She told him about Mike, and Dean's plan to rob houses on the wealthier side of town and the accident she'd caused trying to stop him. Hannah's voice faltered as she described what she'd thought were Dean's final moments, when she left him to die, and the act of kindness from her best friend, Sam, who'd helped her escape in the only way she knew how.

Mark's jaw clenched as Hannah told him that Dean had found her, that he'd come here, to Hawthorne Lane, for her.

"If he hadn't mistaken Christina for me, if Colin hadn't gone after him and killed him once and for all, I don't know what would have happened," she'd said. *That* secret was one she kept. It didn't belong to her. That one belonged to Georgina, and it was one Hannah would take with her to her grave.

"Why," Mark said after a long moment of silence, "why didn't you tell me sooner?"

"Because I was afraid," Hannah replied. "Of so many things. What you have to understand is that I've been doing this a long time. Almost all my life. My mom taught me from a young age that I could never put my identity at risk, that I could never look back. I had to become someone new. And I did. I didn't feel like the same person when I was with you. I *wasn't* that person anymore. And I didn't want my ugly past to ruin this beautiful life we've built together. I was afraid that you'd hate me if you knew the truth, that I'd killed someone and walked away without a second thought. But I was even more afraid that you *wouldn't* hate me. That you'd love me enough to keep my secret, to carry it with you, and you don't deserve that, Mark. What I did . . . it was illegal. I caused an accident that, as far as I knew, killed someone, and I just left him there. I ran... And I didn't want to put you at risk if I ever got caught.

"I thought about telling you so many times. I promise you I did. I hated keeping this from you. But then when those notes arrived, I knew it was too late. Someone knew what I did. I didn't know who, but I knew they were coming for me. That they were going to use my past against me somehow, and I couldn't risk letting them bring you down with me. Knowing the truth would only have put you in danger too.

"But that's over now. Dean is gone. For good this time. And so it's time for me to stop letting my fear of the past dictate my future. You deserve to know the truth. You've deserved it all along. And now that you know it, I'll understand whatever decisions you make from here. Just please know that I love you, Mark. That part has always been true."

Mark's jaw worked as he seemed to mull over everything she'd said. Hannah felt sick to her stomach. She was certain this was the part where he was going to leave her, to tell her that it was time for her to pack her things and go.

"It doesn't matter," Mark said, so quietly that Hannah wasn't sure she'd heard him correctly. "None of it matters. You might have called yourself by a different name, you might have done some things you aren't proud of, but you did what you had to do to survive. I know you, Hannah. I know who you are in your heart. That's enough for me. The rest... the rest we face together. No matter what happens. You aren't alone anymore."

Hannah feels fresh tears welling in her eyes now as she recalls those words—*You aren't alone anymore*—but she pulls herself together, puts on a cheerful smile as she opens her front door.

"Trick-or-treat!" It's a little girl dressed as a daisy. Hannah recognizes her as one of the regulars at the library.

"What a great costume," she says, dropping a handful of candy into the girl's orange bucket.

"Thank you, Mrs. Wilson!" the child chirps as she skips off toward the next house.

Hannah watches her go, lingering in the doorway a moment, savoring the crisp fall air.

Halloween looks different on Hawthorne Lane this year. There is no fall festival. No candy apples or fireworks, no crowds of neighbors gathered on the street. The town has done its best to move on, but no one has forgotten what happened here last year. It's changed them all.

Hannah followed Colin's trial closely. She'd gone to the courthouse, slipping into the mass of people—residents and reporters—that gathered there. Throughout the trial, Colin had maintained his innocence with unwavering conviction. He denied seeing Dean, he denied knowing anything about his death. His insistence was convincing, but Georgina's and Audrey's combined testimony told a very different story, one that painted Colin as a violent man consumed with rage, determined to seek vengeance on the man who'd hurt his daughter. Hannah couldn't tell which way the jurors were going to go, which side they were going to believe.

In the end, Colin had been his own worst enemy, despite his legal training. His temper was the one thing he couldn't control. He scowled at his ex-wife on the stand and grumbled from the defense table as Audrey spoke, his lawyer constantly trying to rein him in. It didn't play well in front of the jury. Colin had made it easy for them to imagine him as the reckless, vengeful monster the two women had described. It also didn't hurt that half the town had witnessed him assault a teenage boy mere hours earlier for simply holding his daughter's hand.

The most interesting part of the trial, Hannah thought, was the part they hadn't accounted for, the stroke of luck that fell neatly into their laps. It came out during the prosecution's case that Colin had taken sleeping pills on top of the copious amount of alcohol he'd been drinking at the fall festival earlier in the day. Several witnesses confirmed they'd seen him drinking just before he lost his temper with Lucas. The district attorney brought in an expert to talk about the dangers of mixing prescription sleeping pills with alcohol and described the known side effects—one of which was memory loss. Hannah listened raptly as the doctor testified that he'd seen patients who had injured themselves or others in this condition but had no recollection of the event in the morning. It was the perfect explanation for Colin's adamant insistence that he hadn't been in the woods with Dean that night and for why he hadn't tried to hide the evidence of his crime before the police barged into his bedroom.

Colin's attorney scrambled to refute the testimony, but it was too late. The prosecution had already offered the jury an explanation they could hang their hats on, something that seamlessly tied together everything they'd heard. And they handed down a verdict of guilty; Colin was convicted of manslaughter in the first degree.

The DA had been hoping for a murder conviction, but the jury found there wasn't sufficient evidence to prove, beyond a reasonable doubt, that Colin went into the woods with the intention to kill Dean that night. (After all, he was only armed with a flashlight.) They did, however, believe that he intended to seriously injure Dean when he swung that flashlight at his head, and in doing so, caused his death when Dean fell backward and hit his head on a rock.

He was sentenced to ten years in prison.

A lot changed on Hawthorne Lane after the trial. Georgina quickly put her house up for sale, and it was bought by a young family with two small children, a girl and a boy. Hannah has seen them only briefly, shared waves from the ends of their driveways.

As Hannah closes her front door, she slips her phone out of her pocket and pulls up the most recent photo Georgina sent. It's of Georgina, her hair cut short, a glass of ruby-red wine in her hand, standing barefoot on the balcony of her new house in front of a California sunset. She looks so much happier there, the smile on her face more genuine than Hannah had ever seen it on Hawthorne Lane. And Hannah is happy for her. She deserves this, her second chance. They don't speak often, but when they do, Georgina tells her that they're doing well, that Christina is blossoming at UCLA, where she was accepted for a fellowship exchange program for creative writing, and that they're all making progress, slowly but steadily, in family therapy. Even Sebastian has started to open up to her about the things he witnessed in his childhood. It sounds as if it hasn't been easy for any of them, but Hannah is glad they have one another to lean on as they heal from all they've been through.

Sometimes Hannah worries about what will happen to Georgina, to all of them, when Colin is released from prison, but she reminds herself things will be different then. Colin's hold over Georgina came from his influence as a lawyer, his threat to turn her children against her, but by the time he's a free man, all of that power will have been stripped away from him. And besides, Georgina is no longer the same woman she was on Hawthorne Lane. She has friends in California, neighbors, classmates from her culinary courses, and she has Hannah and Libby and Audrey and the support of everyone who has now heard her story.

Audrey made sure of that. After Colin's trial, and with Georgina's blessing, she wrote a two-page spread for *Top Cast* titled "Killer in Bed" that featured an inside look at Colin's trial and provided a raw and powerful account of her experience with intimate partner violence and stalking. The piece was brutally honest and unapologetically real, just like Audrey.

Though Audrey's marriage to Seth didn't survive the fallout of her affair, from what Hannah can tell, Seth has been doing rather well for himself since their divorce and subsequent departure from Hawthorne Lane. After a stretch in a rehabilitation center, he'd gone public about his struggle with depression and substance abuse. Though Hannah can only imagine how difficult that must have been for him, she's heard talk that he's booked a national tour of motivational speaking engagements to share his story about the road to recovery. Hannah hopes that both he and Audrey find what they're looking for in their new lives.

"You coming?" Mark calls from the living room.

"Just a second," Hannah replies.

She takes one last lingering look out her front window. At the FOR SALE sign that swings in the breeze in front of Libby's house, Bill Corbin's smiling face beaming out from the placard. She's seen him and his adorable baby daughter in the neighborhood a few times these past months. He seems happy and also completely exhausted.

Hannah spoke to Libby about the night Dean died only once. It seemed to be a tacit agreement among all of the women that they'd never mention it again, but there was something Hannah needed to understand.

She'd approached Libby while she was sitting outside reading a book.

Libby set it down as Hannah climbed the steps to her front porch, a look on Libby's face that suggested she knew what Hannah had come for.

"Why..." Hannah started, searching for the right words. "Why did you help us?"

Libby thought for a moment, her fingers toying with the pages of the book in her lap. "I wasn't sure I was going to go through with it. Right up until I made my statement to the police, I wasn't sure. It's not that Colin didn't deserve what he got, but I just wasn't certain I could do it. I thought about you, and Georgina, and even Audrey. I thought about what he'd done to Lucas and what Pete—er, Dean—had done to me. But that wasn't why I did it. In the end it was something Georgina had said about Christina, that she didn't deserve to have to carry the weight of the truth of what happened that night. She's just a kid. Like Lucas. This really was the least Colin could do for her, for his family."

"I'm sorry," Hannah said. "I really am. For my part in it. For what Dean put you through."

"You know," Libby mused, "it's okay. I jumped into the whole dating thing before I was really ready because I thought it was what I *should* be doing. Because it was what *Bill* was doing. Not because it was what was right for me. For the first time since I was nineteen years old, I'm not in a relationship. Can you believe that? I'm finally getting to know myself not as half of a partnership but for who I am and what I'm capable of on my own. It's made me realize that I can have a fulfilling life without forcing the whole dating thing. I don't need a relationship to define me. I'm enough on my own."

"You are," Hannah agreed, awed by Libby's strength. "You really are."

"I'm not saying I'll never date again or that it'll be easy to open up to someone when I do, but for now, I'm happy to just see where life takes me."

Hannah will be sad to see Libby leave Hawthorne Lane. She imagines what it will be like walking past Lily Lane and not seeing Libby waving to her from behind the counter.

Libby promoted Erica from assistant manager to co-owner. She'll be running the shop once Libby leaves for Maryland. Lucas earned an athletic scholarship to the University of Maryland, and Libby doesn't plan to miss a single game. She's thinking of opening a second Lily Lane once they get settled. It seems that Libby, too, is ready for a fresh start.

"Hannah?" Mark calls again. "Did you get lost?"

"Coming!" she replies, her hand coming to rest on top of her rounded belly. The baby she plans to name after its uncle, Sam, kicks, a flutter against her palm. It was Mark who encouraged Hannah to reconnect with Sam again, to tell him the truth about what had happened here last year. It's all still very new, but Hannah can already picture her life a few months from now, her little family—Hannah, Mark, her old friend Sam—gathered in the yard of the house they've made a home on Hawthorne Lane, a new baby bundled in Hannah's arms. And she knows that the best is yet to come.

ACKNOWLEDGMENTS

To everyone who picked up this book, thank you. Because of you, the reader, I get to continue doing what I love most. Thank you from the bottom of my heart.

This book was the most challenging I've written to date. I first thought of the idea a number of years ago, and after several false starts, I set it aside to work on other projects, one of which later became *The Perfect Sister*. But I knew there was something special about this idea, something that kept drawing me back to it, so I decided to pick it up once again and give it another try . . . This resulted in several more false starts and months of frantic phone calls to my endlessly patient agent, Melissa Edwards, who handled all of my near-breakdown moments with ease and encouraged me to keep going. (I appreciate you, Melissa!)

After I finally managed to pull together a complete first draft, my editor, Jenny Chen, and her assistant, Jean Slaughter, helped me refine and shape it into the book I always hoped it could be. Thank you both for your thoughtful insight, for sharing my vision, and for your enthusiasm for this story.

Thank you also to the rest of my team at Random House—Daniel Denning, Annette Szlachta, Tracy Roe, Alexis Flynn, Belina Huey, Vanessa Duque, and Sarah Breivogel—for all you have done and continue to do to make this book a success.

A huge thank you to all the libraries, booksellers, media supporters, and advance readers who love to talk about books, connect with authors, and spread the joy of reading. Your support means the world to me.

Thank you to my critique partners, Shelby Holt and Tanya Berzinski, for your feedback, patience, and encouragement throughout the writing process. I couldn't have reached the finish line without you!

To my family and friends who are so wonderfully supportive, thank you for checking in on my writing progress, recommending my books, celebrating my wins, and helping me through my losses. Special thanks to my mom, Lori, who tells everyone she knows that her daughter is a writer; to my cousin Ali, who is always one of my first and most enthusiastic readers; to my husband, Giancarlo, who never complains when I talk about fictional people for hours on end; and to Lauren—this one is for you. Thank you for believing in this idea even on the days when I couldn't.

Thank you also to my girls, Christina and Juliana, who are always so excited about my books, even though they aren't allowed to read them until they're adults. Christina, although a character in this book shares your name (as I promised you one someday would!), that's where the similarities end. The character in this story was not in any way based on you (except, perhaps, for her love of reading)—your story will be your own to write.

And finally, I would like to thank my furry writing buddy Dakota, who, sadly, is no longer with us. Her snuggles and comforting presence are missed every day. Thank you for being by my side for so many wonderful years.

THE WIVES OF HAWTHORNE LANE

STEPHANIE DeCAROLIS

A BOOK CLUB GUIDE

AUTHOR'S NOTE

Intimate-partner violence can be a difficult topic to talk or read about, so if you've made it this far, I thank you. As difficult a subject as it is, I felt it was an important one to write about. According to the World Health Organization, one in three women will be subjected to some form of physical violence, sexual violence, or both in their lifetimes.[*] The reality of that statistic is staggering. This is a problem that affects all of us, a conversation we cannot shy away from. And it is one that is near to my heart.

Early in my legal career, I worked on a voluntary basis as an advocate for victims of abuse. I stood beside them in court and helped them plead their cases before a judge, seeking orders of protection, petitioning for supervised visitation of their children, and beginning custody proceedings. The women I met in this capacity came from all walks of life—different cultures, ethnicities, socioeconomic backgrounds—and every story I heard was different than the last. But they all had one thing in common: the strength they possessed to step forward, to try to break the cycle of abuse. Their stories inspired me to keep fighting, to keep having the difficult conversations.

I hope that's what I've done here with *The Wives of Hawthorne Lane*. While the ending of this book is not the path forward, I hope

---

[*] "Violence Against Women," World Health Organization, March 25, 2024, https://www.who.int/news-room/fact-sheets/detail/violence-against-women.

I've started a discussion. I hope I've done their stories justice. I hope that, going forward, we, as a society, can do better.

If you or someone you know is in need of assistance, you can call the National Domestic Violence Hotline at 1-800-799-SAFE (7233). Other resources may also be available in your area.

DISCUSSION QUESTIONS

1. Which, if any, of the main characters did you most relate to? Why? Did any of the characters remind you of someone in your life?

2. How do the different neighbors view one another? What misconceptions did they hold about each other, and how did these misconceptions play a role in the progression of the story?

3. Following Dean's death, in chapter 50, DeCarolis writes: "The four women look at one another, their eyes meeting in the dark, and it's as if they're seeing each other, *really* seeing each other, all the little ways in which their separate lives have become irrevocably intertwined, for the very first time." Why do you think the women didn't fully see each other previously? In what ways might the story have played out differently if they had?

4. Hannah and Georgina had more in common than it first appeared when Hannah moved to Hawthorne Lane. In what ways were their experiences the same? In what ways were they different? Do you think society would treat their situations differently? Why or why not?

5. How did each of the women's childhood experiences affect them? In what ways did their pasts shape the decisions they made in the story?

6. Children who witness or experience violence in their homes are known to be at an elevated risk of developing long-term physical and psychological problems and may also be more likely to become victims or perpetrators of violence themselves.* This is sometimes referred to as the intergenerational cycle of violence. Where did you see examples of this in the novel? In what ways did it influence the plot? How might that cycle have been broken here?

7. Each of the women makes the decision to participate in Georgina's plan to frame Colin at the end of the book. What do you believe were each one's motivations for doing so? Did you agree with their decision? Why or why not?

8. In chapter 51, Detective Olsen wonders "if justice and the truth must always be one and the same." What do you think that means in the context of the story? Do you believe that truth and justice always mean the same thing? Do you think justice was served with the ending of this novel? Why or why not?

9. How did you feel about each of the women at the beginning of the novel? Did your view of them change as the story progressed?

10. What were your thoughts about where each of the main characters ended up at the conclusion of the story?

---

* "Violence Against Women," World Health Organization, March 25, 2024, https://www.who.int/news-room/fact-sheets/detail/violence-against-women. https://womenshealth.gov/relationships-and-safety/domestic-violence/effects-domestic-violence-children.

STEPHANIE DECAROLIS is the *USA Today* bestselling author of *The Guilty Husband, Deadly Little Lies,* and *The Perfect Sister.* She is a graduate of Binghamton University and St. John's University School of Law and currently lives in New York with her husband and their two daughters.

Instagram: @StephanieDeCarolisBooks